Clashing

Jaide Harley

Exquisitely Chaotic Publishing

Edited by Voss Editing

Proofread by On The Same Page Editing

Cover Design by Melissa at Book Love Designs

ISBN 979-8-9869360-3-1 (ebook)

ISBN 979-8-9869360-4-8 (paperback)

ISBN 979-8-9869360-5-5 (hardback)

To all the women who took their power back. I see you, and I'm proud of you.

Content Warning

If you prefer to go in blind, carry on and don't read below. If you are in need of content warnings, find them below and in more detail here: https://www.jaideharley.com/content-warnings/content-warning-for-clashing/

DISCLAIMER:

This book contains themes centered around healing after sexual assault. While the scene itself is never fully depicted except in brief flashbacks, it's a topic that's discussed more than once.

Soundtrack

1. "dangerous woman" — Ariana Grande

2. "Heaven" — Julia Michaels

3. "Chains" — Nick Jonas

4. "Bad Things" — Machine Gun Kelly, Camila Cabello

5. "distance" — Christina Perri (feat. Jason Mraz)

6. "I Can't Make You Love Me" — Adele

7. "Someone You Loved" — Lewis Capaldi

8. "Wrecking Ball" — Miley Cyrus

9. "i hate u, i love u" — gnash (feat. Olivia O'Brien)

10. "Too Good At Goodbyes" — Sam Smith

11. "Powerful" — Major Lazer (feat. Ellie Goulding & Tarrus Riley)

12. "Stay" — Rihanna (feat. Mikky Ekko)

13. "Try" — P!nk

Contents

Also by

CHAPTER ONE

Mystery Man

SCARLETT

I let the dust settle in the dirt parking lot before I hazarded a step outside. The paranoia I'd fought during the fourteen-hour drive crept back in, and I whipped my head around while I white-knuckled my pepper spray. *It's the middle of the day and an entirely new state. You're fine.* Regardless, I kept the spray in my hand and grabbed as many bags as I could carry.

Though I'd never been here, the splintered wooden sign above the bar I'd parked in front of was familiar from pictures. I lugged my bags inside, where a touch of cigarette smoke mingled with whiskey and leather—my comfort smells. The combination reminded me of the days I ran to that smell and found a grilled ham and cheese sandwich with a pickle spear waiting for me. *My safe place.*

The heavy door closed behind me with a loud *thump*, echoing in the nearly empty establishment. Mid-morning on a Wednesday didn't draw much of a crowd.

Wooden walls, floors, and tables matched the polished bar top, which extended from one end of the bottle-covered wall almost to the other. It stopped about ten feet away, the end lining up with an open doorway and a set of stairs leading up.

Swinging half doors—to the left of the stairs behind the bar—opened, and through them entered the man I came to see. The source of the scents. More wrinkles crinkled the corners of his hazel eyes than last time I saw him. The little bit of hair he had left—only on the sides of his head except the beard—was now salt-and-pepper gray. The resting grumpy face hadn't changed. Neither had the build of a Navy SEAL veteran. To anyone else, he might've been intimidating. However, his tough-guy façade faded the moment his gaze landed on me.

Dan's grin reminded me of home as much as the smell of his bar. "My God, look who finally made it!" His exclamation attracted the attention of his three customers, but I didn't care.

Dropping my bags, I ran to meet his quick approach. I threw my arms around him, and he embraced me in the same bear hug he had since I was a kid. *Exactly what I need.*

"You've grown so much, Scarlett. Let me look at you." He held me at arm's length. "How'd you get even more beautiful?"

I giggled and swatted his arm. "Thanks. And again, thank you so much for letting me do this."

"I'm not *letting* you do anything, honey." He snatched most of my bags before I could reclaim them. "I don't even use the place. You're doing me a favor renting it out." He winked, the motion lowering one of his bushy eyebrows. "Come on. I'll show you up."

I followed him, wincing when the limp from his bad knee wavered his advancement. Whether his time as a Navy SEAL or his time in a biker gang was responsible for the injury, I wasn't sure. All I knew was, there was no convincing him to let me carry my bags. Though I did manage to grab the heaviest one.

Dan led me to the narrow staircase. Charcoal drawings and different types of paintings hung on the walls. My work. Dan wasn't much of an art aficionado, but he made an exception for me. Lucky didn't cover it. The man was too good to me.

We reached the top of the stairs, where a window overlooked the alley behind his bar. Dan faced the closed door to the left of the window, and I wiped my sweaty palms against my shorts. *My new place.* He set the bags down and retrieved a blue carabiner clipped on the belt loop of his jeans. I'd given him that carabiner ten years ago when he kept losing his keys. *Can't believe he's still using it.*

He thumbed through the keys on the faded D ring until he reached an especially dark one, then slipped it in the lock of my new home. "Now, it's not much, honey," he twisted the key, and a soft *click* allowed the door to creak open, "but it's something." He gathered my luggage and walked in. "I tried to get it clean, but it was hard on the knees, you know?"

I shuffled in behind him, and the weight I'd carried on my chest for weeks lightened. Over the phone, he'd made it sound like a hovel no better than a cave in the Stone Age, but I *loved* it.

An open floor plan provided a clear view to the living room straight ahead, the dining room beside it on the right, and the kitchen directly to my right. My gaze swept around for points of entry, and the tension in my shoulders eased. The only way in—unless someone scaled the building—was through the same door we'd used. The only other door in the place led to a bedroom.

"Kitchen." Dan wandered toward a single line of counter broken up by a fridge on the end and a stove and sink in the middle. "Dining room." He gestured to the space cornered between the kitchen and living room. Warm light spilled from a giant window that would be perfect for work. "Living room." He jerked his head toward the room holding an old CRT TV and a weathered red couch.

Giddiness fluttered in my stomach. *This is perfect to start over.* Cozy and simple.

The tour took us to the bedroom next. Although it wasn't spacious, it had a walk-in closet and an en suite. Another large window let light in from the left of the bed. A small bed. Didn't matter. It was only me, anyway.

"This is perfect." I dropped my bag and spun around to take it in.

A smile graced Dan's gruff face. "I'm glad you like it. Now, come on." He headed for the front door, and I followed. "Let me show you where to park and how to get in without walking through the whole bar."

Thank God. Not that I wasn't grateful to be here, but I worried I'd have to navigate crowds of drunk people every time I came home.

Home. Moving from New Mexico to California was a big change, but one I needed. I'd never lived alone. Even now, I wasn't *that* alone. Dan lived next door.

As soon as I told him my plans to move, he offered the apartment above his bar and refused to allow me to pay more than the dirt cheap three hundred bucks a month. Maybe he wasn't officially my father or uncle, but he was the closest thing I'd ever had to one. He'd been in my and Mom's life since I was a little girl. Blood didn't make him family. Presence and time did.

We met him when I was a mischievous toddler who wandered into his yard at the trailer park and plucked one of his tulips out of the perfectly lined collection he'd gardened. Mom was wary at first when he offered to help her with me. She was single, worked her ass off as a nurse, and got no help from my deadbeat father. When Mom asked Dan why he'd want to help us, he told her, "You remind me of someone."

A couple weeks later, we learned that *someone* meant his daughter and granddaughter who'd died in a car accident the year before we moved into the trailer next door. In a minuscule way, we helped fill the void they left. Like he filled the dad void in my life.

We missed Dan like hell when he moved to California, but we encouraged his dream to own a bar, just like his father. After his dad died, and Dan inherited the bar, the only thing holding him back was Mom and me. We didn't allow the opportunity to pass him by, and he moved at the beginning of my senior year of high school.

There were many late-night phone calls after he left. It was odd to come home and not find him sitting on his porch with a cigarette, ready to hear any and all problems we had. He listened to my angsty emotions through grade school, even when he moved away to the very bar I now called home too.

We reached the bottom of the stairs, and Dan gestured to a hallway beside the staircase. "Take the car around to the little alley behind the bar. At the end, there's dumpsters and a couple parking places. Yours is the one I'm not in. There's a door I'll open for you. You got a lot of other bags?"

"Two more, but I got it." I pecked him on the cheek. "Don't worry."

It didn't take long to find the alleyway and move my truck. As instructed, I parked next to Dan's truck—the newer version of mine. He bought it the day he gave me his old one, although he had a van too.

Sure enough, Dan waited by the door when I pulled in. He insisted on taking the bags despite hissing at the pain in his knee. I set my hands on my hips and huffed at him.

He chuckled. "I know, I know." He hefted a duffle over his shoulder. "Let me, would you? I know you're capable. It helps me feel less like an old man."

Old man. Pretty sure he was born an old man.

Upstairs, he deposited my bags and held out a key ring with four keys on it. "This is for the front door." He clasped the chain by one key, then switched to the next. "This is for the back door. This one's for your place. This last one will get you into my house." He handed the keys over, and I practically bounced.

New start, here I come. A new start where the only man I allowed in my life was the one in front of me.

"Why don't you settle in, then I'll get you something to eat in the bar, all right?" Dan asked.

I nodded, unable to stop my wide smile. "Thanks."

The moment the door shut with him on the other side, I jumped and squealed. This was everything I needed. Isolated, but not too much. A new town. A new place far away from the drama I left behind.

I'd inherited my mother's horrible taste in men. Many of her exes had been abusive, and so were mine. I only recently told Dan about it because I worried he'd drive there with his rifle to handle it for me. The one time I'd been afraid of Dan was when I came home with a black eye at fifteen, courtesy of my first boyfriend. Dan overheard me tell Mom the jerk had threatened to do worse. That night, Dan sat on our porch, cigarette and rifle in hand. What happened, I never knew, but the guy didn't bother me more, and by the next day, he'd switched schools.

I never heard from him again.

That incident was one of many reasons living near Dan gave me security. The tone of his voice when I finally told him what happened with this last ex, Todd, was ingrained in my memory. Calling to tell him I'd been in the hospital with a concussion and broken ribs was the worst phone call I ever had to make.

Exhausted from the drive, I didn't have enough energy to unpack everything. Essentials came out first, including toiletries and pajamas. Bless Dan, he'd tried to clean, but a lot of corners were dusty. *A problem for future me.*

A shower beckoned, but my grumbling stomach demanded I put it off. I fished out my makeup bag and worked on the dark circles around my eyes, which rivaled the brown of my irises. Tossing my loose brunette curls in a bun, I made my way to the bar.

The later hour attracted more of a crowd, but I still had plenty of space next to the cash register, conveniently located near the staircase.

Dan already had a grilled ham and cheese sandwich with a pickle spear waiting. The added side of fries wasn't the traditional dinner he'd served me as a kid, but I never said no to fries.

Like five years hadn't passed, Dan and I fell into our nightly ritual of dinner and chitchat. I knew I missed it, but I had no idea how much until he was complaining about his hatred for doing the bar's taxes. I could've stayed with him all night if not for the long drive.

"Goodnight, Louise," I said, pecking him on the cheek. He put up with constant *Thelma & Louise* reruns when I was a kid and eventually agreed to be my Louise.

"Goodnight, Thelma." He chuckled and kissed the top of my head. "Give me a holler if you need anything, honey."

"I'll be okay. Thanks."

Okay. I was okay enough.

For the first time in weeks, I fell asleep without clutching my pepper spray. If Todd found me, I had Dan living right next door in his dad's old place.

Even though I barely saw him the following two days, Dan didn't mind. But he'd been lonely without us, and I wanted to keep him company. On the other hand, I was determined to get my shit together in my new home. At least I managed lunch with him each day.

Before I moved, I'd arranged an art show in the next town over and sent all my prints and drawings to Dan ahead of time, so I wouldn't have to travel with them. Of course, Dan already had them neatly set up in my new dining room when I arrived.

On Friday, I rushed around my apartment, packing. I'd opted to stay in a hotel rather than drive back and forth. Thankfully, the art show spanned from Saturday afternoon to Sunday evening, so my inability to leave on time wouldn't impede a punctual arrival tomorrow. It'd work out, but the hour was later than I intended, and that also meant the crowd at the bar started forming by the time I had to take my stuff down.

Lovely.

Deciding it was better to get my largest package over with first, I carefully maneuvered the tall but narrow box into the hall. It held forty-by-sixty prints, and with packaging, the box was taller than me. Not that it said much. Standing a couple inches below five and a half feet sucked. I couldn't reach a damn thing.

Regardless, I shimmied around the box and descended the stairs backwards, easing it down one step at a time. A loud *thud* announced a misstep, and I winced, waiting for Dan's inevitable concern.

"You all right, Scar?" Dan called from the bar. "Need help?"

"No, I don't need help. I'm good!"

My next steps were more careful. The last thing Dan needed was to climb the stairs with his bad knee. I made it to the bottom and sighed. A relief that vanished as quickly as it arrived. The end of the bar with the cash register lined up exactly with the stairway. The box could only get so far before it hit the bar.

I stepped back and tilted my head. I'd need to lift one end or . . . *No. Definitely lift it up and over.*

"Do you need help with that?" A gravelly voice from the other side of the box elicited goose bumps on my arms.

I peeked around the package, and there, sitting at the bar, was the source of the voice—a man too sexy to not be on the cover of a magazine.

My mouth fell open as I took in the giant. His black hair was short on the sides and longer on top. Some hung in his piercing blue eyes, a dark shade reminiscent of the ocean after a heavy storm. The black shirt he wore strained across his broad chest and muscled, tattooed arms. Long fingers curled around a glass full of amber liquid. The bar hid the rest of him from me, but I didn't need to see it to drool.

Past Scarlett would've jumped him in an instant. Those arms. Those lips. Those *hands*. I would've done bad things with him and thanked him afterward.

My gaze finally wandered to his eyes again, only to find him mimicking my actions with a full body appraisal. He dragged his tongue across the front of his teeth. Irritation lifted my chin, though I couldn't be mad. Didn't I just do that to him?

"I'm good," I squeaked. My voice wasn't usually so high, but *damn*.

He arched a brow and surveyed my situation. "You sure?"

"Yeah, I got it." I ducked behind the box to hide from his panty-wetting eye contact. *Good Lord.* He was barely human. More like a god. *He's just a guy.* An attractive guy, but a guy nonetheless. Hadn't I sworn those off?

I set my hands over my too warm cheeks and observed my situation again. I'd need to lift the box over the bar *and* cash register. I gnawed my lip and eyed the bottles of alcohol Dan kept next to the register. If I got distracted by the perfect specimen or made one wrong move, those bottles would shatter on the ground.

Easy does it. I gripped the package, lifted, then lost my confidence and eased it to the ground. Two more attempts later, I braced to lift, but it elevated on its own.

No. Not on its own. Strong hands decorated with scars on the knuckles grasped the sides and hoisted it out of my grip. I followed the path of powerful, inked arms to the mystery man. The box cleared the bar and everything on it with plenty of room to spare. He set it down and when our gazes collided, my body tensed. Stood at attention. The corner of his mouth lifted, and I swallowed against my dry throat.

Leather, sandalwood, and scotch filled my nostrils—a combination a little too close to home.

CHAPTER TWO

Off-Limits

RYKER

Nothing quite captured the homey experience of our regular bar like the smell of scotch, leather, and cigarettes. Add to that the murmur of conversation mingled with classic rock that echoed off the wooden walls and floors, the place was a haven. My crew and I settled into Danny's after an extended ride along the coast. While the others planned to get someone on the back of their motorcycle and into their bed, I wanted a damn drink.

Danny didn't bother asking my order. I'd been coming in since before he took the place over. His father was a good man and kind to us. Didn't assume the worst when a motorcycle club walked in and took up more than half his bar. The motorcycles, the leather, the tattoos—they unnerved the faint of heart. Danny and his father were anything but.

We visited regularly, but tonight, excitement hung in the air. Danny hadn't stopped smiling. He often had a bit of sadness in him. Not tonight. Not even his usual grumpy scowl made an appearance, and I had a guess as to why.

"Your girl finally here?" I asked, sipping my favorite scotch as I adjusted on the oak barstool.

"Yes." He grinned and wiped the bar top with a rag from his back pocket. "Made it in a couple nights ago."

"Bet it's nice to have her around."

"It is. She's been busy, though." He retrieved my scotch and topped off my drink. I tilted it toward him in thanks before taking another sip. "She's got an art show this weekend that's taken up all her time. That and settling in. But," he inclined the glass he was polishing toward me, "she eats lunch with me every day."

A smile fought its way to my lips. He'd been talking this girl up for weeks. He'd told me about both mother and daughter years ago, but he had a new kind of enthusiasm when the daughter decided to move here and take the room over the bar. Never seen him happier.

Dan didn't talk much. More listened to everyone else. Put a couple whiskeys in him, and it was a different story. That's when he told us about them. How they saved his life without knowing it. Gave him something to live for. Apparently, his PTSD from serving got the better of him after he lost his whole world when his girls died. He planned to end it with a gun. Then, a little girl wandered into his yard and picked his carefully gardened flowers.

Since I was also a few drinks deep when Danny got to the point of his storytelling, I couldn't remember *all* the stories or the girls' names. Just that they meant the world to him.

A *thud* from the stairs jerked Danny's attention away. "You all right, Scar?" he called out. "Need help?"

"No, I don't need help!" came the response. "I'm good."

Damn. She had a sweet voice. Even yelling, it was sweet as sugar.

"She doesn't want my help anymore," Danny grumbled as he snatched another glass to polish. "Every time I offer, it's *no thank you, Dan. I can take care of myself.*"

"Sounds like you helped raise her right."

"I know." Danny sighed and braced his knobby hands on the bar. "But it's nice to be needed, isn't it? I almost miss the days she was a little girl, coming to me with every problem under the sun because she knew I'd take care of it for her. Now, I hear about everything afterward." He frowned. "She's not so little anymore, Ryker. She's grown up a lot. What am I supposed to do about that?"

"Let her be. She still needs you. She's here, isn't she?"

He wrinkled his nose. "I suppose, but she didn't call me when that bastard put her in the hospital. You know what she did?" He chuckled and shook his head. "She took self-defense classes, and the next time he tried to hit her, she hit him harder. I don't know whether to be proud or pissed she didn't let me take care of it."

"A little of both seems fair." I remembered him telling me about that asshole. I offered to drive with him to handle it, but he refused. He wouldn't admit that she took after him in not wanting anybody's help.

A bell from the kitchen drew Danny's focus. He tucked the rag in his back pocket and went through the double doors at the same time a girl descended the stairs, battling a box bigger than her.

No. Not a girl. A *woman*. Goddamn.

I had no plans to hook up, but my pants tightened at the sight of that ass. The jeans she wore weren't too tight, but they were snug around her ass. Dark brown hair fell in loose curls down her spine, landing above the hem of her jeans, and *fuck me*. There I was again. Staring at that ass.

What the hell is wrong with you? I shook my head to clear my thoughts as she struggled with the box, ending up on the other side before I saw her face. I prayed she was ugly because God help me if that was Danny's girl.

Fuck. It had to be. She came from the stairs leading to the room I'd helped Danny load a bunch of art boxes into over the last couple of weeks. Unless she had a friend, she was Danny's.

The box shifted a few times, and a huff of frustration later, I spoke without thinking. "Do you need help with that?"

The temptress peeked around the box, and all hope of something being wrong with her went to shit. Her mouth opened like an invitation. Her gaze swept over me, and I took the opportunity to return the favor.

My gaze drifted as I took her in, and *fuck*, was there something to take in. Her tits were as generous as her ass, so much so her shirt stretched over them. A pinch in her waist and hips that flared out gave her that perfect hourglass figure. Curvy and fucking gorgeous.

Before drool slipped out of my mouth, I forced my eyes to find hers. She drew her lower lip between her teeth. I swept my tongue over my lip, imagining what hers would feel like.

"I'm good," she squeaked. Her focus drifted over me once more, and by the time those big brown eyes found their way to mine, a blush dusted her cheeks.

Good to know I wasn't the only one affected.

"You sure?" I asked, eyeing her. She'd have to lift the package over the bar, and she didn't have much height to her.

"Yeah, I got it."

She ducked out of sight, and I leaned over the bar to watch her struggle. The cardboard rose, then dropped. Twice. Like Danny said, she didn't want any help.

The package elevated again, clearing the bar, but not the register. I sighed when it lowered once more. *The hell with it.* The barstool scraped as I stood and sauntered over to her. I grabbed the box and hauled it above the bar and register, then set it down on the other side.

"Thanks," she muttered. "I would've had it."

I shrugged and eyed the hallway. That was most likely her destination unless she intended to carry this box through the entire bar. "Where's it going?" I asked. My attention returned to her in time to find her biting that luscious lip again, and checking me out. For the second time.

If she was going to be blatant about it, I might as well too.

"Out back to my car. I can get it."

"Are there more?"

"Yes." She set her hands on her full hips, and I suppressed a groan. She was a looker. "Like I said, I can get them."

"I know you can. I just don't think you should have to do it all by yourself." I slid the box toward the hallway. "Nothing wrong with accepting a little help, is there?"

No protest. *Interesting.* I expected one. Soon enough, she brushed past me, her arm grazing mine as she stalked ahead. My eyes shut briefly. That skin was *soft*. I bet she was soft all over.

"Fine, but be careful with it," she clipped.

I bit back a smile. Feisty. Voluptuous. This girl was ticking all my boxes a little too well. I followed her into the alley lot, where she opened the back of Danny's van. Yep. Definitely Dan's girl. *Dammit.*

"It's fragile." Her hands hovered over the box.

"I can be gentle."

She cleared her throat and stepped away. Another smile fought its way forward as I eased the cargo inside. She closed the van, and I trailed her inside, where she turned for the stairs.

She paused and pivoted on her heel, staring up at me even though she was on the first step. "You don't have to help."

I crossed my arms. "How many more?" A smirk spread over my face at her lack of answer. Not because she didn't speak but because of why she didn't. She wetted her lips and rubbed her thighs, taking her sweet ass time ogling me. This girl was anything but as innocent as Danny claimed. "Well?" I pressed.

Her eyes widened as they flew to mine. Blush intensifying, she darted her eyes away as quickly as she'd made contact. "Um, well . . . four."

Putting my fingers to my lips, I whistled for the guys and held up three fingers to let them know how many I needed. Three of my buddies approached. "Lead the way."

I knew the way but didn't want to freak the poor girl out. We hadn't technically introduced ourselves yet. It was bad enough I couldn't keep my eyes off her ass swaying as she ascended the stairs.

She let us into her place, and my boys grabbed the boxes, then went downstairs. I set my hand on the last box and glanced around the room to check for more. "That all, sugar?"

"Don't call me that." She leveled a glare at me. "I can't stand pet names like that."

I worked my jaw to withhold the smile. She was somehow sexier when annoyed. That'd be fun to play with. I stepped toward her and enjoyed the way she swallowed, unable to keep eye contact with me.

"No?" I paused inches away from her. "What should I call you, then?"

"Scarlett—Scarlett's my name," she stammered.

"*Scarlett,*" I drawled, testing the name on my lips. "Mmm," I hummed. I could see myself saying that name while she was underneath me. "I like it."

Scarlett blinked. Her pouty lips parted. What really did it was the way she slowly drew her legs together. *Fuck me.* I was about to say *sayonara* to self-control. With the last two working brain cells I had, I left her to process before I did something stupid.

Outside, the guys gave me questioning looks. I shrugged and said nothing. If they needed a reason, we helped because it was Danny's girl. No other motivation.

Scarlett made it outside and offered shy smiles to the guys on her way to the van. Once she opened it, we loaded the packages, and she thanked each of them. I rested the last box inside and leaned against the brick alley wall, tugging on my lower lip when her shirt rode up as she stood on her toes to reach the trunk.

Shit. That skin was warm and sun-kissed. I wanted to see more of it. Touch it. Taste it.

"Thank you." She faced me and wrung her hands together. "It was unnecessary, but thank you."

I nodded and didn't bother hiding my appraisal of her. She didn't in the bar, and damn, there wasn't a bad thing to look at. She shifted her weight and eyed me for a moment, then scurried inside. I chuckled and followed, half tempted to push her up against the wall to see how she'd react.

Good thing I didn't because we rounded the corner and almost ran into Danny.

"You all right?" Danny pushed the back of his hand against her forehead like a nervous mother. "You look flushed."

Her flushed expression has nothing to do with being sick. Your little girl is definitely not so little.

"No, no." She batted at his hand with a nervous laugh. "I'm fine."

"You sure?"

"I'm sure."

I cleared my throat to stop the building snort and took my place at the bar.

"All right, honey," he said, brows knit together. "Got all your things?"

She nodded. Then her eyes widened. "Shit. I forgot my suitcase. And my dress."

Danny chuckled as she raced upstairs. Another bell dinged, and Dan ambled through the double doors to the kitchen. Scarlett returned with her suitcase and a dress thrown over her shoulder. She scanned the bar, and when those beautiful eyes landed on me, I couldn't help myself.

I met her gaze and sipped my drink. "Thought you didn't like pet names, Scarlett."

She rolled her eyes. "I don't."

"Dan called you honey."

"That's different."

"How?"

Her pink tongue darted out along her lip, and my pants tightened.

"It . . ." The words died when I finished my drink and licked the remains off my lips. She watched the movement. The energy crackling between us practically hummed. "It just is."

"Hmm," I grunted. *Bullshit.*

"How would you like it if I called you—" she gestured in a vague circle before her eyes lit up with a victory that wouldn't last "Baby?"

Well, now she was baiting me. "I'd like that quite a bit, Scarlett."

She was at risk of Danny checking her temperature again with how red she turned. The corner of my mouth pulled up in a smirk.

"You're annoying . . ." Her tone implied she was about to full name me, but she didn't know my first name yet. "What's your name?"

Called it. I could be annoying. Especially if it was going to bring out her feisty side. "Ryker, sugar." I winked. "The name's Ryker."

She scowled and crossed her arms. "I told you not to call me that."

"I thought we agreed you'd call me baby, and I'd call you sugar?" I leaned on my forearms over the bar, so I could see more of her. "Or is it that you'd rather we call each other baby? I can work with that."

She pressed her lips together. Her eyes narrowed in a challenge I was too willing to jump on.

Danny came through the doors. "Ready, honey?"

I hid my amusement behind my glass. One moment of a glower was all I got from her before she pecked Danny on the cheek. "Ready. I'll see you in two days. Don't work too hard."

"You be safe driving all that way alone," Danny said. "Call me when you get in."

Everything about her softened, and I was glad I wasn't on the receiving end of the smile she gave him. So warm it would've melted me. *God fucking dammit, who am I right now?*

"I promise." She hugged Danny, then turned for the exit. "Bye."

"Bye, honey." Once she was out of sight, Danny sighed and turned to me. "Isn't she a sweetheart?"

Sweetheart? Not the word I'd use. Thankfully, Danny moved on to other customers, chatting more animatedly than before his hug from Scarlett.

Dammit. Scarlett was off-limits. Danny would kill me. He liked me well enough, but I could only imagine what he'd think if I made a pass at his little sweetheart, and she took it. And she'd take it. I could see it in her eyes.

She's forbidden fruit.

That made me want her even more.

CHAPTER THREE

Roxy

SCARLETT

The art show went better than I hoped. I showed up with over ten large pieces and a handful of smaller ones. I came home with one small drawing. That was a *huge* success for an artist, and I made lots of good contacts thanks to René, a gallery owner in town who encouraged me to move so I could immerse myself in the art community and be featured in her gallery. I met her last year when she scouted talent at my college exhibition. We'd hit it off, and she loved my work. All positive things.

Of course, René was also the reason I had a ceaseless nagging in my head. I gripped the steering wheel tighter, twisting my fists around it. The show went well. I had no reason to overthink. Yet, one single interaction with her stood out amongst all the praise.

"Thank you so much for helping me get in," I'd said to René.

She looked stunning as ever in her black high heels and long, red dress. Everything about her, from her gently waved mahogany hair cascading along her spine to the way she glided toward patrons, screamed *class*. I did my best in the little black number I bought from an off-price department store.

"You didn't need my help." René swirled sparkling wine in her glass, her nude nails scraping against the smooth texture. "You're doing great. I can't wait for your masterwork."

"What do you mean?"

"When you finally figure it out. You're already amazing." She smiled and tilted her glass toward me. "Outstanding, even. Once you figure it out, it's over for everyone else here."

"Figure what out?"

"You know, whatever it is Scarlett needs." She gestured vaguely. "What she wants. There's something holding you back. You're the only one who can figure out what it is. You'll see what I mean."

What I wanted *and* needed? I'd already figured that out. Or I thought I had. She had me questioning my own decisions, and not even blaring music on the drive home quieted my thoughts.

All my needs were provided for. I had a place to live, a somewhat steady income, plus I had Dan. What else could a girl possibly need? As far as wants . . . Everyone wanted something they didn't have. Once upon a time, I'd wanted a life that included a family. I'd wanted a husband who couldn't take his hands off me and a kid I'd spend all the time with that my mom never could with me because she had to provide for us by herself. *Assuming I can have a kid with the PCOS and endometriosis.*

I'd thrown all those hopes out when I swore off men, but it wasn't as if my new life was something to scoff at. I got to live in California, next to a father figure I adored, doing what I loved. It'd be greedy to want more.

I huffed and shook my head. This was getting to me too much. René was a distinguished collector. She knew her shit. Whatever she meant, I needed to figure it out, but I didn't need to get existential about it.

As I approached the bar, I turned early. Dan was working, and that meant his house and garage were empty. I pulled into his driveway and texted him that I was ten minutes out. This was my only chance.

I crept up to the rustic house with faded white paint chipping off the siding. The single, recently planted tree in the front yard provided minimal coverage, so I moved quickly until the side fence shielded me in case Dan took out the trash. I fumbled with my spare key for the side door leading into the garage and twisted it in the lock. The resulting *creak* when it opened made me wince, though logically, Dan couldn't hear it from inside the bar.

Dust greeted me, and I wrinkled my nose as I batted at the stale, hot air. He must've forgotten to turn the light off today because the dim bulb in the middle of the garage illuminated floating particles.

I approached the covered motorcycle that hadn't been ridden in years but was still his baby. Yanking the cover off, I coughed at the dust that lifted with it. My nose tickled until I gave in and squeaked out a sneeze.

"What are you doing in here?"

I screamed and turned. Ryker stood a few feet behind me, boots covered in dust. My heart restarted. Then my brows pulled together. "What are *you* doing in here? I have a key."

He held up Dan's blue carabiner. "So do I."

My shoulders deflated. Was he not only a regular but also Dan's *friend*? That made him an even worse idea. "Oh. Question still applies."

He crossed his thick, tattooed arms, and I needed to fan myself for more than the hot garage air. "I asked first."

"Yeah, well, Dan's practically my family, and this house goes to me, so you're almost trespassing if you don't tell me why you're here."

His lips quirked in a half-smile. "My buddy's bike needs work, and Dan said he had some spare parts." He jingled the keys at me. "Told me to take my pick of anything. Specifically asked I don't touch the bike you just uncovered."

I nodded, avoiding his eyes. "Yep. He doesn't like anyone touching Roxy."

"But you're here touching Roxy."

"Technically, I touched Roxy's cover. Not Roxy herself."

A muscle in his jaw ticked. "What are you doing, sugar?"

I rolled my eyes. "Enough with the sugar thing. What I'm doing is none of your business."

He shrugged. "Fine." He hefted some piece of metal up and made his way to the exit. "I'll ask Danny."

"No!" I ran in front of him and held up my hands. "Don't do that."

He cocked his head. "Thought this place was practically yours. What do you have to hide?"

I sighed and gestured to the motorcycle. "Don't tell Dan you saw me. I came to take pictures of Roxy so I can make something for Father's Day. I want it to be a surprise."

"Ah." He observed the fogged-over lightbulb. "The lighting's shit."

"I know, but I don't want him to hear this prehistoric garage open, so I'll work with what I've got."

"Got a flashlight on my phone." He set down his hunk of metal. "Want a hand?"

I'd like both your hands on me, please and thanks. I cleared my throat and shook my head. "I'm good."

"Do you know how much you're like Dan, or do you two enjoy pretending one is more stubborn than the other?"

"I'm not stubborn."

He arched a brow. "You're trying to get pictures of that old bike in this shitty lighting, and you have an easy way to get help but won't take it. Remind you of anyone?"

I scowled and moved around him. "Fine. Hold up your flashlight. Just don't say anything to Dan."

He whistled low. "Wow. Keep talking sweet to me, sugar. Gets me every time."

"How long have you known Dan?" I circled the motorcycle to find the best angle. Charcoal drawing, definitely. It would fit the rest of his aesthetic. "Hold the flashlight here."

Ryker came up behind me and raised his phone, shining the flashlight on the bike. "Right here?"

"Yeah." I gulped. He stood less than a foot away, his body heat adding to the sweltering room. A heat that grew with the addictive aroma of leather and scotch.

"I've known him since he took over the bar a few years ago," Ryker said. "Knew his old man before that."

"So, you guys are friends?" *Translation: Are you friends and off-limits to me?* Not that it mattered. *No men.* I needed to get that tattooed on my face so I'd remember.

"I'd like to think so. Don't believe many people hand over the keys to their house without a little trust."

I gnawed on my lip and held up my phone for a picture. "Fair enough. How old are you?"

"What is this, an interrogation?"

Sort of. "You're old, aren't you?"

He narrowed his eyes. "Twenty-nine. You?"

"Twenty-two."

"Fuck," he muttered.

I tilted my head. "What?"

"Nothing." He cleared his throat. "Nothing at all."

I peered at him through slitted eyes, but he gave nothing away. "Angle your light to the left, please."

He shifted the phone. "Like this?"

"Perfect." I moved to snap different angles of the bike. I hadn't decided exactly how I wanted it to look, but I had time. "Hold."

The man's patience unnerved me. Given most of my boyfriends lacked it, him possessing a quality I would've appreciated pre-trauma didn't help the *no men* mantra I continued chanting. He waited while I took a dozen pictures, then moved the light again and waited through another dozen. By the time we were done, I was due at Dan's. He'd get nervous if I didn't walk in soon, and worse, this guy being decent wasn't helping my resolve to remain celibate for life. *Vibrator excluded, obviously.*

"I got what I need, thanks." I picked up the cover, and Ryker took the other end. Together, we re-covered Roxy. My phone vibrated. Dan was probably worried. Pulling out my phone, I then opened my messages.

Unknown: *Can we talk?*

My eyes widened. Was that—

It *couldn't* be. Well, it could. Todd had my number. Did he get a new number? *Oh God.* My chest tightened, and I rubbed it like that'd stop the muscles from tensing. I could barely breathe, and I hated it. He didn't deserve to have this power over me, but it wasn't necessarily him. It could be anyone. A wrong number, maybe.

"Hey, you all right?"

"What?" Breathless, I snapped my gaze up. That asshole made me anxious states away. This was exactly why I swore off men, and here I was, ogling a different one.

Ryker's brows drew together. "You look like you saw a ghost."

"No," I squeaked and pocketed my phone. He narrowed his eyes. My stomach turned, and I forced a smile. "I'm running behind on when I told Dan I'd be back. He gets worried."

"Right." Ryker's expression twisted in suspicion, but I held my ground. He nodded to the covered bike as he picked up his hunk of metal. "You ever ride?"

I snorted. "No. I don't ride."

His mouth tilted in a smirk. "Motorcycles, or anything?"

Heat flooded my face and chest.

He sniggered and turned for the door. "See you around, sugar."

CHAPTER FOUR

Sweet as Sugar

SCARLETT

Once I recovered from Ryker's flirtatious comment, I hurried to the van. I parked in the alleyway, then collected my suitcase and the bag with my framed drawing. Entering through the back, I raced around the corner and found Dan typing into his register.

"Scar." He tossed a rag over his flannel-covered shoulder. "My famous artist."

I grinned. "Don't get ahead of yourself."

"Don't undervalue yourself." He gave me a look before refocusing on his customer. "Take it easy." He handed change to the customer, then gestured to the stool by the register. "Sit. We should celebrate. I'll get you a drink. You hungry?"

"I'm starved." I set my hand on my stomach. "But I need a shower. I'll be fast. Then I'll take you up on that drink, and I could use one of those really unhealthy burgers you make with all the cheese and bacon."

Those burgers would probably cause my death, but I didn't care. There was cheese and bacon *inside* the burger as well as on top. A heart attack waiting to happen, but they tasted divine.

"Sounds good." He nodded to the bag in my hands. "Hey, let me look at the last one you got."

"Sure. Don't get grease on it." I handed it over. "I'll be right back."

Suitcase in tow, I hurried upstairs and showered fast at my rumbling stomach's demand. After the shower, I put on the first things I found—some shorts, a V-neck, and sandals to avoid being barefoot.

In the kitchen, I plucked out a glass with intent to get water. However, when I turned the handle, an unusual *hiss* caught my attention. I frowned and opened the bottom cupboard. Sure enough, a leak in the pipe sprayed water at me. Sighing, I snatched a hair tie on my way out and bounded down the steps, throwing my curls up in a bun as I went.

"Dan, do you have tools I can borrow, or can you check out my kitchen sink?" I asked when I hit the last step.

"Sure, honey. What's the problem?" He poured a glass of amber liquid and slid it across the counter.

"I think a pipe is loose. I'd fix it, but I don't have any tools. If you give them to me, I can figure it out."

"I'll fix it for you after closing," Dan said.

"I can look at it, Danny. You shouldn't be on your knees."

Oh no. Shouldn't Mr. Flirty be fixing his friend's bike? I rubbed my sweaty hands over my shorts and tried to avoid glancing at Ryker, who I hadn't noticed sitting at the bar.

"Well . . ." Dan furrowed his brows. "I'd rather it was fixed for her soon."

"It's okay, I can wai—"

Ryker rose from his stool. "Tools in the same spot?"

"Yep. Scar, will you show him the way? This is Ryker, by the way. Ryker, this is Scarlett," Dan introduced. "Ryker helps out around here."

While I couldn't think of an argument, Ryker, that ass, stifled a laugh when Dan was occupied with a customer. Ryker strolled into the back and returned with a toolbox. I glared. He gestured for me to go upstairs.

This seems dangerous. "I can figure it out."

"You don't have to, sugar," he said, climbing the stairs.

Damn him. Damn his nice butt in front of me as I followed him up.

"Don't call m—"

"Oh, right. I'm sorry. My bad, baby." He winked at me over his shoulder as we ascended.

At the top, he leaned against the wall and waited. Huffing, I opened the door and led him to the kitchen. Ryker set down the tools, then turned on the sink. That hissing returned. He crouched and inspected underneath while I tried not to gawk.

He ended up lying on his back, head disappearing under the pipes. Without worrying he'd catch me, I fully appreciated him. His shirt tonight clung to him much like that first night. It rode up as he reached under the sink with a tool.

I salivated. Abs. Abs for days and a dusting of dark hair with a V leading . . .

Thankful he couldn't see me, I fanned myself. My gaze continued over his jeans and thick thighs to his work boots. *God, if he's not the world's most perfect specimen.*

"That should do it." He slid out from under the sink and turned the tap on.

Much to my dismay, he hadn't failed. The water flowed, hiss-free.

He packed away the tools, then straightened and plopped the toolbox on the counter. "Anything else need fixing, sugar?"

I scowled. "How would you like it if I called you sugar?"

"Hmm," he hummed and pushed off the counter, advancing toward me. His hand lifted and I flinched.

Dammit, no. I refuse to be scared of anyone lifting a hand. I held my ground as he tried again, tilting my chin up toward him. He invaded my space with another step closer. His hot breath hit my lips, and my body sparked with awareness.

"I wouldn't mind it, baby. I wouldn't mind it one bit. I like pet names." My lips parted without my permission when he rubbed his thumb over my bottom one. "Why don't you give it a try, and see how you like it?"

An ache pulsed in my lower half. "You're the worst." I scoffed, finding the strength to shove him.

"The *worst*? Really? Come on, Scarlett," he said, drawling my name. "I fixed your sink. You're not going to thank me?"

Oh, I could think of a way to thank him. It included very few clothes.

No! Bad Scarlett. Deciding a response wasn't safe, I rushed out the door. He laughed, but I ignored it and didn't slow down until I found Dan at the bar.

"All good?" Dan asked.

I forced a smile. "Yep."

"Have a seat. Your burger's almost ready. You want a whiskey?"

I hopped on the stool. "Please."

"Here's the drawing." He slid the framed piece across the bar top. "It's really good, Scar. I'm sure someone's gonna snatch it up."

I grinned to myself while he flitted to the kitchen. It didn't matter what happened in my life, praise from Dan would always mean the world to me. I was lucky that he wasn't stingy with it. I reached for the drawing, but another hand claimed it first. Ryker's hand.

"You drew this?" He picked up the frame.

My heart rate sped up. *Why does his opinion make me nervous?* "Yes."

"It's incredible." He rotated it in the light. "I thought maybe Danny talked you up too much. Guess I was wrong. I hear you have some celebrating to do, Scarlett."

It took me a moment to compose myself at his compliment. And the way he said my name, something he had to be doing on purpose. Unfortunately, I found myself staring at him again. He stared right back. Jackass. At least he returned the drawing before Dan approached.

"Your burger." Dan slid the plate in front of me, then poured my drink. "Here's to you, my rising artist." He clinked his glass of water with my whiskey.

"Thanks." I giggled, taking a sip. I returned the drawing to its bag and tucked it next to the register. It was time to dig into my glorious burger. I pointedly turned my body away from Ryker while I ate. Why was he here again already anyway?

"Another, Ryker?" Dan called out.

Ryker turned over his glass to Dan. "Thanks."

"This one's on the house," Dan said. "For taking care of that pipe."

"Not a problem, Danny." Ryker positioned himself on the stool next to mine.

We both sat on the corner, so it wasn't as if we were side by side. Still, irritation straightened my spine. There was plenty of space at the bar. He didn't need to sit *right* next to me. I peeked over to find him glancing over his shoulder, narrowing his eyes at something.

I hated how sexy his glare was. I hated how sexy all of him was. I needed to get him off my radar.

"Are you an alcoholic or something?" I blurted out. *Wow. Smooth, Scarlett.*

Ryker brought his gaze to mine, eyebrows raised. "Are *you*?"

"No." I wiped my face with a napkin. The burger was messy, and the last thing I needed was a verbal sparring match with a slop of ketchup on the corner of my mouth.

"And what makes you think I am, sugar?" He raised his glass to his lips.

I'd like to be that glass. "I've barely been here and have already seen you twice. Plus, you seem to lack memory since I told you more than once not to call me that."

"Well, you called me an alcoholic. I think it's only fair I get to call you *something*, Scarlett."

There it was again. He was saying my name differently on purpose.

I dropped my burger. "Do you like saying my name or what?"

"Yeah, I like saying your name. You know what I like more?" He leaned forward on muscled forearms. "Your reaction to me saying your name."

"I don't react." *Lie.*

"I don't know about that, Scarlett."

Heat enveloped my cheeks. He took a drink of my whiskey while maintaining eye contact. When he pushed the glass into my hands, his fingers very intentionally grazed mine and elicited goose bumps. He had nice, long fingers . . .

"You have good taste." He held up his glass. "Wanna try mine?"

My dry mouth fell open, but nothing came out, and once again, we were locked in a staring contest neither of us could break. Until Tammy, the waitress, hurried over, her sneakers squeaking on the floor. She gripped his arm, sparking a stupid bout of jealousy. Tammy whispered to him, and he nodded, his gaze never leaving me.

She stepped around me, and everything happened fast. Some guy came up behind Tammy, his hand going for her ass. Ryker intercepted it.

He snatched the man's wrist, twisted his arm behind him, and slammed the guy's head onto the bar. "You try to touch her again, you lose your fucking hand. Understand?"

My eyes widened. Gone was the playful Ryker from a moment ago. This was a different one, and he was *pissed*. Moisture pooled between my legs. Here I was feeling jealous when Tammy went to him for protection. How many times had he stood up for her?

The guy whimpered and nodded.

Ryker let him go and shoved him away from the bar. "Get the fuck out of here."

The guy stumbled away until he was out the door. Ryker returned to his seat, and Tammy offered a timid smile.

"Thank you." She rubbed her arms. "Sorry. I thought I could handle him."

"Don't apologize for his shitty behavior, Tammy. You can always come to me."

"Thanks, Ryker." She beamed, then returned to work.

"Did we get another asshole?" Dan asked, stepping through the kitchen doors. "I heard a ruckus."

Ryker drank the last of his scotch. "There're no shortage of drunk assholes, Danny."

Worry lines creased Dan's forehead. "Who?" His gaze landed on me.

"She wasn't the target." Ryker inclined his head to where Tammy was filling a beer from the tap. "Don't worry. He's gone."

"Oh. I'll check on Tammy. Sorry, honey." Dan patted my shoulder. "I'll chat with you in a minute."

"Don't worry about it," I said. "You're busy. I'm good."

While Dan walked away, I processed what happened. Ryker was sexy and annoying but also kind of a sweetie? That wasn't good. That wasn't good at all. Soft heart under rough exterior? A deadly combination. I couldn't think of anything to say, so I did what I did best—avoided it completely.

"You don't call Tammy sugar." I pouted.

That playful glint in his blue eyes returned. "No, Scarlett. You're the only one getting that honor."

I threw my hands up. "Why?"

"Because, sugar," his lips quirked into a half-smile that sent tingles straight between my thighs, "you have such a sweet voice. Sweetest I ever heard. I can't help but wonder, do you taste as sweet as you sound?"

Oh my God. He did not just say that.

He tilted his head. "Should I find out?"

Yes. No. Maybe.

My gaze dropped to his lips, which I wished weren't kissable. I redirected my attention and found him fixated on my mouth as well. He reached under the bar and grazed my knee with his knuckles. I closed my eyes and focused on breathing. The contact disappeared, and when I opened my eyes, his demeanor changed. He angled away, eyes averted. I frowned until I noticed Dan approaching.

Ah, so he was also aware it would be a problem. Interesting.

"How's the burger, Scar?" Dan asked, refilling Ryker's drink without asking and adding more to mine.

"Good." I picked it up in cheers. "Perfect."

"So, what have you planned next weekend?" Dan wiped the counter.

I lifted one shoulder. "Nothing."

"My gun show is next weekend."

I scrunched my face. "Ugh, no. I'm sorry. I love you, but no."

"I wasn't going to ask you, honey." He chuckled. "I know you don't want to go. I was wondering if you could help out at the bar since I'll be gone."

"Oh." I perked up. *Finally*, he'd take me up on helping out. "Of course. No problem."

"Great. I worked out a schedule with Tammy. I'll go over it with you when you're done." He twisted toward the danger to my abstinence. "Ryker, will you and the boys be around to keep an eye on Scarlett?"

"Oh my God." I rolled my eyes. "Stop. I don't need someone watching me."

"You know we will be," Ryker said. "We're here every weekend."

"Thanks." Dan grinned before looking at me guiltily. "Don't look at me like that, Scar. I know you can handle yourself, but drunk people get out of control sometimes. Nothing wrong with someone watching your back." He walked off to serve another customer.

I ground my teeth and sent a glare at Ryker, who didn't try to hide his smugness.

He waited until Dan wandered a fair distance away, then leaned over the counter, whispering quietly enough for my ears only, "Don't worry, sugar. I won't cramp your style. I'll just watch your back and everything attached to it."

CHAPTER FIVE

Clashing

RYKER

Friday night, the boys and I strolled into Danny's. I cursed when I spotted Scarlett. Watching out for her wouldn't be easy. The skirt flowing around her thick thighs barely covered her ass. Besides that, her tank top plunged well into her magnificent cleavage.

Squaring my jaw, I strode to the bar and snatched her wrist before she walked to another table. "Change."

"Oh, fuck off." She twisted out of my grip easily and sauntered past me.

I cursed again and sat at the bar. Almost every pair of eyes ogled her. *Goddamn her.*

She returned with a glass and slammed it on the bar with a loud *thud*. "I know it's scotch, but I don't know what kind." She tapped her long, red nails on the bar.

"You need to change. Right now."

She crossed her arms, pushing her already visible cleavage out more. "It's none of your business what I wear."

"Shit, Scarlett. What would Danny say if he saw you? Everyone in this bar is eye-fucking you." It took all my focus to not stare at her tits. They were a work of art. Supple and round and perfect for anything I could imagine.

"It's also none of *his* business what I wear." She posted her hands on her luscious hips, glare in full force. "Yeah, everyone in this bar *is* eye-fucking me. Including you. Stop staring at my boobs. I thought you were supposed to be watching my *back*?"

She stalked off to another customer, and I couldn't decide if I wanted to yell at her or fuck her really good. Probably both. She went along the line of the bar, getting drinks and throwing flirty smiles. The pain in the ass never got my scotch. I had to flag down Tammy.

After talking to the guys and Tammy, I got Scarlett practically cornered in the bar instead of walking around. We made everyone request Tammy instead. Scarlett tossed scowls my way, and I swear, she made an extra effort to stretch over the counter, giving gracious views of her tits to every customer to fucking spite me.

"You're pissing me off," I warned her after she was particularly flirty with another customer.

"What are you going to do about it?" Her sass made me adjust my jeans.

My mind ran wild with the creative ways I could do something about it. Flattening my palms on the bar, I leaned close enough I got a whiff of her sweet shampoo. "I'm going to bend you over this counter and smack that ass."

Her eyes widened, but she licked her lips. Composing herself, the glint in her eye was all trouble. Then, very pointedly, she rotated toward the tap and bent over in her tiny skirt, giving me a straight view to her ass. My jaw dropped and my cock went painfully rigid.

When she straightened out, a smug smile spread over her face. "Missed your chance." She sashayed away.

She was so not what Danny described. I didn't remember all he said, but the words *shy* and *sweet* stood out. I liked this version much better. Even if it pissed me off.

The night wore on, and I lost all semblance of self-control. Every time she bent over to clean something, I'd get a nice view. I wanted her. Bad. It didn't help that our sarcastic banter tightened the already limited space in my jeans. I liked she had a mouth and kept up with me.

Much to her chagrin, I stayed until closing. She complained while she cleaned, sending me to a corner so she could finish tidying the bar. Around three in the morning, she finally finished. She approached my table with a glass of what I guessed was whiskey and sat.

"You're well beyond your promised hours of babysitting," she muttered, wincing as she removed her heels and pressed her fingers into the arch of her foot.

"You trying to kick me out?" I caught her ankle.

"What are you doing?" she squeaked, pulling away.

"Relax." I rested her foot on my knee and pressed my fingers into the sole. She sighed and threw her head back. Fuck. I could get used to seeing that. "You shouldn't have worn those heels all night."

She flipped me off. "I was trying to get good tips, and it worked, thank you very much."

"Bet the tips would've been higher if you just took your top off. You're halfway to a stripper as it is."

She yanked her foot out of my grasp, eyes flashing in anger. "Who are you?" she snapped. "My parent?"

"No, sugar. Definitely not that." I chuckled, grabbing her other foot. "I guarantee I haven't felt fatherly toward you for one moment."

"Then what do you feel toward me?"

My eyes dropped to her perfect body, then flashed up to her stunning face. She noticed the look, if her rising blush had anything to say about it.

"What do you feel toward me?" I released her foot. "I wasn't the only one checking you out all night, but I'm the only one getting a blush."

Scarlett inhaled sharply and darted her eyes away. "I asked first. You act weird around me. Different than you do around Tammy. What do you want from me?"

"Don't you already know?" I raised my eyebrows. "I want the same thing you want."

"And what's that?"

"To fuck you."

Her mouth fell open, the stain on her cheeks darkening by the second. She smoothed her hand over her ponytail and crossed her legs, avoiding my eyes.

"You can't tell me you don't want it." I reclined in my seat. "You've been staring at me too."

Her slow appraisal of my body had me sitting up like I was a goddamn show pony posing. When her eyes returned to mine, she straightened her spine. "Dan would kill us both."

She was right. *I should back off right now before I make it worse.* But *fuck*, those lips. I wanted to kiss them.

"Danny doesn't need to know." I gripped her knee. Her skin was soft and warm against my palm. I could only imagine how the rest of her felt.

She clasped her hands in her lap. "How do I know you're worth the effort?"

Oh, *that's* how she wanted to play it? I narrowed my eyes at her and rose from my chair. I gripped her hips and hauled her to her feet, then dipped my head to her ear. "Trust me, Scarlett," I whispered. "I'll fuck you so good, you'll miss my cock when it's not in you." I traced her flittering pulse with my fingertip. "That's what you want, isn't it? I bet you're wet already just thinking about it."

Her chest rose and fell rapidly, her soft hands curling around my biceps. That touch ignited flames under my skin. I pulled her flush against me to revel in the burn. She shivered when I kissed her neck, body already molding to mine.

"Don't beat around the bush or anything," she breathed, tilting her head as I kissed along her neck.

"I don't play mind games. I want to fuck you. I want to fuck you hard and long and good. Do you want that, Scarlett?"

She did. I could feel it. She melted into me, and *God*, her body was soft and warm, her curves an addictive presence I worried I'd want to experience again.

"Yes."

Finally. I tossed her over my shoulder, heading for the stairs.

She squealed and smacked my back. "What are you doing?"

"What do you think? I'm taking you upstairs to fuck you." I slapped her ass as I rushed up the stairs. "Stop squirming." She moaned softly when my palm made contact with her ass. My cock twitched. "Do you like that, baby?"

"Yes."

"Fuck. I'm going to have a lot of fun with you." Once we reached the top of the stairs, I set her down and turned her to face the door. "Unlock it." I gripped her hips and ground the erection I'd had all night against her ass.

She rolled back into me as she fumbled with her keys. I smacked her ass again, the work of art turning me into a junkie in need of more hits. "Faster, Scarlett.

I'm not patient. I want to fuck you, and I'll do it right here if you don't speed it up."

She turned the knob, and we stumbled inside. I pushed her against the door to shut it, catching her in a hard kiss. Her plump lips collided with mine, and their softness undid me. She hummed into my mouth, and I dropped my hands beneath her skirt.

"*Fuck.*" I squeezed her thick ass. It was round and firm—a perfect fit in my hands.

She whimpered, and I kissed her again, sliding my tongue into her mouth. She met my tongue with hers and draped her arms around my neck. I lifted her, and when her legs wrapped around me, I couldn't help it, I pinned her hips to the wall with mine and ground against her. *Damn, she smells good.* She shouldn't. She'd worked all day, but she smelled good enough to devour.

"Where's the bedroom?" I asked, biting her skin.

She tapped my right shoulder. "That way."

I carried her through the door and put her down by the bed, then yanked off her shirt and unhooked her bra. Her breasts spilled out, and my cock wept at the sight. Heavy breasts with nipples hard and ready to be teased. I pushed her onto the bed, caught one of her nipples with my mouth, and sucked.

"Ryker." She gasped, tangling her hands in my hair.

I cupped her other breast, pinching the hardened flesh between my fingers. She arched into my hands. Kissing down her body, I tugged her skirt off, leaving her in underwear alone. They didn't last either, and my shirt came off after.

I relished the way she raked her gaze over my torso, her chest rising and falling faster as she did. She sat up and planted her hands on my chest, running them down my stomach before placing a kiss below my belly button. My cock throbbed painfully, and I unbuttoned my jeans.

I shoved my jeans and boxers off. "I need to be inside you."

Soft fingers curled around my cock, and she hummed. Sultry eyes met mine as she licked my hard length. Her warm and welcoming tongue enticed me enough I'd never get to her pussy if I let it go on too long.

"Oh, fuck." I gripped her head as she wrapped her lips around me.

She sucked me to the back of her throat, her tongue caressing the sensitive underside of my dick. *Shit.* If she kept that up, I *wouldn't* be worth the effort.

I tugged her ponytail until she released me. "You can suck my cock another time, baby." I tossed her to the middle of the bed. "I want to feel you." I slid my fingers around her clit, and then inside her soaked pussy. "Fuck, you're so wet for me."

She gasped and raised her hips to my hand, fisting the blankets beneath her. "Ryker," she hissed.

I teased her until her hips bucked before I retrieved my jeans and fished out a condom. I slid it on. "You ready?"

She spread her legs, offering a view of her glistening pussy. "Can't you tell?"

Fuck.

I threw one of her legs over my shoulder and pushed into her. Warmth cocooned my cock, and I groaned. She gasped and squeezed her eyes shut, her hips rocking softly and leg locking around me already. She was as eager as I was. No sense wasting time getting to where we both wanted.

Not bothering with a slow starting pace, I slammed into her. She cried out and dug her heel into my back. My name falling off her lips drove every thrust. It was fast. Faster than I wanted it to be, but she got there so quickly, and when she came around me and cried out my name, I couldn't take it. The heat. The slickness making every thrust even and smooth. The way she tightened around my cock.

I exploded into her. Her inner walls clamped around me and added to the sensation that was already more irresistible than I wanted it to be. Yet, I knew I couldn't stop. Her legs fell away from me, eyes fluttering shut while I disposed of the condom. *Nope. Not enough.* I wanted to ruin her.

I took both breasts in my hands and captured her mouth with mine. She whined in surprise but returned the kiss with fervor, sliding her hands over mine and squeezing her breasts with me.

"I'm not done with you," I said, sinking my hand to her pussy.

She whimpered as my fingers caressed her inside and out. She arched. "Oh, *God*, Ryker."

She gasped when I added another finger, but it was quickly followed with a delightful mew. Her sounds shuddered excitement through me. They were sweet. Just like her voice. Her skin. Probably her pussy, as I'd soon find out.

I never believed much in heaven before, but there was no other way to describe what it was like to have my hands in and on this woman. I trailed my lips between her breasts, past her belly button, and between her thighs. I spread her legs open and dropped my head, circling her clit with my tongue.

She grabbed my head. "Oh yes."

"*Fuck*, Scarlett. You do taste sweet."

Her fingers knotted in my hair, and the pitch of her musical voice grew higher as I fingered her faster while I licked and sucked her clit. Her pussy clenched. She was almost there, but enough time had passed. I was hard again. I stopped before she finished, eliciting a whine from her.

"Patience, Scarlett," I murmured, flipping her over and lifting her ass. Once I secured another condom, I eased into paradise—this time from behind. My eyes rolled back, and I had to focus not to come. This was my favorite position, and her hot pussy didn't disappoint. She took me all until my hips hit that beautiful, round ass. She was more intoxicating than my favorite scotch. An addiction I couldn't afford but couldn't imagine not indulging in again.

"*Ryker.*"

My name on her lips after coming was my undoing. It echoed inside my mind and added sensitivity I wasn't ready for. *Fuck, what is she doing to me?* I slid my hands around to her tits, pinching both nipples. She cried out, and I grunted, placing a kiss on her spine before slamming into her again. Another cry of pleasure from her drove my desire for more. I resisted only so I wouldn't hurt her, but I wanted to pound into her until she wept.

"Harder," she said, meeting each of my thrusts.

I blinked. This was about as hard as I could fuck a girl before they said it hurt, and she wanted more? "You want me to fuck you harder, Scarlett?"

Her voice was low and heady. "Yes."

My cock twitched, and I seized her hips to hold her in place. "Tell me if it's too much." I pounded into her so hard the fitted sheet popped off the edge.

It was a scream this time. A nice scream.

"Oh, G-god. Just like that, baby," she whined. "But faster."

"Did you just call me baby?" I dug my fingers into her ass and enjoyed the unrestrained fucking. Every thrust was rough and punishing, and she took it all so well. "It's about fucking time."

"Shut up and fuck me."

"Whatever you say, sugar."

I pierced into her hard, much harder than I thought she could take. She rewarded me with delightful moans and screams—a harmony that embedded itself in my head in a dangerous space that said I wanted to make more music with her. A second round wasn't enough either. I brought her to the edge where I already teetered. Wanton sounds and a rapidly tightening pussy almost did me in, but I rubbed her clit, refusing to finish before she did.

Her thighs quivered, and I nipped her ear. "Come for me, baby."

She cried out, and her pussy clenched, hands gripping the sheets while her excitement gushed and ran down her legs. Half the bed was exposed now, the fitted sheet unable to keep up with us. Fuck, what a sight. I almost wished she were facing me so I could see her expression twisted in pleasure. I found my own release shortly after, thrusting harder as I finished.

Panting, I pulled out, my hands braced on her hips. She sank into the bed, whimpering lightly. *Shit*, I hadn't had a workout like that in a while. This girl was giving me a run for my money, and I wanted *more. How is that possible?* One night, and I was becoming a nymphomaniac.

"You all right?" I asked, kissing the nape of her neck.

"Mmm," she hummed, causing me to chuckle. "That was amazing."

"So you like it hard, huh?" I smacked her ass.

She turned her head so I could see the side of her face resting against the bed. "Sometimes," she admitted, sinking her teeth into her lower lip.

"Don't be embarrassed, Scarlett. I like it hard." I caressed her ass before slapping it. "Rough too."

She yelped, then crooned, "Me too."

Even in the dim light, her rising blush was visible. I coasted a hand along her spine, enjoying the little sounds she elicited as I made my way down to her ass.

"I also like tasting you." I lifted her hips so her ass was in the air. "Sweet as sugar," I murmured before spreading her legs and licking the length of her pussy. *Fuck me. This is my new favorite flavor.*

"*Oh.*" She spread her legs farther and shuddered.

I couldn't help but taste her again. At some point, I had to have enough, didn't I? I couldn't crave her forever. Her unrestrained sounds filled the otherwise silent room. As if I needed the reminder that she'd somehow become the hottest fuck I'd ever had. How could I accept anything else after her?

I lifted her hips higher and licked around her clit, then plunged my fingers inside her pussy. She clamped around them, and I smiled against her clit. She was so sensitive that she was coming faster now. I continued pumping my fingers in and out of her, my other hand exploring the curve of her ass.

She'd had me in her mouth. I'd been in her pussy twice. There was only one other hole I hadn't filled, and I wanted to fill all of her. If she was a virgin there, I couldn't do it tonight. We'd have to build up to it. She seemed adventurous in other ways. Only one way to find out.

I slid my finger around her anus, and she stilled. "You ever try this, baby?" I asked, waiting for her orgasm to hit.

But it didn't. And suddenly, I wasn't touching her.

"Stop!" She scrambled to face me and backed away. "Don't." She wrapped her arms around herself and drew her knees to her chest. "Don't hurt me."

Jesus Christ. *What did I do?* Her whole body trembled.

"Scarlett." I kept my tone calm and even as I slowly crawled toward her. "It's all right, baby. I wasn't going to do it without your permission, okay?"

Tears poured down her face, and she shook her head, dropping it to her knees. I carefully rested a palm on her hands that held herself so tightly her nails carved red crescents into her skin.

"Scarlett, it's all right. Don't be scared." I pried her nails away before she cut herself with them. "What's wrong? You're all right. Nothing's going to happen."

Agonizing seconds ticked by. She stopped shaking as badly. Her head lifted slowly, and the fear mixed with embarrassment. "I'm—I'm sorry." More tears spilled as she darted out of bed and ran straight to the bathroom, then slammed the door behind her.

What the fuck was that about? I replayed what happened in my head. It wasn't until I touched her *there* that she'd stopped moving her hips against my hand. After I asked her, that's when she freaked. I'd had enough anxiety attacks from PTSD to know one when I saw it. The fear was very real in her eyes.

That could only mean one thing. I grimaced at the door, head spinning with a mixture of anger and sadness. I bet it was the same fucking guy who put her in the hospital. I pulled on my boxers, then picked up my shirt and her panties.

Walking to the door, I tried to remember all the techniques they'd taught me to deal with PTSD. How the fuck I was supposed to translate that to her, I didn't know. The best I could do was what I wished someone would've done with me.

"Scarlett," I said, hoping my voice came out soft enough. "Baby, open up." No answer. I knocked and leaned my forehead against the door. "Scarlett, come on. You can't stay in there forever. I'm not going to hurt you." I tried the knob, but it didn't budge.

"Please go," she choked. "I'm so embarrassed."

My chest ached. I knew what that felt like. I also pushed everyone away, which was the worst thing I could've done. I sighed and glanced around her room. Bobby pins lay on her dresser. God help me. Hopefully it was the right move. I collected two bobby pins and picked the lock. The girl that'd asked me to fuck her harder now sat on the linoleum floor with a tear-stained face. I forced myself to approach slowly instead of gathering her in my arms like my instincts demanded.

Uncertainty danced in her eyes. "What are you doing?"

"Nothing, sugar. I promise." I held my hands up and inched toward her. "I'm not going to hurt you. You're calling the shots, all right?" I draped my shirt and her panties over my shoulder, then offered my hands.

She hesitated but, after wiping her eyes, took my hands. I pulled her up and tugged my shirt over her before crouching and holding her panties open. She stepped into them, and I eased them up, avoiding touching anything but her legs and hips. I stood and opened my arms.

"What are you doing?" she asked, body still trembling.

"Just trying to comfort you, baby." I beckoned her. "Come here."

Her eyes glistened, but she obeyed. Cheeks wet, she rested her head on my chest and cried. I wasn't great with crying, but I couldn't do nothing. She was hurting in a way I at least partially understood. My trauma wasn't the same, but it was still trauma.

Crying could get exhausting, so I carried her to the bed while she clung to me. I sat on the mattress, and she wrapped her limbs around me. Her crying stopped, but the trembling didn't.

"I'm sorry," she muttered into my neck. "I'm sorry I freaked."

"Don't be sorry, baby." I rubbed her back. "A trigger's a trigger. I'm sorry I didn't know about it. I would've avoided it."

"It's not a trig—"

"I'm not an idiot. Was it your ex?"

She went rigid. I wasn't sure she'd admit it to me, but after tense silence, she nodded into my chest. My arms tightened around her, and I rested my head on hers. God help me if I ever came across that motherfucker. The anger coursing through my blood could fuel me to beat him until his heart stopped. Eh, that wouldn't be so bad. I had plenty of people willing to help me hide a body and be an "alibi." Maybe I *did* want him to come around.

"I'm sorry, Scarlett. I'm really sorry." I cradled her head. "I won't bring it up again."

"Don't tell Dan," she whispered. "Please, don't tell him."

"I won't. Don't worry. This stays between me and you. Unless you want to do something about it."

"There's nothing to do. It's my word against his."

I hated how true that usually was. By her response, I assumed she didn't get a kit or anything like that to prove he'd been there. And even then, it was still her word against his on whether it was consensual. I wanted to tell her to fight anyway, and I'd help her, but it wasn't my decision.

"What do you need? What can I do?"

"Nothing. I'm just so embarrassed," she said, shaking her head but keeping it on my chest.

"Don't be. Like I said, between me and you. And you don't need to be embarrassed about anything in front of me. God knows I've seen my fair share of shit and done stupid shit. Don't think on it. I'm not judging you, but hey, look at me." I brought my hand to her chin and eased it up until her face became visible. "I'm not that asshole, all right? I won't hurt you. I'm not going to do anything unless you want it. You don't have to be scared with me, okay?"

Her eyes darted away, but she gave a small nod before hiding in the crook of my neck. I held her close until her shaking finally stopped.

"Ryker?" She spoke so quietly I barely heard her.

"What is it?"

"Would you—would you stay with me?"

Shit. That was against the rules. Rules I'd followed for years to make sure no girl I fucked got too attached. This was different. I couldn't leave her like this in good conscience. *Son of a bitch.*

"Sure, baby." I scooted us more onto the bed, then reclined, adjusting so she lay on top of me.

She shifted slightly, moving one leg off and leaving the other draped over my hips. Her head stayed on my chest, her hand settling over my heart. I wrapped my arms around her, and she relaxed into me.

"Thank you," she whispered.

"Anytime, sugar." The words left my mouth, and I couldn't believe I'd said them. This couldn't be an anytime offer. She couldn't depend on me like this. She needed a therapist and something else, but it wasn't me. I could never be what she needed. I didn't fuck girls more than a couple times. I didn't date. I definitely didn't cuddle.

Yet, Scarlett's head on my chest triggered a powerful surge of protectiveness. Her hand over my heart caused an unusual flutter. Her ponytail spread out behind her, over my shoulders and neck. Her body, soft against mine, fit so well like a puzzle piece. Anytime I got roped into cuddling before I made the rules, it was always uncomfortable, and I made it clear I'd sneak out once they fell asleep.

But with Scarlett, I was comfortable, and as I lay there, listening to her breathing, I found myself drifting into unconsciousness.

CHAPTER SIX

Distractions

SCARLETT

Cold air coasted over my back, and I shivered. I reached out, but instead of finding Ryker, I found the edge of the bed. Opening my eyes revealed his absence. My chest bowed under a heavy weight. He didn't owe me anything. We had a casual fuck. I couldn't be upset he didn't stay.

Did he wait until I fell asleep to leave? *Great. Another thing to be embarrassed about.* Worse, I couldn't avoid him. Tammy told me he and his friends came in every Friday through Sunday, occasionally dropping in during the week as well. Apparently, he was part of a biker club that frequented the bar. They'd all served in the military at some point. Ryker had been a Marine. That explained his insane body and stoic demeanor. *Stoic demeanor when he's not flirting, at least.*

I'd planned to stay away from him when he came in last night, but he sat at the bar watching me, and I grew increasingly horny under his attention. He made it pretty clear he wanted me before he said the words, and it was stupid to deny I wanted him. Being with him was next level.

Until it all came crashing down. I freaked out. Lost control. Hurtled into a different place with a different person. Ryker had been the one with me, but that small touch confused my mind, and when I tried to reassure myself, all I saw was Todd's face. His unwanted intrusion. *Stupid.* Nothing like that had ever happened before. Thinking about it turned my stomach and made me want to cry all over again, but I'd cried enough.

Unwilling to wallow, I forced myself up for a shower and hurled Ryker's shirt into the corner. I made myself get dressed and eat while watching the local channels Dan's old TV received. He didn't upgrade with the times. Only recently did I get him to send a text, and it wasn't likely to happen with anyone but me. Set in his ways, he hated technology.

I can't believe I have to face Ryker after last night. Mortification told me to curl into a ball and not leave my room, the thought of interacting with him abhorrent.

Throughout the day, my pissed-off demeanor shifted focus. Anger at myself overpowered my anger with him. He hadn't done anything I shouldn't have expected. A guy who blatantly says "I want to fuck you" is not the kind of guy who spends the night.

Still, I thought he would since he handled everything so well. Shockingly well. He knew I needed to be covered up and held. Knew what to say. Didn't push and was very sweet.

I almost wished he hadn't been so I could be pissed at him rather than me. Instead of being angry, I wanted him all over again. Last night, before my stupid episode, was by far the *best* sex I'd ever had. Despite being a bigger girl, he threw me around like I weighed nothing. If it weren't for me freaking out, we probably would've gone again. Maybe all night.

Then I ruined it, and he probably didn't want to deal with me again. He probably thought I was weak and needy. I hated looking that way, especially to someone like him. He was all tough guy—rarely smiled, never showed emotion unless teasing—and I cried like a baby on his shoulder.

Could you be more pathetic?

Not only that, now he knew something very personal. Something no one knew except Todd. That fucking asshole. At least I wasn't crying anymore. At least I was angrier than anything else now. Anger was easier than sadness.

My stomach knotted. I'd be lucky if Ryker touched me again. He was probably afraid to lest I fall into tears while he gave me an orgasm. The worst part? I couldn't do a damn thing about it. How he'd act when I saw him tonight or how I'd act, I didn't know. I only hoped he'd keep his word about not telling anyone. He didn't seem like the kind of guy to spread gossip, but I also didn't know him well.

Can't even make it two weeks without creating another problem. Why did I generate drama everywhere I went? I was a magnet for it. The mess with Todd—how did that happen? I inherited my mother's horrible taste in men is how, I guess.

That wasn't fair. I shouldn't blame her. The painful truth was I didn't know what a healthy relationship looked like. I wasn't good at making friends, so I had no one to ask except Dan, who was divorced, and my mother, who only picked douchebags. Tammy seemed nice enough, and despite Ryker being a fucking god, she hadn't batted an eye at him.

Maybe I could try to be friends with Tammy. *How do people make friends?* I only had one friend before moving. I got made fun of a lot in middle school and high school for being a thicker girl. I was always socially awkward. Always too much for people to handle. And last night, I'd been too much for Ryker.

Dwelling on it wouldn't help. I threw my frustration into working at the bar. Dan would be home Sunday, so I had one more night without him. After last night, my self-esteem took a hit. I skipped the short skirts and plunging shirts. Instead, I wore a slightly longer skirt—*still want those tips*—and a blouse that was low but not plunging.

Every time the bar door opened, my heart raced, and I subtly glanced over. A sigh of both relief and disappointment escaped every time it wasn't Ryker. The sun disappeared below the horizon before his usual group swaggered through the door. At first, I thought maybe he was avoiding me since he often entered first, but no, he walked in last with one of the guys, chatting on their way to the bar.

My breath caught as they both sat. Ryker's eyes found mine, and my heart stopped.

A half-smile played on his face. "Hey, Scarlett. Can you get us both my usual?"

Unable to speak, I nodded and placed two glasses in front of the guys. I poured a double of Ryker's favorite scotch, GlenDronach Parliament. Apparently, he had a lot of money because it wasn't cheap, and he always paid in cash with a generous tip.

As I poured their drinks, he didn't look at me again. It shouldn't have bothered me. Yet, it took me a moment to give up and move on to another customer. Unlike last night, his gaze didn't follow me everywhere I went. Was it because of my change in clothes or his change of heart? Or maybe he'd done exactly what he wanted. He fucked me, and now he was done.

Maybe I would've been okay with it if not for my freak-out, and the moment I thought we had while he held me. *No.* He was just being nice. He may be a *fuck them and leave them* type, but unfortunately, he was also a sweetie. It was the second time in one night I'd witnessed his soft side, and I hated it. It would've been a lot easier if he were a jerk.

Serving kept me distracted until I got less and less tables. New people came in, and after their initial greeting, asked for Tammy. I was getting pushed to the bar. Again. I glared at Ryker, but he never spared me a glance. Somehow, he'd done this. I ended up with one single table. Tammy had the rest while I worked the bar.

What the hell? There were way more seats at tables than at the bar. She had more than half the people in here. I couldn't be mad at her because I knew the culprit.

Getting his attention didn't work. Anytime I tried to talk to him, he'd turn away from me and focus on his friend instead. My palm prickled with the desire to slap him.

What's worse, my body responded to him anyway. One look at him in jeans and the black shirt showing off his sculpted body, and I ached. Last night was an *experience*, and despite my annoyance, my vagina remembered his attentiveness. Now, I'd never feel him again. All the sex in my life seemed suddenly boring comparatively.

That jackass.

Needless to say, being stuck behind the bar except for one table and being horny on top of it, with the reason for my horniness inches away, I got crabby. I played it off well with my customers, but the more Ryker avoided me, the more everything about him agitated me. Was he that put off by my display? I knew it was bad, but *come on.*

Fine. If he was going to be that way, I would too. I refused to look at him. Not even when I refilled his and his stupid friend's drinks. Everyone else I chatted—and sometimes flirted—with. Not him. I was done hoping for his attention.

Maybe I needed someone else. I'd already broken my rule of swearing off men. It seemed ridiculous to jump from one guy to another, but Ryker was off the table, and I had a distinctive urge to have my next sexual encounter end better. I couldn't dwell on *that* as the last time I had sex. That, and I might have needed to feel more in control.

The idea rolled around in my head, especially regarding the single table I had left. One guy's gaze had glued to me the moment he walked in. His flirtatious smile was cute. The table had been there for hours, almost since we opened, so they didn't fall victim to Ryker's plan to keep me behind the bar.

Initially, I talked to the flirty guy like anyone else. Then I stood there, cleaning a glass and observing him. He wasn't as average as I'd made him out to be. He just wasn't Ryker.

This stranger had a trim build with an obvious dedication to bicep curls, blond hair, and green eyes. Not a bad combination. *Maybe I'll be a little friendlier when I approach this time.*

Their pitcher of beer dwindled. I adjusted my shirt to show more cleavage and sauntered over, fixing my gaze on Green Eyes. "Another round, boys?"

"Please." Green Eyes grinned. "You know how to take care of a guy, Scarlett."

More than aware I was giving him a look right down my shirt, I bent for the pitcher. "I sure do."

He gave me a once-over, gaze lingering on my tits. I winked, then returned to the bar with an extra sway in my hips.

Maybe I was terrible. Maybe I was pathetic. But I wanted to be with someone tonight to forget about Ryker and my mortifying breakdown. I couldn't be alone in my head. I needed a distraction.

A customer at the bar asked to cash out as I passed by, so I filled my table's pitcher and stopped at the register to print the customer's check. I tapped my nails against the counter as I waited for the old thing to print, making a point to not peek at where Ryker was sitting a couple stools over.

Avoiding him distracted me, and I didn't notice Green Eyes approach until he braced on the counter with a show-stopping smile. "Hey, Scarlett, I was hoping to get something a little extra."

I leaned over the bar, pushing my tits together. "What can I get you, Green Eyes?"

Again, his eyes dropped to my breasts. Good.

"I don't know, beautiful. What do you suggest?"

"I'm a whiskey girl, myself. I could bring you a shot of my favorite," I offered, brushing absolutely nothing off his shoulder. "I don't know, though. You've been drinking beer all night. Sure you can handle it?"

"Oh, beautiful, I can handle anything you throw at me." He grinned before lifting his eyes to mine. "Question is, can you handle me?"

He walked away, and I arched a brow. *Intriguing.* Maybe he was more interesting than I gave him credit for. Once I dropped off my other customer's check, I poured Green Eyes a shot of whiskey and delivered it with the pitcher of beer. I made a point to brush up against him as I dropped off the drinks.

"Well?" I gestured to the whiskey.

He flashed me a smirk, and instead of taking it like a shot, sipped on it with a straight face. "It's good. What else you got that's good, Scarlett?"

"Plenty of things. You just tell me what I can do for you, handsome." I squeezed his bicep and turned to walk away. His hand closed around mine before I made it to the bar.

Green Eyes tugged me to him and set his hands on my hips. "There's a lot of things you can do for me, beautiful. Do you get a break soon?"

Oh, a quickie. I could live with that. It might ease the tension for the rest of the night. But we were busy, and I wasn't handling as many customers as Tammy.

"Sorry, handsome." I crawled my fingers up his chest. "No break tonight. But if you were inclined to stay until closing, well," I kissed his cheek, then walked away, "that's another story."

While I served other customers, I glanced his way. Every time, he was watching me. *Yeah, he'll stay all night for me.*

Time crawled, and the crowd finally dwindled. I'd had to pee for almost an hour. After informing Tammy, I rushed to the bathroom in the hallway. On my way back, a pair of arms wrapped around me.

"Hey, beautiful," Green Eyes cooed. "They can live without you for ten minutes, can't they?"

I turned in his arms, and he pressed me against the wall. My arms snaked around his neck, and his hands slid to my ass, pulling me against his crotch.

I shouldn't have compared but . . . His hands had nothing on Ryker's. Neither did his erection.

Dammit. Stop thinking about Ryker. I shut my eyes as Green Eyes's lips landed on my neck. He left one hand on my ass and brought the other up, grazing my breast. My suggestion to move somewhere more private never happened because his touch disappeared.

My eyes opened in time to see Ryker throw him against the opposite wall, yanking him up by his collar so high the man's feet kicked in the air.

I smacked his arm. "Ryker!" I might as well have done nothing. He didn't budge.

"You and your friends get the fuck out. Don't touch her again," he snapped, pulling the guy away from the wall and shoving him back into it.

"Ryker, what the hell? He wasn't assaulting me. I encouraged him!"

"Scarlett." His low tone almost made me shiver. "Go to the front."

"No, leave him alone!" I insisted, trying to pry Ryker's hands off the poor guy.

Ryker ignored me, turning his glower to Green Eyes, who was stunned to silence. "I'm going to put you down. You're going to walk out there, leave cash on the table, get your buddies, and get the fuck out. If I see you here again, if I see you *look* at her again, I'll beat the shit out of you. Got it?"

Green Eyes lifted his arms in surrender. "Got it, man. She's yours."

Ryker dropped him, and he stumbled to gain his footing, then scrambled out of the hallway. Anger surged through me, and I smacked Ryker's arm hard enough he turned to glare at me.

"What the fuck is wrong with you!" I shoved him. "Why did you do that?"

A muscle in his jaw pulsed. "Careful, sugar."

"Don't *sugar* me, you asshole. He didn't do anything!"

"He had his hands on your ass," Ryker growled. "And he was planning to do a lot more."

"So was I, idiot. Until you ruined it!"

He took a step toward me. "You were planning to fuck him?"

"Obviously. Thought that was pretty clear."

"It was clear." Ryker took another step. "It was clear in the way you touched him, showed him your tits, flirted with him. It was pretty fucking clear."

"Then why did you interfere?"

He clenched and unclenched his fists, nostrils flaring. Eventually, he hauled me into the bathroom, locked the door behind us, and caged me against it, his chest heaving. *Oh, God.* Not thinking about him wouldn't work now. Why did he look so hot when he was angry?

"Listen here, sugar. As long as I'm here, you're not going to fuck random guys. You don't know what they're planning. You don't know what they might do, if they might take it too far. It's fucking dangerous, and you're too sexy for all of them."

"Are you fucking kidding me? That's what this is about? You jackass." I threw all my weight into shoving him. "One time I made a mistake in trusting the wrong person, and you throw it in my face. What the fuck is wrong with you?"

His eyebrows shot up, and he shook his head. "Scarlett, that's not what I meant."

"It's what you said. You think I can't take care of myself? You think I'm stupid? I'm not, okay? I've made mistakes, but I've learned, and I can fucking take care of myself, so don't you dare treat me like a child!"

"You're certainly acting like one right now. I'm aware you can take of yourself. But as long as I'm here, I'm going to do it too. Get used to it." The aroma of leather and scotch wafted more potently the closer he drew. "I have to know. What exactly was your plan? Let him fuck you in the bathroom?"

I lifted my chin. "Maybe. So what?"

"No." He clenched his jaw. "Not fucking happening. Not with him. Not with anyone else."

"What do you mean, *no*? You don't have a say. We aren't together. We did exactly what you wanted. We fucked, you left, and you've been ignoring me all night, so what does it matter to you?"

"I stayed with you, Scarlett. Like I said I would." He cocked his head. "Is that why you're pissed? You thought I left after telling you I'd stay?"

"No, genius, I'm pissed at you for throwing out the guy I wanted to sleep with! And you didn't stay. Not that it matters." I averted my eyes. "I woke up alone."

"Sugar." His tone softened, and he tipped my chin up. "I had to work. I didn't want to leave you, but I had no choice, and you needed sleep after what happened. Didn't you see my note?"

My brows furrowed. "Note?"

"I left you a note on the nightstand."

My shoulders slumped. "There was no note on the nightstand."

"Maybe it fell?"

I didn't think to check. For the second time in less than twenty-four hours, embarrassment burned my face. I jerked out of his grasp and shook my head. "It doesn't matter. The point is, you have no right to tell me who I can sleep with. You certainly can't threaten them. You gonna attack every guy who walks in the bar?"

"You gonna try to fuck every guy who walks in the bar?" He stood over me, his presence domineering in a way I shouldn't have found attractive. "Because then the answer's yes. I'm going to attack every motherfucker who walks through that door."

"Why? You haven't looked at me all night! We had our time, and it's over."

"It's not fucking over." He dipped his head, our faces inches apart. "You want to know why I didn't look at you all night? Because I couldn't, Scarlett. One glimpse, and I'd haul you somewhere to bunch up this fucking skirt. Goddammit, can you not dress normally? Do you have to wear clothes like this?" The muscles in his neck strained. "You're killing me here."

Unsure what to say, I blinked. Rubbed my thighs and tried to ignore the ache building between them at his confession. "Why would it be so bad to be with me again?"

"I don't . . . Fuck, shit," he spat, retreating. "I just can't."

"Because of what happened?" Anger didn't stop tears from stinging my eyes. *Do* not *cry in front of him again.*

"No. That's not—" He sighed, shaking his head. "That's not why. Though I admit, I was surprised to see you encouraging Blondie after the night you had."

"I'm not a porcelain doll." I balled my fists. "I'm sorry you witnessed last night. I *really* am. But it's not your choice if I'm ready to be with someone else. It's *mine*. And I would like to pretend every part of last night didn't happen. Part of pretending means you leave me alone and don't scare away the next guy I choose." I turned and opened the door.

It slammed shut, and Ryker's body pressed against me from behind, his hands sliding to my hips where his tight grip stirred desire.

Oh no. The ache returned with a vengeance.

CHAPTER SEVEN

Addicted

RYKER

"Can you pretend last night didn't happen, sugar?" I asked, nose pressed to her neck. "Can you pretend you don't know what it felt like to fuck me?"

She didn't answer right away, and I knew why. PTSD episode aside, our night was fucking electric. That shit wasn't one-sided. I *had* stared at her tonight, but only when her attention was on someone else. When that fucking douchebag approached her at the bar, I swear she flirted right in front of me to make me jealous. It shouldn't have worked, but then he followed her to the bathroom, and I couldn't stand the idea of anyone else touching her.

"Of course I can," she said.

Lie. Even if I hadn't always been good at detecting it, she sucked at lying. Her chest heaved, and those dilated pupils gave her away. She wanted me again, just like I wanted her.

"Don't fucking lie to me, baby. You said it was amazing right before I tongue-fucked your pussy."

She inhaled sharply. With another girl, it might not have worked, but I paid attention last night. Every time I talked dirty, she ate it up.

"I was—I just said that. I didn't mean it."

You really think I buy that? I dropped my hands to the outside of her thighs, my fingers reaching under her skirt and caressing her soft skin. She leaned back into me, her ass brushing my cock.

"Try again." I slid my fingers to the inside of her thighs. "You can lie better than that, can't you?"

"I . . ." She very deliberately ground her ass against my cock, and I grunted.

"I'm not going to fuck you until you take that back," I growled, kissing her neck. That was fucking untrue. It didn't matter what she said to piss me off, I'd still have her.

"I take it back," she said quickly, rolling her ass against me again.

"Good girl," I murmured, biting her earlobe and cupping her pussy.

She whimpered and threw her head onto my shoulder. My lips landed in the crook of her neck, my teeth scraping her skin. I'd never needed to give someone a hickey so badly. Something to let everyone in the bar know she was off-limits. So I did. She threaded her fingers through my hair while I sucked her skin red.

Turning her around, I tugged down her panties. Her fingers fumbled with my jeans, undoing the button and zipper, then pushing them down. She stepped out of her panties, and I bunched her skirt at her hips before moving my hand to her pussy.

She pushed my hand away and locked her arms around my neck. "I don't want to waste time. I'm wet. I want you right now."

"Fuck, Scarlett, what are you doing to me?" I searched my pocket for a condom that I made quick work of putting on. I kissed her hard, sliding my hands under her skirt and cupping her ass to lift her and brace her against the wall because the door wouldn't hold up against what I was about to do. My cock throbbed and I thrust into her.

"Oh, God." Her head thumped the wall, and she tightened her legs around me. "*More.*"

Her desperate demands dragged me into a state of *needing* to satiate her. I found a spot on the wall and focused on it to stop from coming like a teenage boy losing his fucking virginity. No girl ever affected me like that. I tried to mentally prepare for the sound of her sweet voice and shoved into her again, eliciting a loud whimper.

"Careful, baby. You want to announce what we're doing to the whole bar?"

She buried her face in my neck, muffling her sounds as I fucked her, her heels drawing me closer. She knotted her fingers in my hair and tugged. I groaned, my fingers digging into her ass. It was like she knew exactly how to make me lose my mind.

I pumped in and out of her, grinding myself against her clit until finally, she clenched around me. *Shit. I barely made it this time.* Her pussy tightened on me, and I hardly held myself together. I slammed into her harder, and she cried out into my neck.

Her nails scraped my scalp. *"Ryker."*

"Scarlett." Her name trembled on my lips while I came inside the condom a touch before she gushed around me.

Still made it. Probably the first time in a decade that I'd had trouble not coming before a girl. I usually made them come prior to my cock entering the picture. Scarlett was fucking with my head. I couldn't do this with her. Something about her kept drawing me in, and I wasn't the kind of guy she should be with. I eased her down and intended to set the record straight. I really did. Then she kissed along my neck on her way to my ear.

"Again." Her bedroom voice destroyed my chance at finding inner strength. "As soon as we close."

So much for setting the record straight. I lowered my lips to her shoulder. "You'll be lucky if you make it to closing."

She slumped against the wall and closed her eyes, readjusting her skirt. God, she was beautiful. Her eyes fluttered open, and she fought a smile. "You're still an asshole."

"You're still sweeter than sugar, and I'm looking forward to tasting you again later." I planted a hard kiss on her already swollen lips.

She hummed when I released her and smoothed her hand over her hair. Approaching the mirror, she checked her makeup, then turned for her underwear. Which were stuffed in my pocket, where they'd stay. I dodged her when she reached for them.

"Ryker," she scolded. "Give them back."

"I don't think so. You'll get them back later." I unlocked the bathroom and strode out. She muttered curses behind me and rendered me unable to hold in a smile as I entered the bar, taking my seat next to Gill.

He raised an eyebrow. "Something happen?"

I grimaced at my empty glass. "What makes you say that?"

"Some poor boy ran from the hallway, got his friends, and booked it out of here like he committed a crime." He chuckled and tipped his glass back. "Only you could send someone running like that."

My gaze gravitated to the corner Scarlett rounded. "Don't know what you're talking about."

Fuck. Me. My self-control ceased to exist in her presence. Swollen lips and a flushed face painted a clear picture of what we'd done. A red splotch on her neck stirred pride that I was the one who made her such a mess. My cock twitched, and my jeans tightened to make room for the consequences of my dirty thoughts.

Her eyes met mine briefly, then darted away. As soon as she walked behind the bar, I held my glass up. "Another, sugar."

Gill scooted his glass forward. "For me too, please."

She narrowed her eyes at me and retrieved the scotch. When she returned, she filled Gill's glass and corked the bottle, then slammed it on the bar. Bracing her palms on the counter, she shot me a feisty glare, a catalyst for my thickening erection. "I don't answer to sugar."

Gill laughed, and I bit back a smile as she moved to the next customer, not sparing me another glance.

"I don't believe I've ever seen a woman turn you down." Gill smacked the bar top. "I see why you come here."

I scowled. She wasn't the reason I came here. Or at least she hadn't been part of the equation before. Now?

She had a hold on me that defied logic. Maybe I needed another night with her, undisturbed. I knew what to avoid. I hadn't been done with her when that happened. That's all it was. After tonight, she'd be out of my system.

Gill refused to share his drink and finished when Scarlett walked by again. He lifted his glass, catching her eye. She nodded and refilled his scotch. He abandoned the bar to say hi to the others, leaving me mostly alone with her since the crowd had thinned.

She glanced at me briefly while she printed a check, and I held my glass up, elbow braced on the bar. "Please, sugar?"

She rolled her eyes and shook her head, returning the bottle to the shelf. I leaned forward on my forearms as her red nails clacked against the register.

"I'm sorry, I keep forgetting. That's the wrong term. Please, baby?"

She faced the register but failed to hide her smile. Refusing to look my way, she gave me the finger.

"Is that the finger you use when you're thinking about me? Interesting choice, I must say. Is it because it's longer, and you can go deeper?"

"For fuck's sake, Ryker," she hissed, trying to give me a dirty look despite her upturned lips.

Damn, she had a great smile. She printed off a couple receipts and turned to leave.

"Baby, baby, baby." I caught her arm. "Please, baby?"

She scoffed, and her inability to play it off like she wasn't amused made my own lips curve up.

"Baby, come on. Please, sugar? Baby sugar? Sugar baby?"

She hid her face with her hands. "Oh my *God*."

"Oh, we have a winner. Please, sugar baby?"

"You're the worst," she said through laughs, yanking out of my hold.

"Please, Scarlett?"

She hesitated. Her glare accompanied the pouring of scotch.

I took a sip and held my glass to her like a toast. "Thanks, sugar."

She huffed and stalked away. "Asshole."

I chuckled at her annoyance. I might've felt bad if she didn't purposely annoy me too.

Her refusal to pour me another refill, even after I called her Scarlett, didn't surprise me. She either ignored me totally or said, "Go home and get it yourself, sugar." I cackled at that response.

I admired her shamelessly the rest of the night. Not just because she was fucking gorgeous but because I wasn't the only one who noticed. Now, I was certain she did the 'leaning over to give a view of her tits' thing to bug me yesterday and not for the tips since she wasn't doing it today.

Only a few people milled about after Tammy left. She cleaned her section and said goodbyes. My boys had disappeared a long time ago. I'd rush the remaining patrons out at two, but that was still three minutes away. I blamed my raging hard-on for Scarlett on her damn clothes, but the truth was, the girl could wear a giant sweatshirt and sweatpants, and I'd still want her.

The last group left while Scarlett was in the kitchen, so I cleaned off the tables they were at. I'd been here late with Danny before. It wasn't the first time I helped clean up at the end of the night.

Scarlett reentered the bar. "You don't have to do that."

"Yes, I do. I need to be inside you again. Go lock that front door or risk someone walking in on us."

Cheeks tinting pink, she rushed to the door, locked it, and switched off the neon Open sign. I carried the rag behind the bar and rinsed it before washing my hands. A light flicked off, leaving the place in near darkness except for the bulb leading up the stairs. Scarlett waited at the bottom of those stairs, biting the lip I was about to.

I smirked and stalked toward her. She took the first step up when I called out, "Stay here, Scarlett. I want to come in the bar and remember fucking you right where I sit."

"We can't do that. There are windows!" she whispered, as if anyone could hear her.

"So what?" I shrugged. "I can make you forget about them."

She squeaked and ran upstairs. I sprinted after and caught her on the second to last step. She was one up from me. From here, our height difference didn't matter as much. I could reach her easily.

She glanced at me over her shoulder. "I'm not having sex with you on the bar."

"Fine." I cupped her breast with one hand and lifted her skirt with the other. "Then right here."

"R-right here?"

My hand ascended between her thighs. "Right here."

CHAPTER EIGHT

Edging

SCARLETT

I'd never had sex on stairs, but my quivering thighs told me I'd do it again. Ryker turned my legs to jelly. He offered his hand afterward while I was still bent over and panting. I took it, and he surprised me by tugging me toward him, cupping my face, and kissing me.

Unlike other kisses we'd shared, this was intimate. His lips melded to mine and moved in an intoxicating way I couldn't help but melt under. He held me close, his tongue teasing the seam of my lips. Slowly, he pinned me to the wall with his body, his hand caressing my cheek.

"You feel so fucking good, Scarlett," he murmured against my lips, his hand coasting over my waist and hip. "Where are your keys, baby?"

I barely got my answer out when he pressed a hot kiss to my neck. "It's not locked."

He stiffened. "Why the fuck not?"

"I was basically guarding it all night. What's going to happen?"

"A number of things. Anyone could've come up when you weren't looking or when we were in the bathroom." He snatched my hand and opened the door, peering inside. "Jesus, Scarlett."

"What, are you paranoid?"

"Yes. I am. Get over it." He grunted, tugging me inside but not letting me in front of him. "It was locked last night. Why would you not lock it again?"

Because locks don't just keep people out. Sometimes they trap. I freed my hand from his so he wouldn't notice it shake. I hadn't locked the door yesterday, either. Dan did when he retrieved the sandwich I packed for his drive.

"Because there's no point. I was right by the only way up here. Ryker, seriously, no one's here. Why are you so worried?"

"Scarlett, I don't know if you've noticed," he glared at me over his shoulder, "but men are trash, and you're fucking gorgeous. I wouldn't be surprised if some piece of shit snuck up here."

I let out a long sigh and crossed my arms. "You're so dramatic."

"I'm going to check the bedroom, and when I get back," he pointed at me, "you're paying for that."

I bit my lip and watched him creep into my bedroom, wondering what exactly he meant. My pussy fluttered at the thought. How easily I reacted to him was ridiculous. Pathetic. Yet, I couldn't stay away. Even watching him walk away made me wet. He had a really nice butt.

Knowing I was about to get a workout, I went to the kitchen and filled a glass with water, then noticed the mail I hadn't sorted. I shuffled the envelopes aside, making a pile of things to throw away when something caught my eye.

A letter. From fucking Todd. How did he know where to send it? I'd never told him where Dan's bar was. I never told him I was leaving. I had a restraining order. Wasn't writing to me breaking a rule?

Ryker approached, and I tucked the letter under the other mail.

He tilted his head, gaze darting to the pile. "What's wrong?"

"Nothing." I set my water down. I didn't want him to know about the letter. Not after last night. "Did you find the bogeyman in there?" I clutched my chest and gasped. "Don't tell me, Freddy Krueger?"

His concern-knit brows shifted to narrowed eyes. In two long strides, he reached me, yanked me against him, and smacked my ass. "You like pissing me off, don't you?" His fingers curled around my jaw, and he crushed my lips to his.

I wrapped my arms around him, yelping when his hand hit my ass again. Harder. The sting coursed heat and lust through my veins.

He plopped me on the counter and caged me in with his tattooed arms. "You're going to pay for that."

"Don't pretend like you don't enjoy pissing me off."

He smirked and tilted my chin up. "I do. I like getting you worked up. You're sexier the feistier you get, sugar."

"I seem to recall telling you I don't answer to sugar."

"I seem to recall you answering to it just fine when I had my cock buried in you." He sank to his knees and lurched me to the edge of the counter. His head dove between my legs, tongue circling my clit while his calloused fingers gripped my thighs.

I moaned and grasped the edge of the counter. He pushed two fingers into me and I whimpered and ground against his face and hand. When his fingers curled against my G-spot, I gasped, my orgasm near. I could taste the release when he pulled away.

"Ryker," I whined, clamping my legs together. "What the fuck?"

"I told you." He stood. "I said you'd pay for it."

"You suck." I sank my hand toward the ache to take over where he'd left off.

He caught my wrist and pinned it behind me. "I don't think so, sugar. Don't make me tie you down."

Oh. *Oh.* Maybe I wanted to be tied down. I lowered my other hand to touch myself, and he snatched it as well, pinning it with my other one. *Okay, yeah, I could be tied up by him.*

He pushed his forehead to mine, a challenge clear in his striking eyes. "You testing me, Scarlett?"

"Maybe."

He cursed and captured both my wrists with one hand. With the other, he thrust two fingers into my pussy and pumped them in and out of me at a relentless pace that curled my toes.

His hair tickled my skin where he trailed kisses along my neck to my ear. "Keep your hands where they are."

He continued fingering me and dragged his mouth over my body as he tugged on my shirt, exposing my bra. His mouth closed around my hardened nipple through the lacy fabric. That texture, combined with his wet mouth, made my eyes roll back.

Pleasure scattered through my body, overflowing my nerves until I was sure I'd burst. Still sensitive from the earlier tease, the orgasm built fast. I gripped his head and let out a throaty sound, so close to exploding. Then he pulled away. Again.

"Ryker," I whined, reaching for my throbbing core.

He pinned my hands at my sides. "You didn't listen. I told you not to move your hands."

"If you don't cut it out, I'm not having sex with you."

He chuckled and placed one of my hands over his crotch. His erection twitched against my palm. Thick and ready to fuck. I inhaled shakily, and he brushed his lips over mine. "You were saying?"

That's unfair. I was practically creaming at this point. I'd already had him twice tonight; why did I want him again already?

"Be a good girl, and I'll give you what you want." He cradled my head and kissed me.

How do I become putty in his hands? Worse, he knew I was putty in his hands. He lifted me off the counter, our mouths never parting. I wrapped my arms around his neck and chased his tongue with mine while he carried me to the bedroom and set me next to the bed.

His gaze raked over my body with such focused attention, I could almost feel it. "Strip."

My eyebrows shot up. "What?"

He sat on the edge of the bed. "Take your clothes off."

"I don't—" My cheeks heated. "I don't know how to do it in a sexy way."

"Scarlett, you're taking your clothes off for me. What part of that isn't sexy? I don't care how you do it. I just want to watch." He kissed my stomach. A sharp contrast to a second later when he smacked my ass. "Remember, be a good girl."

The slap electrified my body. Whatever hold he had on me, I couldn't shake it. I stepped away and peeled my shirt off. His gaze lowered to my breasts and hips before returning to my eyes. His studying stare, thick with lust, boosted my confidence. *It's pretty dark in here anyway. It's not like he can see much.*

I unhooked my bra and let the straps fall down my arms. He licked his lips, and his voice came out in a gravelly rasp. "Don't stop."

I coiled my fingers in my skirt and lowered it to my ankles, then stepped out of it. His gaze roamed my naked body, focusing on where excitement glistened at the apex of my thighs.

"Fuck. Come here." I walked toward him, but he held up a hand. "No. Crawl."

"I'm not crawling."

"It wasn't a request. Be a good girl, and crawl to me." He rested his forearms on his thighs. "I'll reward you when you get here."

My throat dried. Unable to help myself, I drew my thighs together. He beckoned me. Part of me screamed to be a brat, but the other part loved the demanding presence.

So, I sank to the ground and crawled.

The closer I got, the more his pupils dilated. The more the muscle in his jaw strained. It urged me forward until I was within reach. He yanked on my ponytail. "Take your hair down."

My pussy throbbed, and I shuddered. "It'll look bad." I ran my hand over my ponytail. "It's been up all day."

"I don't give a fuck. Take it down." He snatched my chin. "I thought you were going to be good for me, so I can be good to you."

Please. I wanted him to be good *and* bad to me. I released my hair from the tie and shook it out, running my fingers through to smooth it as best I could.

Ryker's rumble of approval scorched away my insecurity. "So fucking beautiful." He rolled my nipple between his fingers, and I whimpered. "Your tits are incredible. *Fuck.*" Unzipping his pants, he then eased them and his boxers down, freeing his cock. Before I made a move, he tugged my head forward until my lips pressed against his tip. "Open."

I wanted him to give me another orgasm, I really did. But last night I'd enjoyed having him in my mouth, and as desperate as I was, I wanted him. Without hesitation, I sucked him in, making him groan and fist my hair. I swirled my tongue around his tip before sucking until he hit my throat. I slowly pulled back to his tip, then went down to his base, cupping his balls. He grunted and bucked his hips. "Fuck, baby. Just like that. You're doing so fucking well."

His praise soaked my pussy, and I moved faster, bobbing my head up and down his length. He cursed and urged me forward, rocking into my mouth. His reaction empowered me. I stroked the underside of his cock with my tongue as I sucked.

"Fuck *yes*." He applied pressure to the back of my head and sank deeper down my throat. "Such a good girl."

My eyes watered, but I didn't care. Witnessing him come undone because of me fueled my determination. He let me withdraw to his tip, and when I started sinking, he again pushed my head farther until my throat constricted around his cock.

"That's it, baby," he growled, thrusting deeper. "Take it all."

My pussy wept when he took control. Unable to take the throbbing, I circled my clit with one finger.

"Fuck." Ryker pulled me off his cock and watched me touch myself with bated breath. "You like sucking my cock, huh?"

Chest heaving, I nodded. "Yes."

"That's enough." He picked me up and set me in his lap, then scooted us to the center of the bed. He retrieved a condom from his jeans before kicking them off completely and sliding the condom on. He lay back, hands clamping on my hips. "Ride my cock, baby."

I descended on him, and my lips parted as he stretched me out the farther I sank down. I gasped and rocked my hips, bracing on his thighs. Lifting, I then lowered onto him again and threw my head back, arching my spine. The angle allowed him to go deeper. I already trembled from the stimulation. His teasing left me so sensitive, every invasion of his cock rippled pleasure through my body.

"You're so sexy, Scarlett." Ryker sat up and kissed my breasts.

Breathless, I bounced on his dick. "Ryker."

"Fuck, baby. This pussy." He lay back and groped my breast. "This body. You're a fucking work of art." His other hand played with my clit, and I whined, the pleasure almost too intense.

I lost momentum at the attention but regained it a few seconds later, rocking my hips faster as I uttered "I'm close" between whimpers.

"Come for me, Scarlett."

I cried out, clenching around him as my orgasm knocked into me like a tsunami. It obliterated any memories of previous orgasms, each wave more powerful than the last, each crashing me into a state of ecstasy that bordered on overstimulation.

Ryker thrust up into me a few times before he finished with a groan. "That's right." My hips bruised under his fingers when he slammed me onto his dick. "So fucking good."

"Fuck." I collapsed onto his chest, body twitching and nerves humming with pleasure. "That was so intense. Why was it so intense?"

He draped a heavy arm over my back, trapping my naked, sweaty body against his. His other hand drifted lazily along my spine. "You've never been edged before?"

I hid in his chest. "I don't know what that means."

"Don't be embarrassed. It's what I did. Bringing you to the edge of orgasm but not letting you have it. If I'd done it more times, you would've come harder."

"Oh, God, I don't think I could take harder than that." I raised my hips enough for him to slide out before collapsing on him again.

"Mmm, I bet you could," he murmured.

The orgasm tapered, and my limbs went limp, my eyes fluttering in satisfied exhaustion. I needed to get off him so he could go, but my muscles were unresponsive, and his body was comfortable. *Five minutes.* Five minutes, then I'd get up and let him leave.

I woke in the morning to my phone ringing, and cursed the world. My beef with the universe ended, however, because Ryker's arm tightened around my waist. My stomach flipped. He'd stayed. I'd fallen asleep on him, but he could've easily lifted me off.

He hadn't.

"What the fuck is that?" he grumbled.

"My phone. Sorry." I rolled off him and snatched the offending device from the nightstand.

Dan's name flashed across the screen, and I tensed. I knew he'd call in the morning, but I hadn't planned to talk to him while Ryker was lying in bed with me. Naked. I started to answer when Ryker's arm curled around me, the heat of his body firm against my ass and back, a contrast to the cool sheets tangled around us.

Ryker buried his face in my neck. "Don't answer it."

"I have to. It's Dan."

"I don't give a fuck. He'll live. Don't answer it."

"I give a fuck." I pinched his arm, then answered the call. "Hi, Dan."

"Hi, honey. How's everything going? Did I wake you?"

"Fine, everything's fi—" I inhaled sharply. Ryker's fingers swirled over my clit. "Fine." I cleared my throat before covering the microphone and glaring back at Ryker. "Stop it!" I hissed. "I'm on the phone."

He grunted, his erection thick against my lower back, his finger continuing to circle my clit while he peppered open-mouthed kisses across my neck. He caught my skin between his teeth and bit. "I told you not to answer."

I pressed my lips together to hold in a moan. "You're the worst."

"Everything go okay last night?" Dan asked.

Ryker's fingers stroked my entrance. My breath hitched, and my voice squeaked. "It went great."

"You all right, Scar? You sound funny."

"Because I'm finger fucking your perfect little sweetheart," Ryker whispered in my ear, sliding his finger inside me.

Oh, God.

"I'm good. You did wake me, so I'm just," I inhaled, biting down on my lip and squeezing my eyes shut as Ryker curled his finger against my G-spot, "trying to wake up."

"Sorry, honey. I just wanted to let you know I'm leaving in a couple hours, so I should be home by eight. Think you can stay out of trouble 'til then?"

It took all my focus to conceal my labored breath. "Totally."

"All right. See you tonight," Dan said. "Love you, Thelma."

"Love you, Louise," I managed before hanging up. The moment I did, I rocked against Ryker's hand. "Fuck, Ryker, *really*?"

"You should've listened to me." He ground his erection against my ass. "You're so fucking wet. I need to be inside you. You gonna take me again, baby?"

I shouldn't say yes. I shouldn't give him the benefit. "Yes."

He rolled me over and climbed above me, nipping at my neck as his cock stretched my tender pussy.

CHAPTER NINE

Frustration and Secrets

RYKER

Well rested. I hadn't experienced it since I finished my tours as a Marine. Things happened, and I hadn't been able to sleep well. Last night, with Scarlett on top of me, her naked body blanketing mine, I slept like a baby. No nightmares. No anything except bliss.

I wasn't supposed to stay the night, but it was so goddamn comfortable. I wasn't supposed to wake up and immediately fuck her again, but I couldn't keep my hands off her. Acting like this was misleading her. I wasn't a relationship guy. I didn't spend the night or cuddle. So why the fuck did she have this effect on me?

"Ryker, are you listening to me?" Conrad asked.

I blinked, the whir of his old desk fan a reminder of the bail bondsman I sat across from. "What?"

"I said he's in Nevada." Conrad dropped a folder in front of me on his laminate desk. Sunlight filtered in through dusty blinds and illuminated stagnant dust mites.

"Got it." I snatched the coffee-ring-stained folder. "I'll take care of it."

"What's going on with you?" Conrad reclined in his office chair and clicked his pen.

"Nothing. Just didn't sleep much last night."

He smirked. "Another girl?"

"Something like that." I pulled at my collar and stood. This office was stuffy, and he never wanted to open a window. "You got my check for the last one?"

He nodded to the plastic bin on the right of his desk. "In the bin."

I picked up the envelope with my name and inched toward the exit. "I'll call when I have him."

"Take it easy, Ryker. Get some sleep for Christ's sake."

"Yeah, yeah." I waved at him as I exited.

Conrad paid each time I brought a criminal in after they skipped out on a court date. I worked with others, but Conrad was the most consistent and bugged me the least.

I stuffed the file in my jacket and zipped up before getting on my motorcycle and heading to the bar. Going there was always something I looked forward to, drinking and hanging out with the few people I tolerated, and sometimes taking someone home.

Now, though, my shoulders tensed because Scarlett was there, and I had to tell her no more hooking up.

I didn't want to. I wanted to have her several more times. I wasn't sure what it would take to get her out of my system. If a whole night with her didn't do it, what would? She was still on my mind too much.

It had to stop. I only hoped she wouldn't be pissy about it. I parked in my usual spot and went inside, bracing myself to see her. Except, Tammy was at the bar, and Scarlett was nowhere to be seen. Tammy's eyes lit up, and she waved me over.

I nodded to her. "What's up?"

"There's something wrong with the light in the storage room." She drummed her fingers against her tattooed arm. "Scarlett's been trying to fix it, but we can't get it to come on. We already tried a new bulb."

Alone in the dark with Scarlett. That felt like a fucking trap. I'd have to keep the door open.

I shoved open the saloon doors leading to the kitchen. "I'll take a look."

"Hey, Ryker!" Dave, the cook, yelled as I passed by.

"Hey, man, how's it going?"

"Good. Gonna fix the light?"

"We'll see."

Continuing, I turned the corner and came face to face with the storage room door. It was already open a crack, so I slipped inside without much noise. Finding Scarlett bent over a counter, watching a tutorial on her phone about lights, stopped me in my tracks. She had a little lantern in the center of the room that provided light for me to appreciate and curse the vixen. Her forearms rested on the counter, her ass sticking out of her booty shorts, waiting to be smacked and mounted.

She didn't notice me when she paused the video and climbed a stepladder. Flashlight in hand, she studied the socket. As she reached up, her shirt lifted, and I wondered if God existed and was fucking with me.

No. Be strong. I could do this. She was just a woman. I'd faced worse than a woman. I paused behind her and frowned at her attempts to identify the problem.

I rubbed my jaw. "What are you doing?"

She gasped, and when she spun around, lost her balance. I reached out and caught her before she fell, which brought her tits right into my face. Yeah, some deity was fucking with me. "Happy to see me?" I asked, looking up at her, leaving my chin between her tits.

"It—" She licked her lips. "It was an accident."

"Hmm." *Let her go. Get your face out of her perfect tits.* Instead, I kissed one, then nuzzled between them and kneaded her ass.

"Ryker," she mewed, her hands knotting in my hair. "I'm working."

"Working too hard. Time for a break." I lifted her off the stool and carried her to the counter she'd been bent over.

Twisting my fist around her hair, I pulled her mouth to mine. My tongue chased after the taste I couldn't get enough of, and my hands roamed the body I itched to touch again. I squeezed her ass and pulled her flush against me. Her hands snaked under my shirt, fingernails scraping my back.

Oh, fuck it. One last time.

"What if someone comes in?" she breathed against my mouth.

"I guess we better make it fast." I turned her around and palmed her breast while I cupped her pussy. "Are you wet for me, baby?"

Breathless already, she ground her ass against me. "Yes."

"That's my girl." I undid the button on her shorts, then yanked them down.

Bending her over, I pushed my finger inside her pussy.

My cock twitched at the generous coating of arousal. She was soaked already. *Goddamn her.* I stroked inside until she squirmed, then undid my jeans and shoved them down. The moment my cock freed, I slid on a condom and thrust into her.

"Ryker," she whimpered, clawing the counter.

"Scarlett," I panted, adjusting to her warm, enticing pussy. "Brace yourself, baby. I'm going to fuck you hard."

She gripped the counter, and I slammed into her, making her moan too loud for where we were. Possessiveness reared its head, and I covered her mouth. No one else got to hear her sweet voice.

"Shh." I pounded into her. "Someone will hear us and tattle."

Her sounds muffled by my hand, she rolled her ass against me again, sinking me deeper with each thrust.

I wasn't gentle. I didn't build up to anything. I fucked her with reckless abandon, and she let out noises that echoed in my head better than any song. Even muffled, they fucked me up and made me so sensitive I'd come too soon. Again. To avoid embarrassing myself, I played with her clit.

Finally, she came, and I followed immediately after, unable to hold it in anymore. I uncovered her mouth and smacked her ass. She let out a guttural sound and arched her back. I smacked it again. And again. Each time, she released a noise of pleasure so exquisite I needed more.

"Scarlett." I wrapped my hand around her throat and pulled her against my chest. "You're so fucking sexy. What the hell am I going to do with you?"

She closed her hand over mine. "Whatever you want." She tipped her head back until our gazes collided, hand tightening mine on her throat. She inhaled sharply, her mouth parted and eyes pleading.

If I wasn't fucked before, I certainly was now. She was as depraved and insatiable as me.

"Fuck." I squeezed her throat until she gasped. "Get in the bar before I fuck you again. I can*not* be alone with you."

Spinning her around, I lowered my mouth to hers. She sighed into the kiss and walked her fingers underneath my shirt.

Her mouth dragged off mine and drifted to my neck. "Maybe I want you to fuck me again," she whispered, raking her nails over my torso.

"Fucking hell." Potent desire almost clouded my judgment. "I can't right now. Get your sexy ass out of here."

A swift smack to her ass later, she squeaked and she lifted her brown eyes to meet my blue ones. Unable to tear my gaze away from those bedroom eyes, I dropped my forehead to hers.

She cupped my face and brushed her thumb across my cheek. "I'll have a scotch waiting for you." Her soft lips teased my cheek with a kiss that lingered on my skin long after she strolled out.

It made no sense, but what she did—her hand on my face, a kiss against my cheek—it spread a warm sensation through my chest. Staring in her eyes like that . . . It was so much more intimate.

I didn't like intimacy. I liked fucking.

Yet, she'd infiltrated my thoughts. As if that wasn't bad enough, her saying to do whatever I wanted with her threw out all hopes of this time being the last. I had to have her again and make good on her offer.

One more night. No more. Danny would return tonight, anyway. It would have to be over after that, and I'd have to make that clear to her before we started. It wasn't fair to do it any other way.

Once I fixed the stupid light, I returned to the front. Music and chatter greeted me when I stepped through the doors and scanned the room for Scarlett. I found her at a table with some of my guys, throwing her head back with laughter. My jaw clenched, and I walked over.

"Ryker." She swept her tongue over her lower lip. "Are you going to sit here?"

"Yes," I said gruffly, grabbing a chair.

"I'll get your scotch." Her hand grazed my shoulders as she walked away. My skin tingled from the contact, and I rolled my eyes at myself. *Why is her touch so powerful?* My gaze remained on her until she was a fair distance away, then I turned a glare on the rest of the table.

"Easy, you don't need to say it." Francis held up his hands, light reflecting off his bald head. "We know."

I narrowed my eyes. "Say what?"

Benny sipped his drink, blond hair falling across his eyes. "That she's off-limits."

"Right." I set my hand on the table. "Because of Danny."

"Danny?" Nick arched a scarred brow and drummed tattooed fingers against the table. "Come on, Ryker. Danny may be oblivious to the two of you, but trust me, no one else is."

I grunted and folded my arms over my chest. "What's that supposed to mean?"

Francis chuckled. "It means you two make eyes at each other every time you're in the same room."

"And the shameless flirting," Benny said. "You'll have to ease up on that when Danny gets back."

"That's fucking ridiculous," I scoffed. "She's off-limits because of Danny."

"Just because of Danny?" Nick nudged me. "Well, Danny doesn't need to know, so I guess I'll make my way over and get to know her a little better."

My lip curled. "Don't you fucking dare."

Nick's smug expression as he sipped his drink boiled my simmering irritation. The other two mirrored it. I closed my hand into a fist against the table so I wouldn't throw it at their faces.

"Here you go." Scarlett placed a glass in front of me.

"Thanks, sugar."

I reached for the drink, but she swiped it and stepped away. Cocking her head, she planted a hand on her hip.

I *tsked*. "Oh, come on."

She retreated another step and shook her head. That fiery spark in her eye warned me she could do this all night.

"Thanks, *Scarlett*."

"That's better." She returned the drink and sauntered off.

Her hips and ass swayed as she walked, providing a view no sane person could ignore. She disappeared behind the bar, and I tugged on my lower lip. All three of the assholes with me sniggered.

I scowled. "What?"

Francis cleared his throat. "Nothing."

I dipped my fingers in my glass and flicked scotch at him. He didn't speak again.

Nick did. The cunt.

"Just that you're so fucking pussy-whipped after a few days with this girl."

I swallowed my drink in one gulp. "I'm not."

"No? She didn't just make you call her by her name?"

Collecting my glass, I stood. "Shut the fuck up."

"Hey, man, it's all good. The guys really like her, anyway," Francis said.

"What do you mean by that?" I worked my jaw. She was mine.

"Not like that." Francis waved his hand. "They enjoy talking to her. She's a sweetheart and has a good sense of humor."

"It better be the talking they like," I muttered, heading to the bar. I sat on my stool, and Scarlett approached with more scotch.

"I would've gotten you a refill." She filled my glass and pouted. "You didn't have to come over here."

Fucking hell. That pout.

"I got tired of their company." I shrugged, taking a drink.

She giggled. "That didn't take long."

Fucking hell. That giggle.

"I'm not that social, Scarlett."

"But you always show up with a group of people."

"I like them in small bursts. I like to drink alone."

"Why?"

"I just do."

"You're weird. Do you want anything to eat?" She braced her elbows on the bar and dropped her chin to her clasped hands. The position made her tits press together, and her shirt hung low enough to show her lacy, black bra.

She was *killing* me.

I inched forward, my nose almost touching hers. "Just your pussy, sugar. I'm craving something sweet."

Pink blossomed on her face in record time. "Dessert later is all yours. But do you want something right now?"

"I'll take a burger like you had the other night. You made it look damn good."

She bit her lip, but it didn't suppress the smile. Flipping me off, she walked into the kitchen and out of sight. I was still staring after her when Danny ambled around the corner.

"Hey, Ryker." He grinned. "You take care of my girl?"

I mean, in a way.

"Danny," Tammy greeted before I could, wrapping her arms around him briefly. "Is there a reason some guy would call asking for Scarlett, and then she'd freak out and ask how to block the number?"

I tensed. Why didn't she tell me he called?

Danny clenched his fists. "Did he give a name?"

"No." Tammy's sandy blonde ponytail swished as she shook her head. "When I asked, he said to tell her it was an old friend. Then when I gave her the phone, she freaked out and hung up real fast."

"I'll talk to her." Danny gritted his teeth and disappeared behind the doors.

Tammy turned her attention to me. "I don't suppose *you* know?"

"Why would I know?"

"Next time, shut the door," Tammy said, wrinkling her nose. "Actually, no. Next time, don't do it on shift. Surely you can keep it in your pants long enough to wait until after work."

"Don't say anything," I hissed.

"What do you take me for?" Tammy huffed. "If you hook up in the supply closet with the door open, you're kind of asking to get caught. You're lucky Danny didn't arrive a few minutes earlier."

She had a point. Tammy returned to work, and I really wasn't concerned she'd say anything. She wasn't a gossip.

That wasn't the problem at the forefront of my mind. My problem was I had a pretty good guess who'd called for Scarlett, and a stupid nagging in the back of my brain wouldn't stop asking why the hell she didn't tell me.

Chapter Ten

Overprotective

Scarlett

Seeing Dan had always warmed my soul. This was the first time my shoulders lifted from tension, and my stomach knotted. Dan being here meant I couldn't get distracted ogling Ryker. I couldn't make eyes or tease or really acknowledge his presence because I didn't trust myself not to give it away. Difficult before, but even worse now that I knew what he felt like. Sex with Ryker was an otherworldly experience.

Dan would freak if he found out. Especially since Ryker wasn't only a regular, he also helped Dan out. A friend was worse than a regular. Dan never let anyone help with anything, so it spoke volumes that Ryker found a way around his stubbornness. I was shocked when Dan let him fix my sink. Then, when the light went out and a new lightbulb didn't do the trick, Tammy said Ryker would take care of it as if it was normal.

He did take care of it. *Add "make Ryker teach me how to do handy tasks" to the list of things I want from him.* As if that list wasn't long enough.

Dan sat at the bar and made small talk about his gun show. After I brought him a burger, my nerves heightened. His stern expression dredged up memories of me as a young girl, awaiting a scolding I probably deserved.

Dan ignored the burger. "You got something you wanna tell me, Scar?"

Oh God, he can't already know. I glanced at Ryker, but he wore a similar disapproving frown. My gaze returned to Dan, and my brows furrowed, unsure where the sudden animosity from both of them had developed from.

"Uh, I have another art show coming up?" I tried.

Dan hmphed. "What'd you do this weekend?"

Ryker. Several times. Guilt kept that information at the forefront of my mind. Dan couldn't know. Ryker didn't seem nervous—more tense, like Dan.

"I worked and . . . Okay, for fuck's sake, tell me what you're trying to get out of me." I threw my arms up. "Because I don't know what it is, and you're making me nervous."

Dan released a doubtful huff. "You don't know what it is?"

"I truly don't. Spit it out. What's wrong?"

Gaze assessing, he sat up straighter. "Who called for you today?"

Oh, fuck. Tammy, that traitor, must've told him. To be fair, I didn't tell her not to say anything. Still, though. I curled my arms around myself. "Your tone implies you know."

"Were you not going to tell me?" Whether he was more annoyed or hurt, I couldn't tell.

"No. I wasn't going to tell you. What are you going to do?"

He ground his teeth. "There's plenty I could do."

"It's not like anything happened. He called, I blocked the number, that's it."

"I thought he didn't know where you were."

"I didn't think he did, but so what? He's not going to cross two states to find me."

"Then why's he bothering you?"

"I don't know. Because he gets off on fucking with people?"

"You're too nonchalant about this." Dan wagged a finger at me. "Is this the first you've heard from him, or has he contacted you already?"

I opened my mouth to say no, then slammed it shut. *The letter. The text.* Dan's eyes sharpened, and I cursed myself for not being more stoic. Now I had to tell him, and I couldn't put into words how much I didn't want to ever talk about Todd again.

I gnawed on my lip. "It's not a big deal."

"How did he contact you?"

"He sent me a letter and a text, but I blocked the number."

"A letter *and* a text? Jesus, Scarlett. What did he say? Where's the letter?"

"Burned. I don't know what it said because I burned it without opening it."

Dan scowled. "You shouldn't have done that."

"Would you please chill?" I snapped. I couldn't talk about this anymore, or I'd tear up. "He lives almost a thousand miles away. He's not going to come all the way over here to mess with me." *He won't come find me.* If I said it enough, maybe I'd believe it. "You worry too much."

"I worry enough," Dan said, standing. "We're not done talking about this. I just have to use the bathroom."

Dan stalked off, and I rolled my eyes. Turning to serve another customer, I was interrupted by Ryker grabbing my arm. I arched a brow. His clenched jaw implied he was as pissed off as Dan, if not more.

"Last night you were going through your mail and I asked you what was wrong, and you said *nothing*. Why the fuck did you lie to me?"

"Seriously?" I yanked out of his grip. "You too?"

"Why did you lie to me?"

"I didn't lie to you. Nothing was wrong because nothing happened. It's just a letter." *Let it go.* The more we discussed it, the heavier that weight on my chest suffocated me.

"Bullshit, Scarlett." He stretched over the bar and lowered his voice. "Danny's right. You shouldn't have burned that letter. You could use it against him. Don't you have a restraining order? He's violating that by contacting you."

"I'm not an idiot, Ryker. I took a picture of the envelope and sent it to the police. His parole officer said he'd deal with it. Not that it's any of your fucking business."

On my retreat this time, I dodged his attempt to stop me. Now I had two overprotective freaks to deal with. *Wonderful.* I served the other customers at the bar and was making a drink when Tammy sidled up beside me and scooped ice into a glass.

I dropped my third lemon, and Tammy nudged me with her elbow. "Are you okay?"

"Why did you tell Dan about my call?" The words came out clipped. "That's *my* business. You don't need to tell him."

"Whoa." Tammy held up her hands. "I'm sorry, Scarlett. I got worried. You seemed really scared when you got on the phone."

I massaged my temples. Being a bitch to Tammy wasn't the answer. I smoothed my ponytail and offered an apologetic smile. "Sorry I snapped, but you have no idea how overprotective he is." As I said it, I spotted Ryker and Dan whispering to each other out of the corner of my eye. *Fantastic.*

"He as in *Danny*, or he as in *Ryker*?" Tammy asked. I gaped, and she laughed. "Next time, close the door. Or, like I told Ryker, don't do it on shift."

"Oh, God." I buried my face in my hands. "I'm sorry. Please don't say anything to Dan."

"I wasn't going to." She finished making a drink, then pivoted toward me. "Look, I'm sorry I told Danny about the phone call. I'm not a nark. I won't tell him about you and Ryker. I just worried because you went white as a ghost on the phone, then clammed up and wouldn't say anything when I asked about it."

I made a face and finally finished making the drink without dropping another lemon. "I get it. But, for future reference, don't say anything to him, okay? I can take care of myself despite what Dan's told you."

"Danny's never said you can't take care of yourself." Tammy set her completed drinks on a tray. "All he ever talks about is how proud he is of you and how strong you are. He's not protective because he thinks you can't handle yourself. He loves you."

She left, and a new kind of guilt swirled in my stomach. Overprotective or not, Dan cared a lot. I served a couple more customers, then returned to peck him on the cheek. His burger was practically gone, and I didn't want him going home with awkwardness between us.

"You don't need to treat me like a child, but I'm sorry for not telling you, okay?"

He stiffened but relented. "Okay. You'll tell me if he tries again?"

I didn't miss the vulnerability and concern there. "I'll tell you."

"Good." He wiped his hands with a napkin and stood. "I'm tired. It was a long drive. Come over for breakfast?"

"Sure." I nodded. "Not too early, though."

"I've known you long enough to realize you're not a morning person." He chuckled and circled the bar, then pulled me into an embrace and lowered his lips to my head. "You know I love you, don't you?"

"I know." I squeezed him tight. "I'll see you tomorrow."

"All right, honey. Sleep good." He nodded to Ryker. "See you, Ryker."

"See you, Danny."

Dan disappeared around the corner, and I turned my attention to the register. Prickling on the nape of my neck alerted me to Ryker's relentless stare.

I tore my eyes away from the register. "What?"

"You know what. I don't appreciate you lying to me."

"What does it matter to you?"

The glower on his face would become permanent if he wasn't careful. "Next time he bothers you, tell me."

"Or what?" I scoffed.

"Don't fuck with me, Scarlett. Next time he bothers you, tell me."

"You're being ridiculous. He lives hours away. He's not motivated enough to come all the way here."

"Never underestimate assholes like that, Scarlett. They don't know boundaries."

The sarcastic retort I had planned died on my lips at the frown marring his face. *He's actually worried.* Pissed, but concerned. "It's fine. Seriously. Don't worry about it."

"Promise me you'll tell me if he bothers you again."

"What are you going to do if he does? He doesn't live here."

"Trust me, baby. You don't wanna know." A humorless smile replaced the glower. "State lines have never stopped me, and they're not about to start, so don't you dare keep it from me if he bothers you."

His predatory look elicited a gulp. Tammy had informed me that Ryker bounty hunted for a living. When I first moved here, I was concerned about Dan's reaction to Todd but Dan was getting older and, with his knees, could only do so much if Todd showed up.

Ryker, on the other hand . . . That dark smile? Yeah, I wouldn't want to be on the receiving end. Curiosity mingled with trepidation. What lengths would he go to if Todd contacted me again?

CHAPTER ELEVEN

Keeping Tabs

RYKER

The sun beat down hot enough to melt the walls. Heat waves radiated in the distance, and businesses advertised air conditioning inside. I almost took up the offer of the store I slouched against for ice-cold lemonade. I cursed myself for wearing a black T-shirt that enhanced the already unbearable heat. Sweat dripped down my neck, and I checked my watch.

Any minute now.

I ran my hand through my hair, annoyed the action coated it in sweat. I fucking hated summer. A little bell dinged, alerting me that someone had exited the shop. I glanced to the right and found it wasn't my hit. It was a woman.

Normally, she'd be my type. Curves, a bright smile, and pretty eyes. Except she did nothing for me. Not even when she batted her eyelashes. Scarlett never batted her eyes at me. Scarlett's eyes were easier to get lost in.

Annoyed, I tore my gaze away and clenched and unclenched my fist. One look at a girl, and my thoughts ran back to Scarlett. She had no right to occupy so much space in my head, but I couldn't get her off my mind.

The bell dinged again, and out shuffled an elderly woman. Her walker scraped the ground as she hobbled to the traffic light, hitting the button to cross. Any other day, I'd offer to help her, but I couldn't leave my post.

Another ding, and the door swung open. This time, a shaggy-haired asshole stepped out, a Danish pinched in his teeth, a coffee in one hand, and his phone in the other. Bafflingly, my bounties either seemed to be drastically unaware of how easy they were to find or went to incredible lengths to keep themselves hidden. There was no in between. This guy was plain stupid.

I reached into my pocket and retrieved the picture, confirming it was him by the scar on his left cheek and the tattoo on his hand that read his last name—*Harvey*.

Stuffing the photo in my pocket, I followed him. Idiot was oblivious to my presence. Pocketing his phone, he chewed his Danish and paused at a streetlight. I stopped beside him.

"That you, Jerry?" I asked.

His expression went blank. Some of them made this so easy, it hurt. "Uh, yeah." He faced me with a frown. "Sorry, man, your name's escaping me."

"Come on, Harvey, don't tell me you don't remember me?"

I needed him to not deny the last name, and then I could make my move.

He rubbed his chin. "Did we go to high school together?"

"Nah, Jerry, we didn't." I smacked the Danish and coffee out of his hands before pinning his wrists behind him and cuffing them. "You missed your court date for that assault and battery case with your ex. Let's go."

I ushered him forward, expecting a fight. These dumb motherfuckers must have some handbook on how to fight against a bounty hunter because they all tried the same thing. I saw it coming and gripped the nape of his neck before he threw his head back. I wasn't surprised at his next move. He crouched to escape my hold, and I let him. Then I shoved him to the ground, and he fell face-first onto the pavement.

"I can do this all day, Jerry," I warned, grabbing the cuffs and yanking him up. "Either way, you're going in, so I suggest you make it as painless as possible."

"Fucking twat," he spat.

Eh, I'd been called worse.

Jerry was an annoying little shit. Tried to get in my head by calling me names, asking for a fight. I laughed. Scrawniness didn't intimidate me. I could knock him out with one hit.

I got him to the police station, and they booked him while I waited for Conrad to arrive. I tapped my fingers against the counter near the reception desk, glancing at the door every time it opened. Usually, I didn't wait for Conrad, but he happened to be in the area. He had a previous check for me and promised to give me the one for Jerry as well if I sat tight. Finances weren't an issue, but I had a buddy who was struggling. I planned to send him the money to help him out.

An easygoing grin spread over my face when a familiar man rounded the corner from behind the desk. Ray had rich brown skin, barely any hair, a potbelly, and the best sense of humor. He approached the counter with a cup of coffee. "Ryker, hey."

"How's it going, Ray?"

I was grateful for Ray. Some police officers had a problem with bounty hunters, but he didn't.

"Doing good, doing good." He slapped a newspaper on the laminate counter. "Who you bring in today?"

"Jerry Harvey."

"Oh, that piece of shit." He took a gulp of coffee. "Glad to have him locked up again. How you been?"

"I'm good. How's the family?"

"Good. Jada is turning thirteen this weekend. Can you believe that?"

I couldn't. The last time I saw Jada, I was pretty sure she was only ten.

"How's thirteen turning out for you?" I asked, aware Jada had a rebellious streak since she was a baby.

"Lord help me, Ryker, it's not easy. She's full of eye rolls and *whatever Dad* comments. It's driving me nuts. I love her to death, though." He grinned. "What about you? Any chance you'll settle down soon?"

"I don't intend to. You know that."

"It's a shame. A real shame. There's nothing like having your woman by your side as you get older. You mean to tell me not one girl has caught your eye?"

Only one giant pain in my ass. He didn't need to know that. Though thinking of her reminded me . . . A quick sweep of the room showed no one nearby, but I still lowered my voice. "If I give you a name, can you tell me who they have a restraining order against?"

"Not legally." Ray peered at me over the computer he shuffled in front of, hands hovering over the keyboard. "But out of curiosity, what's the name?"

My lips twitched up. *Knew I could count on him.*

"Scarlett Solis."

His smile widened as he typed. "Oh, so there *is* someone."

"It's nothing. A friend's niece. I'm doing him a favor."

As I said the words, I got that feeling—the muscles in my neck tightening. The urge to avoid eye contact. The same sensation I experienced anytime I lied. I hated that feeling. But I wasn't lying. It *was* nothing. Maybe I half lied because I didn't intend to share the information with Danny, but I was doing it for Scarlett's safety, which was technically for Danny.

Yep. That's all.

Ray swiped his coffee and took a sip. "Do you know a birthdate?"

"No. She used to live in New Mexico, now lives in California."

He nodded and typed into his computer, then scrunched his face. "Can you give me anything else? Solis is a common last name."

"I don't know." I racked my brain for what her mother's name was. Danny had said it before. I remembered it being something with a *D*. "Diana is the mother's name. I'm pretty sure."

"That helps." The keys clicked fast under his fingertips. "I think I've got her. A restraining order against a Todd Haverson for . . ." He frowned. "You know what this is for?"

I knew a hell of a lot more than that report said. "Assault and battery, bad enough to put her in the hospital. Should also mention something about him contacting her recently."

"Right." Ray nodded. "I do have a note from the parole officer saying he texted her, wrote her a letter, and called her. You planning to do something about this?"

"Don't worry, Ray." I patted the countertop. "I'm not making you an accomplice to anything. I only wanted the information. I got some buddies in New Mexico who can keep tabs on him and let me know if he leaves the state. That's all I want. Fair warning if he tries to come here."

"In that case, tread carefully. It might be pertinent for you to know he has two registered guns, and this isn't the only restraining order he has against him."

Of course it wasn't. It never was with these kinds of assholes. The guns didn't scare me. I rarely didn't have a gun on me, and I was confident after being a Marine for eight years that he couldn't possibly be a better shot than me.

"Don't worry, Ray," I said. "If he comes around, I can handle him."

Handle him by beating the shit out of him until he doesn't know his name anymore.

Another officer walked in, and Ray quickly closed out of his window, picking up the conversation about his daughter like we were right in the middle of it. This was why Ray was one of my favorites.

After Conrad finally showed and paid me, I stepped outside and called Dustin, a friend in New Mexico who I'd toured with. He didn't answer, so I left a message.

I didn't intend to go to the bar until the weekend. The moment I stepped inside, Scarlett would suck me in. Yet somehow, after the police station, I ended up parked in the familiar dirt lot and cursed myself while I pondered this unrelenting hold she had over me. She had me caught in a lightning storm, too dangerous to stay in but too beautiful to look away from.

She was a bigger pain in my ass than anyone had ever been. That was the only thing different. At least, that's what I told myself.

The bar door creaked, and I spotted Scarlett sitting alone, drawing. Ignoring her would be the wise thing to do, but noting Danny's absence, I stopped at her table and grabbed a chair. A loud scrape announced my presence. She looked up. Red stained her cheeks when I settled on the chair.

"Hey." She caught her lip between her teeth. "It's not the weekend."

"Am I only allowed to come on the weekend?"

She scoffed. "Obviously."

My sarcastic retort never came. My eyes widened at her work. While nails digging into a muscled back wasn't elaborate, that's not what reduced me to awed silence.

It didn't resemble a drawing. The shading and clean lines gave it more of a black-and-white photograph feel. Jaw hanging open, I watched as she made it come more alive with every scrape of her pencil. Part of me wondered if that's what it looked like when she did that to me while I thrust into her. *Shit.* Less than five minutes, and I already had to adjust myself.

I scrubbed my hand over my face. "That doesn't look like a drawing."

Brows pinched together, she tilted her head.

"I mean, because it's so good, it looks like a photograph."

"Oh." Her shoulders relaxed, and a smile played on her lips. "Thanks. My anatomy's a little rusty. I'm not as good as Cath Riley, but," she shrugged, "I try."

"I have no idea who that is."

"She's my favorite artist." Scarlett lunged for her phone, tapped the screen, then turned it toward me. "She does super realistic drawings. The reason I got into art in the first place. She's my idol. It's my dream to go to one of her shows."

Her screen showcased a photo of a hand gripping a thigh. Except it said it was a charcoal drawing, not a photo. *Impressive.* Though I disagreed with her.

I returned the phone. "I think you're just as good, sugar."

"Sure you do."

"I *do*."

"Do you know anything about art?"

Like I said, goddamn pain in my ass.

I dragged my tongue over my teeth. "You wanna take this argument upstairs?"

A smirk formed at her parted lips and dilated eyes. I leaned over the table, and her gaze darted to my mouth. My ringing phone interrupted our moment, and when I retrieved it, Dustin's name flashed across the screen.

"Is Danny around?" I asked, standing.

"I'm supposed to have dinner with him."

"And after dinner?"

"After dinner," she gazed up at me with those bedroom eyes that annihilated my self-control, "I guess I'd like dessert, but not with him."

"Jesus Christ." She too easily got me where she wanted me. "I'll get you dessert, baby." I hooked my finger on her shirt collar and tugged. "I gotta take this." I held up my phone, then trudged outside so she wouldn't hear.

I accepted the call, and during the small talk greeting with Dustin, I watched through the dusty windows as Scarlett picked up her pencil and brought it to paper. Pushing her hair out of her face, she left a streak of black across her cheek.

"Everything okay, Ryker?" Dustin asked.

"Fine." Try as I might, I couldn't tear my gaze away from Scarlett. There was no way in hell that fucker was getting his hands on her again. "I need you to do something for me. You got a pen to write down this name?"

Chapter Twelve

Rougher

Scarlett

Eating dinner with Dan was one of the most chill parts of my day. He had a way of making things easy. Except he noticed something up with me, and that part made my palms sweat.

"Meet anyone with potential to be a friend?" Dan asked as I picked up our dinner plates and carried them to the sink. They were the same mismatched plates he'd had since I met him. In fact, aside from the slight difference in orientation, this kitchen resembled the one he had in New Mexico. Same round table. Same wooden chairs. Same lack of curtains on the window over the sink.

"I don't know." I snatched a towel to dry the dishes while he washed them. "I haven't been out much. Tammy's nice."

"I thought you were joining some group."

"I was going to but I—shit!"

Dan's knees buckled and he crumpled, barely catching himself on the counter.

I slipped my arm under his and helped him to the closest chair. "What happened?"

"Damn thing gave out on me again." He rubbed his right knee and winced.

"Ice?"

"Nah, just give me a minute."

"You need to go to the doctor—"

"No." He straightened his knee, a determined frown on his face. "No doctors."

"Stubborn as a fucking mule, I swear," I muttered, returning to the sink.

He scoffed. "Look who's talking."

A witty retort died on my lips when he hissed in pain. He really needed to do something about his knees before he couldn't walk at all.

I finished the dishes and said goodbye to Dan with a kiss on the cheek. On my way to the bar, I spotted Ryker reclined against the wall in the alley with his thick arms on display over his chest.

My heart raced. His fervent stare stopped me in my tracks. Eyes dark, he uncrossed his arms and beckoned me. It shouldn't have been that easy for him to get me over there, yet my feet wouldn't stop moving.

The moment I was in reach, he seized my hips. His warm, calloused hand cupped my face, and his lips caught mine in a kiss that sparked tingles all over my body. His hands slid down and claimed my ass with a tight squeeze. Breaking the kiss, he slipped his hands into my back pockets as he nuzzled my neck.

"This is just fucking." His teeth scraped my skin. "You know that, right? It won't turn into anything else."

"I know." I angled my head and lost my fingers in his dark hair. "I don't want anything else."

"Good." He smacked my ass. "You're coming home with me tonight." He grabbed my hand and had me halfway around the building before I processed his statement.

"Wait, I need stuff."

"What stuff?"

"Uh, keys? My car?"

"You don't need your car, and I already locked your door." My keys dangled from his finger, and I gaped.

"Seriously? Do you know any boundaries?"

"Well, *you* weren't going to do it."

"Dude, you need to get over that."

He halted and dragged my body to his. "Scarlett, if you keep pissing me off, I'm going to edge you all night and not let you come."

I licked my lips, and his gaze darted to the movement. He groaned and pulled me into another kiss, his tongue sweeping over my lips. "You're going to be the death of me, I swear," he grumbled, taking my hand again.

I formed a retort in my head, but it vanished the moment he handed me a helmet. I paled at the motorcycle we paused in front of. "Uh, no." I shoved the helmet into his arms. "I don't think so."

"Why not?"

"Why don't I just bring my truck?"

"What's wrong?" His lips lifted in a smirk. "You scared?"

"I'm not scared. I just don't like motorcycles."

"You're such a bad fucking liar. Come on, sugar. I promise I won't drive crazy. Live a little."

I scrunched my nose at the beast of death he called a vehicle. He gripped my neck and kissed me, his tongue plunging between my lips and caressing mine. "Come on, Scarlett," he murmured against my mouth. "Have a little faith."

My insides fluttered in demand for more kisses. A demand I didn't have the strength to deny. "Fine."

He secured the helmet on my head, then swung his leg over the bike. *Hmm.* Motorcycles scared me, but a muscled hunk on a motorcycle? Different story.

I flipped up the visor. "Where's your helmet?"

"On you." He positioned the bike upright, then patted the space behind him. "Sit."

"That's silly. You wear it."

"No. Let's go, Scarlett. I don't have all night." He drummed his fingers against his bike. "Do you want me to eat you out again or not?"

Obviously I wanted him to do that. I shifted my weight while he tapped a piece of metal behind his foot. "Put your foot here. There's one on the other side too."

One bracing breath later, I climbed on the bike. I adjusted on the seat, sliding closer to him and wrapping my arms around his waist.

"Hold on tight." He revved the engine, and we lurched forward.

A squeal erupted from my mouth, and I tightened my arms around him. He didn't drive crazy, but he did drive *fast.* I rested my head against his back and shivered at the wind whipping around us. Despite the cold, I didn't hate it as much as I'd expected.

We rode for about twenty minutes before we turned onto a long, dark road. Trees shrouded us for most of the street but thinned when a building came into view. A sleek, modern house. Not huge, but it could've fit both the trailers I grew up in with plenty of room to spare. Black and brown framed the boxy structure. Sharp corners and floor-to-ceiling windows made up the second floor, while the ground floor appeared to be a cement garage.

Ryker stopped in front of the garage and reached into his pocket. A *clank* announced the metal door lifting, and two dogs ran out. Ryker hushed them as he walked the bike inside and cut the engine. Curious noses sniffed me the moment my feet hit solid ground.

Once I removed the helmet and set it down, I crouched and extended my hand to let them smell me. Ryker crouched as well, ruffling one's head. They preened under his attention but returned to lick my hands.

"Who are these two?" I giggled, dodging a lick on the face.

"Grayson." He patted the gray-and-white pit bull. "And Demon." He scratched behind the rottweiler's ears.

"Demon?" I stifled a laugh. "Really?"

"He's only friendly because I brought you. If you came around without me for the first time, you'd see why he has that name." He stood. "Come on."

They followed him through the alarmingly neat garage. Gray coated the ceilings, walls, and floors. One side of the space stored locked cases and the other side housed shelves organized with tools and a long workbench. A punching bag hung in the middle of the room across from a weightlifting bench. Ryker led the dogs past the locked cases near a door. They sat when he told them to and never moved while he filled their metal bowls.

"All right, eat."

They sprinted forward and ate from their separate bowls.

I approached Ryker and rubbed my arms. "Wow. You've trained them well."

"They're good dogs. Cold?"

"A little."

"Wouldn't have happened if you weren't half-naked."

"Uh, actually, it wouldn't have happened if we rode in a real vehicle."

"Please." He opened the door and waved me ahead. "You enjoyed it more than you thought you would."

I rolled my eyes on my way upstairs. We ascended to another door, and Ryker reached around me to open it. My mouth fell slack. His home made the garage look messy. Despite the dogs downstairs, every surface was spotless. The leather couches, the coffee table, the shelves flanking the big screen television—all of it was sleek and polished like it'd never been touched. Dark, hardwood floors didn't boast a single scuff. The open floor plan allowed a view into his massive kitchen with marble countertops. A fireplace sat to the right of one of the bookshelves, between the kitchen and living room.

"Wow."

Ryker caught my wrist when I advanced to explore more. "You haven't seen the best room."

He kissed me, and his warm arms eased the chill from the ride. I greedily pressed myself against him for more body heat. Something he granted by lifting me. I wrapped my legs around his waist, not paying attention to where he took us until he dropped me on a bed. He caught my jaw before I took in my surroundings.

Darkened eyes drifted to my lips, then back to my eyes. He dipped his head and kissed the corner of my mouth, then along my jaw to my neck, leaving my skin hot and begging for more. He continued past my breasts and stomach as he undid my shorts. He slid them and my underwear down at once. I shuddered when he kissed my inner thighs and slung my legs over his shoulders.

"Ryker," I murmured, losing my fingers in his hair.

His tongue darted to my clit, and I arched my spine. Guttural sounds tumbled out of me with the precise and relentless attention of his tongue. He was ridiculously good with his tongue. His hands. His . . . well, everything.

The sucking and licking made me needy enough, but then his fingers slid inside me. His other hand caressed my outer thigh and tingles crawled their way up to my pussy, which quivered more with every stroke of his fingers and tongue. It didn't take long for the pleasure to explode.

My legs still twitched from the orgasm when he climbed over me and kissed me. My excitement lingered on his tongue and lips—a new but not unwelcome experience. In fact, the longer he kissed me, the more it turned me on. He untangled my hands from his hair and pinned them over my head. A jolt of excitement shot through me when I tried to move my hands, and he squeezed them tighter.

"Do you like that?" he asked against my lips.

I locked my legs around his waist. "Yes."

"Do you trust me?"

It was insane to say yes, but the truth was, I did. Dan trusted him, and he'd given me no reason to doubt him.

"Yes."

"Good." The tender kiss he gave left me chasing after him when he pulled away. "Because I want to get rougher with you. But I want you to know, you can tell me to stop if it's too much."

Rougher with me? *Yes, please.* I nodded. "Okay."

His lips claimed mine again, this time fiercer. I sank into the bed, and he sucked my lower lip into his mouth, then dragged his teeth off it. My shirt and bra were discarded, and he sat up on his knees, removing his shirt, then his belt. My breath accelerated with my heart rate. I'd never had a man turn me into a hypersexual addict like he did. I forced myself not to dwell on it because if I did, I'd realize he'd singlehandedly repaired my enjoyment of sex after I thought it'd vanished forever.

He set the belt down and clamped his hands on my hips. How I ended up lying on my front, I didn't know. He tossed me so effortlessly, it dampened my pussy and yanked me out of my wandering thoughts. He took my hands hostage and leather tickled my skin. I glanced back to find his belt snug around my wrists. I wiggled but couldn't break free.

"Okay?" He glided his hand over my spine and goose bumps followed.

"Yes."

He hummed in approval and placed a hot kiss against my neck, caressing my ass. "Good girl."

My pussy clenched. Other guys I'd been with made me feel weird about liking this—if I even had the courage to bring it up. He was the first one taking the lead. I wouldn't tell him, but I'd get on my knees anytime he asked.

He caressed my ass before lifting it. I shivered as his hand brushed the sensitive skin of my inner thighs on its way up. He alternated between circling my clit and sliding his fingers in and out of me until my whimpers echoed off the walls, the release so close I could taste i—

He stopped.

"Ryker," I whined.

"Patience, Scarlett." He kissed my spine. "Remember how hard you came the other night?"

My breath trembled, and my eyes slid shut. *Yes.* I wasn't about to forget that any time soon. Or ever.

His lips drifted over my butt to my pussy, where he gave me a languid lick. I arched, giving him better access. My reward was an approving caress over my ass while his tongue toyed with my clit, and his fingers plunged into me. Again, he had me panting, my toes curling. Then he fucking stopped.

I needed a release too badly to care how desperate I sounded. "*Ryker.*"

He smacked my ass, and I yelped. "Keep complaining and it'll never happen."

His fingers found their way to my most sensitive parts once again. He edged me twice more, leaving my body pleading for consistent attention. Excitement dripped down my thighs, my nerves on high alert at what could happen next. The fact I couldn't see what he was doing, couldn't finish myself off, all of it added to the scorching heat he continuously stoked.

Ryker stopped touching me, and the restraint on my wrists loosened. I shuddered when the leather wrapped around my throat instead. Fabric rustled behind me. I hoped his clothes were coming off. Strong hands rubbed against my ass, then . . . *Yes.* It was clothes because his tip teased my throbbing pussy.

He nudged inside me and closed his hand around my wrists, pinning them to my spine. "This what you want, baby?"

I'd come just from him filling me. It was inevitable with how sensitive I was. "Yes."

"Promise me you'll keep your hands where they are, even if I let go."

My insides vibrated with need. "I promise."

Fingers digging into my hips, he jerked forward and his cock penetrated me. Dropping my forehead to the bed, I moaned. He yanked me up by the belt which tightened it around my throat and forced my back to arch. Wrapping the belt around his fist, he tugged it toward him as he thrust in so deep I screamed.

"Oh, *God.*"

"You like that?" His thrusts grew harder.

Unable to speak through the whimpers, I nodded. "Words, Scarlett," he growled, smacking my ass.

"Yes." I gasped as he rammed into me. "Just like that, but harder."

"Fuck," he groaned, and his skin slapped against mine when he shoved into me. I cried out, pleasure assaulting my senses until stars danced in my vision.

He jerked me back toward him, and his fingers clasped around my wrists. Hot breath skirted over my skin, and when he tightened the belt around my neck, I almost came.

"Baby, I'm going to make it so you can't walk tomorrow." His lips grazed my ear. "Every time you step, you'll feel that ache and miss my cock in you."

Having trouble walking never sounded so good.

CHAPTER THIRTEEN

The Whole Package

RYKER

*O*ne more night. The futile chant didn't improve my self-control. My plan to set things straight with Scarlett and end all this sneaky hooking up backfired when she answered the door to her apartment in sweats and a T-shirt. The T-shirt hung loose everywhere except her chest, and the sweats rested low on her hips, like a temptation to pull them down. A lack of revealing clothing didn't diminish her irresistibility. Especially not when I ripped those clothes off her.

That night, I told myself *no more*. I trudged in on Friday planning to tell her and of course, it went to hell. I snuck up after closing, and she answered the door all sleepy and adorable, wearing a tank top that did nothing to hide her perfect nipples and shorts that might as well have been underwear. Pretty clear I didn't end it that night.

Saturday's the day. Another attempt failed when she returned from an art show wearing a little red dress. It clung to her curves and ended mid-thigh, showing off legs I wanted wrapped around me again. I invited her to my place and told her to keep the dress on. I now had *a lot* of good memories attached to that dress. I only hoped she'd spare me and not wear it again.

Sunday's inability to locate self-control marked the fourth week of hooking up, which I'd *never* done. I usually got bored, but there was nothing boring about Scarlett—her retorts, her attitude, her body. I loved pulling those needy sounds out of her, loved watching her writhe and whimper. Her responsiveness enraptured me.

The addiction had gone too far. We talked about birth control and stopped using condoms. Another thing I'd never considered before but when she asked, the image of taking her raw shoved responsibility out the window. Fantasies of my come spilling out of her drove my decision to say *fuck condoms*. That kinda thing was relationship-level shit. I had to end it.

Another week passed, but this time I arrived with a plan. I prepared a speech and spent the whole drive thinking of the most unsexy things. Grandparents doing it. Green beans. Danny naked. *Yeah, that'll do it.* I just had to stay focused.

Cigarette smoke and greasy but delicious smells from the kitchen filled my nose when I strolled into Danny's. With Scarlett nowhere to be found, I sat at the bar and Tammy dropped off a drink. I expected Scarlett to appear at any moment since Dan said she'd work weekend nights—barring an art show— to help with the NBA crowd.

Thirty minutes passed. Dan emerged from the kitchen with crackers and ginger ale but abandoned them behind the bar. Muttering a curse, he stalked to a new group of customers who planted themselves at a corner table.

While Danny and Tammy rushed around, I racked my brain for a reason behind Scarlett's absence. She knew weekends were hard for them.

Dan refilled my scotch, shaking his head. "Sorry, Ryker. Swamped today."

"Isn't Scarlett supposed to be helping?"

"She's sick." His concerned gaze flicked to the ginger ale and crackers. "I meant to take this up to her an hour ago but haven't been able to."

"Want me to take it?"

"Would you?" He inclined his head toward another group who sat at the bar, gazes glued to the TV mounted above the liquor. "I have to get these new guys."

"No problem." When his attention diverted, my shoulders slumped. This wasn't part of my plan.

Crackers and ginger ale in hand, I stomped upstairs and knocked. No answer. Trying the door, I found it unlocked. *Damn her.* She never fucking listened.

Static voices sounded from the CRT TV, but no Scarlett. Then I heard it. Retching.

I should leave this and get out of here. She could be contagious. Even if she wasn't, I wasn't her boyfriend. We fucked. There was no reason to stay and check on her. Except the retching continued, each one more violent than the last.

Ah, fuck.

I slogged to the bathroom and found her lying on the linoleum floor, pale and clutching her stomach. Sweat gleaned on her forehead, and she curled into a ball. A horrifying thought seeped dread into my chest and stomach.

"You're not pregnant, are you?" I asked.

"Jesus, what are you doing here?" she whined, hiding her face. "Go away."

"You're not." My heart thundered against my ribs. "Right?"

"No." She tightened her arms around her stomach. "*Christ*, Ryker."

"Are you sure?"

She sat up, glare furious and almost intimidating. "Pretty fucking sure."

"Because you took a test?"

A kid at this point in my life? I couldn't even fucking take care of myself.

"No, jackass, because I'm on my fucking period." She barely snapped the words out before her eyes widened. She dragged herself over the toilet and vomited, one hand haphazardly holding her hair back.

Cursing myself, I collected a hair tie from the counter. I waited until she stopped throwing up, then braided her hair. "Look, I got three sisters. None of them were this sick on their period." I caressed her spine. "Are you sure that's all it is?"

"Oh my *God*." She sneered at me. "Can you not be a total prick? I know my body. This is my body on my period. If you want me when this is over, I suggest you leave me the fuck alone and stop being a dick."

Whether I was more annoyed with myself for breaking the rules *again* or with her, I couldn't tell. Either way, I frowned and stood. "Fine. Jeez. You're being the real poster child for bitchy women on their periods."

"Get the fuck out before I claw out your eyes."

"There's ginger ale and crackers on the table." I walked out, not so sure she wouldn't actually claw out my eyes if I didn't haul ass. "You're welcome."

Another retch halted my advancement to the front door. *Leave her alone, Ryker.* I tried to tell myself that. I really did. The fact was, my sisters were sick on their periods, but nothing that brutal. It still sucked. I still helped them. *She's not my sister.*

So I left.

And returned an hour later with a bag from the store. Standing outside her door, I wondered what the fuck was wrong with me. How could she have this hold on me? My hand lingered on the doorknob. *I shouldn't do this.* It'd give her the wrong idea. Yet, I twisted the knob, and it wasn't locked even though I locked it on my way out. Now she was being a pain.

I entered, relieved to find her on the couch, nibbling crackers and watching TV. She peered over the sofa and scowled.

"*What?*" She narrowed her eyes at the bag. "Ryker, I swear to God, if that's a fucking pregnancy test . . ."

"It's not." I kicked the door closed behind me. "This door was locked when I left."

"I know."

"Why isn't it anymore?"

"Oh, *I don't know.*" At least she wasn't too sick to allow sarcasm to drip into her tone. "Maybe someone picked the lock and snuck in."

I white-knuckled the bag as I circled the faded red couch. "When you feel better, you're paying for that."

"What do you want? Come to tell me more about how I don't know my own body?"

"Jesus Christ." I lifted her legs and sat down, then draped her calves over me. "You're in a real crappy mood."

"You barged into my bathroom while I was vomiting and demanded to know if I was pregnant. What did you expect?"

She had me there. "Sorry," I muttered, scratching the back of my neck. "I panicked."

"Well, next time don't." She timidly sipped her can of soda. "This is normal for me. I won't have you freaking out every month."

"The violent vomiting is normal?"

"It's *my* normal."

"That's horrible."

"No kidding."

"Can't someone give you something to help?"

"The medical field doesn't give a shit about women, Ryker. No one does research to help. The most they do is give you painkillers and anti-nausea pills and say good luck. Pills are pretty useless when you can't keep anything down."

I pictured Scarlett lying on the floor every month and flexed my hand. "All right, I'm not trying to be a dick, but what the fuck? Three sisters, never saw shit like that."

"I have everything wrong with me a girl can have." Her face reddened before she looked away. "My periods are like periods on steroids."

"What does that mean?"

"It means I have PCOS, PMDD, and endometriosis."

"I don't know what any of that is."

"It's bullshit. Bullshit and pain." She stroked her lower stomach with a grimace. "Also why no matter how hard I work out," she patted her tummy, one I knew she was insecure about because it wasn't flat, "I can't get rid of this."

"Don't get rid of anything. Your body's perfect."

"Perfect at causing me immense pain."

Can't argue with that. I retrieved the electric heating pad from the bag I brought and knelt next to the closest outlet.

"What's that?" She craned her head to see what I was doing as I plugged it in.

"A heating pad."

I rested it on her stomach after setting it at a medium heat. Her eyebrows nearly touched her hairline.

"What?" I asked.

"Nothing. Never had a guy who didn't get squeamish at the mention of a period. Or one who knew how to help."

"Then you haven't been with men; you've been with boys."

She giggled, and I didn't realize how much I missed her smile until that moment. "Thanks. You didn't have to do that."

"I owed you for the pregnancy freak-out."

"That's for damn certain."

"So, what the fuck is that shit you listed?"

She tilted her head. "You seriously want to know?" I gestured for her to continue. She arched a brow. "Um, okay. You're a first for me. Guys usually treat me like I have the plague when I'm on my period."

"I told you, they were boys. If you were with a guy who couldn't handle hearing about a period, then he was a fucking child. Real men buy tampons and chocolate."

"Real men buy tampons and chocolate? Is that what else is in the bag?"

I tossed her said bag. "Obviously."

"That's so sweet." She peeked inside. "How'd you know what kind of tampons I use?"

"Don't read into it. I was a dick to you earlier. I'm making up for it. And there was a box in your bathroom."

"It's still sweet." She lowered the bag to the ground, then hissed and flattened her palm over the heating pad.

"Are you done throwing up?"

"I think so."

"Did you take something for the pain?"

"You're being a real mother, you know that?"

"I don't see the point in letting yourself be in pain."

"This is my pain on painkillers, Ryker." She sighed. "This is my normal. PMDD is like PMS but a million times worse. Endometriosis is when the tissue that should shed every month grows where it isn't supposed to and more than it's supposed to. And PCOS means I get cysts on my ovaries."

"Sounds like something out of a horror movie." My lips twisted downward. "What happens to the cysts?"

"If I'm lucky, they dissolve. If I'm not, they burst, and it hurts like a motherfucker."

"They burst?" My eyes bugged. "*Inside* you?"

"No, I give birth to them, and they burst afterward." She rolled her eyes. "Yes, they burst inside me. That's why it hurts so much."

"Is that what happened this time?"

"No." She adjusted, rotating her hips and wincing as she pulled her knees up. "That happens when I ovulate. You know, so the pain is nice and spread out over the whole month."

"Jesus Christ," I muttered.

"Yep. The extra pain right now is the endometriosis. Fingers crossed it doesn't keep moving up into my stomach and require surgery."

I eyed her stomach warily. I liked her body, but I didn't care for the way it seemed to attack her. "It's growing into your stomach?"

"Mm-hmm. In the intestines already."

"Why don't they take it out?"

"There's no point unless it threatens my life. My mom had it too, and she did the surgery three times. All three times, it started growing again before she recovered. Unless you get a surgeon that actually knows what they're doing, it's not worth it."

"Why isn't there a standard?"

"Why, indeed."

I rubbed gentle circles against her leg. "I'm sorry, sugar. That sounds shitty."

"It is shitty." She inhaled sharply, her face contorting in pain. Tucking a pillow between her knees, she rolled onto her side. "You don't have to stay. Apology accepted."

"What're you going to do?"

She gestured to the TV. "This."

"Watching this boring station is what you're going to do all night?"

That embarrassed flush returned. "It's the only one I get."

"That's ridiculous." I stood and crouched beside the TV. "You have an antenna." I adjusted the device, and the picture flickered. As was typical for these things, it had a delicate nature, and I had to keep moving it until it finally calmed down. I tightened the connection, then tried another station.

"I tried to fix it," she whined. "No fair. That's it. You're teaching me how to do stuff around the house."

Returning to the couch, I plopped down and draped her legs over me again. An action so natural it startled my spine straight. *What the fuck am I doing?* This was more relationship-level shit. Yet I couldn't leave her helpless and in pain. "What do you need to learn for when you have me?"

Why'd I say that? I couldn't be at her beck and call. But I hated the idea of her never needing me for anything.

"I like being self-sufficient," she grumbled. "You're no longer allowed to fix anything without explaining what you're doing."

I saluted. "Yes, ma'am."

"Don't call me ma'am. I'm not old yet."

"Sorry. Yes, sugar baby."

"Be nice to me." She pouted. "I'm sick."

"Fine. Yes, my poor sick Scarlett."

She shook her head, battling amusement.

I shouldn't have stayed. But every time she curled up with a whimper, I couldn't find the motivation. *It's because she's vulnerable and won't lock the fucking door, meaning anyone could come up here.* She was in no position to defend herself.

So I stayed. Much longer than I should've. It only made everything worse because I cracked sarcastic jokes, and she fired retorts back. I knew I was in too deep when she fell asleep, and I couldn't stop staring. Why did she have to be the whole package?

I laid a blanket from her bed over her, then turned off the TV and locked that goddamn door on my way out. I waited at the stairs until Dan vanished, the creak of the kitchen's swinging doors informing me the coast was clear.

I settled into my regular seat, and Nick approached. He sat next to me with raised eyebrows.

"What?" I snapped.

"Careful, Ryker. You're going to get caught."

"I'm not going to get caught. Besides, it's over. I'm ending it. I only didn't because she's sick."

"Yeah, I usually go shopping for sick girls I'm about to tell I won't fuck anymore."

I glowered. "Fuck off."

Nick gave me a side-glance with a knowing guffaw that balled my fists. Thankfully, he left, and the crowds died down, so I was able to get more scotch. I normally looked forward to Dan being available to chat for a minute but going behind his back changed that.

Unfortunately for me, he noticed. Fortunately for me, he wasn't the type to pry, and I left without many questions.

I had to end it with Scarlett. The best time to do it was while I couldn't fuck her. So, I returned on Wednesday, figuring after three days she couldn't be as sick. Dan took the night off and I'd seen the light in his house on as I drove by. Without him around, I hurried straight up to her apartment.

I knocked on the door. No answer. Again, I knocked, but the result didn't change. *Maybe she's not home.* I started down the stairs but paused. She would lock it if she wasn't home, wouldn't she?

Returning, I tried the door and took a deep breath when I found it unlocked. I sighed and pushed it open. I'd lock it, and if she forgot her keys, too bad. She could ask Dan.

Inside, I found her in the kitchen, cooking. She looked a lot better, given she was standing and swaying her hips. *God, please let her still be on her period.*

Not only did she not lock the door, she also had headphones in. She wouldn't notice if anyone snuck in. I flung the door, and it shut with a loud *slam*, but she didn't react. *That's it.* I couldn't let this slide.

I tapped her on the shoulder. She squealed and pulled out her headphones, retreating so hard she rammed her lower back into the counter.

"Oh my God." She placed one hand over her chest, the other rubbing the spot where she hit the counter. "You scared the shit out of me."

"I wonder how. Couldn't be because your door isn't fucking locked."

"God, you're so bossy." She wrinkled her nose. "What are you doing here? I'm still riding the crimson wave, but it's not as bad. The first three days are the worst."

Thank God. "I need to talk to you, but first, how hard is it to lock a door?"

"*Really?*"

"I entered your apartment without you noticing until I fucking touched you. That doesn't bother you?"

"No." She stirred the contents of the pan over the stove. "You come up here all the time. Do you want it to bother me that you came into my apartment?"

"That's not the fucking point. The point is I could be someone else. A robber or worse."

"But you're not, so why are you making such a big deal about it?"

"Because I *could've* been."

"Yeah, and this building could catch fire, I could shatter my hand and not be able to do art anymore, and someone could break into my truck. *Could.* You need a chill pill." She waved her spoon around. "Lots of things could happen. If we worry about that shit all the time, we'd never have any fun."

"Those are different scenarios. This is basic knowledge to protect yourself from shitty people."

"Okay, sugar baby. I'm sorry." Her mocking tone twitched the hand that demanded I spank her raw. She laughed. "You're seriously a poster child for *man*opause right now. Stop being so bitchy. Is it that time of the month? Are we synchronized?"

A muscle in my jaw ticked nonstop. "I want you to remember this moment. When your period was the only thing keeping me from making you scream my name until your throat hurts and your ass turns purple. Probably the only time in your life you'll be thankful you're on your period."

"Man." She exhaled overdramatically. "It's that sweet talking that gets me every time."

"Scarlett." I pinched the bridge of my nose. No one could piss me off like she could. "Would you please lock the fucking door? It's not that hard, is it?"

"I'm a creature of habit and locking my door isn't habit." She lifted a shoulder, and I wanted to scream. More so when she pouted at me. "Aw, are you *worried* about me?"

"In the same way I'd worry about a child who's about to stick their finger in a socket."

"Jeez, Ryker. Lighten up. What are you doing here anyway? What'd you want to talk about?"

She approached and slid her hands up and down my arms. Although my brain recognized she was on her period, my cock did not. I inhaled slowly, reminding myself why I was here.

"I need to talk to you about . . ." I paused, trying to remember the speech I'd prepared, wondering how I could possibly pull it off when her hands were curling around my biceps.

"You seem stressed." She kissed my cheek and uncrossed my arms. Pressing her body into mine, she rested her cheek on my chest and circled her arms around me. "What's wrong?"

Fuck. I hadn't mentally prepared for a hug. I tried to form words, but every word I planned flew out the window with her in my arms. Then she was guiding me to the wall and logic didn't care what I came to do.

I snatched her wrists when she reached for my belt. "What are you doing?"

"Helping you relax." Her sultry smile loosened my hold. "And thanking you."

"Thanking me?" She undid my belt and unbuttoned my jeans, lowered the zipper, and caressed my cock on the way.

She kissed my neck and shoved my jeans down. "For being so sweet the other day."

Instead of pushing her away like I should've, I reveled her full hips in my hands and hauled her closer. "You're on your period."

She dropped to her knees, tugging my boxers with her until my cock sprung free. "You're not."

Fuck. Confronting her now was supposed to be safe, a time she couldn't seduce me. Except her hand wrapped around my cock and she licked the tip while staring up at me with those beautiful brown eyes.

"Scarlett," I groaned. "You don't have to do that."

"I want to." She licked the entire length of my cock. "I like to."

Her lips wrapped around me, and my head thumped against the wall. Half of me wanted to worship her for being so good with that smart mouth, and the other half cursed her as she sucked me deep and eliminated any chance of self-control winning.

Tell her to stop. That would be the right thing to do.

Instead, I grabbed the back of her head and sank deeper.

CHAPTER FOURTEEN

Art Lessons and Texts

SCARLETT

Early afternoon sunshine illuminated the white tiles and walls of the gallery. Floor-to-ceiling windows offered natural lighting for the front room, though a few spotlights aided in accenting artwork. A curved, sleek black counter with a glass top served as the front desk off to the right. To the left, I mounted my last painting. Although it seemed even, I climbed on the stepladder and placed my little level on the top. The bubbles inside the green liquid informed me it tipped to the left. I adjusted the frame, then climbed down and stepped back.

René, the curator, approached, her straight, dark hair tied in an elegant ponytail. "Looks good. I'm excited for Friday. You've created a wonderful centerpiece."

I beamed while I folded the stepladder. "Thanks."

"Month after next, I'm doing a charcoal drawing theme centered on the human body. Have anything to show me?"

Sweat formed on my palms. Practicing human anatomy had gotten lost in my recent obsession with creating full scenes. However, I'd been drawing Ryker a lot. Nothing spectacular. I couldn't capture that perfect body in a drawing, and despite what he said about that one charcoal he saw, it lacked.

"I'm not sure my stuff is up to your standards." I snapped a few photos of my painting on the wall for Dan. More acrylic paintings hung beside it—some my work and some not. The show would be for all kinds of paintings. I had more over in the oil and watercolor collections, but this was my big one. "I only recently picked up human anatomy again, and I have a lot to learn."

"I have a friend who teaches a phenomenal class, if you want to brush up those skills. Hera's a fantastic teacher. I've had people who couldn't draw stick figures come out with incredible talent."

A lightness spread in my chest at the thought of continued education. I missed my classes. Being around others pushed me to work harder. "Really?"

"Yeah. It's a six-week course. Mondays, Wednesdays, and Fridays from four to six. She has two openings left. Here, let me get her card for you." She dug into a drawer on the inside curve of the glass desk. "It's a little pricey, though."

I picked at my phone case, and the aroma of roses and vanilla wafted from the glass bowl of potpourri on the counter. "How much?"

"Eighteen hundred." My eyebrows shot up, and René offered a sympathetic smile. "I know it seems like a lot but trust me, she's amazing. You know that new artist taking off, Marvin Jarkus?"

"Yeah, he's skyrocketing."

She handed me a colorful business card. "After he took her class."

"Seriously?" I took the card and scanned the information. "Why haven't I heard of her?"

The bangles on René's wrists clinked together when she braced an elbow on the counter and rested her chin in her hand. "She's a great artist but not an *exceptional* artist. She is, however, an exceptional *teacher*. Marvin credits her all the time. She's a master at teaching and critiquing."

"Damn." I tapped the card against my palm. "Okay. I'll try to get the cash together. When does it start?"

"In a couple weeks. She'll give you up until a couple days before class starts to pay in full as long as you provide a small deposit up front to hold your spot."

I nodded. "Thanks, René."

"No problem." She clicked her French-manicured nails on the counter. "I need all the artists here by five on Friday. I'll see you then."

I waved at her over my shoulder as I strolled out the front door. "See you Friday."

So far, my art shows had been successful. Unfortunately, not successful to the point I had a spare eighteen hundred dollars. I did have almost a thousand saved. *Could I pick up the difference in the next two weeks?* Maybe if I got more commissions and shifts at the bar.

Retrieving my phone, I updated my social media, stating I'd give ten percent off commissions for the next week. That usually got me some business.

After a hot drive home courtesy of the awful summer weather, I sat at the bar near the register where the rumbling A/C offered respite from the heat.

Dan emerged from the kitchen and grinned when he spotted me. "How'd it go?"

"Good." I tied my hair up in a messy bun. "Do you need extra help this week? I heard there's a fight that a lot of people will be watching."

"Yeah, on Thursday. I've been advertising. You want to work?"

"Please. What about the weekend or any other days this week except Friday?"

His lips tugged down. "Do you need money, Scar?"

Oh, God. Here we go. I squared my shoulders and looked him dead in the eye. "No."

His chest puffed out more than it needed to. "It seems like it."

"I don't. What's wrong with wanting a little extra money?"

"There something you can't afford?"

"Oh my God." I braced my elbows on the counter and dropped my head in my hands. "Nothing I want you paying for. Do you need help or not? And don't cut any of Tammy's hours to do it."

"I wouldn't. If anything, I'd take more days off."

I arched a brow as he limped to a glass and a bottle of amber liquid. "As you should."

"I will for you." He slammed the glass in front of me and poured a shot of whiskey. "Not because I need to."

"Whatever." I rolled my eyes. "Which days?"

"I'll look at the schedule. *If* you tell me what you need money for."

"I don't *need* money. I want it for an art class. That's all."

"What art class? Who's going to teach you anything?" His brows pulled together. "You're already the best."

I sipped my whiskey and fought a smile. "Says the man who only has my art in his house and never looks at anyone else's."

"It's because I'm a distinguished man of taste and yours is the only art that measures up to my standards."

I laughed. "You're so full of shit, Dan."

"How much does the class cost?"

I inclined my head to the water pitcher behind him, and he obliged, pouring me a glass. "None of your business."

"How much, Scar?"

I gulped the icy water. "Eighty cents."

"Eighty dollars?"

"Sure. Eighty dollars."

He sighed and stroked his beard. "Come on, honey. Why can't I help you out sometimes?"

"You already do too much for me. You're letting me live here for ridiculously cheap, and you keep buying my art supplies when I tell you not to." He pouted. I covered his hand with mine. "Okay, tell you what. I'll let you help me if you let me take you to the doctor for your knees."

He scowled. "A doctor can't tell me what I need."

"Sure, I mean, they only have doctorates and machines that can tell you why you can barely walk, and medicine and therapy to help, as well as years of experience, but yeah, I get your point. What do they know? The silly bastards, trying to help people." I scoffed. "The *nerve*."

He pointed at me as he scooted toward an approaching customer. "Watch the sass."

"What are you going to do? Chase me around the bar? Which bad knee is going to hold up the best?"

He threw me a dirty look before greeting his customer. Swirling my drink, I considered what I could sell to get the money. Dan welcomed a few more customers, then returned with a determined glint in his stubborn hazel eyes.

"If you tell me, I won't pay the whole thing." He held his hands up in a false show of surrender. He would absolutely pay the whole thing. "Why don't you tell me how much you're short?"

"Not happening. I'm an adult, and I like taking care of myself. Like *you* taught me."

"I didn't think you were actually paying attention," he muttered. "You were always painting your nails."

"Painting my nails *and* listening?" I gasped. "I pursued art when I should've been performing acts. No one would believe I could multitask those two things." I leaned across the bar dramatically, my hand to my chest. "Could you imagine the ticket sales?"

His flat expression showed no amusement. "Definitely more than you'd get going into comedy."

"Oh, come on, you used to love the comedy nights I did!"

"They were cute when you were nine and had much less attitude."

I stifled a laugh and arched a brow.

He sighed. "All right, you always had an attitude. But it was less directed toward me." He gestured to himself as if he were mortally wounded. "You get pictures of your wall for me?"

"I did." I snatched my purse.

"Send them to your mama too."

"Yeah, yeah." I dug through every crevice and pocket of my purse but came up with nothing. "Crap, I think I left my phone in the truck." I handed him my bag, and he tucked it behind the bar. "I'll be right back."

Summer heat slouched my shoulders when I stepped out into the alley and hurried to my car. Unsurprisingly, my phone sat in the cup holder. Retrieving the device, I stuck it in my dress pocket with a stupid grin. This sundress was my favorite because it was cute but also had pockets. I sunk my hands in them because I could, and my phone vibrated. *Maybe someone already ordered a commission.*

A message notification from an unknown number stilled me. I didn't recognize it, but I did recognize the area code.

Unknown: *Did you get my letter? I want to talk.*

Screenshotting the text, I then sent it to the officer I'd been in contact with about Todd trying to get ahold of me. Once it sent, I blocked the number and dropped my phone in my pocket like it infected me. Like he did.

No. I refused to allow him to control me through fear. I took a few deep, shaky breaths until my heart stopped trying to escape. Everything would be fine. *He can't hurt me anymore.* One more meditative breath later, I entered the bar through the rear door.

Ryker exited the men's bathroom as I made my way down the hallway and we almost collided. I stumbled and he steadied me, his gaze doing a full body appreciation. *It's ridiculous how easily this man distracts me.* I clenched as his eyes darkened.

His fingers dug into my waist and his biceps flexed, making the ink etched on them come alive. "How you feeling, sugar?"

Oh, God, I missed his hands on me.

I flattened my hands on his chest and caught my lip between my teeth. "Good now that it's over."

He grunted, glanced around, then retreated into the bathroom and yanked me with him. The lock clicked into place seconds before he caught me in a kiss so hard it pinned me to the wall. I moaned into his mouth, and he groaned, bunching up my dress. His teeth dragged off my bottom lip as he moved to my neck, his tongue and teeth scraping my skin.

I lost my fingers in his hair, a heat I didn't mind so much coursing through my nerves. "*Ryker,*" I hissed when he yanked my dress to the side and bit my shoulder, all while his free hand groped my ass like he hadn't touched one in years.

Calloused fingers hooked in my underwear, and he knelt, peeling them off as he lowered. I stepped out of the underwear, and he threw my leg over his shoulder, then reduced me to a puddle when his face dove between my thighs.

His tongue traced all the paths he'd laid out before, ones that turned me into a heaping mess. My knuckles bleached, my fingers tangling in his hair tighter and tighter, as if that'd help me stay quiet under his delicious assault. I was close to the edge when a thrill skittered up my spine at the sound of his zipper. I muffled my moan with my hand. One last flick of his tongue pushed me over the edge. The waves of pleasure didn't subside before he picked me up and slammed his cock into me.

"*Oh,*" I whimpered, clutching his shoulder and wrapping my legs around his waist.

"Fuck." He buried his face in my neck while he fucked me, the light stubble on his jaw scratching my skin. "I missed your tight pussy."

It was very Ryker-like. Hard and fast, his thrusts so deep I struggled to keep my scream in, his dick creating a permanent imprint inside me. Each thrust granted friction that left me craving more, somehow never sated. His touch electrified me, igniting a spark I didn't think could burn after the Todd fiasco.

A second release danced on the edge, then toppled off in a beautiful show of pleasure that ricocheted through my nerves. Ryker thrust harder until he finished, challenging my ability to stay quiet so we didn't rouse suspicion. He stayed inside me for a moment, panting. A few seconds passed, and he crashed another hard kiss on my mouth, one that whispered we could go another round. *Or three.*

He eased out of me, then let me down. I slumped against the wall to catch my breath while he fixed his pants and held my panties open for me to step into. His hands caressed my legs as he glided the underwear up. Once they were in place, he dropped his forehead to mine and squeezed my ass so hard I gasped.

"Yeah, I'm gonna need to make up for lost time." A teasing kiss to my lips nearly coaxed a whimper out of me. "Make up an excuse to Dan. You're coming home with me. Right now."

I clenched, my insides buzzing at the prospect. "He's going to want to talk to me for a little bit."

Ryker dropped his mouth to my neck, his words low and rough. "Make it fast. I'll meet you outside." He caught my jaw, his grip almost as bruising as the kiss he planted on my lips. "Don't keep me waiting, or you're going to be begging me to let you come all night."

Oh God. Yep. I already wanted him again.

He peered out first and checked the hallway, then waved me out. On my way to the front, he smacked my ass. As much as I enjoyed it, I sent a glare over my shoulder. It didn't last long. The way he looked at me held so much promise, my pussy fluttered. *Thirsty bitch, didn't he just take care of you?*

I made it to my seat in time for Dan to return to the register. He leaned over the counter, looking at me expectantly. *Why is he looking at me like that?*

Silence ensued. He held out his hand. "The pictures?"

Shit. *Right.* The pictures.

I pulled up the photos on my phone and handed it over. He swiped through, praising me much more than I deserved. My leg bounced, a little sting on my ass a reminder I needed to get moving which meant all my answers to Dan's questions were short.

"You got somewhere to be?" he asked.

"I'm supposed to meet a friend." It wasn't *totally* a lie. Ryker was kind of my friend.

"Why didn't you say so?" A grin spread on his face. He'd been encouraging me to meet people. "I'm glad you're making friends. Who is it?"

There were exactly three times in my life I'd ever lied to Dan. All during my rebellious teenager phase, and they didn't last long because guilt made it unappealing. I couldn't lie.

"So nosy." I circled the bar and pecked his cheek. "Don't wait up."

He nodded, but a slight narrowing of his eyes made me scurry away faster. I almost made it around the corner when he cleared his throat in *that way*. The way that warned he wouldn't let me off the hook. "Is your friend a male friend?"

Amazing how the man could threaten with simply the tone of his voice.

"Maybe?" I squeaked. "Bye. Love you!"

I raced down the hall, but every step grew heavier. This wasn't good. It wasn't technically lying but it *was*. I was going behind his back and I wasn't okay with it. I told Dan stuff I couldn't tell my mom. He'd always been my confidant. He was a little weird about men, but I couldn't blame him. My track record wasn't a lot better than Mom's. I simply got out of my situations faster than she did.

I couldn't do this to him anymore. I'd have to tell Ryker. We either had to admit to Dan we were hooking up or stop.

That was all well and good. Easy in my head. Not so easy when I exited the bar, and summer didn't burn me as hot as he did. He waited on his motorcycle, eyes devouring and hands flexing like they did before he threw me around like a ragdoll. When he finished scrutinizing every inch of me, his darkened eyes met mine, and tingles coursed through my body.

Yeah, easy in my head. Impossible when he looked at me like *that*.

CHAPTER FIFTEEN

Irresistible

RYKER

I hit the punching bag once. Twice. Three times.

Seven weeks. Seven fucking weeks and I couldn't stop. Not only could I not stop fucking her, I couldn't stop *thinking* about her. I spent a great deal of the day with a throbbing cock that'd only answer to one person. The torment didn't subside for a second. Another girl would pass by and all I'd think about was how Scarlett's walk made her hips sway, a reminder of how well they moved with mine.

Sweat dripped down my face while I took my frustration out on the punching bag. *I should stop.* I'd gone longer than I should. No matter what I tried, I couldn't get her out of my head.

The muscles in my arms, shoulders, and back screamed until I relented. I braced my hands on my knees and panted. In the corner, the dogs watched me with knowing looks.

I waved my hand at them. "Let it go." I shouldn't have gone so hard but . . .

It was Friday. There was no escaping her.

Once I cleaned up, I rode to Danny's. While I waited at the stoplight right before the bar, I spotted Scarlett in booty shorts. She fussed around a big object with her tailgate open. I cursed her in my head but when the light changed, I parked in that very alley.

I dismounted my bike, removed my helmet, and approached. The big square thing turned out to be a stereo, and she already had it covered with a sheet in the truck bed. She secured a tie over the top.

I stroked my jaw. "Moving?"

"No." She caught her lip between her teeth, her gaze sensuous and dangerous as it crawled over me. "Selling it."

Fuck, I loved the way she always checked me out. "Why?" I leaned against her truck, arms crossed. "You love listening to music."

Her apartment always had music playing, and she'd asked me to put some on at my place a couple times. She didn't care what kind. She just wanted noise.

"Yeah." She lifted a shoulder. "But I need money, and I have my headphones, so I'll live."

"What do you need money for?" She shouldn't sell her shit. "I can lend you money."

"No." Her firm tone aggravated me. She'd accept my cock, but not my help. *Why does that bother me?* "No one's lending me money. I can take care of myself."

So much like Danny. I drummed my fingers against my bicep. What if some asshole took advantage of her? "You won't get a fair deal at a pawn shop."

"I'm not going to a pawn shop. I listed it online and someone wants to see it."

"Wait." A muscle in my jaw ticked. "Are you about to meet some stranger from the internet?"

"Oh, God." She braced her hands on her hips and preemptively rolled her eyes. "Here we go."

"Yeah, Scar, here we fucking go. Why would you do that by yourself? Wearing those fucking shorts?"

"Jesus Christ, Ryker." She slammed the tailgate shut. "It's not a big deal. I'm meeting him in a public plac—"

"*Him?*"

She retrieved her keys from her pocket, and they clanked together when she pointed at me. "Relax, psycho. I'm meeting him in public so there's people around, and he doesn't know where I live. I'm not an idiot."

"*We're* meeting him." I held out my hand. "Keys."

"What? No." She stepped back, and I wanted to spank her until that stubborn glint in her pretty eyes muted. "You're so overprotective."

I followed as she retreated. "Keys."

"Ugh." She stomped to the driver's side. "You can tag along, but you aren't driving my truck."

"I'm going to smack that ass raw."

She flipped me off and climbed into the truck. I sat in the passenger seat and was about to speak but she started the ignition and blasted the music, then smacked my hand when I reached for the volume knob.

"Goddammit, Scarlett," I growled.

"What?" She pointed to her ears. "Can't hear you."

The cheeky smile she gave before the vehicle lurched forward made me question whether I wanted to kiss or punish her. *Both.* Definitely both. She rolled down the window and let her hand hang out, bobbing her head to the music. *Why do my lips twitch up when she does that?*

Ten minutes later, we pulled into a grocery store parking lot. Scarlett parked, then retrieved her phone. She killed the engine, and the music turned off with it. Her curly hair stuck to her neck as she pushed it out of the way and lifted her phone to her ear.

"Hey, it's Scarlett. You here?" The mumble of his response made my fist tighten. Scarlett twisted in her seat to look out the rear window. "Oh, I see you. I'm in the faded green truck. I'll be right out."

She ended the call then turned to me with one of her iconic glares. She had this special kind of glare that you didn't only see but *felt.*

"Listen, overprotective freak." She poked my chest. "I'm a grown ass woman. You're here and that's more than adequate. Stay in this car or so help me, *I'm* not going to let *you* come."

I scowled but she didn't spare me another glance. She strode to the back of her truck where the stranger approached, his smirk a little too wide, his eyes drifting a little too much. I clenched my fist as he drew nearer. She opened the tailgate and untied the stereo. As she reached for the sheet, his gaze slid to her ass. If he didn't move that hand off the tailgate so close to her, *I* would remove it.

Fuck it.

I opened the door and the asshole's wandering eyes widened. He retreated at my approach, and I cracked my neck. He gulped. Scarlett straightened out, her gaze flicking between us.

She smiled at the guy over her shoulder, then grabbed my arm. "What are you doing?"

"Nothing, baby." I crushed her body to mine and planted my lips on hers. "I missed you."

I knew she'd react. She always reacted to me. She moaned softly and I slid my hands into her back pockets, squeezing her ass before pulling out of the kiss.

My gaze slid to the creep, who had the decency to pretend he couldn't look at my girl. "I thought you might need help."

He frowned and avoided our eyes. Scarlett recovered and sneered at me before she returned to the guy with a friendly smile she'd never send my way.

"Sorry. Ignore him." She tossed the blanket off the stereo. "It's in good condition."

The guy nodded, eyeing me while he took wary steps forward. Logically, I recognized that he drew closer to examine the stereo. *A good excuse to get close to her.* I snaked my arm around her waist and pulled her snug against me. My lip curled. He noticed, swallowed, and looked away.

Good.

Less than thrilled, Scarlett pinched my arm. *Hard.* It hurt but I didn't budge, much to her dismay, evident from the little huff she exuded. Being this pissed at me, she'd be *extra* fun in bed tonight.

The guy asked questions about the stereo, and I kept her firm against me, despite her subtle attempts to escape. I could only imagine the fury she'd unleash after this. The thought rushed blood to my groin and Scarlett stiffened when I hardened against her ass. The stranger inspected the stereo and the fucking tease rolled her ass against me. I held in my groan and dug my fingers into her hips.

The creep wanted to make sure the stereo worked, so we plugged it into an outlet outside the store. After a few minutes, he offered cash and retreated quickly, a nervous tremble in his hands as he eyed me. It wasn't until we were in Scarlett's truck that she swatted my arm.

"What the hell is your problem?" she hissed, smacking me with her purse. "He didn't do anything!"

"He stared at your ass and stood way too close."

"You mean like you do all the fucking time?"

"It's different when I do it."

"How is it different?"

I caught her wrist when she tried to land another blow. "Because you *want* me to stare at your ass. That's how it's fucking different."

"You're so anno—"

"Annoying? Yeah, so you tell me." I grunted and yanked her toward me by her wrist, pulling her within reach of my lips. "And you have no sense of self-preservation. It's pissing me off."

Scarlett jerked away and started the car, then pulled out of the parking lot and headed toward Danny's. "Kiss my ass."

I wedged my hand between her ass and the seat and pinched. She squealed.

"I will." I set my palm on her inner thigh, where her skin scalded mine. "I'll do more than kiss it."

"You're the worst." Even as the words left her mouth, she pulled her thighs together and licked her lips.

"We'll see if that's true when I slide my cock into your already wet pussy." I nudged her thighs apart and palmed her through her shorts.

"*Fuck.*" She gripped the steering wheel and gasped. "I'm driving, Ryker."

I applied more pressure. "Then drive."

She whimpered and rocked her hips against my hand. "If we get in an accident, it's your fault, and you're paying for it."

She had a point. *It's not my fault you're irresistible.*

Reluctantly, I returned to my spot high on her bare thigh. God, that skin. "The fuck you need money for anyway?"

"An art class."

"Do you have what you need now?"

"Almost." She chewed the inside of her cheek. "I have a couple other things I can sell."

"Jesus, Scarlett, let me loan you the money."

"No."

"Come on, baby. Why the fuck does it matter? It's a loan." I shrugged to mask how much this bothered me. I liked her leaning on me for orgasms. I shouldn't want her to rely on me for other shit, yet the urge to encourage her to wouldn't simmer down. "I'm not giving it to you."

"I don't need it."

"I have no doubt you'll find a way to get the money but why sell your shit when you have another option?"

She parked behind the bar and twisted toward me. "Ryker, drop it. This is me, okay? It's the way I am. I don't like depending on people. I don't like being rescued. I don't like owing anybody anything. I'd sell my bed before I'd borrow money from you."

"That's fucking insane." I petted circles against her thigh with my thumb. "Everybody needs help sometimes. You literally bitched about how Danny won't let you help him."

"That's different. He's in actual pain because of the shit he does by himself. He isn't capable of some of the things he needs done. I'm capable and handling it, so stop being such a prick." She got out of the car, the slam a testament to how done she was with this conversation.

Muttering under my breath, I got out and followed her toward the bar's rear door. "Don't meet another stranger without me."

"You don't have a say, Ryker. I'll do what I want, and you can suck it up."

"You're fucking asking for it." I snatched her arm and threw her against the brick wall, then caged her in with my arms. "You're not going without me. End of discussion."

She got right in my face. "You don't control me. End of discussion."

"I'm not controlling you, Scar. I'm protec—"

"I don't need protection," she snapped. "I'm good. I'm fine. I take care of myself."

I pinned her to the wall with my body and wrapped my fingers around her throat. "You take care of yourself?"

Despite glistening sweat on her skin sticking strands of her hair to her neck and face, goose bumps erupted on her arms. She fisted my shirt, her breathing shallow. Hooded eyes destroyed my decency.

"You don't always take care of yourself." I ground my cock against her. "I take care of you."

She bit her lip, her eyes fluttering. "I take better care of myself."

Now she was *really a*sking for it.

"You do, huh?" I eased back and slipped my hand between her thighs.

She gasped, and I touched her through her shorts until she ground against my hand with a low moan.

"You do this better?" I rubbed her harder, and her pupils expanded. "You can't do this." I planted my lips on her neck and sucked until she hissed. "You can't do this." I crashed my lips on hers.

She curled her fingers around my biceps and mewed into my mouth. I rubbed her faster, harder. She whimpered, falling out of the kiss, eyes squeezed shut. I knew her body well, and when she was close, I stopped.

She whined and shoved against my chest. "You're such a dick."

"What's that? You want my dick?" I placed her hand over my bulge. She flushed and traced my throbbing erection. "If you want it, you have to ask nicely."

Her hand tightened around my cock and all thoughts of telling her this thing between us had to end flew out of my mind.

CHAPTER SIXTEEN

Crisis

SCARLETT

Tuesdays became dinner night with Dan no matter what. He made sure we both had the day off and we alternated cooking. While he made the same grilled cheese every time it was his turn, I didn't mind. I liked his sandwiches, and the food wasn't the point.

The only thing that sucked was the stomach-knotting guilt from sneaking around with Ryker. Dan wasn't stupid. He knew something was up and, unfortunately, knew me well enough to know a guy was involved. The fact that I wouldn't tell him worried him. I hated that.

Creaking above alerted me that Dan was on his way downstairs. I braced myself as I finished the fajitas, trying to think of new and creative ways to dodge his questions for the night because I couldn't tell him yet. I had to talk to Ryker first.

I shut off the stove and gathered plates from the cupboard when Dan shouted. The floor creaked louder, and then there was a loud *thud*, followed by several others, then a *crash*. Dan cried out, and I sprinted to the foyer.

Panic seized my muscles, freezing me for a few seconds. Dan lay on the ground with a cut on his temple. Blood streamed from the wound, dripping onto the floor. The plates from my hand clattered to the wooden boards, shattering.

"Dan!"

Rushing to his side, I then turned him over. He groaned, his face contorting in pain. My hands hovered over him, afraid to touch in case I made it worse.

"What happened?" I scrambled for my phone.

He cringed, his eyes dazed. "My knee gave out."

His slurred tone knotted my stomach. He hadn't started drinking, yet his voice was slow and odd. I forced back tears and started dialing 911, but he huffed.

"No ambulance. They're too expensive."

"Are you serious?" I gaped. "You fell down the fucking stairs. You're bleeding!"

"We can go to the hospital but no ambulance." His stubborn tone contrasted with his vulnerable demeanor as his eyes slid shut again, his breath short and harsh.

My heart raced and I swallowed, eyeing the gash on his head. *How the hell does he expect me to get him in a car?* He probably broke something. Or some*things*. I didn't want to make it worse.

I dialed Ryker's number without thinking. He answered after the first ring and the words tumbled out of me faster than my tears spilled. "Dan fell down the stairs."

"What? In his house?"

"Yes." I scrubbed away the tears and set my hand on Dan's trembling shoulder. "He's hurt bad, and he hit his head, and he won't let me call an ambulance."

"Hang on, sugar. I'm at the bar. I'll be right there."

The call ended and the phone fell from my shaking hand.

Dan winced with every breath. "Who was that?"

"Ryker. He's coming over." I took in a long inhale to steady my voice. He needed me to be strong, not panicky. I traced the wound on his head. "I can't move you by myself. I'm afraid I'll hurt you."

Grunting, he gave a light nod. "Don't worry, honey."

God, he could have a concussion.

Ryker stormed through the door with two other guys. He knelt next to Dan, scanning the various injuries. "Hey, Danny, you awake?"

"I'm awake."

Awake, but his words slurred more.

"Stay awake for me, man. Where does it hurt?"

"Everywhere." Dan laughed, then hissed and clutched his ribs.

"Scar." Ryker's calm but firm tone snapped my attention to him. "Go upstairs and get two fitted sheets. Strongest ones he has."

Scrambling to my feet, I rushed upstairs to the linen closet. I returned with the least worn sheets. Ryker instructed me to arrange them on top of each other beside Dan. Once I had them down, Ryker and his friends cautiously moved Dan onto them. The four of us carried him outside, each grasping a corner. Thankfully, Dan hadn't put the seats back after I borrowed his van, allowing space to lay him down.

Ryker and I sat with him as Ryker's friend raced us down the street. During the drive, Ryker called the hospital and explained what happened, asking them to be ready for us. Dan lay quietly, one of his hands sandwiched between mine.

When we arrived, they wheeled Dan away on a bed and didn't let me follow. Ryker stayed with me in the waiting room. As much as I liked being strong and taking care of myself, I needed his arms around me and didn't fight him when he sat and pulled me into his lap. I tried not to cry but Dan was my *world*.

Ryker held me while we waited. Pale linoleum floors squeaked from the sneakers of people running by. A telephone perpetually rang with small absences, and the constant bustle of doctors in and out of doors made me jump every time, hoping one of them was Dan's doctor.

The sun set by the time they let me see him. *Just* me, since I was family. Well, not technically, but the closest thing he had, and thankfully he told them I was his niece.

The doctor pulled me aside and informed me Dan would be all right. I thanked him for telling me ahead of time because the relief at that news made me burst into tears. Dan didn't need to witness me crying. I got a hold of myself before I entered the room to find him sound asleep. A pile of beeping machines reassured me he was all right.

Although I could breathe because he'd be okay, the list of injuries wasn't anything to scoff at. A concussion. A broken arm, leg, and a couple ribs. It could've been worse, but he had to get his knees fixed whether he liked it or not. Otherwise, he wouldn't be able to walk. He wasn't in any position to use crutches, so they informed me they'd keep him for a couple days but would send him home with a wheelchair.

He's going to hate that.

I stayed well past visiting hours and nearly passed out on the chair by Dan's bed. The nurse gently encouraged me to go home and get some rest. She took my number, promised to call if anything changed, and said she'd tell Dan to call me when he woke.

Stiff limbs protested movement after staying tense in one place for so long. I stretched as I made my way to the waiting room, and only then realized Ryker didn't have a way home. Someone picked up his friends earlier and he stayed with me, but he didn't have his motorcycle, only Dan's van.

I sped up and found Ryker still waiting, seemingly much more awake than I was. He stood at my approach.

"I'm sorry." I rubbed my eyes, swollen from tears. "I didn't think about how you wouldn't have a ride."

"Don't be sorry. I could've had someone pick me up." He closed his arms around me, blanketing me in comfort I needed as badly as I needed Dan to be all right. "I'm here as long as you're here."

I melted into him. "Thank you."

Ryker stroked my hair. "How is he?"

"Fine. He's asleep. He's going to be in a wheelchair. I'm sure that's going to piss him off when he wakes up." I trudged toward the exit. "He's not going to like sleeping downstairs."

Ryker's hand enveloped mine on our way to the parking lot. "We'll figure it out." He squeezed my hand as we approached the van. "Give me the keys, Scar. You're barely awake."

Normally I'd fight him, but emotional and physical exhaustion stole my energy. I handed him the keys, but he guided me to the passenger side and helped me in before he hurried to the driver's side.

The cool glass from the window I rested my head against didn't wake me up. I barely registered the drive. At some point, Ryker's hand landed on my thigh. I appreciated his show of comfort but speaking required too much of me, so I said nothing, and Ryker being himself, remained silent.

We arrived at the bar, where Ryker parked the van in the alley next to my truck. I pivoted toward Dan's house, and Ryker followed. We stepped inside and a lump caught in my throat at the blood pooled at the bottom of the stairs.

"Hey." Ryker squeezed my shoulder. "Go to bed. I'll clean up."

"No. It's okay. I can handle it."

I got a rag from the kitchen, but before I could do anything with it, Ryker snatched it out of my hands and crouched beside the blood. There was still the mess from the dropped plates as well, so I found a paper bag and the broom. Glass scraped against the floor, scratching the already scuffed wooden planks. A lot of the pieces were big, so I crouched and carefully plucked them by hand, then dropped them in the bag.

Ryker covered me with his body from behind and closed his hands over mine. "Stop. Come on, Scarlett." He pulled me to my feet. "You need sleep."

"I have to clean it up."

He turned me to face him. "I'll clean it up."

I desperately wanted to *not* cry but tears fell anyway. Dropping my head to his chest, I let it out. He wrapped his arms around me and though it brought comfort, it made me cry harder. "I was so scared."

"I know, but you did well, and he's okay. He'll be home before you know it." His lips pressed to the top of my head. "Come on, sugar. Let me put you to bed."

"I want to stay in the house," I mumbled into his chest.

Strong hands gripped the back of my thighs and lifted me. "All right."

My legs locked around his waist, and he carried me upstairs into the spare bedroom. He laid me down, and I knew I should let him go but I didn't want to. I caught his hand, tears in my eyes, the plea of *stay with me* unable to escape my tight throat.

Regardless, he understood. We'd always communicated better physically than verbally.

Ryker lay beside me and pulled me to his chest. A heavy hand stroking my spine eased the panic, and the light forehead kisses made me cling to him, absorbing every ounce of comfort he gave. "He's okay, baby. You did good. You handled it well. It's going to be all right."

My racing heart slowed under his affection. I'd never been more comfortable, and I still wore shoes.

I must've been *very* comfortable because when I woke up, I couldn't remember falling asleep. Daylight filtered through the curtains, revealing I'd been asleep a while.

There was an empty space beside me where Ryker had been. He must've left. It shouldn't hurt. He didn't owe me anything and he helped a ton yesterday. But my heart ached at his absence. I reached into my pocket for my phone and found nothing. No messages. I couldn't wait for the nurse to call. I'd have to check in for my peace of mind.

My eyelids slid shut, my body exhausted and protesting my desire to call the nurse. A *thud* snapped my eyes open. A knocking, almost. I frowned and sat up. The rhythmic *thud* continued, like someone hammering.

I forced myself out of bed and toward the door where more noises persisted. Voices. I shuffled down the hall, then peered around the corner down the stairs.

Ryker stood at the bottom with several guys I recognized from the bar. Regulars who always arrived with Ryker. My brows furrowed as they snapped rails off the stairs. One of them spotted me and nudged Ryker, who jogged upstairs.

"Hey, sugar. Sorry if we woke you. We had to get started to finish before Danny gets released."

"What are you doing?"

"Installing a wheelchair lift so he can get up to his room and downstairs." He gestured at the new device they'd screwed into the wall. "We have to make the stairs bigger or it won't fit. Don't worry, we've all done this kind of thing before. We'll get it done right."

Tears stung my eyes. Dan would be so *relieved*. Ryker took my hand and led me down the hallway, out of view of the other guys.

"Hey, it's okay." He wrapped his arms around me and cradled my head into his chest. "He'll be home soon."

"It's not that." I blinked back tears but they caught in my lashes. "You're so sweet for doing this. I don't know what to say."

"Don't say anything." He kissed my head. "It's nothing. Danny's done plenty for us. We're returning the favor. Watching out for our own. But hey, it would probably be a good idea for you to not stay in that room or you'll end up trapped here while we're working. Why don't you go to your apartment?"

I shook my head and pulled back from the arms I wanted to bury myself in for a few hours. Or days. Or weeks. "I want to help."

He arched a brow. "Do you know what you're doing?"

"No." I batted my eyelashes, fully aware I looked like a train wreck, and it shouldn't work. "But you do."

He sighed but took my hand and led me to the stairs. "Fine. Come on."

We rejoined his friends, and they packed on the niceness, even more than when I served them at the bar. One handed me a breakfast burrito from a stack they'd picked up on their way over. Ryker started working again but not before glancing at me over his shoulder with a smile that left me breathless. Ryker didn't smile.

Air rushed from my lungs. That smile. His tenderness. All the things he'd done for me and Dan. The way he stepped up . . .

I was falling for him. Hard.

The realization left a pit in my stomach. Only a few days ago, he reemphasized our relationship was only about sex. He'd said that before and I didn't have a problem with it because I liked having sex with him. I didn't want a relationship anyway. We promised we'd tell each other if feelings developed and I was certain they wouldn't because he pissed me off most of the time.

But now?

I watched him, and it wasn't only because he was unbelievably sexy, his muscles flexing as he worked, his eyes a striking blue, and body exhibit worthy. It was that he was also funny and ridiculously sweet and loyal and dependable. I didn't want only sex anymore. People showed their true colors in a crisis, and he certainly had. He was everything I needed and more last night. And this? Installing that for Dan?

Shit.

I was in trouble.

CHAPTER SEVENTEEN

Too Close

RYKER

With the help of my guys and Scarlett, I installed the wheelchair lift before Danny got out of the hospital. Scarlett stepped up to any challenge and impressed me with how fast she learned. She did as much work as anyone else, if not more, because on top of helping with the construction, she made sandwiches, tea, and lemonade for lunch. Pizza for dinner. *Made* pizza. Didn't order. It pissed me off because it tasted delicious. I didn't need another reason to be attached.

The more time I spent with her without fucking, the more I realized my attachment had never only been physical. Yes, she caught my eye immediately because she was fucking stunning, but that's not what did it. The fiery attitude. Her ability to keep up with my banter. Her soft side that only showed around Dan.

I had it bad. After this, I'd distance myself because my growing affection sounded alarms. It drove me nuts how many times she caught me staring at her.

As if it couldn't get worse, she had my guys eating out of the palm of her hand. She snapped back at every remark with a better one, had them laughing their asses off so much it interfered with our progress, and on top of that, she had them coming to her with their problems. *Ridiculous.* Yet it heightened my attraction. She could handle my friends. *She* was becoming friends with them too.

Scarlett was the complete, whole, beautiful package and it was bad news. I couldn't be in a relationship. It was insane enough she spent the night half the week. I considered myself lucky I hadn't had a nightmare with her in bed with me, but I was kidding myself to think it wouldn't happen. What if my brain confused her for an enemy I was supposed to leave overseas? I couldn't be with anyone. Not after I served and became the version of myself I had to protect people against.

Scarlett would never look at me the same if she learned those secrets. What I'd done as a Marine. I couldn't be with her and hide all that shit. Anything more than sex would mean more time with her and a stronger likelihood that she'd discover that part of me and run.

Not to mention I wasn't boyfriend material and didn't want to be. Spending time with her outside of sex put me on edge. That had to be the reason I thought about what it would be like to be with her. I needed to get back to normal. Hook up with her and get rid of some of this fucking tension.

Unfortunately, that had to wait. The lift took priority, and she spent all her time either working on it or going to the hospital.

I helped her bring Danny home when they finally released him. Although his face was a mask of emotions when he saw what we did, he appreciated it. He'd had a shitty few days, so we left them alone not too long after he arrived and thankfully, Scarlett stayed in the house that night.

I told Dan to call me if he needed anything and stayed away from the bar. I tried a different one on the weekend and hated it. I liked being at Danny's. Some truly beautiful girls approached me, but they weren't Scarlett.

I just need to get things back to normal between us. No more cuddling or holding or any of that shit. Fucking only. And God help me, I wanted her again. It was the longest we'd gone without having sex and I craved her. I craved the way she looked while she came undone. I craved the way her nails dug into my back, the way her skin felt against mine, the way she uttered my name as I sank into her. I craved all of it so much I was losing my fucking mind.

I gave up on distancing myself after a few days and called her. Asked her to meet me outside. Her quick response had an unusual effect on the beat of my heart. I picked her up from the bar and took her to my place. Even my damn dogs had gotten attached. They loved it when I brought her home because she fawned all over them.

Add another thing to the list of reasons she was perfect for me. Problem was, I wasn't good for her. I never would be.

I pushed out all the confusing thoughts, all the frustration. I took it out on her in the bedroom with relentless fucking. She egged me on, told me she wanted more. Harder. *My perfect match.*

I had her under me, her cheek pressed into the bed as I fucked her from behind. I hoped it would help to not be face to face with her. One hand pinned her wrists to her back. The other wrapped around her throat.

"Ryker," she moaned. "That's s-so good."

I grunted and tightened my hand on her throat, my skin slapping hers in a satisfying sound I chased after. I knew her body. Her eager responsiveness told me when I did something she really liked. It's how I knew her orgasm wasn't far. It's also how I knew she liked it when I yanked on her hair.

"Come for me, Scarlett."

Her cry of release was an addictive melody bound to get stuck in my head. I pounded her through my own release and shuddered as I emptied inside her. I couldn't seem to get tired of the way it felt to come inside her, to know I filled her with a raw declaration of possessiveness. As soon as I finished, I let her arms go and released her hair. She moaned and sank into the bed. I lay over her, kissing her shoulder and neck, exploring the body I thirsted for no matter how often I enjoyed it.

"Not too much?" I asked. I always expected it to be.

We had an arrangement in place, of course. She had a safe word. We communicated hard nos. What hung me up could've been an unrelated issue. A part of me that worried I'd be too much in other ways, so why wouldn't I be here?

"No." Her eyes fluttered. "It was amazing."

I ran my hand down her side, and she shivered. I smirked against her skin and nipped her neck. "You tired yet?"

She angled her head toward me, that fierceness I'd grown attached to sparking in her big brown eyes. "Are you?"

"No, baby, I can fuck you all night," I murmured, sucking on her neck. "I'm only worried you'll be too sore for me to fuck you in the morning."

She rolled her ass against me. "I'm not sore."

Damn her.

I flipped her over, and she was *perfect*. My gaze glided away from her hypnotic eyes and down to her breasts. I dipped my head and sucked a nipple into my mouth. She whimpered and arched her back, threading her fingers into my hair.

I palmed her other breast and rubbed my thumb over her hardened peak. She moaned softly and I moved my lips over her stomach, past her belly button, between her legs where the taste of our come mingled together drove me wild. I could spend hours tasting her and I'd never tire of it. I dragged my tongue along her clit, and she gasped and bucked her hips. That was the other reason I loved eating her out. Nothing was as satisfying as coaxing her to desperation.

Teasing her, I brought her to the edge and stopped. She whined but didn't protest when I did it several more times. By then, my cock had hardened. I sat up on my knees and draped her leg over my shoulder as I slid into her.

I groaned, loving her warmth, her wetness, the way she closed around me like I belonged there. I pumped in and out slowly before I returned to the gruff, short, rough thrusts. She clawed at the sheets, face twisted in pleasure. *Fuck, I love this view.*

I needed more. I needed to be deeper, so she'd feel me after we finished. I lifted her other leg and started bringing it up over my other shoulder. Her eyes snapped open. It was a new position for us, but I'd learned its intensity from experience.

I caressed her calf. "Trust me."

She screamed. Not from pleasure. From terror.

CHAPTER EIGHTEEN

Healing

SCARLETT

One leg over the shoulder was a good position for me, one I always enjoyed. Then Ryker lifted my other leg and panic seized my chest. I tried to breathe through it. He wasn't Todd. This was Ryker. I trusted him. He'd never hurt me like that. Still, I opened my eyes to remind myself it was Ryker. Then he spoke.

"Trust me."

Trust me.

Somehow, I wasn't with Ryker anymore. Todd loomed over me. I didn't remember taking my clothes off, but they were gone, Todd's sheets cool under my naked body. The room spun, my drunk mind unable to slow it or make sense of how I'd gotten here. I slurred a *no*, rolled off the bed, tried to open the door, but the lock slowed me down and he hefted me to the mattress.

I must've wanted to be here. The anxiety clutching my chest wouldn't let me convince myself it was true, though. "Trust me." Todd draped my legs over his shoulders, and I told myself I wanted it. I told myself I must've encouraged him, but the alcohol made me forget. Then he adjusted to shove into a different hole, and I squirmed, pleading with him not to because I wasn't ready. Alcohol made my limbs too heavy to fight him and—

Blood. Blood and pain. Even with my pleas to *stop*.

"Scarlett!"

That dark night with menacing shadows and a laughing Todd transformed. Ryker's powerful voice guided me to the present. To his neat room—the opposite of Todd's.

I gasped, scrambling to cover myself but I'd already been covered. Ryker stood beside the bed, hands up in a show of surrender.

My heart hammered against my chest and even though I wasn't in that night anymore, panic rose, some deep part of me splintering into shards and spreading the pain. Though I tried to shove it down, I couldn't stop the tears. Couldn't catch my breath. The strain on my heart tore and ripped me apart inside.

I had my knees to my chest, my arms wrapped around myself. When did this blanket cover me? When did Ryker put boxers on? What the hell had I been doing when that happened?

"Scarlett, baby," Ryker said softly. "You're okay. You're safe."

Tears poured down my cheeks. Shaking my head, I hid my face with my hands. I didn't want him to see me break.

"I'm sorry," I cried. "I'm sorry. I don't know what happened."

I dropped my head, unable to look at him while a sob tore through my chest. What the hell was my problem? It was *Ryker*. Ryker had never done anything to me I didn't want. Yet here I was. Unable to stop the tears, the shaking, the images from that night.

God, would it *ever* stop haunting me?

Ryker brushed a gentle hand over my shoulder. "Scarlett, can I hold you?"

"You don't have to be nice to me. I freaked out." I laugh-cried. "I'm sorry."

"Stop apologizing. Let me hold you." He sat on the bed beside me. "Come here."

Safe, open arms awaited me. Ryker beckoned me forward. I hesitated, but the pressure and comfort of an embrace would help stop my shaking. I tightened the blanket around me, then lunged into his arms. He caught me and pulled me into his lap, hands outside the blanket.

Okay tears, please stop. "I'm sorry."

"Stop." He kissed the top of my head and caressed my spine. "You have nothing to apologize for."

The waterworks upgraded their show but not because of the flashback. Because of Ryker. Because he was patient and gentle. I'd never been with anyone so understanding. At first, I thought I couldn't stand to be touched but the thing about Ryker was he knew exactly how to embrace me. He held me tight enough to keep me together but loose enough I could pull away if I needed to.

He stayed quiet while I got a hold of myself. His embrace remained constant, his heartbeat a steady rhythm mine strived to meet. It could've been hours that I let him hold me. Not once did he let go or tell me to calm down. He held space for me while I let it out in a way I hadn't allowed myself before. A real, thorough, ugly crying session I'd probably needed for a long time but hadn't been able to express.

The crying slowly subsided and my eyelids drooped, exhausted and heavy. Ryker smoothed a hand over my hair. "What happened, sugar? Was it the position? Was it something I said?"

I shook my head, and he sighed. "You gotta tell me, baby. I don't want to trigger you. I need to know so I don't do it again. You can tell me." His voice softened to a tender tone. "I'm not going to make you feel bad about it."

I hated he was right. If I kept having sex with him, I couldn't keep doing this.

I swallowed and my eyes went downcast. "I think it was . . . both the position and you saying 'trust me.' The two together, I guess," I muttered.

"I won't do it again." His arms tightened around me. "You're safe with me. You know that, don't you? I won't hurt you. Any other triggers you know of, tell me so this doesn't happen again, okay?"

"I don't know what they are." I peered up at him, shame warming my face. "I don't know what they are until they happen."

"All right. Don't worry about it." He brushed a light kiss over my forehead. "You want your clothes? I'll leave the room so you can put them on."

"Can I have your shirt?"

"Sure, baby." He maneuvered me onto the bed and secured the blanket around me before he stood.

Ryker tossed me the shirt he'd been wearing earlier, then closed me in the room alone. Not wanting to be by myself, I dressed in his shirt and my leggings then rushed out. The dogs greeted me with licks as soon as I exited, eyes full of concern.

They pawed at me until I crouched to give them love and the licks increased as they sandwiched me between them. My chest swelled and I hugged them. Clanking glasses led me to the kitchen where Ryker set out two crystal cups.

Whiskey glugged into the glasses, and I perched on one of the stools. Securing the cork on the bottle, Ryker pushed one of the glasses toward me. I didn't take it. Mainly because he leaned forward on his forearms, gaze unrelenting. I squirmed in my seat, not enjoying the observed-under-a-microscope stare.

He sipped his whiskey. "Take the drink, Scar. You're going to need it."

My stomach knotted and I closed my hands around the cool glass.

Ryker tipped his head back, emptying half his glass in one go. "You're probably going to get pissed at me for this," he lowered the glass to the counter, "but I'm done dancing around the topic. So, get pissed, but listen. You never talked to anyone about what happened, did you?"

I averted my eyes and took a sip. The alcohol didn't burn my throat as badly as my mortification.

"Didn't think so." He crossed his arms. "Am I the only one who knows? Your mom doesn't know? No friends?"

I shook my head. "I don't want to talk about it."

"Too bad, sugar. We're talking about it. Because that," he gestured to the bedroom, "can't keep happening. I can handle anxiety attacks so don't twist this shit and convince yourself I'm saying something for my benefit. I'm not. I'm telling you, if you don't talk to somebody, this will consume you. Pretending it didn't happen doesn't work. It'll fester and get worse."

I curled my arms around myself. "I'm handling it."

"No, you're not. You're pretending it didn't happen. You're having nightmares. You're having this." He flung his hand toward the bedroom, but his tone softened. "You don't have to live like that. There are people who can help you cope and heal. You're not healing because you're refusing to see it as a problem and that's going to make it hurt more. You gotta face it, Scar. No matter how scary it is."

"I don't want to see a therapist." I hated the tears blurring my vision. "I don't want to talk to anyone. I want to handle it myself."

"I know." He dragged his hand over his face. "You take care of yourself. I'm aware. But sometimes you need help. PTSD isn't a joke. It fucks with you. It'll affect other parts of your life. It's going to be harder to hide the longer you let it go untreated. Listen, I know personally that pretending it's fine makes it worse."

"I don't have PTS—"

"Don't give me that shit." He stretched his hand toward me. "I know what it looks like. The sooner you admit it to yourself and to someone who can help you, the better."

I eyed his waiting hand. If I was honest, I knew I might have to do this at some point, but I didn't want to. I couldn't. Ryker rounded the counter and turned the stool until my body faced his. He cupped my jaw and made me look up at him.

"I know it's scary," he said softly, brows knitting in concern. "It's not easy. I don't think it is. It takes a lot of strength and bravery to face something like that and open up to someone about it. But you have to, Scarlett. You *have* to. You're strong, baby. Don't let fear stop you."

"I wouldn't know where to look," I whispered.

"I can help." He caught my tears with his thumbs. "If you want to find a therapist, I'll tell you the best ones closest to us. If you're worried about money or you want someone specifically tailored to your needs, there's a crisis center not ten minutes from the bar. I'll take you if you don't want to go alone."

I nodded and tried to turn away, but he held me in place and brought his forehead down to mine. "Look at me."

I did. I looked into those sapphire eyes and wondered if anything had ever been so beautiful.

"I won't push it. You gotta go when you're ready to go. I know that. So I won't push, but it needed to be said, okay? You're not alone." He hugged me, his arms a respite from the pain. "You tell me when you're ready. Because you haven't lost all control in your life, Scar. No one has that power over you. Especially not him. You call the shots for you. No one else."

I nodded and he circled the counter to pour himself another drink. Grayson laid his head in my lap, whining softly. I pet his head, and Demon turned the corner toward Ryker. Ryker's lips turned up and he gave Demon an affectionate pat.

His dogs were like him. Intimidating to look at but so attuned to people. If anyone else told me what Ryker just did, I wouldn't have taken it well. But he knew what to say. He knew what to do. He knew I needed to be covered. He seemed to always know what I needed. Then he looked up at me with a reassuring smile and it hit me harder than it did before.

I was so in love with him, it hurt.

CHAPTER NINETEEN

Feelings

RYKER

I expected Scarlett to be mad at me for encouraging her to get help, but she was more resigned than anything. That was good. It meant part of her already recognized that we'd reached this point. Not wanting to push her after an episode, I didn't initiate seeing her for a few days. Letting her come to me was best.

She didn't initiate for over a week, then one night she stopped me on my way out of the bathroom and said she wanted me to take her against the wall. I wasn't going to say no to that. So I did and of course, it was amazing. It always was with her. It felt great at the time but later in the night, I wondered if it was the right thing. Her eyes were off, their usual spark muted.

I decided to tell her we should hold off until she figured things out. She seemed vulnerable and I wouldn't be some jackass taking advantage of her. So, I rode to the bar early and found her outside, loading canvases and bags splattered in paint into her car. It was better to be in public, where saying no to her was easier. I parked my motorcycle next to her truck. She'd already turned to face me by the time I removed my helmet.

"Where's that crisis center?" she asked, wringing her hands together.

Oh shit. All right.

I gestured to the street behind her and dragged my hand to the right. "Down that way. Take a left on Washington. It's on the right side. Purple sign."

She gnawed her lip. "Okay."

"Want me to come?"

"No." She straightened her spine and took a deep breath. "I need to do this for myself."

I've never been prouder in my life. That shit wasn't easy. It took guts to face something you'd rather pretend was a nightmare. "All right."

"Did you want to talk to me about something? That's usually why you park back here."

"It can wait. Why don't we talk when you get back?"

"Okay." She waved at me as she got in her truck. "See you later."

I waved and she drove in the direction of the crisis center. *Good for you, sugar.*

The thing was, I should leave her alone while she worked on this. She didn't need to get distracted, and my attachment couldn't continue. This was the perfect time to end our arrangement. It was the last thing I wanted but it wasn't about me. Not only did she deserve better, she *needed* better.

I moved my motorcycle to the main parking lot and shuffled inside the bar. Danny hired another person since he was still on the mend, so Tammy was training some new guy I'd only seen a couple times. She told him to let me in anytime, regardless of whether or not Dan's was open.

Once she poured me a drink, Tammy continued her training while I tried to work out what the hell to do. Several whiskeys later, the liquid courage sank in, and I resolved to talk to Scarlett tonight. When she returned.

Time ticked on. People filled the bar. Some ordered food and left. She didn't show and my guys kept sending me disapproving frowns. Some of them were aware I was about to break things off and weren't happy. They thought she was good for me. She was, but that wasn't the problem. I wasn't good for her. Being with her would be selfish.

I went to the bathroom and stared into the mirror reflecting the wall where I'd had her six times. *Not helping.* I splashed my face with cold water and returned to my seat. I almost started to worry when another hour passed, and she didn't show.

Nick noticed my fidgeting and took a seat beside me. "What's up?" he asked, lifting his glass to signal another refill.

My leg bounced. "Wondering where the fuck she is."

"She's here." Nick inclined his head to the stairs. "She arrived like an hour ago while you were in the bathroom."

I scowled and rose from the stool. "Why didn't you say anything?"

"Because no one wants you to break things off."

"Not your decision."

Nick said something else I didn't catch and had no patience for. I had to focus on telling Scarlett this had to stop. That nagging inside me whispering *maybe we could be more* needed to die. I *couldn't* be more.

I made it to the top of the steps and didn't bother knocking. She almost always had her headphones in, anyway. Opening the door, tomato, parmesan, oregano, and other heavenly aromas wafted into my nose. Scarlett stood at the stove, stirring a wooden spoon in a pot.

"Hey, I'm making food." She held up the spoon with sauce on it. "You want some?"

"Nah," I said, although yes, yes I did. It smelled incredible.

"Come on." She pouted and held a hand under the spoon, then carefully carried it over to me, blowing on the sauce. "Try it."

"Fine." I gripped her spoon and hand and tried to ignore the electricity sparking between us while I sipped the sauce. "Fuck, that's good."

"Right?" She returned to the pot and resumed stirring. "Sure you don't want some?"

"Fine. That's easily the best sauce I've ever had. Where'd you learn to cook like that?"

"Dan and my mom. For this specifically, my mom." She stood on her toes and reached into a cupboard for two ceramic bowls. "She worked at this Italian restaurant for a while. A legit one. Owned by Italians who'd immigrated. They taught her all their recipes and secrets, and she taught me." She shoveled food into the bowls. "So, this is almost-authentic Italian cuisine."

She really is the whole package. For the first time in a long time, I wished I were different. Years ago, I wanted to be different but lost my resolve after serving overseas. I lost hope for anything good. I lost the belief I deserved anything good. I definitely didn't deserve someone as amazing as Scarlett.

She retrieved forks and brought the pasta to the kitchen table. We sat, and I grudgingly ate the best pasta I'd ever had. Damn her.

"So." I cleared my throat. "How'd it go?"

"It wasn't that bad." Her tone implied it surprised her as much as it did me. "I thought it'd be terrible, but it wasn't. We didn't get too deep into anything yet. I don't know. Is it fucked up to say it's nice to not feel so alone? I don't wish it on anyone, but I wasn't the only one there. It made me feel less crazy."

"You're not crazy. Don't ever think that."

"It's a little easier not to feel that way now." She stared into her bowl for several seconds, then shifted her gaze to me. "Thanks for encouraging me to go."

"It was nothing."

"It wasn't nothing to me."

She was off tonight. I narrowed my eyes at her, wondering what the hell was on her mind. She clearly wanted to speak, and she'd never held back before. Her eyes darted away, her mouth opening and closing several times.

"Spit it out, Scar." I swirled noodles around my fork and raised it for a bite. "Promise I've heard worse, whatever it is."

"I have feelings for you."

I stopped with the food halfway in my mouth. My appetite vanished and I lowered the fork.

"I'm sorry." She wrung her hands together. "I know we said we'd say something if feelings got involved and I thought I could ignore them but . . ." She caught her lip between her teeth and avoided my eyes. "I can't. You've been so amazing to me and Dan. Ryker, I have feelings for you. Strong feelings. I want to be with you. All of you. All the way."

My fork landed in the bowl with a clatter. *Feelings.* She couldn't have feelings for me. What the hell did I have to offer her?

I slumped in my chair and pondered what the fuck happened. I was used to girls being attracted to me, but I wasn't boyfriend material. Not in the slightest. I couldn't comprehend how she could have feelings for me. *Feelings.* Physical attraction was one thing, but this?

"Please say something." Her quiet voice pulled at my heart. "I know I dropped it on you but please say something. You're killing me here."

Say something. What the hell could I say? She was perfect in every way, but I was too fucked up. She'd grow to resent me the same way I resented myself and I wanted her to only feel good things when she thought of us.

"Scarlett." I clasped my hands together to keep them steady. "I'm not that guy."

"I think you could be that guy. I think you'd be great at being that guy."

"I wouldn't. That's not me, Scar. I don't do relationships. I don't do feelings. This. What we've been doing." I gestured between us. "That's all I got. There's nothing else in here."

"But you show up. You always show up. It wouldn't be that different."

"I'm not boyfriend material, all right?" *I would never make you happy, and it'd kill me to watch you slowly start to hate me as much as I deserve.* "I like having sex with you, but I can't do the relationship thing."

"Have you ever tried?"

"Not since high school."

"Then you don't know. Maybe you could." She lifted a shoulder. "I'm not that needy, Ryker. I'm not one of those people who wants constant attention or nice things. I want you the way you are. I want exactly what we currently have, only with a firmer commitment. Literally nothing has to change except I get to call you my boyfriend and you—" Pink tinted her cheeks. "You call me your girlfriend."

I'm no good for you. I couldn't fuck up her life like that. Having sex was one thing. Matters of the heart? That was a story that wouldn't end well. She'd outshine me and hate herself for wasting time on me.

"I can't do it, Scarlett."

"So you don't have feelings for me at all? It's all sex all the time?"

Of course it's not. My attachment to her, my *pull* to her, the electricity that crackled between us was undeniable. It had been from the moment I laid eyes on her. At first, I wanted her for shallow reasons, but now? It wasn't about fucking anymore. Telling her would only make it more complicated. So, for the first time since I met her, I lied to her.

"No. I don't have feelings for you. I like messing around with you." The words tasted bad leaving my mouth—a bitter residue left on my tongue because I never wanted her to believe anyone could experience her without wanting more. I should've been more careful. Necessary or not, my wording was insensitive. I braced for the anger I deserved.

"Okay."

I blinked. She said no more. I expected a much bigger fight. "You're not mad?"

"No." She met my gaze, and my heart flipped. "That wouldn't be fair. You can't force feelings that aren't there and you've been clear with me what this was from the beginning. I'm not mad, Ryker, but I can't do this anymore."

"What do you mean?" It shouldn't matter. I was about to tell her we had to slow down. Why did I feel the persistent need to fight her on this?

"I can't sleep with you anymore. It makes the feelings stronger, and I can't handle that." She folded her hands in her lap. "But I want to be friends. Because you mean the world to Dan and I'd hate myself if I were the reason you stopped coming here. So please don't stop. I can be normal. I promise."

I can't. "It probably seems you can't handle it because you have so much going on." Scarlett was slipping away from me, and it was worse than I thought it'd be. She was sand spilling between my fingers while I desperately tried to catch every grain my dumb ass had come up here to let go of anyway. Now actually faced with it? My heart thundered, the roaring of blood in my ears too loud to think straight. "Let's give it time and what you think of as feelings for me will go away. Seriously, Scarlett, we piss each other off more than anything. You're leaning on me because I'm safe."

Weak attempt. We did piss each other off but I enjoyed it. *She* enjoyed it. Fighting exhilarated us.

"That's not what it is." She shook her head. "I know when I have feelings for someone. I have a level head. I don't go back and forth. I know how I feel. The circumstances don't matter."

"But—"

She held her hand up. "I can't. I'm sorry. You won't stop coming to the bar, will you?"

Her resolve stunned me. I couldn't agree, but I couldn't argue. The sand was almost gone, and she stared at me, waiting for an answer while my stomach turned to lead.

My chest crumpled in on itself. "I wouldn't stop hanging out with Danny because of you."

"Good." Her shoulders lowered. "Then we can be normal."

"Normal." Normal sounded fucking terrible.

The world's best pasta rested unfinished in our bowls. She picked at it with her fork but didn't take another bite. I'd never turned down good food but the longer I sat there, the more I couldn't breathe. I pushed the bowl away and stood.

Her response was like everything had been between us from the beginning—a strange sense of having known each other longer than we had. She always knew what I was doing. Always somehow in my head. So when I stood, she did too and approached the door, aware of my intentions.

She opened it and waved me ahead but none of it seemed real. It was more like we were actors playing parts. I paused in the doorframe. The ache in my chest built to an unbearable pressure. I needed it to release, and she was the only way it could. Turning around, I cupped her face and kissed her.

Her lips molded to mine, their shape perfectly made to fit against my mouth. She moaned and that unforgettable sound echoed in the chambers of my mind where I hoped it continued bouncing for eternity. I *needed* her.

"One more time," I murmured against her lips. "Let me have you one more time, Scarlett. *Please.*"

The sadness in her dark eyes knocked into me so hard, I almost stumbled from the impact. She gazed up at me for a moment, biting her lip. I knew that look. She felt it too. The crackling between us. I was certain she'd say yes but then she backed away, shaking her head.

"I can't." She gripped the door. "I'll see you around."

The last grain slipped between my fingers and my knees threatened to give out. She gave me a small smile that didn't have a hint of genuineness, then shut the door. I remained outside it, the touch of her soft lips lingering on mine.

My throat thickened and I stuffed my hands in my pockets, every step away from her an agonizing pierce through the chest. "See you around."

CHAPTER TWENTY

Mom

SCARLETT

When I was fifteen, I thought I was in love. We had nothing in common, but he was the first boy I had sex with and a weird part of me thought that meant I should stay with him, even though I was miserable. My mom pointed out that staying with him for that was insane and I distinctly remembered telling her, "You don't understand. I'm in love!"

Except I wasn't. He broke up with me and I laughed. He was confused. I was happy he did it so I wouldn't have to. Definitely not love.

With Ryker? It'd only been a couple months, and we weren't together. But my heart split when he said he didn't have feelings for me. When he left, I shattered. It couldn't be anything but love. Ryker crashed into my life like a lightning storm, each strike vibrant and powerful but gone too quickly.

I told him I could be normal. I could, but I needed time.

Regardless of it not being a real breakup, I treated it like one. A week went by, and I avoided the bar so I wouldn't see him. I stayed in bed crying. I listened to depressing music to cry more. However, it wasn't all awful. A pile of commissions came in and I finally got the money I needed for that class. I had things to look forward to. Things to focus on.

By the end of the week, my tear ducts almost dried out and I poured my energy into a deep clean of my apartment. Mom took off work to care for Dan and would be here any minute. Dan acted annoyed about us fussing over him, but he was excited to see Mom. As was I. I could use a mom hug and the therapy I'd started made me realize I needed her for that too.

I planned to tell her what happened with Todd.

While I organized my pencils, charcoals, and brushes on my art desk, the familiar faded red of an old Honda caught my eye out the window. A squeal erupted out of me, and I sprinted to the kitchen sink to scrub the charcoal off my fingers. Within seconds, I flung open my door and raced downstairs.

I lifted my foot off the last step and the bar doors swung open. Dark, curly hair piled on her head and a worn Van Halen shirt took me back to my younger days and the familiar comfort she always provided. A wide smile spread across her face, the kind that whispered *home* without words.

She opened her arms. I ran.

"Mom!"

I didn't care about the scene we created. I fucking *missed* my mom. Dropping her purse, she wrapped her arms around me in that way only a mom could. Snug, warm, and powerful enough to melt the tension in my shoulders.

She kissed the side of my head and swayed us. "I missed you so much, sweetie."

I might've been suffocating, but I refused to let go. "I missed you too."

"Let me look at you."

She tried to ease back but I pulled her in tighter. "Not done."

She laughed and returned the enthusiasm, nearly squeezing the oxygen out of me. She kissed the side of my head again and I slumped against her and inhaled her familiar perfume. When I believed I wouldn't burst into tears, I loosened my arms.

She held me at arm's length and arched a brow. "Is this how you've been dressing?"

I tugged at my paint-stained shorts and tank top and smiled sheepishly. "I was cleaning."

"I shouldn't be surprised." She clicked her tongue and winked as she picked up her purse. "You never clean unless I'm going to be around."

"I clean."

A weak defense we both knew to be untrue. I hated cleaning. I became friends with the dust in my apartment. We respected each other's space.

"God, you got more beautiful."

I almost giggled because Dan had said the same thing to me. They were so alike. She yanked me into a one-armed hug and planted her lips on my temple. "I came to see you first. Wanna help me get my bags to Dan's?"

"Yeah. I'll show you where to park."

Once we moved her car to the alley, we gathered her bags and entered Dan's house. Dan couldn't hide his excitement when Mom ran to him. One gentle hug was all she offered before switching into nurse mode, asking about his meds, schedule, physical therapy, and what kind of routine he was supposed to practice. While Dan complained the whole time, a glint shone in his eye.

They bickered and I sat on the couch, stifling laughter. Mom would say something, and he'd roll his eyes but smile when she wasn't looking. I forgot how much I loved the three of us being together.

The rest of the day was spent catching up until Dan needed to go to bed. Earlier than Mom and me, thankfully. It'd only been two months, but it felt like forever since I'd seen her. A couple times I thought I might bring up what happened and therapy, but the night was full of laughter and reminiscing. I couldn't do it. I wanted a happy night before I broke her heart.

And happy it was. Especially because I spent it in the guest room with her.

When I was younger, she was often gone all night for work. The nights she had off, we slept in the same bed. It was a way to feel close to each other. The long hours weren't her fault. She raised me by herself while trying to get out of the debt she fell into escaping my dad. She may have worked a lot but the time she gave me, she gave me all of it. I didn't know how she did it for so long. Never had time for herself but made sure our time together was the best.

A quick breakfast was all I could offer Mom and Dan before I rushed out the next morning. I had some commissions to finish before my first class.

I hadn't taken an art class in a long time, and I was so bad with people, my stomach fluttered nervously while I gathered my supplies. Bag packed and social anxiety high, I drove to the studio and actively forced Ryker out of my mind anytime a motorcycle passed on the road.

Focus on your future.

Entering the studio, I paused. The small class elevated my already high heart rate. Thankfully, René was right about the woman teaching. Hera. She flitted over to me, brown hair streaked with pinks and purples and fingers black with charcoal. She spoke animatedly as she led me to an empty seat, then addressed the rest of the class.

"We'll have a nude model tomorrow," she said.

My eyes bugged. I'd learned to draw off models online, so I wasn't unfamiliar with the human body, but it was a different experience to have that model in the same room. A lot of artists learned this way and I wanted to improve so . . .

Here we go, I guess.

Regardless of my awkwardness, the girl beside me started a conversation before class. Hannah. She was sweet, outgoing, and exactly what I stereotypically pictured when thinking of an artist. Funky glasses, hair in a messy bun, a very colorful jacket, and paint-stained jeans. I liked her immediately.

Class ended, and Hannah and I exchanged numbers, much to my relief. I worried my awkwardness ruined any potential friendships. Apparently not. *Is this how people make friends?* I didn't know. I had one friend back home. *One.* I'd never been great at any kind of relationship.

I returned to Dan's to find him and Mom already eating and a plate waiting for me. They asked about my classes and when I told them about Hannah, their jaws dropped before over-the-top excited questions started. *Yeah.* That's how much I never made friends. I was almost twenty-three, and they were excited about a possible friend.

Mom and I spent the night together again, but I couldn't work up the nerve to tell her about Todd. Partially because I was already nervous for my first shift back at the bar.

No more avoiding Ryker.

Minutes before my shift, I fiddled with the end of my lacy shorts and adjusted my blouse, telling myself to stop wondering if I looked good. Fidgeting with my ponytail, I twisted it into a bun instead. All the memories of Ryker fisting that ponytail while fucking me didn't need to cycle through my mind tonight. Despite my sadness, that memory sparked right between my legs.

This is gonna be a long night.

I prepped the bar to open, and Tammy introduced me to the new guy, Peter. He was nice, but got distracted every time a hot biker strolled in. Considering that comprised most of our customers, he spent half the time fanning himself and talking about which regulars were the hottest. Luckily, when Ryker's name came up, Tammy shut it down. So, she knew our fling ended. Ryker must've said something because I didn't.

Throwing myself into work helped occupy my mind. Mom stopped in and sat at the bar during Dan's nap. The distraction she provided was welcome and I chatted with her between customers, never giving myself a moment to worry about anything else.

It worked until *he* walked in. Ryker ran his fingers through his hair, shaking it out as he always did after removing his helmet. I forced myself not to gawk and told my vagina to cool it the fuck off because it wasn't happening.

I faced the shelves of liquor to avoid watching his approach. Not that it mattered. I was so in tune with him, I *felt* his eyes on me. I sensed him taking his usual seat. Drawing a deep breath, I snatched a glass and the scotch he liked, then turned to face him.

I swallowed hard when our eyes met. Apparently, his rejection didn't matter. Those eyes, those lips, that body . . .

Dammit. Focus, Scarlett.

I set the glass down and poured the scotch. Stepping back once I finished filling it helped nothing. We were magnetized, and I couldn't resist the pull.

Striking blue eyes remained unrelentingly on me. "Thanks, Scarlett."

Please don't say my name like that.

Whipping around, I returned the bottle to the shelf. "You're welcome."

"Did you forget about me?" Mom asked, holding up her glass.

"Shit." I retrieved a bottle of her favorite gin. "Sorry."

With her gin and tonic made, I slid it across the bar. Mom squinted, first at me, then at Ryker. *Uh-oh.* I should've known there was no hiding from her.

"I'm going to check on the other customers," I squeaked, my exit less than graceful. *She knows.*

A busy crowd provided a convenient excuse to avoid both Ryker and my mother. Until the buzz died down and I had no choice but to return to the register-end of the bar where they both sat. I refilled Ryker's glass, and he thanked me every time, but that was all we said to each other. I hated that I missed him calling me sugar.

As the night slowed, I took a moment to hydrate. The wrong moment, it seemed.

"So." Mom crossed one leg over the other, her gaze bouncing between Ryker and me. "How long have you two been sleeping together, and does Dan know?"

I spat out my water, and Ryker choked on his scotch.

"We're not," I said quickly. She shot me a look. "Anymore." I ignored the pang in my chest. "And no, Dan doesn't know. It should most definitely stay that way."

"What's wrong with you?" Mom turned a scrutinous eye on Ryker. "My girl isn't good enough for you?"

I stifled a giggle as Ryker's mouth fell open, his eyes wide. I'd never seen him scared. Mom maintained eye contact and he opened his mouth several times but couldn't get anything out.

"Mom, please don't. We're friends."

"Friends." Mom scoffed. "Good luck with that. You don't like beautiful women? Is that it?"

"Mom," I hissed.

"I'm the one who's not good enough," Ryker finally spoke. "Good luck finding any man who's good enough for her." His gaze flicked to me briefly and that, coupled with his words, stunned me. I blinked and he swiped his glass, emptying the contents in one go. He slid the glass to me. "Another." He inclined his head to my mom. "I have a feeling I'll need it."

I poured the scotch and tried to sort through what he said. What the hell did that mean? *He* rejected *me*.

"Don't bother him." I sent Mom a scolding look that had no impact whatsoever. "He hasn't done anything to me, and he likes to drink alone and in silence. Leave him be."

Mom put her hands up in surrender and Ryker gave me an almost smile as I passed the glass back to him. "Fine," Mom conceded. "But remember how nice I was about this when I tell you what I'm about to tell you."

"Oh no." I paled. "Don't say it."

"I—"

"No, no, no." I put my hands together in a plea. "Please don't."

"—have a boyfriend."

"For fuck's sake." I dropped my elbows to the counter and my head into my hands.

"You don't know him!"

I glared at her. "He's trash."

A pout on her lips, she crossed her arms. "Thanks for the vote of confidence."

"You swore off men!"

"So did you, and yet, this is most *definitely* a man," she said, gesturing to Ryker who snorted and choked on his scotch for the second time.

"Mom," I whined. "Can't you be a spinster?"

"What happened to being nice?"

I made a face and straightened out. "Fine. Who is he?"

"His name's Mike."

I fished my phone from my back pocket. "Mike what?"

She massaged her temples. "You're going to internet stalk him?"

"Of course I am. I'm going to cyberstalk the shit out of him and learn all his dirty secrets."

"You don't know that he has dirty secrets!"

"Everyone has dirty secrets. *You* taught me that. Last name." I tapped the counter. "Now."

"Michael Frasier." She dropped her chin in her hand with an overdramatic huff. "He's a doctor at the hospital I work at."

I winced. "He's not your boss, is he?"

"No, give me a little credit. Jeez." She rolled her eyes and shook her head at Ryker. "Some people's kids."

"Don't give me that. You dated your boss before."

"You have a job to do." She jabbed her thumb at a group who entered and sat at a table. "You can go crazy stalker on him later."

"Fine. But I *am* going to go crazy stalker on him. In fact, you might as well give me his home address." I planted my hands on my hips. "'Cause I'll find it either way. And if he hurts you, he has me to deal with. Tell him that."

"God, for all your bitching about Dan being overprotective, you're just like him."

Ryker lifted his glass in cheers. "Hear, hear."

I clicked my tongue and swatted Ryker with the dirty bar rag. He threw his arms up, but I didn't care.

"I gotta get back to Dan." Mom slid cash across the counter. "Be nice to your customers but, you know, maybe not *too* nice." She winked at both me and Ryker.

And that's how he ended up choking on his scotch for the third time in one night.

"I'm not like Dan," I huffed as she walked away.

Ryker cocked his head. "Yeah, you are." I turned to glare at him, and he stared back unapologetically. So unapologetically, he repeated the words. "You *are*."

"Whatever," I grumbled.

New customers provided an excuse to get away from him while I tried to sort out that interaction. At least we'd spoken, but I cringed to think that this would be our new normal. I glanced back at him, surprised to find him already staring. Except he snapped his head forward the instant our eyes met.

This was a shitty new normal.

CHAPTER TWENTY-ONE

Worth the Risk

RYKER

Life without Scarlett was unbearable. Before we stopped, I slept well half the week. Without her, I was back to nightmares and tossing and turning. Back to doom and gloom. Back to storm clouds without the bursts of lightning she emitted.

A whole week passed without seeing her. She said she could be normal but avoided me. I didn't see her until the day her mother arrived, and she was so excited to see her mom, she didn't notice me.

Then she did, and it was awkward as fuck. I wanted our banter. I missed her attitude and sass, missed everything about her that had driven me nuts.

Even my dogs missed her. Every time I came home, they'd wait at the garage door like they expected her to show up. It irked me. Why were they so attached? She was only here a few times a week at most.

Not anymore.

I caught glimpses of her on her way to art class. She spent a lot of time at the house with her mom and Dan. I'd see her return to her apartment at around eleven each night. If she looked at me, she'd offer a timid smile.

I hated the fake cordiality. Most of all, I hated how much I missed her. Not because I wanted her body, which I did. *Badly.* But more than anything, I wanted our normal. I wanted her sarcastic remarks and ferocity. I wanted to fight with her, piss her off, have her piss me off. I wanted us to yell at each other, then make up in bed like we'd done over the last few months.

The following Sunday was Father's Day, and a lot of our crowd stayed home with their children. Some brought their kids with them if they were over twenty-one. I didn't see Scarlett and didn't expect to. I'd stopped in to visit Dan and he feigned annoyance that Scarlett insisted on doing Father's Day for him every year.

"She makes too big a deal out of it," he grumbled while her mom, Diana, smirked a knowing smile.

For all his complaining, he was excited to see what she did for him this year and I swallowed back a throb in my chest because I already knew what she'd done. That charcoal drawing of Roxy. Just like that, I was transported to before we ended things.

All that to say, since I wouldn't see her going up and down the stairs or working the bar like she usually did on Sunday, I almost didn't bother coming in. However, Fred, one of our guys, got real depressed on Father's Day.

He refused to discuss it, but his daughter had died overseas serving in the Air Force. No one knew her name. Fred was closed off about it. But I wasn't stupid. *On a day like this, he shouldn't be alone.* So, he sat at the bar with me, and we drank and talked like normal.

In fact, more guys sat at the bar to be closer to Fred. They cracked jokes and got half-assed chuckles out of him. *Better than nothing.* Even my spirits lifted a little until—

She walked in.

A white sundress clung to her curves and complemented her golden skin. *Damn, she looks good in white.* She approached us and gave me a small nod before addressing Fred.

"Here," she said, extending a box with a card on top.

Fred stared. Blinked. Spun on his barstool to face her. His lips twisted down and our whole group silenced.

"Just because your daughter's an angel daughter doesn't mean you're not still a dad." She pecked him on the cheek, then opened the small box. "Happy Father's Day."

A cupcake read *Happy Father's Day* in elegant blue frosting. He made no move. She set the cupcake on the bar and held out the card. I almost thought he wouldn't take it, but he did. He opened it, and for the first time in my life, I thought he might cry.

"Thanks, Scarlett." We all pretended we didn't hear the waver in his voice.

She threw her arms around him. He hugged her while we snapped our open mouths shut. Fred never showed affection, nor did he respond well to anyone bringing up his daughter. But Scarlett hugged him, and he hugged her back, and the rest of us gawked like baffled weirdos.

As if that wasn't surprise enough, when she pulled away and turned to leave, he spoke up. "Do you want to see a picture of her?"

Someone nudged me but I didn't move. Scarlett faced him, expression soft and welcoming. She nodded and the two of them sat at a table where he pulled a picture out of his wallet.

"How did she do that?" Nick asked, staring after them.

She's a fucking angel. "I have no idea."

No one had ever managed to get Fred to talk, but there he was. Talking. Sharing pictures and almost smiling. *God.* That open heart of Scarlett's drew people in.

The guys shot me a look every time I glanced her way. I scowled at them to no avail. Unable to handle so many pairs of eyes saying *why the fuck would you let her get away*, I found solace in the bathroom. Splashed cold water on my face and tried to remind myself—and my dick—that it was over. I couldn't have her, and I needed to let it go.

The universe must've wanted to punish me because I exited the bathroom at the same time Scarlett started down the hallway. We awkwardly sidestepped each other and she gave me another one of those shy smiles.

I hate this.

I had to walk past and ignore how gorgeous she was. With much effort, I tried. But I couldn't ignore the other thing.

I paused and flexed my unsteady hands. "Scar?"

She stopped.

"Thanks for doing that for Fred. He doesn't usually open up like that."

She lifted a shoulder. "Sometimes it takes the right person with the right words."

Right. She was definitely the right person. And I was the wrong one.

I nodded and kept walking because looking at her was too fucking difficult. Returning to the bar, I ordered another drink. Then another, ineffectively trying to erase the image of her in that dress.

"You think drinking is going to help?" Francis asked, taking the seat next to me.

"Don't fucking start."

"What's wrong with you?" Francis pushed my drink away. "Go fucking get her."

"I can't." I snatched my glass.

"Yes, you can. You're being a coward."

"I'm not being a coward. It's best for her. I'm not good for her. Drop it."

"Pretty sure it's her decision to make on whether or not you're good for her." He shook his head and stood. "A girl like that does not stay available, Ryker. And you're going to feel like shit the day she shows up with another guy when that guy could've been you."

He left me there alone. Pissed off. Frustrated. *Hurting.* I pulled out my wallet and dropped cash on the bar, unable to take anyone else's shit today.

Going home without Scarlett on a Sunday plunged me deeper into depression. She always came home with me on Sundays. I entered the garage, and the fucking dogs sniffed around my motorcycle then stared out the door expectantly.

"For fuck's sake, she's never been here without me." They whined. "If she were here, she'd be here when I pull in."

They didn't care. Instead, they lay on the ground and watched down the road.

"Fucking traitors, I swear." I yanked open the door, then trudged upstairs.

A bottle of scotch later, I stumbled to bed. My phone pinged. A message from Nick that made me throw my phone on the ground because it wasn't *her*. I fell back on my mattress and my stomach sank at the scent of Scarlett's perfume lingering on the sheets. I couldn't escape her.

I don't want to escape her.

My phone vibrated again and a small, delusional part of me hoped it'd be her. Groaning, I rolled over and retrieved my phone from the floor. No Scarlett. Only a message from Francis. I dropped my phone, and it thudded on the ground.

Fuck, I should answer one of them. Otherwise, they might show up at my house. I reached blindly and patted the ground. Instead of finding my phone, I found something softer. Lifting the object, my heart skipped. A hair tie of Scarlett's.

"Give me a fucking break." I hurled it under the bed before flopping down in my empty, cold sheets.

The bed didn't offer much rest by the time sunlight filtered in my windows. I threw myself into work, getting as many bounties as I could in one week. Conrad was happy but it changed nothing for me.

I went to the bar on Thursday but spotted her from the street, gliding to Dan's house with a covered pan in her hands. Probably cooking him dinner because that pain in the ass was also a complete sweetheart when she wanted to be.

I couldn't fucking take it. I drove home and sat on the couch with the dogs. They laid their heads in my lap and looked up at me with sad puppy eyes they should've outgrown by now.

"What?" I snapped.

Demon whined.

"Shut up." I reached for a bottle of scotch.

Grayson whined.

"Let it go. Both of you."

They both whined.

"I can't have her, all right? She's too good for me. What do you want from me?"

Demon snorted and laid his head in my lap again. The fucking jerk. I stared at the TV I hadn't bothered to turn on. Most of my free time recently had been spent with her. I didn't know what to do with myself.

Grayson whined again and I patted his head. It spoke volumes that they could tell I was upset. Not because they couldn't always, but because that made it evident what bad shape I was in.

Was I *that* terrible for her? She didn't think so. She said I always showed up. But she didn't know my dark secrets. *What if she can't handle them?* What if she learned that shit and was done? Then there was the nagging thought in the back of my mind. *Isn't she worth the risk?*

She absolutely was.

"Fine." I petted the dogs' heads as I stood. "You win."

I was too drunk to do this with her tonight, so I staggered to bed and formed a plan to talk to her the next day. She had worked Fridays before but since her class started, her schedule changed. Still, I could catch her coming home from Dan's.

Except, what do I say? I wasn't good with words. I tried to come up with a speech, but it sounded like such bullshit. After writing several different options, I crumpled them all and buried them at the bottom of my trash can. The words would come to me when I saw her.

I'd been to Dan's bar a hundred times and sat on the same stool, yet that night, I couldn't stop fidgeting. I drummed my fingers against the bar while I waited. She usually showed up after her class before going to Dan's place. I tried not to fixate on the time or the hallway. I was only on my second glass when Dan appeared down the hallway, being wheeled by Diana.

My eyebrows shot up. "Danny."

"Hey." An easygoing grin he only had around Scarlett and Diana stretched across his face. "Thought I'd see how it's going over here. I needed to get out of that fucking house."

I chuckled and stood to shake his hand. "I don't blame you. Nice to see you moving around."

Several people flocked to Danny. Followed him to the table Diana claimed. Isolating Scarlett wouldn't be easy. I'd have to wait until Danny was gone, then if Scarlett wanted to try this with me, I'd let her decide how to tell him.

If she still wanted me.

Time crawled and she didn't show. I needed to see her, even if it wasn't the right moment to talk. I sipped my drink, and a hand landed on my shoulder. I didn't need to look—I recognized those long nails.

I shrugged off her hand. "Natalia." *Shit.* Her timing couldn't be worse.

"Ryker," she said smoothly, taking the seat next to me and rubbing my leg.

Not good timing at all. Natalia and I usually hooked up whenever she was in town for work. She was married, but her husband was a tool who cheated on her constantly. As she sat, I remembered she'd texted me earlier this week and told me she'd be here. I'd ignored it because I was hoping it was a message from Scarlett.

"You didn't answer but I figured you'd be around." She inclined her head to the door. "Wanna get out of here?"

"Not tonight, Nat." I pushed her hand off my leg. "Sorry."

Her lips pulled down. "Why?"

"There's—ah, fuck. There's a girl, all right?"

"You don't settle down."

"Not usually."

"So . . ." she asked, fingers trailing up to my shoulder.

"So," I removed her hand from my arm, "she's different."

"Oh, come on, Ryker. We're good together. It's only physical. Are you in a relationship?"

"No, but I might end up in one if I don't fuck it up. Back off, Nat. I mean it."

"I never thought I'd see the day," she said, shaking her head as she stood. She leaned over my shoulder. I was going to push her away but then she whispered in my ear, "I'm having a shitty week. At least drive me to my hotel. I took a cab here."

Her voice cracked, and I cursed because I couldn't say no. Not with how fucked up her situation was.

"Fine." I exhaled and stood. "What happened now?"

"Nothing new. Another case of I'm not doing enough for him. I need to get another surgery. I need this and that."

She acted like it didn't bother her, but it did. Asshole constantly put her down, told her she needed to change to be good enough for him. I felt bad and rested my hand on her back on our way out.

"I'm sorry, Nat. When are you going to divorce him?"

"I have a lawyer working on the papers."

I focused on my motorcycle so I wouldn't roll my eyes. "Right." I'd heard that before.

"I'm really going to do it this time."

"Good." I passed her my helmet. "I hope you do."

"I am. I mean it."

"Good." I mounted my bike. "Then do it."

She pulled the helmet on and climbed on behind me. "You think I'm full of shit."

"I hope you're not this time."

The plan was to take her to her usual hotel and rush back. But she cried and admitted he'd also slapped her this week. I couldn't leave. She needed a reality check—a serious talk about *actually* leaving for real this time.

In her room, I made her call her mom to explain what'd happened. Knowing her mom, there was no way Nat would return to that house. I glanced at the clock and grimaced. I wouldn't make it to Scarlett tonight until it was late. Probably too late.

Tomorrow, then. Tomorrow I'd talk to her no matter what.

CHAPTER TWENTY-TWO

Friends

SCARLETT

Drawing a nude model was as embarrassing as I feared. For me. No one else wore a bright red face and hid behind their easel. Not even two weeks of drawing the naked man helped me stop fidgeting.

Over the course of multiple sessions, I'd managed to finish his lower and upper halves. The middle I hadn't gotten to yet, mostly because I'd never drawn a penis, but also, the man was hot as hell. Not as hot as Ryker but unfortunately, no one would ever measure up. Regardless, he was attractive with his sculpted body, green-blue eyes, and dirty blond hair. *And naked.*

Hera's loop to check on each student's progress ended with me. She paused behind me. I tensed but forced my gaze to stay forward and my hand to keep moving. *I don't usually let people watch me work.*

"You're very good, Scarlett." She leaned closer, a mischievous smirk playing on her lips. "You're missing a vital piece, though."

"I'm getting there," I said, blowing a piece of hair out of my face.

"The thing that scares you the most is always the thing you should do first."

Ugh. She was right, but *ugh.* "Got any other tips for me?"

"No. You've improved greatly already. I'm impressed. Next circle around I hope to *see* a tip, though."

Oh my God. I moved to hide my face with my hands but stopped because they were a mess of charcoal. I peeked around my drawing to get a look at the piece I was missing. It wasn't a bad piece.

My face burned the entire time, but I added that vital part before the session ended. After washing the charcoal off my hands, I hurried to pack my stuff. Hannah made it to my easel before I put away the drawing and gasped.

"Wow." She stepped closer, mouth hanging open. "That's amazing!"

"Thanks." I chewed my lip. "This class is my first time working with an actual nude model."

"Well, it doesn't look it." She waved the model, *who was still putting on his pants*, over to us. "Collin, come here."

Oh God. Oh no. I didn't want him to see it.

"What's up?" He circled the easel, and his eyebrows shot up. Letting out a low whistle, he nodded to Hannah. "Yours?"

"I wish." She scoffed. "Scarlett's."

The model's gaze swept over me, and he offered his hand. "I don't think we've met. I'm Collin."

I accepted his hand. "Scarlett."

"You're damn good, Scarlett." He examined my drawing and stroked his chin. "Damn good," he repeated, softer.

I shifted my weight. "Thanks."

"Scarlett, you should go out with us tomorrow!" Hannah said.

"Out?"

"Yeah, we're going drinking and dancing downtown." She bounced on her toes. "Come! It'll be fun."

"Oh, um . . ." Shit, why did I always freeze like this? *Yes, say yes, Scarlett. This is how normal people make friends!*

"You should." Collin tugged his shirt on, and the fabric fell over his abs. "Might make you less nervous to look at me if you get to know me." He winked as he walked away.

I blinked, then ducked behind my easel. "Oh my God."

"You're so cute." Hannah giggled. "Seriously. Come. I'm new here and desperate to make friends, especially those with common interests. We'll have a blast. What do you say?"

I know the feeling. I'd never been good at making friends. This was an opportunity to change that. And occupy more time so I didn't wallow over Ryker.

"I'll go. I usually work the bar Saturdays, but you caught me on an off week."

"Yay!" Hannah clapped. "I think Collin has his eye on you."

"What?" I recoiled. "I don't think so. Today's the first day I talked to him."

"Yeah, but he's noticed you." She wiggled her eyebrows. "He asked me about you."

I covered my face with my hands and laughed. "He's probably asking because I'm so weird hiding behind my easel."

"He doesn't think it's weird. He thinks it's cute. What's wrong? You don't like him, or you got a boyfriend?"

"Uh . . ." I picked at my nails, and we wandered outside. "No. No boyfriend."

"I hit a nerve. Ex?"

"No." My chin dipped to avoid eye contact. "It's this guy who's friends with my uncle. I've been hooking up with him for a while. It was supposed to be no strings, but I fucked up. I caught feelings and he didn't and . . ." I lifted a shoulder. "So, that's that. I wish I were fully over him, but I'm not. He's not the kind of guy you get over easily."

"Maybe you need another guy over you to forget about him." She nudged me. "Plus, if he didn't have feelings for you, he sounds like an idiot."

My lips twitched up. "Thanks, Hannah. I don't know if I'm ready to be with someone else. He really did a number on me."

"Let's see how tomorrow goes. If you're not feeling it, ignore Collin's flirting because he'll definitely be flirting. If you are, then good. Rebounds are healthy. Hey, why don't I pick you up and we get ready at my house together, then we can carpool?"

"That sounds good."

I wasn't great at makeup, but maybe she could help me.

"Okay, girl, call you later." She skipped off to her car.

For the first time in a while, I entered the bar with a smile on my face. I had *plans.* With potential friends. Actual plans. Like normal people. Typically, I was a social recluse, but I did crave some kind of connection. *Having a girl to hang out with is nice.*

I had an extra spring in my step as I made my way along the hallway toward where Dan would probably be surrounded by regulars. Unfortunately, I couldn't help but glance toward a certain someone's regular seat.

My world halted. My stomach churned.

A beautiful woman in a show-stopping dress stood with Ryker, her hand on his shoulder as she whispered to him. Then he stood. Turned. Followed her toward the exit.

I'm gonna be sick. Right before they stepped outside, he put his hand on her back.

We weren't together but did he have to flaunt it in front of me like that? He could have any girl at any bar, but he picked her up *here*? Where he *knew* I'd be? I balled my fists and forced back tears as I approached Dan and Mom. I had to be nice for Dan's sake.

Dan grinned up at me, the most he'd smiled in weeks. "Hey, honey."

"Hey." I pecked his cheek. "Having fun?"

"I am." He glanced at the bar. "Ah, they're gone already. Was hoping to ask Ryker for a favor."

Now the universe was baiting me. *Don't ask, Scarlett. Don't ask. You don't want to know.* No, I didn't want to know, but I couldn't help myself. "Do you know who that was?" Maybe I misread the situation. Maybe she was a relative, and I was upset over nothing.

"That was Natalia. Ryker's married friend." Dan chuckled, shaking his head. "We won't see Ryker for the rest of the weekend. Those two are like rabbits anytime she's in town."

Like rabbits? Married? "She's married?" The blood drained from my face. I didn't see him as that kind of guy.

"Yep."

And now the spiral plunged deeper. If she were some random girl, sure, but he'd been with her before. They had history. And he was here with her when he knew I could see them.

Mom pursed her lips, but I shook my head. *Be nice. Divert. Talk about* anything *else.* "I'm going out tomorrow with Hannah and a couple other people from my class."

"Oh, good." Dan patted the seat next to him. "Don't drink too much."

"Define too much." I mostly said it to bait another lecture because I didn't have it in me to focus for banter.

My gaze drifted to the door. How could he do that to me? He'd been so sweet, then he did *that*? We weren't together but it was insensitive. I told him I had strong feelings. The least he could do was not flaunt his latest fuck right in front of me.

Dan elbowed me. "Scarlett."

"What?" I snapped my gaze to him.

"I asked where you're going tomorrow."

"Oh, uh, some club I don't know. Hannah's picking me up and we're going to her house early to get ready, then we're riding together."

A regular approached, and I mentally thanked them for stealing Dan's attention. My eyes stung, but I breathed through it. Finding a different focus backfired. I caught a glimpse of Francis's face, which made my stomach sink. Pity filled his eyes. As if that didn't hurt plenty, Tammy stopped by with a double shot of whiskey and gave me the same piteous look along with a squeeze on my shoulder.

Apparently, she knew too. They all knew, and I was an idiot.

CHAPTER TWENTY-THREE

Not Mine

RYKER

Getting Nat help took way too long and especially ticked me off because she tried to seduce me again. I let it slide because she'd been a friend since high school, and I felt bad for the situation. Vulnerable, hurt people rarely acted logically. Her mom promised to make sure Nat did what needed to be done. It sucked to pull her mom into it, but Nat couldn't stay in that relationship. It was a disaster already, but violence was too fucking far.

I barely slept once I got home because another bounty I needed to chase was in the area. After a couple hours of rest, a friend called saying they saw him leaving a gas station not ten minutes from my place. This particular motherfucker had beat up his boyfriend to the point the guy was in the hospital. Then he didn't show up for his hearing. *I won't be gentle with this one.*

Catching him wasn't difficult. The cocky type who beat their partners never were. The asshole pulled a knife, but I saw that coming. It didn't take me long to have him cuffed and enraged in my trunk as I drove to the police station. Conrad was pleased when I stopped by to pick up the check from the last time. He tried to chat, but I wasn't in the mood.

There was only one person I wanted to talk to.

I stood outside the bar for a good several minutes. She always worked Saturdays so there was no way I wouldn't see her. Inside, my heart palpitated out of control and every step took effort. Planting my ass on my usual seat, I glanced around the bar and spotted the new guy working but not Scarlett.

Shit. Was he working with her and Tammy or taking over for Scarlett tonight? I glanced around once more, searching for those beautiful dark curls. Something hard hit the bar, and I turned, finding Francis beside me.

"She's not here." His clipped tone raised my eyebrow. "Shouldn't you be with Nat?"

"I wasn't *with* Nat."

"You went home with her."

"Not like that." I scowled. "She had trouble with her husband. The asshole hit her. I talked sense into her. I didn't fuck her. I came here yesterday to talk to Scarlett, and Nat showed up."

Francis grimaced. I cocked my head, and he scratched the back of his scalp. "Uh . . . from other viewpoints, it looked like you picked her up and took her home."

Oh *no*. No fucking way. "Scarlett wasn't here." I almost fucking passed out with how little my body wanted to function. "I watched for her."

"She came in around the time you two left." Francis winced. "Then Danny told her about you two. Including that Nat's married. Said you fuck like rabbits."

"For fuck's sake." I dropped my head to the bar, then thudded it against the surface several times. *With the rabbits comment, Danny? Really?*

Francis clapped me on the back. "Sorry, man."

"It's fine." I massaged my temples. "She's not unreasonable. I'll tell her the truth. Where is she?"

"She went out with friends. She said so last night. Ryker, she was really upset. I'd approach carefully."

"Of fucking course." I dug the heels of my palms against my eyes. "I'll wait for her."

"She was going out drinking, man. There was talk that she may not make it home tonight. She might stay with some girl named Hannah."

"Great. Perfect timing. Thanks, universe."

"You were really going to talk to her?"

"Yeah." My heart rammed against my ribs. "Is she working tomorrow?"

"As far as I know."

"Fuck." I pinched the bridge of my nose and Tammy approached with my scotch open. "Fill it up, please."

"He told you?" Tammy asked.

I groaned. "You too?"

Tammy folded her arms across her chest. "Did you have to bring Nat here in front of her? I'd be thinking of ten ways to castrate you if I were Scarlett. You may have rejected her feelings, but you didn't have to flaunt your other fuck buddy in front of her."

"I didn't fuck Nat," I snapped. "I helped her with something with her husband. God damn you two."

"Oh." Tammy's shoulders lowered. "Yeah, it looked terrible. And Scar seemed really upset. I honestly don't know how Danny didn't pick up on it."

Francis scoffed. "Danny's been oblivious to these two since the beginning."

Tammy lifted a shoulder. "Maybe he subconsciously knows and doesn't want to think about it."

"That's enough." I gulped my scotch and reveled in the burn down my throat. "Go away."

Tammy cleaned out a glass. "You better hope she doesn't hook up with Collin tonight."

Francis tensed.

My blood simmered. *Collin?* "Who the fuck is that?"

"Some guy her friend was talking about when she picked her up," Tammy said. "Her friend is weird, by the way. Cute, but weird. She said the dress Scarlett picked out was going to make Collin salivate over Scar more than he already does."

"Uh-oh." Francis looked up to the heavens, as if they could save this man if he touched my Scarlett.

"Do we know where they were going?"

Both shook their heads, and I gripped the glass tighter.

"You shouldn't have taken so long to do something about her." Tammy ground her teeth. "I love you, Ryker, I do. But you messed this up. She's good for you and you pushed her away."

"Stop being my shrink, Tammy."

She rolled her eyes and strolled off, leaving me frustrated, irritation prickling the back of my neck. Scar wouldn't hook up with someone else already, would she?

She might if she thinks I have. Fuck me.

Regardless, I stayed as late as possible, hoping she'd show. Tammy let me stay after closing while she cleaned but Scarlett didn't come home. At three thirty in the morning, I finally left. I called her all night, but she never answered. I texted her but received no response.

Images of her with whoever Collin was played on repeat through my brain. *Collin.* Stupid fucking name. I didn't doubt he'd salivate at whatever she wore because that damn girl could make a potato sack look good.

I went home, but the likelihood I'd sleep knowing she was out and possibly with a guy? Yeah, that wasn't happening.

I tossed and turned all night, not falling asleep until the fucking sun rose. I'd never thought about a girl this much. That was the problem and for whatever reason, I'd decided I wanted to make it a bigger problem by keeping her in my life. *My mind's a mess.*

I got up later than I wanted to after sleeping so long and took the dogs for a run before I left. By the time I got to the bar, the stupid NBA playoffs crowd was there. Thankfully, Tammy always kept my seat closed off.

As soon as I entered, I scanned the bar for Scarlett. My search ended at a corner table where she dropped off drinks. She had her hair in a loose bun and wore sinful booty shorts and a low top that fit her figure. *God,* I missed seeing her like that. It'd been ages since I'd seen her normal.

I made my way to my seat, and she turned with her empty tray, headed to the bar. She didn't notice me at first but when she did, her lips pursed and she whipped her head away, not giving me a second glance.

I stretched over the bar as she passed. "Scar."

Nothing. No acknowledgement.

Tammy patted me on the shoulder and left a drink in front of me but for the first time possibly ever, I was uninterested in it. Scarlett avoided passing me as she loaded drinks onto a tray and took them to another table. Then another. *All right, fine. Ignore me.*

She couldn't do it all night. I bided my time until she had to linger by me to access the cash register.

Determined eyes remained glued on that register. She tapped the screen, posture tense while I leaned on my forearms over the bar.

"I need to talk to you."

"I'm busy," she clipped.

"Scarlett, come on. You're not going to let me explain?"

"Explain that I told you I had feelings for you, and you flaunted your other fuck buddy in my face?" She finally faced me, hands planted on her hips. "No, Ryker. I don't need a fucking explanation for that. And in case you've forgotten, this," she gestured between us, "isn't a thing anymore. Nor will it *ever* be. So, you don't owe me an explanation. Fuck someone else's wife to your heart's content." She stalked off before I could respond and I clenched my jaw.

It hadn't looked good, but she could give me a fucking chance. If every stool and chair in the place weren't occupied, I'd grab her and make her listen. I flexed my hand and stayed where I was, reminding myself that getting frustrated wouldn't help. She and I had a bad habit of colliding tempers at the worst moments. Always clashing.

She bustled around and I remained silent so she could get her work done. As soon as it died down, I'd talk to her, and she'd understand. She *had* to. I missed her so fucking much. Her pissed at me was better than nothing.

Sort of. She wouldn't refill my drinks and blatantly flirted with any guy who gave her eyes. *So pretty much all of them.* Only once did she spare me a glance and maybe I shouldn't have glowered at her because she flipped me off on her way to flirt with another customer.

Damn her. She knew how to push all my fucking buttons, and she was pushing them all at the same time.

A piss was a good excuse to leave the bar and take a breath. Both of us angry at each other was a recipe for disaster, and I wanted to make up. Bring her home with me tonight and make the dogs' night, then make her and my night.

Don't be an asshole. Handle this maturely. I returned and Tammy refilled my drink. Thank God. I needed it to endure douchebags eyeing Scarlett's cleavage all night.

My mantra to remain patient faltered when she returned to the register. *Fuck,*

I didn't want to wait until it slowed down. I wanted to clear the air, but she wouldn't look at me.

She turned her back to me and I scrubbed my hand over my face. I'd never fought with a girl like this before and didn't know how to fix it. If I were upset with her, all it'd take for me to forget it was a blow job. Something told me this wasn't the right time to ask her if I could lick her clit until she wasn't mad anymore.

"Hey, you good?" Tammy approached, gaze flicking toward me as she addressed Scarlett. "You want a break?"

Thank you, Tammy.

"I'm good." Scarlett dropped a lime in one drink then poured vodka into another. "I don't need a break."

"I heard your favorite artist is having a show a couple hours away." Tammy typed on her phone. "Are you going?"

"I wish. It's ridiculously expensive and at this point, it's probably sold out." Scarlett's shoulders deflated. "Maybe when I'm not paying for an art class. It would be a dream to go."

My phone buzzed.

Tammy: *You're loaded. Buy tickets to Cath Riley's art show and take her. She can't say no to that, upset or not. The artist is way too important to her.*

I owed Tammy big time.

They moved on with their drink trays and I tried to get tickets, but Scarlett was right. Sold out. But I knew people. *I might be able to work something out.* Even if I couldn't, I had to talk to her tonight. I couldn't stand this tension. Couldn't stand her thinking I'd treat her that disrespectfully.

An opportunity arrived when the crowds died out. Scarlett returned to the register and my heart thudded. Waiting until she was off her shift flew out the window. I stretched over the bar and closed my eyes at the smell of her perfume, the warmth of her body close enough to touch.

"Scarlett, I didn't sleep with Nat last night."

She stiffened and sent me a doubtful glare.

"I didn't. I swear I didn't. I wouldn't do that to you, sugar. I've never lied to you and I'm not about to start." *Well, except that one time about not feeling anything for you.*

Her expression softened a fraction, but she refocused on the register. "Whatever. It doesn't matter. It's none of my business," she muttered, tearing off a receipt. "You're not mine to feel jealous over." The last part was barely audible under her breath as she stalked away.

After dropping off a check and taking an order, she breezed past me into the kitchen. Groaning, I dropped my head into my palms. *You could've avoided this if you hadn't turned her down the first time. Idiot.*

"Rough night?"

The unfamiliar voice dragged my attention to the right, and I resisted the urge to curl my lip. I hated nosy people.

"Something like that." I tipped back my glass, swallowing a gulp.

"You served?" He pointed to the Marines tattoo on my arm with the years served underneath it.

"Yep."

"So did my brother. Same years almost. What battalion and platoon?"

"1st Battalion, 109."

"Ah, he was in 1st Battalion but a different platoon." He scratched the back of his neck. "I don't suppose the last name Loughty means anything to you?"

"Loughty." My eyebrows shot up. "Not . . . Phillip Loughty?"

He grinned. "That's the one."

"Phil's your brother?" I asked. He nodded. "That must make you Collie."

"I'm not a fan of that nickname." He rolled his eyes, but the grin remained intact. "I can't believe the bastard carried that nickname through his term."

I chuckled. "He did say it was to piss you off."

"So, you do know him?"

"Yeah. We worked a couple missions together. How is he?" I rotated on my stool to face him. "He didn't actually go through with that winery thing, did he?"

"He's good. He did, actually." Collie laughed. "Yeah, he's doing all right with it. Bought a vineyard off this older couple over in Napa Valley. He loves it. Keeps him busy."

"That's great. Next time you talk to him, tell him Harding says hello."

"Harding." Collie cocked his head. "Ryker?"

"He's mentioned me?"

"Yeah, he says you saved his life!"

"It wasn't just me."

"Still, dude." He clapped me on the back. "You're part of the reason my brother made it home. Let me buy you a drink."

I started to answer but Scarlett walked in from the kitchen and her mouth fell open. "Collin?"

His grin turned a little too friendly as he focused his attention on my girl. "Hey, Scarlett."

Collie.

Collin.

Oh, *fuck*.

CHAPTER TWENTY-FOUR

My Lightning Storm

SCARLETT

Collin showing up at the bar would've shocked me any day. Collin showing up and talking to Ryker *stunned* me.

Once my heart restarted, it beat out of control with no consistent rhythm. My gaze bounced between the two like a ping-pong match while I struggled to get words out.

"Uh, hi." I settled on Collin. "You two know each other?"

Did I want the answer? Not so much, but heartbroken over Ryker, I'd drunkenly kissed Collin last night. Calling it a kiss was generous. It was sloppy and lasted all of three seconds, but I'd *die* if he and Ryker were friends.

"Not exactly. He saved my brother in the Marines."

I fiddled with my apron. *Saved?* "Oh." *Is that better?*

I cleared my throat. "What are you doing here?"

"Came to see you." He held up a pair of heels. "You left these in my car last night."

Tension rippled off Ryker, and I licked my lips. *He better not be an ass to Collin.* Jealous, uncommitting asshat.

"I'm sorry." My laugh rattled with nerves as I circled the counter and plucked the heels from him. "I was a little wasted. Thanks for bringing them and for getting me and Hannah home."

"Not a problem." He chuckled. "It was pretty fun for me, actually."

"Yeah, taking care of drunk people is *fun*."

His eyes twinkled, smile wide. "When they're as funny and adorable as you, it is."

This man is flirting with me. I'd decided to move on from Ryker, but I didn't want to do it in front of him. No reason to stir that pot more than it already had been.

"Well, thank you." I inched toward the stairs. "I probably shouldn't have these sitting out while I'm working."

"For sure." He inclined his head to the stairs. "Got a minute? Seems kinda slow."

"Oh, uh . . ." *Don't look at Ryker. Don't look at Ryker.* I held up the heels. "We could talk while I put these away, but then I gotta get back to work."

Collin grinned. "Sounds good."

I started upstairs with him close behind. At the top, I tossed my shoes in my apartment, then faced him with a sheepish smile. "Look, I'm *really* sorry about last night. I'm so embarrassed. I wasn't in a good place."

"I'm not complaining." He shot a lingering glimpse at my lips. "I'd like the opportunity to have you kiss me when you're sober, though. That's why I came. To ask you out. The shoes were an excuse."

My mouth fell open. I couldn't do that. Collin was cute but I wasn't over Ryker even if I was pissed at him. If the timing were different, I would've loved to go out with someone as sweet as Collin. I had a great time with him last night.

This is your fault. You led him on by kissing him. Guilt twisted my stomach. "Collin . . ." The words wouldn't form. I didn't want to say no.

"Before you answer." He held his hands up. "I have a proposition you can't possibly refuse."

Huh. Now I was half interested, half annoyed, half impressed at his cockiness. *That's too many halves.* Whatever. It was all three. I arched a brow. "What's that?"

"I may have asked Hannah about you." His sheepish expression made my lips twitch up. "And Hannah may have told me you want to go to the Cath Riley exhibit this weekend."

Of fucking course I do. Cath Riley was the reason I got into art. I *adored* her.

"Yeah, but it's probably sold out." *And out of my price range.*

Collin raised two tickets, the corner of his mouth curving up. "Not if you know the art director."

I gaped. "Are you serious?"

"Completely." He stashed the tickets in his jacket pocket. "But I'm afraid if you want to go, you have to go with me. As my date. And to dinner beforehand. A very date-like dinner. Spoiler alert, there might be flowers because it's definitely a date."

Damn, he was good. *I shouldn't say yes.* I definitely shouldn't. But it was *Cath Riley.* She was my hero, and I'd probably never have another opportunity like this.

Fuck it. Ryker didn't want me anyway.

"For Cath Riley, I suppose I could endure that."

"Don't flatter me too much." He set his hand over his chest. "So, you'll go out with me?"

My stomach fluttered nervously at the idea of going on a date, but it was trumped by my excitement to see Cath Riley. *Oh my God, am I dreaming? Cath Riley!* "Yes."

"Good." Collin stuffed his hands in his pockets. "I'll pick you up early since it's a two-hour drive. Three o'clock okay?"

"That works." I inclined my head to the stairs. "I'm super excited, I really am, but I better get back out there." *And I need you to leave so I can properly fangirl without embarrassing myself.*

"Yeah, of course."

I bounced downstairs ahead of him, barely keeping my giddiness under control. *Cath Riley!* She was astounding. She was what I strived to be. *I can't believe this is happening.*

We reached the bottom of the steps and Collin sent me a charming smile as he walked toward the exit. "See you Saturday."

"Saturday." I pressed my lips together to contain the squeals demanding release.

"And make sure to be hungry because I'm taking you to French Laundry."

"Uh, what?" *Talk about fancy.* I'd never been there, but I'd heard of it. "You need reservations for that."

"I know."

"There's no way you made reservations at that restaurant this late."

"I didn't. I made them two weeks ago. The first day I saw you."

I narrowed my eyes. "What made you think I'd say yes?"

"I saw Cath Riley in your style. That, and your sketchbook has a Cath Riley sticker on it. It was pretty obvious you'd have to say yes even if you weren't immediately interested. Then I could get you interested by spending time with you."

"You planned ahead." My brows pulled together. "And paid attention." Now I was impressed. "You're good."

"A girl like you deserves the best, Scarlett. See ya."

He strode out the door. *Damn.* He really *was* good. Should I be annoyed or impressed? It didn't matter because the only thing that mattered was Cath Riley.

I squealed and jumped up and down, not caring about the confused looks from the customers.

"Why are you beaming?"

I spun around and grinned wide at my mother, who'd rounded the hallway corner.

"Mom," I squeaked. "You know that art show Cath Riley's having?"

"The one you've been talking about incessantly for months?" She poked my side teasingly. "Yeah, I know about it."

"I'm going!"

"What! How?"

"A guy from art class knows the art director and has tickets!"

"Baby, that's great!" She tugged me into a hug. "That's on your bucket list, isn't it?"

"It totally is!" I squealed, unable to keep myself from bouncing. "Okay, I'm good." I inhaled a deep breath, but my smile only widened. "Cath Riley!"

"I know." She laughed and squeezed my hand. "I'm so happy for you. It'll be a night to remember."

I clutched my stomach as it erupted with butterflies. I was going to see her work. In *person.* "It's surreal."

"The best things often feel that way." Mom pecked me on the cheek. "You have to finish your shift, and I have to turn in. I came to say goodnight."

"Okay." I gave her another quick embrace. "Goodnight. Love you."

"Love you too, babe." She waved at me on her way out.

I danced to the bar. *Nothing* could kill my mood.

Well . . .

Ryker remained on his usual stool. His glower implied unhappiness. He stared at me like he expected me to say something.

I wouldn't give him the benefit. I owed him no explanation. We weren't together and he didn't want to date me. He said he didn't sleep with that woman, but he also didn't tell me why they left together.

Shit. It didn't matter what happened and the fact was, he was involved with a married woman. I wasn't okay with that. Plus, he told me he had no feelings while I wanted a relationship. I shouldn't feel guilty. I *shouldn't.*

But I did. A little.

His gaze burned into me for the rest of the night and unfortunately, I was closing. Which meant no escaping if he decided to stay.

He stayed. Of course he stayed.

I avoided him at every opportunity, but the bar fell silent when the last patron left. I had to face him. "We're closed." I flattened my palms on the bar and met his intense gaze. "Go home, Ryker."

He crossed his arms. "You're going out with that guy."

I wished he wouldn't cross his arms. It put them on display, and I had more important things to think about. Like *not* sleeping with someone who didn't want to be with me.

I lifted my chin. "Yes."

His jaw clenched. "No."

"It's not your choice."

"Still a no."

"Still not your choice," I snapped, pointing at the door. "Go home. We're closed."

He stood, nostrils flaring. "You're not fucking going out with him."

Damn him being hot when mad. This was ridiculous. I leaned over the counter. "You have no say!"

He leaned over the bar as well, fingers almost touching mine. "You're not going."

"You can't control who I see."

The arguing brought us closer, enough his warm breath coasted over my lips. So close I spotted the flutter of his pulse against his neck. Our glares faded as electricity sparked between us. His eyes darted to my lips, and I couldn't stop myself from licking them.

Grabbing the back of my head, he crushed my mouth to his. I should've pushed him away, but my nerves ignited. A moan toppled out of me and his tongue slid between my lips. He bit my bottom lip and sucked it into his mouth. I whimpered and he dragged his teeth off, his gaze meeting mine in a way that reminded me why I had such a hard time saying no to him.

"You're not going," he growled, hopping over the counter. "You're mine."

He caught my face with his hands and kissed me again. Pushing him away would've been the wise thing to do. But I wasn't wise. I wrapped my arms around his neck, pulling him closer while my eyes stung. I missed him *so* much. I missed kissing him. I missed *feeling* him.

He groaned, lifted me, and dropped me on the counter. Yanking my legs apart, he nestled between them and pulled me closer, right against his erection.

God. I missed him all right. He fisted my hair and pulled my head back, exposing my neck. He planted his lips on my skin, sucking where I was most sensitive. He clamped his teeth on the hollow of my throat, and I whimpered, wrapping my legs around him.

"Fuck, I missed you," he murmured.

My heart ached. *Missed me.* He missed me. I clung to him, deepening our kiss. His hand lowered to my inner thigh, and I clenched. His fingers grazed my core, and I broke our kiss, letting my head fall to his shoulder.

"You're *mine*, Scarlett." He fumbled with my shorts. "If anyone's taking you to that show, it's me."

His. I wanted to be his and I wanted him to be mine. Some of the fog cleared. This wasn't going to help me get over him. I couldn't sleep with him again. He knew what I wanted. I knew what he wanted, and I couldn't give that to him anymore. Our physical attraction couldn't distract me. While great for my body, it was terrible for my emotional state.

I pushed his hands away. "Stop."

His face crumpled, his arms falling to his sides. "Why?"

"I can't do this with you." I slid off the bar. "You need to leave."

"Don't." He cupped my face, blazing emotion flickering in his eyes. "Don't tell me to leave."

"Ryker." I retreated from his touch, unwilling to cave. "Go. I can't do this. I'm going out with Collin on Saturday. This isn't okay."

"Scarlett, don't go out with him." His hand stretched toward me without making contact and I told myself I imagined the longing in his voice. "I'll fucking take you to the show."

"We don't want the same things."

"That's bullshit! You want me and I want you. Stop complicating it. You can't date someone else."

Amazing how quickly he could jerk me from horny to pissed off. *I swear.* No one got under my skin like he did.

"Why not? You didn't want me!" I threw my arms up. "Now someone else does. You can't have me do whatever you want and not commit to me. That's not fair. I told you what I wanted. You're being an asshole and a hypocrite. You left with a woman last night!"

"I told you, *nothing* happened. I didn't sleep with her, Scarlett. I came here to talk to you, and she showed up and told me her husband hit her. That's why I left with her, but I made it damn clear we wouldn't be sleeping together or anything else. She was in a bad place and needed a ride to her hotel. I was being *a friend* to her. Nothing else."

A married friend you go at it like rabbits with. It didn't matter. He wasn't mine. "Ryker." I pinched the bridge of my nose. "It's not my business what you do. And it's not your business what I do. I'm going out with Collin, and you have no say. Now, go home."

"So your feelings for me are gone? Just like that? I thought they were strong, but you say yes to the first guy who comes your way? Some fucking feelings."

"Don't be an asshole," I hissed. "For your information, I probably would've said no if it weren't for what he planned for us to do. You didn't want me, Ryker.

Did you think no one ever would?"

"I never stopped wanting you, Scarlett." He flexed his hand. "Not once."

"You don't want me like I need to be wanted." I snatched his arm and pushed him toward the door. "I need someone who wants me for more than sex. I need more, and Collin's offering that. He's taking an interest in my interests. There's nothing wrong with me exploring that."

"Give me a fucking break, Scar. He doesn't care about your interests," he snapped. "I saw the way he looked at you. He's hoping this stunt will get him in your pants. That's what he wants. To fuck you."

Anger boiled through my veins until my hands trembled. He didn't think of me as more than that and assumed no one else would either. I was *tired* of this. Tired of fighting. Tired of defending myself when I didn't need to.

Ryker came into my life like a lightning storm, beautiful and exciting but dangerous up close.

Thinking about it made me more pissed off. Pissed off and hurt that he didn't see me as anything but a fuck.

"You're such a prick!" I shoved him toward the door. "Is it so hard to believe he has a genuine interest in me? I'm not a sex doll. I know you don't think of me as more than that, but he does. At least he's showing me some fucking respect, which is more than I can say about you. Stop trying to make me feel bad and get the fuck out."

"Scarlett." He didn't budge no matter how hard I shoved him.

"Goddammit, Ryker." Tears blurred my vision, and I jabbed my finger at the door. "Get out. I can't look at you. I'm not nothing, so stop treating me like I am."

"Scarlett, I'm sorry." He stepped toward me. "Don't push me away. I want to talk to you. Hear me out. Let me say what I wanted to say Friday."

Normally I gave into him. Normally I let things slide. Today, I couldn't.

"I said get out!" I backed away and wrapped my arms around myself. "I'm not going to fuck you if that's what you're thinking. I regret *ever* doing it in the first place. That's all you want from me and you're not getting it, so *leave.*"

"Fuck, Scarlett, let me talk. I don't—"

"Dammit, Ryker, leave!" I turned away, embarrassment heating my face as the tears spilled. "I hate that you're seeing me like this. I don't want to hear what you have to say. Leave me alone."

If he tried again, I'd die right there. Silence suffocated the space between us for too long, then the front door shut. I slid to the floor and dropped my head in my hands, my heart cracking because of him. *Again.*

Chapter Twenty-Five

I'll Always Want You More

Ryker

Throwing myself into relentless workouts didn't help. Neither did burying myself in work. Drowning in a bottle didn't help. I still tried because I needed *something*. Anything to get Scarlett out of my head.

I couldn't return to the bar. Time had passed. She had her first date with *him*. I drank a lot that day. I'd been drinking a lot in general, which was why I nursed a hangover before I took the dogs for a run. My dogs who missed her too and wondered why I wasn't myself.

I never said the right thing. I never *did* the right thing. It's why I'd convinced myself I couldn't be with her in the first place. I wasn't good enough for her. That became painfully evident the last night I saw her, when she yelled at me. Said I didn't respect her. *When I made her cry.* I hurt her like I was afraid I would if we started a relationship.

I never wanted to be the reason she cried.

As usual, I fucked it up. I got so angry when she disappeared with Collin. It took concentrated effort not to storm up there. Then she bounded downstairs with the biggest smile I'd ever seen. Bigger than any smile I'd ever gotten out of her, and he'd gotten it from a few minutes of talking. Jealousy consumed me and I made her feel like I didn't respect her, which couldn't be further from the truth.

He gave her what she wanted. He *knew* what she wanted. What did I know?

What she wanted in bed. That was it. I didn't know that artist they talked about. Scarlett had mentioned her before, but I didn't fucking know art. He was good for her.

I hated him.

I let my anger and jealousy get the best of me and hurt her. It confirmed I couldn't be with her. It wasn't fair to put anyone through that. Especially not Scarlett.

Scarlett. God, I missed her in ways I hadn't fathomed a person could be missed. I missed the crinkle between her brows as she worked on details of a drawing. Seeing her new work and distracting her from it. Her defiant looks, the way she'd stick her hip out and plant her hand on it. The way she'd bite her lip. The way she always had a comeback.

Most of all, I missed having her in my arms. I missed the way she'd curl into me while she was asleep. She became a thousand times cuddlier. Awake, she didn't seem to care. Asleep, she'd cling to me, and I missed it like part of me had been cleaved off. I missed the way all of her wrapped around me, held on like she was afraid I'd leave. I missed waking up before her and watching her sleep.

It was a stupid thing to miss but watching her sleep gave me a glimpse into the parts of her she never let show. She wore a mask all the time. Not when I was inside her, not when she was having an anxiety attack, not when she was asleep. Those moments were *real*. I didn't like the anxiety attacks, but I did love the way she'd lean on me. I loved when she'd let me hold her in her most vulnerable moments.

But for the first time during that fight, she told me to leave. She didn't want me to comfort her. She didn't want me to see her vulnerable. Before, she'd say no at first but then run to me. That night, she hid from me. She didn't want me to see her without the mask. That hurt more than anything—shutting me out when she'd normally run to me.

Normally. I scoffed at myself. I hadn't known her long. There was no room for normal. Didn't it take more time to have a normal?

The thing with Scarlett, it didn't feel like two months. She understood me, like I understood her. Like I'd known her forever. Like she'd uncovered all my secrets, even though she hadn't. Being with her was fighting and pissing each other off and saying the wrong thing. But it was also easy. I didn't have to hold back. She welcomed my rough edges, encouraged them. She took all my shit and threw it back at me without hesitation. No one had ever been that way with me. No one could handle me the way she did.

She always called me out on my shit. Wiggled her way into places no one else could. I'd never been more comfortable with anyone in my life. And now she wanted nothing to do with me. While I couldn't blame her, I couldn't move on.

At first, I was angry with her for not giving me a chance to explain. For not listening when I said I could take her to that show. I could do all the shit she wanted.

Then I pulled my head out of my ass and realized it was my fault. She didn't want to hear me out because I'd given her no reason to. At least it ended before I got too attached.

Too attached. Fuck, if this wasn't too attached, I didn't want to know what it felt like.

Time passed. I texted her to apologize for the shitty things I'd said. I kept it simple and brief: *I'm sorry for making you feel like I don't respect you. I do. I think you deserve everything good, and I'm sorry I didn't show you that.*

I obviously couldn't return to the bar. Except Danny called me while I was out and left a voicemail, asking me to fix a leak in his kitchen. No more avoiding it.

I told Scarlett I wouldn't abandon Danny because of her, and I meant it. That didn't make it easy to return his call and tell him I'd fix the leak. I had to be there soon and didn't want to go.

What if she's there? I didn't know how to act. It was Saturday night and if her date went well with Collin, she'd probably be out again. I probably wouldn't see her.

So I got my ass up and brought my tools because I liked using my own. I didn't bother knocking because we were past that and Danny didn't need to worry about answering the door. Inside, I followed the sound of the TV. Diana's time off must've been up because her car wasn't outside and she wasn't there, nor was any of the stuff she had lying around the house when she first arrived.

Following the TV worked. I found Danny sitting on the couch. Alone, thank God.

"Ryker." He patted the seat next to him. "I haven't seen you. Where you been?"

I plopped next to Danny and shrugged. "Had some pretty intense cases the last couple weeks."

I did. Not enough to stay away, but he didn't need to know that.

"You got hurt." Danny nodded to my bandaged arm. A stab wound I let happen because I couldn't beat the shit out of myself for hurting Scarlett, so I had to get creative.

"Barely a scratch." *Sort of.*

All right, it required stitches and hit a nerve, but it wasn't the end of the world.

Danny made small talk, and I responded to the best of my ability. Thankfully, he laughed off my disinterest as not having a drink to make me talkative.

Whatever show played on the TV sucked Danny in, and I wandered to the kitchen and checked the sink. Nothing complicated but definitely something he couldn't do in a wheelchair.

A few minutes of tightening loose pipes did the trick. I wiped my hands on my jeans and tried the faucet, letting it run for a minute to make sure it didn't leak. Truth was, all his shit was old and needed replacing but he was stubborn as fuck.

Satisfied it was the best I'd get it, I turned off the water, spun to put my tools away, and froze. Scarlett stood in the doorway, gorgeous as ever in skinny jeans and a top that accentuated her hourglass figure.

Our gazes collided, shattering what remained of my heart. I didn't like the way we looked at each other. Like strangers. I closed the toolbox and tore my gaze away from her as I strode past her for the door.

"Ryker, wait."

Her hand landed on my arm and the simple contact from her soft, warm skin reminded me what I'd missed the last two weeks. Electricity coursed through my veins and made me more alive than I wanted to be. Normally I loved the way she brought me to life but now, I preferred numbness. It was the only way I could handle the chasm between us. I faced her, swallowing hard.

Her hand fell away, leaving a cold void behind. "I'm sorry." Her pretty lips pulled down. "For yelling at you. It wasn't fair to yell and not let you talk. I'm really sorry."

That, I wasn't expecting.

"*You're* sorry?"

"Yeah." She curled her arms around herself. "The yelling, the being pissed at you for Nat, it wasn't fair. I just . . ." She pinched the bridge of her nose. "I'm sorry, Ryker. It wasn't fair to treat you like that. We made an agreement, and I lost my cool. I told you I'd be normal, and I wasn't. I have a lot on my plate and—look, you can't kiss me anymore." Her expression stomped on the remains of my heart. Decided and firm, like there was no chance she'd change her mind. "You can't. Thank you for the apology, but you need to respect my boundaries. Which means you don't kiss me whenever you feel like it and you don't tell me what to do or wear or who to see or anything because it's not okay. I'm my own person." She gestured to herself. "Do you understand?"

"Yes." I forced myself to hold her gaze even though shame compelled me to break eye contact. Nothing she said was unreasonable, but there were a lot of unreasonable things I'd done. "I do."

She sucked in a shaky breath. "I know you haven't come to the bar because of me, and I don't want it to be that way. Please come back. It's not the same without you. Dan misses you and I miss seeing you. I know there can be nothing between us anymore but don't stop coming because of me."

I gaped at her for far too long. Words failed me. I didn't expect her to apologize. Another reason she was way too good for me.

"I'm sorry too, Scarlett. I wasn't so great to you myself." *Understatement.* "You deserved much better than how I handled things. I want you to know I know that."

"Thanks." She averted her eyes. "I don't want you to be gone from my life, Ryker. I don't want you to be gone from Dan's life. How can I get us to be friends?" Desperation filled her tone, and it broke me.

I didn't want her out of my life, either. I couldn't do friends. Or, I thought I couldn't. But that hopeful glint in her eyes told me pretend friends would have to do. Because I'd fucked up and I owed her *something*.

"You don't have to do anything." I offered my hand. "Friends it is."

She almost smiled. "Really?"

No. I'll always want you much more than that. "Really."

She shook my hand and thankfully took hers back quickly. I couldn't handle the physical contact for long. Not with her. Her eyes dropped to the bandage on my arm and a concerned frown pulled on her lips. "Did you get hurt?"

"It was nothing."

She bit her lip and nodded. I had a hate-love relationship with her lip-biting habit. Right now, I hated it because I couldn't do anything about it. We stood in awkward silence until her phone rang. She pulled it out of her back pocket and silenced it before speaking. "Well, I gotta go." She clasped her hands together. "I'll see you, right?"

I can't fucking breathe. "Yeah, you'll see me."

"Okay." She darted her eyes around nervously, meeting my gaze only briefly. "Later then."

She gave a small wave and walked out the door, taking my sanity with her.

CHAPTER TWENTY-SIX

Normal

SCARLETT

Finding a normal with Ryker was a challenge. We'd been attracted to each other from the beginning. It was our thing. Fight-flirting. I didn't know how else to be around him. But not being around him sucked. It also opened up more free time.

I told my mom what happened with my ex. What he did, and how he continued contacting me. Though I hadn't heard from him in a while. I hoped that meant he'd given up.

I never doubted that telling Mom would break her heart, and it did. At least I comforted her with the knowledge Todd seemed to be backing off, and I was getting help to heal. I had Ryker to thank for that.

Ryker. That frustrating part-time sweetheart, part-time asshole. I was honest with my apology. While he was definitely an asshole, I didn't handle things right either. At first, I was too hurt and angry to think straight, but then I attended a therapy session and parking in front of the building reminded me I probably wouldn't have had the courage to go if it weren't for him.

Like I said, part-time asshole, part-time sweetheart. It'd be nice if he could pick one and stick with it.

Since that awkward conversation in Dan's kitchen, things were as normal between us as they could be. He started coming in again, and we were polite to each other, but I missed our banter. *I guess I can't have that anymore.*

Things with Collin continued. Spending time with him was always enjoyable, and he wasn't a part-time sweetheart. He was *full*-time. There was nothing wrong with him but . . .

He didn't set me on fire like Ryker did. Probably no one ever would, and I couldn't use Ryker as a standard for other guys. Especially considering Ryker didn't have it in him to do more than fuck.

I tried to avoid any run-ins between Ryker and Collin. Whether or not it was the right thing to do, it seemed the safe thing to do. If I didn't enjoy seeing Ryker with Nat, I doubted Ryker enjoyed seeing me with Collin. Collin did, however, meet Dan, who actually liked him. That spoke *volumes.* Dan never approved of any guy I dated. Him warming to Collin reinforced that I needed to try harder and stop pining after someone I couldn't have.

Because I had to put effort into not thinking about Ryker, I didn't allow things to move forward with Collin. We dated, but I told him we needed to wait on any official labels or commitments. I refused to be a girlfriend to one man while thinking about another. Which made progress slow.

Polar opposite to my experience with Ryker. It'd been three weeks, and we hadn't done anything but make out. No sleeping over. I told him the truth—that I had some hang-ups and didn't want to commit to him or ask him to commit to me until I worked them out. The man had the patience of a saint. Patience I appreciated while my gut swam with nauseating guilt.

The only thing keeping me going was the fact I didn't catch myself thinking about Ryker as often. I didn't want to jump his bones as much. I needed to focus on Collin instead, anyway. Ergo, I was currently spending way more time dolling myself up for him than I ever had for Ryker.

We had a date tonight and I'd learned makeup tricks from Hannah. I got that smoky eye thing down and put on red lipstick to match the dress I'd picked out. Checking the time on my phone, I stilled. Dropped my lipstick.

A notification from an unknown number waited.

Chills racked my body. Not opening it wouldn't make it go away. My thumb hovered over the screen for a moment before I tapped the notification.

Unknown: *Stop ignoring me. We need to talk. You can't avoid me forever.*

My stomach churned and I took a screenshot of the text, sent it to the officer in charge of the case, blocked the number, and deleted the text. Hands trembling, I lowered my phone to the counter and practiced the breathing exercises I'd learned in therapy.

I can't be shaken before my date with Collin. He didn't know Todd existed. I preferred it that way because I didn't have to relive it and didn't have to worry he'd look at me differently.

Allowing myself exactly three minutes to chill out, I took off my robe and retrieved my dress from the closet. The silky fabric chilled my body, and I stretched my hand back for a zipper I couldn't reach. A knock on the door startled me.

Dammit. Collin was early. I intended to avoid Ryker witnessing him pick me up, so I usually rushed out before Collin arrived. Unfortunately, Collin noticed that I always waited outside and insisted I wait for him to come to the door. I blanched at the thought of explaining why I didn't want him to, so I told him I was punctual. Total lie. I was late for *everything.*

I worked on the zipper on my way to the door but couldn't catch it. Collin and I may not have had sex, but he had his hands under my shirt enough that zipping me up shouldn't be a problem. I opened the door and turned.

"I'm almost ready. Can you zip me up?" I glanced back over my shoulder and the blood drained from my face.

Oh *fuck.* I spun around and held my dress closed behind me. "Ryker," I squeaked.

His striking eyes might as well have conjured a bolt of lightning as they drifted up and down. "I don't think I'm who you were expecting, but I'll zip you up."

"It's o-okay." I backed away and contorted my arm to reach the zipper. "What are you doing here?"

"Danny said you've got a problem with a light switch." He held up his faded red toolbox. "He asked me to check it out for you."

"Oh." My finger almost grazed the stupid little metal slider but not *quite.* "You don't have to do that."

"It's not a big deal."

"I don't want to bother you."

"Jesus, Scarlett. If you want us to find a normal, me helping around here *is* normal. Now, stop being stubborn and turn around." He snatched my wrist and twisted me. "I've seen and touched more of you than this."

"You're so annoying," I huffed, ignoring the tingles as his hand rested on my back.

"There you go. That's normal." He glided the zipper up. "You accusing me of being what you are."

"Asshole." I snapped the word, though in reality, I internally cheered because *this* was normal. So much better than fake niceness.

"Takes one to know one," he said. I scowled, and he almost smirked. "Which light switch?"

"In the dining room."

He followed me and flipped the switch on and off a couple times, eventually leaving it off.

"Wow, that was amazing." I folded my arms. "Are you an electrician?"

He glared at me and set his toolbox down. "Shut the fuck up and go turn off the breaker for this room."

"So *bossy*."

I did as he asked, though. I needed a functioning light, especially in my makeshift studio. When I returned, he had a flashlight mounted on the fixture, already working on wires behind the switch. *Huh. I should learn more about electricity.*

"Take a picture, Scar." A hint of amusement danced in his eyes. "It'll last longer."

"I don't want to break the camera."

"I can't be that bad, or you wouldn't keep staring."

"I have zero interest in you. It's what you're doing I'm curious about."

"Oh, so you're watching what my hands can do?"

Bastard. I bit back the grin and he almost smiled. Yeah, this was normal. Though also a little flirty. *I should cool it.* A knock eradicated Ryker's amusement and shattered the moment. *Probably for the best.*

I hurried away, thankful for the distance from him. Opening the door, I gasped. Collin held a bouquet of roses, his eyes wide as they took me in.

"Wow," he breathed. "That's some dress." He offered the flowers. "These are for you."

"Thank you! That's so sweet." I pecked him on the cheek. "I'm basically ready. Only need my shoes."

"You're good." He checked me out while I filled a vase with water for the roses. "Seriously, you look amazing."

"Thanks." Dropping the blooms in the water, I then spun and fanned out the skirt. "I do like this dress."

"It's a good dress." Ryker emerged from the living room and my stomach dropped. I forgot this was the red dress I wore on one specific night with him. *Shit.*

"Uh." I fiddled with my hair. "Ryker was fixing my light switch."

"Oh." Collin nodded. "What's up, man?"

"What's up?" Ryker strode between us and faced me. "It was a loose wire."

"Thank you. I appreciate it."

"Anytime." He stalked out without another word of acknowledgment.

Collin's gaze, however, burned into me as I fussed with the roses. I hadn't told him about my history with Ryker.

"Shoes," I murmured as I slipped past him for my bedroom. He followed and leaned against the doorframe while I retrieved my heels from the closet.

"How come you called him to fix your light?" Collin hooked his thumbs in his belt loops. "I could've looked at it."

"I didn't call him." I sat on the edge of my bed and worked a heel on. "Dan did. It's nothing, Collin, honestly. Ryker fixes a lot around here. He was doing it for Dan long before I moved in."

"So, there's nothing between you two I should know about?"

I put on the second shoe, then stood and smoothed out my dress. The dress Ryker had done incredible things to me in. I should've chosen a different outfit.

"Full disclosure," I held my hands up, "we hooked up a few times." *Several times.* "But it was never serious." *For him, at least.* "It wasn't a relationship or anything. And it stopped before you asked me out."

He pushed off the doorframe and approached. My nerves prickled when he tucked a lock of hair behind my ear, expression unreadable. "You're sure it's over? It seems like he wants you."

"It's over. We talked. We agreed to be friends because I can't avoid him. He and Dan are close, and I don't want to come between them. Oh, also, Dan doesn't know, and he should *never* know."

"Got it. Shouldn't be a problem since you're with me now anyway." He circled his arms around my waist and drew me close. "Ready?"

"Ready."

He took my hand and led me toward the front door. "Come on."

I resisted the urge to fuck up my lipstick by gnawing on my lip. "Are you mad?"

"Of course not. There were other guys before me. It's fine. There were other girls before you too. It's a little weird he's in your apartment fixing things but you were honest with me, so," he shrugged, "it's cool."

See, brain? Forget Ryker. Collin's so much better for us. "Thanks."

That was the best response he could've given. He wasn't jealous like Ryker. He trusted me.

Once we survived escaping the bar with Ryker's friends staring, we carried on with our night. Dinner with Collin always went well. He had good taste and liked art, so we never ran out of things to discuss. Our conversation continued outside, where we strolled downtown, observing the neon lights and advertisements for bars and shows.

"Are you going to try for that show René is doing?" Collin asked. "The charcoal anatomy one?"

I wish. "I'm not sure if I'm ready."

"You're ready. You've made amazing progress. Even Hera thinks so and that means a lot coming from her. What are you afraid of?"

My laugh held a touch of insecurity. "Failure. Always have been afraid of failure. It's a problem. You might as well know. I almost never do anything unless there's practically no risk of failure."

"Live a little, Scar." I hated that his words reminded me of Ryker convincing me to ride his motorcycle. "You can't wait for things to be perfect or you'll never do anything. You can only achieve great things if you take risks."

He has a point. I chewed on the inside of my cheek, and he grasped my waist, pausing our walk.

"Besides, there's practically no risk. You're an amazing artist. Whatever's holding you back, don't let it. Just jump." He nuzzled my nose. "Not everything needs to be perfectly planned out. You don't have to have all the answers right away. Sometimes winging it works, and if not, at least you won't regret not trying."

My nervous expression softened to a smile. He always said the right thing. *He might even be right in more ways than one.* I should try for the art show, but I was also holding back with him. Afraid I wasn't ready to be with someone else. I'd been dodging his advances and . . .

Maybe it was time to stop thinking so hard and jump. I wrapped my arms around his neck and pulled him down for a kiss. "You're really sweet, you know?"

"I try. Come on." He broke our kiss. "I'll take you home."

I hesitated. *Just jump. Don't overthink it.*

My heart thundered against my chest. "Or we could go to your place."

His eyebrows shot up, but a sultry smirk formed. He gripped my hips, and I let go, hating myself for having to force thoughts of Ryker to the background.

CHAPTER TWENTY-SEVEN

My Kryptonite

RYKER

Days blurred together, each as inconsequential as the last. I crept out of the unfamiliar bed, careful not to wake the thin blonde who drank with me all night, but nothing else. Over the last week, I'd tried to get Scarlett out of my head to no avail. I couldn't get it up for anyone. Tried girls who looked like her, girls who were her opposite. It didn't matter.

Meanwhile, Scarlett spent more time with Collin. Danny informed me they were still dating though not officially together. Part of me wondered why. Part of me wondered if she held back because her feelings for me lingered.

Fuck. That line of thinking was too dangerous to explore. If she wanted me, she'd say it. She spoke her mind. I was holding onto something I'd already lost.

You're going to feel like shit the day she walks into this bar with another guy when that guy could've been you. Francis's words haunted me almost as often as memories of the girl who got away. One who wouldn't have gotten away if I'd manned up. Instead, I slumped into this rut of trying to move on without really living. Life was dull without her spark in it.

As if I didn't have enough to worry about, Fourth of July—aka, the worst holiday in the world—approached. New Year's was the second worst. I hated resolutions. Mostly, I hated fireworks. My dogs hated fireworks. If it were up to me, the damn things would be outlawed.

Every year, Danny had a barbecue with strictly no pyrotechnics. Too many of his close friends couldn't handle them. Instead, we drank, ate, and told war stories. We weren't close to any fireworks, but they'd go off in the distance and put me on edge. I only went to the barbecue one year, and even though it wasn't as hellish as I'd feared, I wouldn't go this year. Not with Scarlett and Collin there together.

Fuck, I hope I don't run into them.

Danny called and asked me to look at the grill in the bar. His father had given me a key years ago and Danny didn't see any reason I shouldn't keep it. This way, I could get in for repairs if no one was there.

I unlocked the door and headed to where the old-ass grill sat because Dan was too stubborn to replace it. After looking it over, I discovered a heating sensor problem. I could fix it, but I needed the right part. I was washing my hands when footsteps jerked my focus backwards.

Collin. Collin in boxers, no shirt, blinking sleepily.

Fuck. He spent the night with her. I didn't want to see that.

"Oh, hey." He ruffled his stupid hair. "I, uh . . . Scarlett said it was too early for anyone to be down here."

I turned off the faucet and dried my hands. "Usually is."

"Right." He rocked back on his heels. "Anyway, Scarlett said to steal eggs from the fridge."

"She does practically own half the place."

Everything Danny had, he was leaving to that girl. He'd already added her to the business's bank account. She refused at first but he told her it was so she could help with bookkeeping. That was bullshit. He wanted her name on it in case something happened to him.

Collin offered an awkward smile before digging into the fridge. I picked up my toolbox and got the fuck out of there. The situation couldn't be more strained and if I didn't escape, I'd be sorely tempted to punch him for no good reason except he had what I wanted.

The universe had it out for me, though. As I walked out, Scarlett ambled downstairs. Wearing nothing but *his* shirt. She froze when she saw me, gaping.

"What are you doing here?" she squeaked, wrapping her arms around herself.

I raised my toolbox. "Fixing the grill."

"Oh." She averted her eyes. "Sorry. I didn't know you were here."

"Clearly."

She blushed and tugged on the end of the shirt, which barely covered her thighs. Collin's entrance into the room amplified the tension.

"Got the eggs, babe," he said, waving the carton.

"Thanks." Scarlett's blush darkened. "Uh . . . thanks for fixing the grill, Ryker." She snagged Collin's hand and pulled him upstairs.

I clenched my jaw and turned for the door but called over my shoulder, "I'll be back in an hour. Be dressed if you're down here."

I intended to go get the part and fix it right away. Except seeing them together boiled my blood. *Look at what you could've had, you dumb fuck.* Knowing my mood was a recipe for disaster, I went home and beat the shit out of my punching bag.

Babe. It sounded so stupid coming out of his mouth. She hated pet names. She gave me shit about it so why didn't he get shit about it? I punched the bag harder. I didn't stop until I could barely breathe. Until my knuckles hurt. Until my muscles screamed. Until at least some of the razor sharp edge of seeing her with someone else faded.

I crouched, trying to catch my breath and erase the image of them from my mind. The dogs ran over, licking and nosing me.

"Go away." I pushed them off. "I'm not in the mood."

Grayson whined, and I sighed.

"You're such a fucking baby." I scratched behind his ears until a smile pulled on his goofy face. "Pit bulls are supposed to be scary. Don't you know that?"

He dropped his head and peered at me sadly. Yeah, Grayson being scary, *that* was a thing. I petted and kissed him until the dejected look disappeared. He didn't deserve me snapping. I needed to get my fucking head on straight.

I showered again before leaving. *Please let him be gone. Please let them both be gone. Please no more half-naked run-ins.* Once I returned, I rushed to the back. Scarlett's room was directly above the kitchen. If I heard anything, I'd either vomit or commit murder and one was unappealing while the other would be a headache to clean up.

Thankfully, silence awaited me. At first. When I'd almost finished swapping the heat sensor, a creak made me tense. Upstairs, a door opened. Footsteps, and a quiet mumble of an exchange followed. Seconds later, the kitchen door swung open, and Scarlett walked in. Fully dressed, thank God.

"He left. I'm sorry." She averted her gaze. "I didn't know you were here. If I did, I would've been more careful."

"It's fine." I wiped my hands on a rag as I stood. "Not like I thought you'd never fuck him if you continued dating."

"Yeah, but—" She pressed her lips together. "I guess you're right. Did you fix it?"

I scoffed as I turned on the grill to check. "What do you take me for?"

She lifted a shoulder, a teasing glint in her eyes. "An overconfident ass, mostly."

"I'm not overconfident, Scar. I'm confident in everything I have reason to be confident in." Flicking off the grill, I faced her, arms crossed. "So, *babe*, huh? Really?"

She wrinkled her nose. "Shut up."

"You don't actually like that, do you?"

"It's whatever." She picked at her cuticles. "He started saying it last night."

I worked my jaw and packed my tools. "It's a stupid pet name."

She planted her hands on her hips, a move that turned me on every time because it meant her sassy attitude was coming out to play. "How's it worse than sugar or baby?"

"You want me to remind you why I called you sugar?"

Red stained her cheeks and made the corner of my mouth quirk up. My hold on her wasn't gone. *I should probably stop flirting.* But I didn't want to. I wanted her. I *really* fucking wanted her, and I was selfish enough I didn't care if it meant stealing her from someone else. She didn't belong with anyone else.

"Baby was your doing." I closed my toolbox and hefted it onto the counter. "You said it first."

"I was making a point."

"That worked out real well, didn't it, sugar?"

"Oh my God." She covered her darkening blush with her hands. "You're the worst. Those are as bad as babe."

"If you say so. I mean, it's the name of a pig. If you don't mind being called a pig, it's not so bad. Oh, and your mom calls you babe. If you wanna think of him like that, I guess it works."

She dropped her arms to her sides, eyes narrowed into slits. "Really?"

I winked. "And now that's all you'll be able to think of whenever he says it."

"Asshole." She tapped her foot. "Why aren't you coming to the barbecue on Thursday?"

Talk about killing the fun. Gritting my teeth, I snatched my toolbox and brushed past her. "I don't socialize."

"It's basically the same people you come with to the bar every night." She followed me. "How is a barbecue different?"

"I don't like Fourth of July."

"Why not?"

"Jesus, Scarlett. Drop it. I just don't like it."

"Is it because of Collin?"

That was definitely part of it but not the whole thing. I didn't need witnesses to my inevitable freak-out once the fireworks started.

"If it is, you should know Collin won't be there," she said. "He had plans to go to the coast before we started dating and I wanted to stay with Dan."

That didn't help a lot. Without him there, I'd have an even harder time not flirting with her. Like right now.

"The world doesn't revolve around you, Scarlett. I don't want to go. That's it." I spun to face her, and she almost knocked into me. "But while we're being nosy, why is it still dating?"

Her lips pulled down. "What?"

"You guys have been dating for a while." I stepped closer. "Why isn't he your boyfriend?"

She stepped back and averted her eyes. "He hasn't asked."

"Why haven't you?" Another step closer, and her floral shampoo invaded my senses. "Why haven't you asked him to be your boyfriend? I thought you wanted a relationship."

Each step I took, she took one back until she bumped into the wall. She inhaled sharply when I braced my palms on either side of her head. Fuck, I *wanted* her. We had something. Something that couldn't be broken. The desperate idiot inside me took the wheel because I had an effect on her and couldn't let it go.

It's not all gone.

"It hasn't been that long." Her blush spread down to her rapidly falling and rising chest. "What are you doing?"

"Curious." I dipped my head, and her warm breath fanned over my lips, the heat between us crackling hotter by the second. "If it's not exclusive, doesn't that mean you're allowed to be with other people?"

"Ryker." She pushed me back. "I'm not that girl."

"I didn't mean me," I lied. "How would you feel if he were out with another girl? Have you made those rules with him? For all you know, he's out with someone else right now."

"Stop trying to sabotage this." She swatted my arm. "That's not what you meant."

"It is. Although, I'm wondering why you assumed I meant me. You want me, sugar?" I cocked my head. "Seems like you do." I rested my hand over her chest, where her heart thrummed against my palm. "Look how hard you're breathing. Am I making you nervous, Scarlett?"

"God, Ryker." She shoved me back. "I don't appreciate you doing this. Just because *Nat* doesn't mind being unfaithful, doesn't mean I'm okay with it."

I groaned and leaned one shoulder against the wall. "You're not going to let that go, are you?"

"It's not you." She curled her arms around herself. "I don't see you as that guy."

"Why not?"

"Because you're a good guy and sleeping with someone who's taken is sleazy."

"I'm not a good guy, Scarlett. Far from it."

"Bullshit." She pursed her lips. "I know you. You're an asshole but you're also a good guy. So, why are you sleeping with a married woman?"

It's always going to come back to this. She couldn't get past it, and I didn't know what to say.

"You don't know me, Scar." I forced myself to grab my toolbox and move toward the exit. "Don't pretend you do. Us fucking for a couple months," *sixty-seven days,* "doesn't mean you know shit."

"Why are you being so defensive? I'm trying to understand."

"No, you're not. You're not trying to understand. Just like that night. You jump to conclusions. Don't tell me you think I'm a good guy when you got pissed at me before you gave me a chance to explain."

"Here's your chance." She stopped in front of me, blocking my path. "Tell me the truth. Tell me what happened."

"It doesn't fucking matter anymore, does it?" My laugh held no humor. She had someone better and the fact she was pushing me when I couldn't have her pissed me off. "You have pretty boy Collin now, who brings you flowers and does everything a perfect boyfriend should, right?"

"Stop being such an asshole," she hissed. "Why do you always do this? Why can't you talk to me?"

"You're not mine to talk to, Scarlett," I growled, clenching my fists.

"Whose fault is that? You didn't want me!"

"Yes, I did!" I snapped. "You don't know what happened that night. You never let me tell you. You want to know why I left with Nat? Her husband slapped her around, and she needed a friend. *Nothing* happened. I wasn't at the bar for her. I was at the bar for *you*. Waiting for you to come home to talk to you and tell you I—" I sucked in a breath and shook my head. I couldn't do this with her. I'd keep hurting her. We'd continue this awful fucking cycle of fighting. "Stop fucking saying I don't want you, Scarlett. I'm sick of hearing it. Like anyone in their right mind wouldn't want you." I squeezed past her. "Being friends isn't an option. We can be cordial, but I can't do anything else. Leave it alone."

That finally shut her up. Never in my life had I needed someone so badly. Needed, and couldn't have. I bolted outside and cursed myself for losing my cool. Only she burrowed under my skin like that.

My fucking kryptonite.

CHAPTER TWENTY-EIGHT

Fourth of July

SCARLETT

I thought I was doing well. I thought my attraction to Ryker had faded. Until he backed me against that wall, close enough to kiss, to touch . . .

I wanted him as badly as before.

But of course, we fought. A small, fucked-up part of me liked fighting with him. It made me feel alive. It made us passionate. It made me believe we could get through anything because we weren't afraid to be our worst selves.

This fight was different. At first, I was pissed at him for losing it like that, for closing off and getting angry instead of talking to me, but another emotion lurked beneath the armor of anger.

I'd hurt him. I'd hurt him and hadn't considered the ways my actions affected him. He had such a stoic exterior. So rough around the edges. I sometimes forgot he had soft spots.

I shouldn't. He'd shown me more than once. Our first night together. When I was on my period. When he went with me to sell my speaker. When Dan fell. When I freaked out again. When he encouraged me to get help. More than anyone, I should know he had soft spots. *I guess I didn't think he had one for me.*

He told me he had no feelings, yet that fight wasn't all anger. He was hurt that I'd assumed the worst and didn't let him explain. For that, remorse plagued my every waking thought.

I wanted to chase after him but my heart split. I was with Collin. Not officially, but I liked Collin. Had the timing been different, he would've been perfect for me.

Now I was confused. Although Ryker and I could barely have a conversation without fighting, he invigorated me. Challenged me. *Knew* me. Would the same thing happen with Collin if I let it? Maybe I'd feel as much for Collin as I did with Ryker if I gave it time.

I don't believe that.

Ryker was different, and I didn't want to string Collin around. He deserved better.

Fourth of July, I plastered on a fake smile and helped Dan get the grill ready, along with the refreshments spread—chips and dips, beer, veggie and fruit platters, a huge bowl of Dan's famous macaroni and cheese, and corn on the cob. The regulars showed up with some of Dan's other friends. All people I was comfortable around. People I could laugh with.

Laughing was the last thing I felt like doing. My mind kept returning to Ryker. Was it because of me he didn't come, or did he really hate the holiday?

Music boomed over the fireworks exploding in the distance. A few guys struggled with the sound thanks to PTSD, but the loud music and company kept them grounded. I sat alone on the porch steps, watching them play horseshoes, throw tomahawks, eat, and laugh. Normally, I'd love this, but guilt ate at my stomach. For jumping to conclusions. For thinking about another man when a perfectly good one wanted me.

Dammit. No matter what I felt about Ryker, no matter how confusing, I owed him an apology. I'd been unfair. He was being a dick too and I wouldn't let him get away with that. We had a habit of setting each other off instead of talking through things rationally. Neither of us seemed to be good at calm but one of us *had* to be the adult. I hated that he said we couldn't be friends. I didn't want to lose him all the way.

Packing a plate of food might not have been a fully conscious decision, but I did it. With Dan distracted by his friends, it was easy to sneak out. Not until my truck engine rumbled to life did I realize I'd never driven to Ryker's house before. *I think I know the way.*

Nervous butterflies kept my stomach unsteady, and my heart beat out of rhythm. By the time I found his dark road, my palms were sweaty. My leg wouldn't stop bouncing. The brief relief of finding the right street offered only a second of reprieve from my vibrating nerves.

I parked outside the garage and the dogs barking curved a bittersweet smile on my lips. *I miss them too.* I knocked on the garage door and Grayson's whine flipped my smile to a frown. Why was he whining? Was Ryker not home?

"Demon, open the door."

A trick Ryker had taught him in case he ever forgot his keys. I'd seen him do it once when he left his garage opener at my apartment. Demon ran up and jumped on the wall, pushing the button with his paw. I wasn't sure if he'd do it for me, but the door rumbled and lifted. The dogs yelped and whined, circling me.

I knelt down and petted them both. "What's wrong, sweeties?"

Maybe it's the fireworks. I was surprised Ryker would leave them here alone if they had issues with fireworks. Grayson gave an especially loud whine and sprinted to the door leading to the house.

Tilting my head, I approached and tried to calm him with scratches, but another firework boomed, and a whimper startled me. Not from the dogs. One from the other side of the door.

Oh no. Ryker was a veteran. He hated Fourth of July. *How dumb are you, Scarlett? There's literally a whole group of people who struggle like him at Dan's house!*

I yanked open the door and concern rippled through my chest. Ryker sat on the floor, head between his legs, body shaking.

I knelt beside him, my pulse thrumming. "Ryker."

The dogs rushed to his side and licked him in between concerned whines. I set my hand on his shoulder, and he flinched. His head snapped up, eyes red and expression twisted between agony and confusion. "What the fuck are you doing here?"

"Bringing you food. Hey." I squeezed his trembling shoulder. "It's okay. You're okay."

"I don't need your fucking pi—"

Bang. Another firework exploded and he jolted, hugged his knees to his chest, and rocked. "Dammit!" He punched his leg, and I swallowed.

"Ryker." I walked my fingers up to his neck and caressed his out-of-control pulse. "Don't shut me out. It's going to be okay." I pulled my earbuds from my pockets and tried to turn his face toward me. "Come here."

"Get out of here, Scarlett. It's not your problem."

Yeah, and it wasn't your problem when I freaked out in bed. "I'm not going anywhere." I brushed his hair back. "Let me help, Ryker."

Vulnerability danced in his usually stoic eyes. His hands quivered. His chest rose and fell too fast. Every small noise made him twitch.

I held up the earbuds. "I can help."

"I can't use those," he snapped, dropping his head between his knees. "It freaks me out."

Another explosion, and he sucked in a breath, cursed, then slammed his fist against the ground. His knuckles split. Demon whined as he licked at the wound. *I can't leave him like this.*

I stood and offered my hands. "Ryker, come here."

He shook his head. "I can't."

"Yes, you can, baby. Come here." I unfolded his arms and placed his hands on my shoulders. "You can do this. You're not powerless. Come on."

His Adam's apple bobbed. He didn't move, but I did.

I held his hands to my shoulders and began to stand. I petted his wrists and pretended I didn't notice the tear escape the corner of his eye. "You're safe with me."

Unsteady, he rose to his feet, and I locked my arms around him. He almost returned the embrace, but another firework went off. Ripping away from me, he smashed his fist into the wall, opening more cuts on his already bloody knuckles.

"Scarlett, *leave*. My brain isn't in a good place. I might hurt you." His voice cracked and he dropped his head into his hands, fingers digging into his scalp. "Just fucking leave."

"You wouldn't hurt me." I pried his hands from his hair. "I'm not leaving."

I wrapped an arm around his waist. He resisted at first but let me pull him out to my truck. I settled him in the passenger side and opened the tailgate. "Come on, sweeties." I patted the bed of my truck. "We're not leaving you alone with all this noise."

They barked and sprinted over. Once both jumped in, I closed the tailgate and shut the garage door. Another firework detonated as I climbed into the driver's seat, and Ryker released a shuddering, heartbreaking sound.

"Ryker." I gripped his bicep. "Come here, baby." I tugged him until he laid his head in my lap. "It's okay. I've got you."

Ryker turned his face toward my stomach and snaked his arms around my waist. I started the car and combed my fingers through his hair. I didn't know where to go. There were too many events and parties. I needed to get him away from it *all*, so I got on the highway and drove out of the city.

More fireworks went off and his trembling arms tightened around me. I turned on the radio and found a station to drown out the sounds. Hoping to keep him fully distracted, I sang along with the music.

Ryker's shaking slowly subsided. Whether it was the music, the growing distance between us and the big parties, or my fingers in his hair didn't matter. All that mattered was it helped.

Time ceased to exist as I drove until everything around us quieted and no colorful fireworks illuminated the sky. Exiting the highway, I found a dirt road that didn't seem to lead anywhere. Darkness and silence greeted us as dust danced in my headlights. I stopped the truck and killed the engine, my heart thudding as I waited for the crack of a firework.

Please let this be far enough from everything. I waited five minutes. Ten. Fifteen. *Nothing.* If we were going to hear explosions, we would've by now.

Ryker's arms constricted around me, his eyes squeezed shut. "I can't breathe in here."

"Let's get you some fresh air." I opened my door and guided him out. Taking his hand, I pulled him with me into the bed of the truck. The dogs yelped as he climbed in, both jumping at him. After petting each of them, Ryker sank down, head hung between his knees. The dogs cuddled beside him, and I returned to the cab.

Dan wanted me prepared for anything and insisted I keep a bag with blankets and a bunch of other stuff for emergencies. In that moment, I appreciated his paranoia. I dug the bag out from behind my seat and returned to the truck bed.

Ryker hadn't moved. I draped a plaid blanket over his shoulders and one over mine before sitting next to him. While he slouched forward, head down, I rubbed gentle circles against his back. *I wish I had something comforting to say.* He'd never opened up to me about this part of his life.

I almost gave up on the rubbing, but he finally took a deeper breath, the tension in his shoulders relaxing a small amount. I scooted closer, wrapped my arms around him, and rested my chin on his shoulder. "What can I do?"

In a twisted way, the question almost made me laugh. It's what he'd said to me our first night together when I freaked out. *What do you need, sugar? What can I do?*

Fuck. Definitely not over him.

"I'm tired." The tremor in his voice clamped a vice around my chest. "I haven't been sleeping. I'm so fucking *tired*, Scarlett."

My eyes stung at the raw vulnerability. Despite not wanting to, I released him to roll my blanket into a makeshift pillow. Stars twinkling above us, I scooted forward, lay back against the blanket, and beckoned him toward me. "Come here."

I expected a fight but didn't get one. He let me direct his head onto my chest. I draped the blanket over both of us and hugged him. His body slumped against mine and burly arms curled around me.

"It's okay." I kissed his head. "I've got you."

Both dogs cuddled against Ryker's side and rested their heads on his back. Silence filled the vast space around us. Evidence he was awake came from the occasional wince, then he'd squeeze me tighter.

I pushed my fingers through his hair. "Do you want to talk about it?"

"There's nothing to talk about."

I hesitated, nerves buzzing with uncertainty and concern. "Do you want to tell me why you can't sleep?"

At first, he didn't answer. He cuddled me like he never had before. Draped his leg over mine and pulled us so close, nothing could've come between us.

"Nightmares. Nightmares *every fucking night*."

"Nightmares about what?"

"Things I did. People I killed." His voice croaked. "One person in particular."

I pursed my lips so I wouldn't push. If he wanted to tell me more, he would. As much as I wanted to know, the last thing I wanted was for him to reopen a wound.

"He was only a little kid." His words came out whispered and broken, the tremble in his body returning. "I didn't mean to, Scarlett." He choked on the words. "He got caught in the crossfire. I didn't know he was in the house. When the shots came at me and my friends . . . I shot back to defend us. I didn't know they had a kid in there. Who the fuck shoots at armed soldiers with a goddamn kid in the house?"

My stomach dropped and I shut my eyes to keep the tears from escaping. "It wasn't your fault. You were defending yourself. It was an accident."

"An accident that ended a kid's life." His warm tears dripped onto my skin.

"Oh, Ryker." I twisted toward him. "I'm so sorry that happened. I'm sorry it haunts you like this."

"I deserve it," he muttered. "I didn't know you could sing."

I could've pushed it, but he didn't need that right now. If he needed to change the subject, I'd let him.

"I've been in choirs most of my life." I rested my cheek against his head. "I like singing."

"Sing again." He buried his face in my neck. "Please."

I did. Until he fell asleep. I would've sung all night for him.

Chapter Twenty-Nine

Crossing the Line

Ryker

Waking up to Scarlett's perfume for real instead of clinging to the scent she left in my sheets relaxed my muscles. Liquid warmth spilled through my exhausted nerves. *Maybe I'm asleep. Maybe I'm dreaming.* I didn't want to find out.

Mustering the courage, I opened my eyes. My face rested against her soft chest. Internally, I groaned at the comfort of her supple skin. All this time, I let her sleep in my chest when I should've been taking advantage of hers. Glancing up, I found her deep in slumber. Dark lashes fanned out over cheeks that I missed watching turn red. *All that time you had to appreciate her, and you didn't, you damn fool.*

Regret for letting her slip away twisted knots in my gut. I wanted to appreciate every part of her. Her small details, her passion, what her muse was. I wanted all of her.

Not a dream. She was here. Grayson lay beside her with his head nestled over her shoulder against her neck, also asleep. Demon's familiar presence against my back almost elicited a smile.

Almost.

Memories from the night before flooded my mind until I drowned in humiliation. I'd never let anyone see me like that. I'd never told anyone what happened overseas. Panic and shame twisted nausea to the point bile crawled up my throat.

I fucking *cried*. She'd never respect me again.

I disentangled from her, ignoring Demon's light whine as he moved so I could shimmy away. Sitting up, I scrubbed my hands over my face. A loose curl dangled across Scarlett's cheek, and I traced it while I cursed myself. I was such a fucking idiot. So *weak*. What would she think of me? I didn't want to know. Things were already bad between us, but *now*?

I lost my last chance of ever getting her back. She'd learned what a piece of shit I was. It was over.

The sun crept above the horizon, providing hope for those who deserved it. It would've been a beautiful morning, waking up in fresh air with Scarlett in my arms and the dogs lying next to us. Except I ruined it. Like I ruined us. I clenched my fist and wished I could clone myself to beat the crap out of me. I hated showing weakness around anyone, especially the person whose opinion mattered the most.

Sighing, I bent my knees and dropped my head between them, then laced my fingers over the back of my skull. Same position as last night. I should've been able to handle the stupid fucking fireworks. I expected them. *So why couldn't I fucking ground myself?* It'd been three years. When would it end?

Anger simmered in my veins. At first, anger at me. Then anger at her. She was so reckless last night. I wasn't in my right mind. Other guys had hit people who tried to comfort them. They'd *hit* people they cared about because they'd gotten stuck in a memory and reflexively swung. I could've *hurt* her. She was so fucking stubborn. This girl had no goddamn sense of self-preservation. I'd bet money her apartment was unlocked.

"Hey." Her soft, sweet voice both fueled the rage and calmed it. Calmed because her voice could soothe every bad thing that'd ever happened. Fueled because it reminded me how easily she could've gotten hurt last night because she didn't fucking listen when I told her to get away from me.

She squeezed my shoulder and once again, I bounced back and forth between extremes. Her touch relaxed and tensed me. *Always a game of extremes with her.* Dammit, why did she never prioritize her own safety? Why did she never think of herself?

She rubbed my back. I didn't deserve it. She shouldn't *be* here. She should be somewhere safe. "You okay?"

I snapped my head up, frustration narrowing my eyes. "No, I'm not fucking okay, Scarlett. What the hell were you thinking?"

Her hand retracted, her mouth open. Silence fell between us and guilt crept up my spine, but I was tired of her doing reckless shit when she wasn't stupid.

"Ryker." Her brows furrowed. "What's wrong?"

"What's wrong?" My fists clenched and cracked the dried blood from punching the wall last night. Right in front of her. I shouldn't have done that and the fact I did proved I was way too out of control for her to be vulnerable around me. I hopped out of the truck. "What's wrong is you can be so fucking dense."

Worry lines creasing her forehead, Scarlett climbed out of the truck bed. "Are you mad at me?"

I couldn't look her in the eye. Shame, frustration, and concern all converged to a dangerous point. I was angry at me. At her. She shouldn't have taken that risk last night.

Fuck, stop being unfair. I needed to calm down. Only this woman propelled me from zero to a hundred so fast.

I dropped my forehead against the passenger window, craving the coolness to counteract the hot anger. *Don't be an idiot, Ryker. Don't lose your shit on her.*

I closed my eyes. Tried to get my breathing even. One deep breath after the next. My anger with her was misplaced. She worried me all the damn time, and while I couldn't stop her from getting hurt ever again, the thought she could be hurt by *me* was too much to handle. I'd already done that, and I'd have to take a fucking gun to my head if I did it again.

Breathe. She probably doesn't realize how dangerous last night could've been. She was trying to help, like always. And like before, I was ruining it. *Don't be an asshole. You could have a real chance with her again.* Bull-fucking-shit. Not after I told her what I'd done.

Breathe. I waited until the adrenaline stopped vibrating in my blood. The fight response subsided to a reasonable worry I could ignore until I got home. Thankfully, Scarlett stood quietly. Didn't try to make me talk. I couldn't have handled her talking while I calmed down.

My eyes fluttered open and I took one last deep inhale. When I released it, the shine of sunlight reflecting off metal on the passenger seat caught my attention.

Her keys. Sitting on the passenger seat for anyone to steal. I yanked open the door and a muscle in my jaw pulsed. Unlocked. *For fuck's sake, am I the only person who gives a shit about her safety?*

"Dammit Scarlett, do you *want* to get hurt?" I waved the keys at her as she approached.

She froze, hurt flashing in her eyes. "What's going on with you? Why are you acting like this?"

"Because you're being fucking stupid." I snatched her wrist and pulled her toward the passenger seat. I needed to get out of there. The combination of emotions I normally shoved down was a bad situation—add in a woman who got under my skin like she had her own private entrance?

"Ryker, what the hell? Are you mad because of how I saw you last night? I won't tell anyone. That stays between us."

Picking her up, I plopped her in the truck. "That's not the fucking point."

I slammed the door before she said anything. The dogs whined. I ignored them and circled to the driver's side. An alarm in my brain went off. *You know when you ignore the dogs' whines, nothing good happens.* They whined to warn me I'd reached a breaking point, but I didn't have anywhere to fucking break. I had to get home. I had to get Scarlett away from me before the shrapnel from my inevitable explosion cut into her.

A mission made more complicated when I had no choice but to sit beside my greatest weakness and greatest igniter. I climbed into the truck, and she twisted toward me, lips pressed together and arms crossed.

"How about instead of freaking out, you tell me why you're so mad?"

"I don't know, Scarlett." The engine roared to life. "Maybe it's because of how fucking reckless you are."

"I'm not reckless. You can't be this mad about keys. Jesus, Ryker, we were *in* the truck with *guard dogs*." She jabbed her thumb back at the window where Demon and Grayson watched from the other side of the glass. "You think with Demon and Grayson here, someone would've approached the truck, gotten in, gotten the keys, and . . . what? Driven away with us? What could've happened?"

What could've happened? The question screamed through my mind when I'd sat beside that kid's body. I fired at adults, not a child. What could've happened to put him in the crossfire? I asked it over and over again because I needed a reason. I needed something else to blame, but I was the only one responsible. That kid shouldn't have been there. *Goddammit.*

"Anything!" I yelled and brought my fist down on the horn as I sped over a dirt road. "Fucking *anything*, Scarlett. You should always be ready for the worst-case scenario. *Always.* The second you aren't, you get fucked. And you're so fucking unprepared and trusting that you're going to get fucked over by the world a thousand times if you don't learn some fucking self-preservation."

I pulled onto a real road instead of a dirt one. Signs from the highway pointed me in the right direction, and I sped onto it, pedal to the floor. I had to get home. Tremors started in my hands. That rage within me, the world, *everything*, became too fucking loud to think clearly.

Heavy, roaring silence dominated the truck for the entire drive. I couldn't decide if that was good or bad. Bad because the tension radiating off Scarlett was palpable. Good because I wasn't in my right mind and the last thing I wanted was to push her further away.

So why do you keep doing it? I didn't know. Maybe because if I pushed her away, it didn't hurt as badly as her choosing to leave.

Not until we turned down my private road did she speak. "I'm sorry you've been through so much that you feel the need to be ready for the worst all the time. That must be exhausting." She massaged her temples. "I understand you're going through a lot, but you don't need to yell at me. Can't you talk to me?" Warm fingers curled around my arm. "I know you're probably embarrassed but you don't need to be, okay? Nothing has changed about how I see you. *Nothing.*"

It should. "I have nothing to fucking say to you. You're so reckless it's infuriating."

"I'm not reckless," she snapped. "Stop saying that."

"Stop acting like it, and I won't say it."

"Oh my God. *Why* are you mad at me? Seriously, why? It can't be because of the keys. For once, tell me what you're feeling."

"I'm feeling pissed off." My hands cramped from gripping the steering wheel so tightly. "Pissed off because you're so fucking naïve. I could've hurt you last night. How can you not see that? I could've *physically* hurt you, Scarlett. You can't fucking trust someone who's having an episode like that. You have to let it happen. You can't play savior. It isn't safe. Not with someone like me."

"You wouldn't hurt me. I trust you. I'm sorry that you don't trust you, but *I* trust you, Ryker."

I parked in front of my house and twisted toward her, rage boiling through my veins, elevating the frustration. *Trust me?* How could she trust me? This woman needed a better trust radar.

"You trusting me in a moment like that is unbelievably fucking stupid." I gritted my teeth. "I'm trained to react quickly, Scarlett. I might've reacted and hurt you. It's like you want to be hurt."

"I don't want to be hurt." She threw her arms up. "You've never given me reason to think you'd physically hurt me. You'd never be that far gone. That's not you. Maybe other guys do that, but you wouldn't. And nothing happened so why are you again focusing on what could have happened instead of what actually did?"

"Because you have to be ready for that shit! You have to be ready for the worst. Who leaves keys sitting in their unlocked car while they're unconscious? Who does that! Is your apartment locked right now? For fuck's sake, Scarlett, it's like you intentionally set yourself up to get hurt when you've already been hurt and should know better. Stop being so fucking stupid about basic safety, and I won't be so goddamn mad."

She sucked in a breath. A sound that reminded me of someone being stabbed. They didn't scream. They gasped.

You fucking idiot. How could you say that to her! I opened my mouth, but nothing came out. As if any of it was her fault. I didn't for one second believe what happened to her was her fault, but my word choice didn't convey that.

I thought I'd seen her hurt. I was wrong. This was so much worse.

I wanted her to yell. I deserved for her to yell and scream at me for uttering such horrible words. But she didn't. She stared at me like she couldn't believe what I'd said. I couldn't either. How could I say that after how good she treated me?

"Scarlett." My chest caved in and every nerve in my body pricked with deserved pain. "Baby, I'm sor—"

"Get out of my truck, Ryker." Although calm, her voice quivered.

"Scarlett . . ." I reached for her, but she jerked back. "I'm sorry, I—"

"Get. Out."

"Scar—"

"I'm *not* stupid." Her sharp, hurt tone pierced my rapidly disintegrating heart. Her voice trembled, eyes red and glistening. "Stop talking to me like this. A locked door is what kept me from escaping when Todd attacked me, you *asshole*."

Oh fuck. Oh no.

"So, forgive me if I get uneasy locking doors now. Just because I don't take care of myself the way you think I should, doesn't mean I'm stupid."

"No, I know. I know you're not. I'm so fucking sorry, I—"

"Get out."

"Scarlett, please—"

"Get out!" she screamed, tears spilling—each one a punch to the gut.

Scarlett covered her face with her hands, her shoulders quaking. I couldn't leave her like this. I *couldn't*. I barely touched her shoulder, and she shrugged it off.

"Get out," she choked, shoving my arm. "Right now."

I didn't want to, but I was the reason for her pain. She'd looked out for me last night and I fucking hurt her. I exited the truck. She didn't move until I finally coaxed the dogs out. I opened my mouth to say I was sorry, but she scooted over to the driver's side, glanced over her shoulder, backed out of my driveway with a squeal, and sped away, dust kicking up behind her wheels.

She didn't look at me. Not once. And I couldn't blame her.

I was such a fucking prick. This was what fucking up looked like.

This was crossing the line.

CHAPTER THIRTY

Buying Time

SCARLETT

I lied about being on my period, so Collin stayed away. He wasn't Ryker. Like every other guy I'd dated, he left me alone, no questions asked. I'd hardly heard from him since. Though I wasn't menstruating, I might've preferred that.

I thought I knew heartbreak when Ryker told me he didn't have feelings for me. That was *nothing*. This hurt cracked down to my soul. He took one of my most vulnerable moments and threw it in my face. Made me feel small. Made me feel stupid, like it was my fault.

Tears flowed endlessly. My chest was sore from sobbing. My throat tender. My eyes swelled shut and my head throbbed from too much crying. My lungs constricted to the point I couldn't remember how it felt to breathe without pain.

I knew Ryker had issues. He'd been through a lot, but trauma didn't excuse cruel behavior.

Days passed, and I finally stopped crying, though I wasn't in great shape. I lay on the couch, staring at a switched-off TV, and pondered what about myself I needed to fix so I'd stop being an asshole magnet.

Ryker called. About a hundred and fifty times. He called and texted nonstop since I left his house. I deleted every text and voicemail without reading or listening because *nothing* excused the way he'd treated me. He came to my apartment several nights in a row, but I'd actually locked the door. His annoying persistence backfired because I didn't acknowledge a single time he knocked.

I'd barely seen Dan, who wasn't fully mobile. Disappearing under my blankets forever wasn't an option. Dan's worry made me get myself up. Although I would've liked to couch-rot forever, I showered and dressed. Before leaving, I descended into numbness so I wouldn't cry if I ran into Ryker on my way to Dan's.

I didn't bother with makeup. Sweats and messy hair had never been a problem for the only man in my life I'd been able to depend on. I walked to his house with my arms wrapped around myself, hoping he'd accept that I was having an extra bad period and not pry. Inside, the murmur of his TV led me to where he'd been spending most of his time. He didn't have a lot else to do while healing.

"Scar." Dan sat up straighter when I entered the living room. "You okay?"

Didn't I say I was numb? So why did him asking that fill my eyes with tears?

"Oh, honey." He set his beer down and opened his arms. "What's wrong?"

I crawled onto the couch, laying my head on his lap and hiding my face as the tears returned. Again. *When will I run out?*

"What's wrong?" He rubbed soothing circles on my back. "Talk to me, honey."

"It's nothing," I cried. "I'm having the worst period. I feel like shit."

"Doesn't seem like that's all it is. Did you fight with Collin?"

"No. I'm having a bad emotion day."

One of the many good things about Dan? He pushed when he needed to and never did when I couldn't handle it. He didn't ask again. Instead, he stroked my back while I cried. Eventually, I stopped, and he told me to order us takeout and that my favorite ice cream was in the freezer. It always was because he was amazing. My life might fall apart, but I'd always have Dan.

We ordered Chinese and I rested my head against him while we waited for it to arrive. Dan draped an arm over my shoulders and let us watch TV until he came up with a solution I believed to be a guise to get me to talk.

"You need a drink?" he asked.

"God, yes." I didn't care if it was a guise. I wouldn't talk to him about Ryker. Nothing could make me that stupid.

"I'm almost out." Dan gestured to the nearly empty bottle resting on the coffee table. "Do you wanna get a bottle from the bar?"

I stretched as I stood. "Okay."

I paused at the bathroom to check my reflection in the mirror. Messy hair and puffy eyes, but it was Wednesday, so the bar wouldn't be full. *I hope Ryker's not there.* His presence during the week had always been erratic. I crept through the back and peered around the corner. Thank fuck Ryker's usual chair sat empty.

Sneaking into the supply room, I nabbed a bottle of my and Dan's favorite whiskey and escaped without anyone noticing. I shuffled out the rear door but paused when it didn't crash shut behind me. I glanced back. Ryker stood a few feet away and my spine straightened. I snapped my gaze forward and sped-walked toward Dan's house.

"Scarlett, wait."

"I don't want to talk to you," I muttered, hugging the whiskey to my aching chest.

Ryker stepped in front of me and widened the crack in my heart.

"Ryker, *fuck* off," I snapped. "I mean it. I don't want to talk to you."

"I'm sorry, Scarlett." His expression crumpled, though not nearly as badly as my soul had. "What I said was fucked up. I didn't mean it and I don't think it. I was angry and it was stupid. I'm so sorry."

"Apology not accepted." I sidestepped him, but he moved in front of me again. The devastated look in his eyes almost matched mine, but the wound bled too freely to give in.

"Scarlett, I'm so *desperately* sorry." He flattened his palms together in a plea. "What can I do? I'll do anything. Baby, it was wrong and untrue and not fair. It was a fucked-up thing to say. I don't think any of what I said. I wasn't in my right mind, and I'm sorry. I wish I could take it back. Let me make it up to you. Tell me what to do, Scarlett. I'll do *anything*."

"You can't make that up to me, Ryker," I seethed and stormed past him. "How can you possibly make that up to me?"

"I'm aware how fucking awful I was." He caught my arm and twisted me toward him. "I don't for one second think what I said was true or acceptable. It absolutely wasn't. I regretted it the instant it left my mouth." He raked his hand through his messy hair. "Everything's so much more intense with you. Not that it's your fault," he added quickly. "It's *my* fault. There's no way to justify what I said. I'm so fucking sorry. I hate myself for doing that to you."

I wrapped my arms around my waist, though it wouldn't hold me together. "Why did you say it?"

"I don't have a reason, Scarlett. I was ashamed and embarrassed and convinced myself the bigger issue that morning was you not taking precautions because it was easier to focus on. I was angry at myself but convinced myself I was angry at you. It was easier than admitting that I—" He shook his head and looked away.

"That you what?"

"That I needed you." Eyes as blue as my battered heart clumped emotion in my throat. "I don't like needing people but that night, I *needed* you. I've never let anyone close to me like that, Scar. *No one.* No one's ever seen me have an episode. No one else knows that story."

I said nothing. Both because he wasn't done, and I didn't know what to say.

"It scared the shit out of me," he whispered, meeting my gaze. "That you could calm me down and that I could say what happened out loud. It scared the shit out of me that I actually felt good when I woke up with you. It scared the shit out of me that I could've hurt you because you may trust me, Scarlett, but I don't fucking trust me. The thought I could've hurt you fucked me up so much I took it out on you." His shoulders drooped. "Then I hurt you anyway. What I said was bullshit. Not the truth. Not warranted." My heart pounded in agony at his glistening eyes. "I'm sorry, Scarlett."

I swallowed, uncertain how to respond. We were both too emotionally charged for a mature discussion, and I wasn't about to fight with him again. I couldn't handle more pain. I couldn't handle *this*.

"Okay." I blew out a puff of air. "You're sorry. Dan's expecting me."

"You're going to hate me forever, aren't you?" His vulnerable tone rattled me, though it changed nothing.

I was tired of being hurt and didn't trust him not to make it worse. "I don't know." I shifted my weight. "I need time, Ryker. That wounded me. More than you understand."

"Help me understand." He reached for my hands. "I'll do anything to get you back. I'll do anything to make this better. Scarlett, I'm such a fucking idiot sometimes, but I swear you're important to me. You have no idea how important.

I never want to be the reason you cry. Tell me what to do. I fucked up so bad, I'd do *anything* to fix this. You want me on my knees?" I sucked in a breath when he sank to his knees, begging for something I couldn't give right now. "I'll get on my knees every damn day, Scarlett. There's no limit to what I'll do to get you back."

"What does that even mean? We weren't together and you told me you didn't want to be friends. So what does having me back mean? I can't do this weird back and forth with you. I can't do this lashing out bullshit. Pick a fucking speed, Ryker. You can't tell me we're friends one second, then try to kiss me the next, then be unbelievably cruel the next."

He stood on unsteady legs. "I want to be here for you like you let me before. I want to hold you. I want you around. I was stupid for saying I didn't. Scar, I want you, all right? I want to be good to you. I want to make up for my shitty behavior. Fuck, I'll go back to therapy and work every second of the day to become someone good for you. I'll do *anything*." I resisted the shiver when he tucked my hair behind my ear. "I want to be the reason you're happy. I'll take you however I can get you, Scarlett. I'll be your friend if that's what you want, or if you want more, I'm in. The only thing I can't do is not have you in my life."

"I don't know what to say." My legs weighed heavy as I stepped back from him. I had to. One tiny show of affection shouldn't make me want to curl up in his lap and be held. Especially after what he'd said. The smallest contact made me crave his hugs—he gave damn good hugs—but I wasn't a doormat. "I . . . give me space. You ignoring my space isn't helping. I'll come to you when I'm ready."

"Will you?"

I lifted a shoulder. "Probably. Like you said, I'm stupid."

"I don't think that, Scar. I was talking shit because I was mad at myself. You're not stupid." His Adam's apple bobbed. "You're strong. I wish I were as strong as you."

"Oh, I'm strong now?"

"Yeah, you are." His gaze met mine, intense like it was when he brought out his unfiltered opinions. "You didn't let the dark shit make you paranoid about everything. You didn't let it turn you into an angry person who lashes out at the people you care about. You're bright and hopeful. It takes a lot of courage to be hopeful after seeing how dark the world is. You overcame it better than I could hope to. I wish I were more like you, Scar. You're anything but stupid. *I'm* the one who's stupid. You're incredible. The most fucking amazing person I've ever met."

A cacophony of emotions screamed different advice from every angle. I couldn't respond. I didn't know how to. We stood there and all I could do was shift my weight from one foot to the other. My resolve slipped, but I wasn't ready to give in.

"I don't want you to think I don't respect you. You've said that before." He flexed his hand. "I respect the hell out of you. Me being a piece of shit has nothing to do with you. That has everything to do with me and my insecurities, but I don't blame you for feeling like I don't respect you after the way I acted. So, as much as I really don't fucking want to do this . . ." He stepped back and sucked in a quivering breath, his tone uneven as he continued. "Take your space. And know that I'll wait for you. I mean it. I'm done fucking things up. You're too important to me. I don't care how long it takes. I'll always want to fix this and be close to you again. We're forever, Scarlett." My lips parted. "I know that in my bones."

He tore his gaze from mine, hesitated, but walked away. I took an involuntary step toward him but didn't take another. We were so toxic. I was surprised he was even capable of saying the things he said.

Part of me wanted to let him grovel and see if it eased the ache in my soul. My mind spun. He wanted to wait for me? We were forever? How could he say that when we weren't anything? Worse, why did I feel like I knew it in *my* bones?

Conflicted and hurt, I forced my legs to move toward Dan's house. If I let Ryker off the hook after how badly he wounded me, he'd always think that's how it would be. So, I let him walk away. And I walked away, pretending every step didn't tear another piece of my heart open.

I drank so I wouldn't dwell on Ryker's words. I didn't know what to make of any of it and I was too exhausted to try. Instead, I drank with Dan and watched *Thelma & Louise* reruns.

Dan hadn't been drinking much because of his medication. He only got cleared to drink a few days ago. The break chipped at his alcohol tolerance and around one in the morning, his snores overpowered the TV's volume.

I never outdrink him. I sniggered for all the shit I'd give him tomorrow. Standing, I swayed and blinked. Not drunk, but definitely tipsy. I gathered the food we hadn't eaten and put it away, but kept the whiskey to take back to my apartment.

I draped a flannel blanket off the couch over Dan before kissing his cheek. Once I turned off the TV, I tiptoed out.

Since it was a weekday, the bar didn't stay open as late, and we never got much business after midnight. I unlocked the back door and relocked it behind me. Darkness enveloped my creaky trudge upstairs. When I made it inside my apartment, I fell back against the door to shut it. *What a night.* Massaging my temples, I pushed off the door and dropped my keys on the table.

The lock drew me back. Sighing, I twisted it and slumped my forehead against the cool surface. Half of me wanted to replay the way Ryker sank to his knees for me. The apology. The sincerity in his eyes and desperation in his voice. The hurt part of me shied away from it to nurse the still fresh wound.

My throat burned as I took a big swig of whiskey and wandered toward my desk. My art supplies lay untouched the last several days. I needed to do some work for my upcoming display. The only thing I could show René right now were charcoals of Ryker.

I'd drawn him many times. In the first couple weeks we hooked up, I'd snuck out of bed and drawn him while he slept. I became so familiar with him, his expressions, his posture. His body claimed a permanent residence in my mind.

Those drawings got tucked away in hiding once Collin and I started dating.

Collin. I could draw him. Except I couldn't. I had to end it. The way I was with Ryker while dating Collin wasn't okay. Besides, I wasn't in a place to be with anyone. That meant I'd have to call him and set up a breakup date. I hated breakup dates, but he'd been good to me. I owed him at least that.

A weight settled over my chest as I took another sip of whiskey. I glanced out the window, where maybe another person's life was less of a mess. Someone out there had their life together, and I pretended that meant one day I would too. Maybe I'd even see one of them walk by. Maybe—

My brows pulled together, and I focused on a figure outlined below a flickering street lamp. A person. A person who stared up at my window. I leaned over my desk, squinting.

The whiskey fell from my fingers and shattered on the ground, spilling liquid everywhere. My heart stopped. The figure stepped forward, more into the light. Fear seized my body into a rigid state.

Todd.

No. He started walking, and I fumbled for my phone. I had a restraining order against him. He wasn't allowed to be this close. I quickly dialed the police.

"Nine one one, what's your emergency?" a woman answered.

"There—there's a man outside my apartment." I peered out the window, watching him draw closer to the bar, every step an acceleration to my heart rate. "Someone I have a restraining order against. He's walking closer to the building."

She asked me questions. I tried to stay calm while I gave her details. She pulled up the file from when he put me in the hospital. Promised she'd send a car. Offered to stay on the phone but it freaked me out more to think I'd be distracted if he made it inside.

He can't get in. The doors downstairs were locked. My door was locked. I was panicking for no reason. *No way he'll break in.*

Logically, I was safe. He couldn't get into the bar *and* my apartment. *Unless he could.*

My wooden kitchen chair scraped along the ground as I dragged it to brace against the door. I made sure it was snug, then backed away, white-knuckling my phone. Fright spilled through my body like a paralyzing poison. It crawled over every inch of my skin, freezing one muscle after another until I couldn't move.

No matter how hard I breathed, I couldn't take in the air I needed. I'd tried so hard not to let fear consume me after what happened. I'd tried not to be paranoid about everything. I didn't want to give him that power. And yet, there I stood, consumed, my legs barely holding me up.

He can't get in. He can't get in. He can't get in.

Glass shattered downstairs, and my blood turned to ice.

Okay, maybe he can. Hands shaking, I dialed the first number I thought of.

"Scarlett," Ryker answered. "I'm glad you called. I—"

"Todd's in the bar." My voice croaked as hot tears streamed down my face.

Ryker's tone dropped to a growl. "What?"

"He broke in. He broke in and—" The stairs creaked. "Oh, God. Ryker, he's coming upstairs!"

"Baby, breathe for me, okay? Did you lock the door?"

"Yes." I nodded. I didn't know why. He couldn't see me. "I braced it too."

"That's good, baby. You're doing good." His even tone almost tricked me into being less scared. How could he be calm right now? "Take a deep breath and grab two more chairs. You need to barricade yourself in your bathroom, okay? Brace your bedroom and bathroom doors. You can do this, Scarlett."

I nodded again. Why was I nodding? I lunged for a chair, and the creaking on the stairs stopped. *Knock. Knock. Knock.* An involuntary whimper escaped me.

"It's okay, baby. I'm going to be right there." Ryker's voice reminded me I was supposed to be moving, not freezing. "Get those doors braced. Take a knife from the kitchen. Worse comes to worse, you defend yourself."

Oh God. I couldn't process. Couldn't understand through the racing thoughts tying my mind into complicated knots. "That's so many things."

Another knock. Todd's angry voice oozed through the door. "Scarlett, open up."

"Baby, listen. You gotta breathe." Ryker's tone was so much nicer. Calmer. Softer. "We gotta buy some time, okay? The more obstacles you give him, the more time it gives me to get there. You can do it, baby. You're so damn strong."

I nodded because apparently it didn't matter he couldn't see me, I couldn't think straight. I took as deep a breath as I could manage and followed it up with several more.

"Good girl." Ryker's reassurance made the next breath easier. "Now, get a knife from the kitchen."

I almost tripped over my own feet as I scrambled for a knife, cursing myself for refusing to let Dan give me a gun to keep in the apartment. They made me so uncomfortable, but right now, I wished I could shoot Todd through the door.

"Scarlett!" Todd beat on the door so hard I jumped and dropped my phone.

When I picked it up, Ryker's panicked voice awaited. "Scarlett! Baby, are you okay? Talk to me."

"I'm fine. I dropped my phone."

"*Fuck*," he spat. "Okay, Scar, grab two chairs and go to your bedroom."

"Okay. Hold on."

I tucked my phone into my back pocket and dragged two chairs into the bedroom. I braced one against the locked door. Once I'd done the same thing in the bathroom, I gripped the knife and backed away.

Heart thundering, I retrieved my phone and pressed it to my ear. "O-okay. I did it."

"Good. I'm almost there, baby. Keep breathing. It's going to be okay."

My voice quivered and more tears spilled down my cheeks. "I called the police."

"That's good, Scarlett. I'm so proud of you." I choked on a sob. "I know, baby. I know you're scared, but it's going to be okay. You're so strong, and you did everything right." His voice was so soothing. How the fuck was he pulling that off in a situation like this? "Breathe, baby. I'm almost there."

A loud *thud* and *slam* startled me. I almost dropped my phone but clutched it tighter and pressed myself against the wall farthest from the door. "He's trying to get in."

"He's not getting to you before I do, Scarlett. No way." His confidence eased a fraction of my fears. "He can't. It's too much shit for one person to get through that fast. I'm so close, baby. Hang on."

I stared at the door and fought the awful memories trying to resurface. "I'm scared."

"I'm pulling into the parking lot right now. I've got you. He won't lay a finger on you ever again, all right? I won't fucking let him. I—"

A loud *crash* and crackling wood paralyzed my body. Todd's shouts grew louder.

Closer.

He was in the apartment, banging on my bedroom door.

CHAPTER THIRTY-ONE

Anything for Her

RYKER

Two bullets.

That was all it took to eradicate Scarlett's living nightmare. Two bullets I should've fired months ago. The first day I learned what he'd done, I should've gone after him. I should've known he'd come back for her after those damn letters.

Should've. Should've. Should've.

So many aspects of my life with Scarlett were full of *should haves*, and I was tired of it.

That fucker got into her apartment but never made it into her bedroom. Sirens wailed in the distance as I crept up the bar stairs. He didn't see me coming. Didn't hear the creak of the old floorboards over his yelling and pounding on my woman's door.

Technically, I didn't have to shoot to kill.

He died as pathetically as he deserved to. Crawling and begging after a shot to the kneecap. I told the officers he fired first, something easily believed given his criminal record and the fact I staged a few shots with his gun before they arrived. I told them I shot his kneecap first in the hopes it'd get him to back down. Definitely not because it was one of the most painful places to be shot, and I wanted him to *hurt.* I told them it didn't work. I had to shoot him a second time.

The moment one of Scarlett's biggest sources of pain left this world, I called her to take the brace down. My chest caved in when the door opened, and she stood there with tear-stained cheeks. I wanted nothing more than to crush her in an embrace and carry her home. Hold her until she fell asleep. Make her breakfast. Wrap her in fucking Bubble Wrap. Anything to make her feel safe.

I could've lost her. Really lost her in every fucking sense of the word.

I'd lived through plenty of horrors overseas, but fear had never seized my heart the way it did when I considered the possibility I might lose Scarlett forever. Of fucking course the weekend Todd decided to make a move was the weekend my friend keeping an eye on him went camping.

I could've wept when Scarlett threw her arms around me. I'd stayed calm for her, but the truth was, I almost crashed my truck when she told me he was here. My truck, because the forces of the universe stopped hating me for one day. I never had my truck, but a buddy needed help moving. Having the truck let me stay on the phone with her the entire time, and now she was here. In my arms. *Safe.*

"You're okay." I curled my arms around her and breathed in her familiar shampoo to calm myself. "You're safe."

The cops' arrival was an ordeal thanks to all the gunshots, and I had to admit I did, in fact, kill someone. We both had to provide statements and while I should've prepped Scarlett, I didn't need to. She made our stories work together to paint me in an innocent light. I'd have to go through some legal shit, but it wasn't my first time killing in self-defense. It'd happened when tracking bounties. I had a record for only using deadly force when absolutely necessary, and that helped my case.

The police wanted to talk to Scarlett alone, but I kept them at bay until she had a better hold over herself. I would've stayed with her, but they made us give statements separately at the station, so all I could do was stand outside and wait. Considering she lived through a fucking nightmare, she handled it well. Another testament to her resilience and strength.

Of course, the police weren't the only ones with questions. Dan scrambled over and half crawled upstairs with a gun when the shots went off. Once he settled down, he accompanied us to the station, and a couple hours later, we returned. Danny and Scarlett reassured each other for over an hour while they sat in the bar with shattered windows.

I called some of my boys to board up what the asshole broke. Scarlett convinced Dan to go back to his house, only with the promise I'd walk her over there when she was ready. Hours passed before the police left and forensics allowed me to run in to find Scarlett a few clothes and toiletries before they taped the apartment off and warned us to stay out until we were given the okay.

The first hints of daylight gave the horizon a light blue glow by the time we left the bar and walked to Danny's. We made it two steps into his place before Scarlett buried her face in her hands and sobbed. I caught her when she started to slide to her knees and carried her to the couch. There, I held her in my lap until the crying turned to sniffling, the sniffling to silence as the sun rose. If not for her iron grip on my shirt, I might've thought she'd fallen asleep.

I stroked her spine and rested my cheek against her head. "You wanna talk about any of it?"

I was familiar with the conflicting feelings about death. Not for Todd. I should've taken him out a long time ago. Regardless, complicated emotions dominated the death of a bad person whom the world was better off without. Sometimes a sense of relief that in some ways made a person feel guilty, even if they had nothing to feel guilty about. I'd be damned if Scarlett sank into anything like that.

"I did everything I was supposed to." She shuddered, fists twisting in my tear-soaked shirt. "I moved away. I told them he was still bothering me. I told them every time he contacted me." Her voice cracked, and I tightened my arms around her. "I wish I knew what I should've done different."

"You didn't do anything wrong, Scarlett." I kissed her head. "You didn't do *anything* wrong. He was a fucking psycho. You never know what people like that will do."

"I don't understand." She curled into me and snuggled me. "I didn't encourage him to keep talking to me. He had a *gun*. What was he going to do?"

"I don't know. But baby, it's not your fault." I tried to tip her face toward me, but she stayed tucked into my chest. "Scarlett."

"Don't," she whispered. "I can't look at anyone right now. I'm so . . ." She sucked in a breath and muttered something too quiet to hear.

"So what, Scarlett?" I frowned. "Don't tell me you're stupid or embarrassed. This wasn't your fault. You know that, don't you?"

Her silence might as well have been a thousand knives slicing through my chest. I was part of the problem. She might've found a way to blame herself anyway, but I made it worse with the stupid shit I'd said.

"Scarlett." I tucked her head under my chin. "I'm sorry for what I said to you, but it wasn't anything except displaced anger. It was bullshit. So far from the truth. You didn't do anything wrong. You're not stupid. You're not reckless." I stroked her hair. "You're perfect. This is all on him. *None* of it is your fault."

Silence again. That was okay. If she needed me to sit here in silence, I would, for however long. She could ask me to hold her for an eternity, and I would. I never wanted her hurt again. Never wanted her in danger. Whether she kept me as a friend or more, I'd spend the rest of my life watching her back, even if I had to do so while someone else made her happy.

"I'm tired." Her hoarse voice was so far from the sweetness I'd grown used to.

I adjusted my hold on her before standing and turning for the stairs. As I did, the front door caught my attention, and I thought back to the damage at her apartment. Splintered, broken doorframe. Lock ripped out. I'd set her up with a much stronger lock and door after forensics released the apartment.

Not wanting her to wake with a headache on top of everything else, once I laid her down in the spare bedroom, I hurried to the kitchen and filled a glass with water. All that crying was going to turn my girl into a raisin. Maybe she couldn't take care of herself right now, but I could.

I returned with the water and knelt beside the bed. She sat up and drank the whole thing in one go. *Yep.* Thought she might need that. I took the empty glass and stood. "More?"

"No." She curled up. "I want to sleep."

"I can stay. I'll sleep on the couch."

I didn't want her to send me away but if she did, I'd respect her wishes. I'd camp out in front of the house to ensure no one came near it, but I'd give her whatever space she needed.

Considering how we parted ways before this disaster, I wasn't sure what to expect. She shook her head, and my stomach dropped. *It's what she wants. You can at least give her that after everything you and that asshole put her through.* I'd sleep outside.

"Can you stay with me?" She patted the bed, eyes glistening with fresh tears. "I don't—" She gasped and clutched her chest. "I don't want to be alone. We can lock the door, so Dan doesn't come in."

The relief almost stole my consciousness. I locked the door, crawled onto the bed, and gathered her in my arms before more of her tears fell. "Of course I can."

We sank into the mattress, and she wrapped all her limbs around me. I tucked a blanket snug around her and cradled her as close as possible. Her chest vibrated with the agony of her cries, and my chest rattled in response. She didn't deserve this.

"It's all right," I murmured, kissing her head. "You're safe. No one's gonna come near you. I'm not going anywhere."

It took a while for her to relax into sleep. She tossed and turned the entire time. Woke up with dark circles under her swollen eyes and missed calls from her mother.

Of course, Danny told Diana. I understood he had to. But a distraught Scarlett had to call her back and sit there in the bar, exhausted and reliving the entire night. All while Danny fussed and hovered. I couldn't blame any of them, but she was so fucking drained. She needed a minute to breathe. She was keeping it together because she was herself, but it was too much to put on someone.

Then, because it couldn't possibly get worse, fucking Collin showed up.

He asked a thousand questions, and I wanted to punch him even more than I had that day he came downstairs in his underwear. Scarlett told him she couldn't talk about it anymore and he backed off, but the police returned.

How many times do they plan to make her relive this traumatic experience before she gets some fucking rest to process it?

"For fuck's sake," I muttered, walking over to Scarlett. "You don't have to do this now. They'll understand. We'll tell them you need a day."

"It's fine."

Fine. It wasn't fucking fine.

We returned to the police station with an even bigger group, thanks to Collin's presence. Scarlett sat there with a blank stare until they called her back. Her shoulders slumped hours later when she exited the interrogation room. That usual fire in her eyes was reduced to a barely there ember.

"Ryker Harding?" one of the officers said, looking up from a paper.

"Yeah?"

"Can we talk to you again about what happened last night?"

If she could do it, I could do it. "Sure."

I was taken back, and I retold the story for what seemed like the fifth time. Kept the details the same, both at the police station and at the bar when they finally let us go. Danny was so relieved I'd shown up for Scarlett, he hadn't asked why I was the one she called, but he did eye me skeptically when I explained the shot that killed Todd was self-defense.

On the other hand, Collin gaped when he heard me explain that Scarlett called me because I'd been with her and seen her at the bar, which meant I was close.

I was sure he'd ask her about it, and while I understood, I also wanted to tell him to fuck off. She didn't owe anyone explanations right now. It was out of hand already. I snapped when Tammy and the new guy showed up and wanted to know what happened.

Enough is enough. Scarlett murmured she needed the bathroom, and I waited until the door closed before I confronted the room. It was my boys, Tammy, the new guy, Danny, and Collin. Scarlett was probably suffocating under the amount of people.

"All right." I crossed my arms. "When she gets back, we need to send her to bed and not ask any more questions. This is too much. She's barely slept. Stop bombarding her and let her have a moment."

"You're right." Danny's chin wobbled. "I need to get some things from the store. Things that help her relax."

"I'll run to the store for you, but for fuck's sake, *no* more questions. She needs to breathe."

My gaze pointedly landed on Collin. He didn't say anything, but I could tell he wasn't happy with me calling the shots. Too fucking bad. It wasn't about me or him. It was about her.

Scarlett shuffled toward us and Danny smiled lightly, though no one believed that smile.

"Hey, honey. How about we go back to the house, and you get some rest?"

"I am tired." She yawned.

Danny rolled his wheelchair toward her. "Let's go."

Her gaze drifted to Collin. "I'll call you later, okay?"

"Take your time. Whenever you're rested and feeling up to it." Collin squeezed her arm. "Let me know if you need anything, and I'll be here."

She thanked the guys for their help, then walked out with Danny. I almost wondered if Collin would say something to me, but he didn't. He left the moment she was out of the building.

"You should probably sleep too," Francis said.

"Not yet. I have things to do first."

I'd asked Danny for years to set up an alarm system. Now he couldn't argue. Not with Scarlett living here. When I dropped off what he wanted from the store, I told him I was installing one. He agreed without argument.

After calling around, I found a place to fix the window that day. Next, I went to the hardware store and inspected about a hundred locks and doors before I was satisfied. The door was bigger, so I'd have to adjust her frame size, but it wouldn't be that difficult.

I called buddies who did cabling to set up the security cameras and the alarm system. They all owed me favors and rushed to get it done before sunset.

I couldn't work on her door until forensics took the tape down, so I left the supplies in the hall. The new locks were stronger and the door itself more solid. Since I had to get a wider frame anyway, I made sure it was sturdier with long screws to hold it in.

Without being able to actually install the door, I ran out of excuses to linger. I packed up to go home since I was a fucking zombie by then, but my phone rang. Danny's name flashed across the screen, and I answered.

"Everything okay?"

"Yeah. She slept. We're ordering dinner. She's a little jumpy. I thought maybe if you stayed here, it might help. You know, a guy in a wheelchair isn't very intimidating." He laughed, one laced in something he didn't have to explain because I understood. It frustrated the hell out of him he couldn't do more. "I need her to feel safe, Ryker."

"I'll stay. I'm at the bar, so I'll be right there."

"We'll order dinner for you. Thanks, Ryker. For everything."

"Anything for you, Danny."

Anything for her.

It took me less than five minutes to get to his place and find them on the couch. Scarlett sat next to Dan with her head on his shoulder, her feet up on the cushions, tucked in close so the space beside her was open. She gave me a small smile that confirmed my suspicions.

She wasn't okay. That wasn't her smile. She was trying to be strong, like always. I sat next to her, thankful she was in the middle and there was nowhere else for me to be except beside her.

Danny mouthed *thanks* over her head before resting his against it. From this angle, Danny couldn't see her feet and legs. I wanted to hold her hand but that was too visible, so I adjusted and set my hand on her calf, caressing circles with my thumb.

Expression unreadable, her gaze flicked to me. Those eyes drooped every several seconds but snapped open like she was afraid to keep them closed too long. If it weren't for Danny, I'd pull her into my chest and run my fingers through her hair until she fell asleep. Anytime I did that, she passed out within minutes. I didn't get why she found it so comforting until Fourth of July when she'd done it to me.

For now, I'd have to settle for touching her at all.

She stretched, her hand drifting down and hooking around her leg. Then, after a few minutes, her fingers reached for mine.

Our fingers laced together, and for the first time since that panicked phone call, I could breathe.

CHAPTER THIRTY-TWO

I'll Be That for You

SCARLETT

As soon as we got off the phone, Mom raced over. Not alone. Her new boyfriend drove her. Lucky for her, I was in a tumultuous emotional limbo and didn't have the energy to cyberstalk him.

Moms held magical power because when she arrived early in the morning and climbed into bed with me, her soothing voice gave me hope I'd be okay. Someday. Not anytime soon, but *someday*.

We stayed in bed most of the day while I tried to process what happened without falling apart. Individual aspects created a horrifying picture I hoped would recede into dark corners of my mind where I never had to remember the fragmented details. The dumbest things set off bursts of crying. Someone bumping into a wall. A glass clinking. A door opening.

At least I already had a therapist because I sure as fuck needed one.

Six days Mom and I stayed at Dan's place. Six days, and every day, Ryker showed up to check on us. A couple times he brought food. Offered to go grocery shopping. Offered to fix things around the house and bar. Since forensics cleared access to the apartment, he'd already repaired and cleaned it, he said. After our sixth night at Dan's, I decided to brave that space again.

Although it wasn't true, I told Mom I wanted to face my apartment alone. I didn't. I didn't want her to go because I wanted a moment with Ryker. He'd saved my life. Slayed my demon and comforted me after, and I hadn't had a spare second to properly thank him.

I ascended the steps to my apartment and there he waited, shoulder against the doorframe. He pushed off the wall as I approached and offered a key. This key unlocked a much heavier door compared to the last. Inside, the pools of blood and holes from gunshots had vanished. He showed me the different locks he'd installed. Taught me how to set the alarm and access the security cameras if I wanted.

Silence fell between us afterward. When I hazarded a glance at him, he was already staring. I hated how beautiful he was. I hated I couldn't deny I was still in love with him. What he said cut me deep and should've evaporated all feelings. It didn't. Any hopes of getting over him shattered when he killed the man who hurt me.

More than anything, I hated myself. Even if Ryker and I never became anything, I had to end things with Collin. It wasn't fair to him that I was in love with someone else.

"Thank you. For everything." I broke the silence and toed the ground. "I don't know what to say except thank you. I appreciate you. Everything you've done."

Ryker nodded and took a step toward me. One that danced the edge of too small and too big. "Do you think you'll be able to sleep here okay?"

The natural instinct to move closer to him shuffled my foot forward a step. Once again, too small and too big. "I mean, I have like fifty locks on my door now."

Another step from him. My soul begged to fall into his arms. "All the locks in the world won't make you feel safe if you're uncomfortable somewhere."

"I guess we'll see." I lifted a shoulder and took one small step. "I won't know until I try."

"You can call me." His step closer was far bigger. It shrunk most of the distance between us. "If it's not working or you don't want to be alone, I'll come for you."

"Thank you."

That usual crackle between us emitted warmth instead of a blaze. An offering of comfort and safety. I peered up at his eyes, unrelentingly on me.

Fuck it. It was just a hug. I curled my arms around his middle. He returned the embrace and rested his chin on my head.

"Thank you," I murmured against his strong chest. The chest I'd slept on after one of the worst nights of my life. The chest I'd slept on after every hard night since I'd arrived. After my first freak-out. After Dan's fall. Ryker was *always* there.

His lips pressed to the crown of my head, and my eyes stung. "Anything for you."

A shuddering breath escaped, and I let myself sink against him despite the conflicting emotions. I still loved him. Despite his assholery, I loved him. I couldn't *stop* loving him.

The problem was, I always let things go when people hurt me and ended up getting hurt worse. Except he'd shown me he could be good too. He acknowledged and owned up to his fuck-up. Was it enough to soothe the pain he'd caused? I didn't know. All I knew was that I wanted his arms around me because they were the fortress of safety I craved.

Ryker's embrace tightened after another shuddering breath. "Scarlett?"

My eyes slid shut at my name on his lips. "What?"

"I'm sorry. I'm so sorry for what I said. I don't think any of this is your fault or that you brought it on yourself." He eased back and pleading eyes found mine. "I mean it. If you give me a chance, I'll make it up to you. Let me be here for you."

He cupped my face, and my pulse stumbled out of control. His touch held a power over me I couldn't deny—an electric charge that ignited the darkest parts of me and coaxed them out.

"I know you're not okay, and this will be difficult to recover from." His thumb swept over my cheekbone. "If you're pissed at me, that's fine. Be pissed at me, but let me be here for you. Scarlett, I'd do anything for you. I know I hurt you, and I'm so fucking sorry." He swallowed. "But, baby, *nothing* matters more than you. I'd do anything to make you feel better. I'll be what you need. I can be your friend. I can be more than your friend. I can back off. Tell me what you need me to be, and I'll be that for you."

My heart ached with every fluttering beat. The genuineness in his eyes stunned me. I opened my mouth, but nothing escaped.

A knock at the door made me jolt, and Ryker adjusted his position to stand between me and the door. My heart gave another bittersweet thud against my ribs.

Although the knock startled me, I knew who it was. Backing out of our embrace, I wrangled what little energy I had left after the last several days. Everything was out of control, but unfortunately, life didn't offer breaks. There were things I had to handle, even if I didn't feel like handling them right now.

"It's Collin." I hugged myself. "I have to talk to him."

Ryker's lips pulled down, but he nodded. "Okay."

I didn't expect him to give in so easily, but he brushed the pad of his thumb over my cheek one last time, lingered for several agonizing seconds, then turned for the door. He opened it to a surprised Collin, who he muttered a quiet greeting to before slipping past.

Collin entered the apartment when Ryker's echoing footsteps faded. If the look on his face said anything, he knew what was coming. *I'd like to crawl into a hole now.* He was perfect. He was everything a good man should be, and he deserved better than the mess I was.

Maybe that's why Ryker and I fit so well. We were both messes, and we both had to heal. Maybe our messiness made us more comfortable with each other because we didn't *have* to be perfect. We could be a mess and still find beauty.

Regardless of the obvious awkwardness, Collin pulled me into a hug. Sweat formed on my palms because I thought I'd figured out what to say, but in his presence, my confidence faltered. I hated hurting people, and I had no way of doing this without hurting him.

"I gotta use the bathroom."

He nodded and I scurried away like a coward. I splashed cold water on my face and gripped the counter while I sucked in deep breaths. Never in my life had I considered it possible I'd have to end things with a man who was so good. Dumping assholes, I was a pro at. But a good man? There was absolutely nothing wrong with him. Any girl would be lucky to be with him.

You're stupid for letting him slip away. Maybe. But my heart only sang for one person, and Collin deserved more than to be someone's second choice.

Deep breaths didn't make my legs less wobbly when I exited the bathroom and found Collin in what used to be the dining room but was now my studio.

I froze as he thumbed through my depictions of Ryker. He lifted one and rotated it in the light. A candid of Ryker and Dan. Dan pouring a drink with a small smile hidden beneath his bushy beard. Ryker grinning back. A quiet moment they shared every time Ryker came into the bar, usually toward the end of the night when people had a few too many and started acting silly. It was too beautiful not to capture.

"Why did you call him?" Collin returned the piece to my desk and twisted toward me. "Why did you call him and not me?"

I wiped my damp palms against my jeans. "Ryker knew about my ex, and I ran into him on the way to my apartment. I figured he'd get here fastest."

Collin scrunched his face. "That's not why."

No. It wasn't why.

"I'm sorry." I clasped my hands together and let myself marinate in the remorse I deserved. "I thought I was ready. It's not you. You're amazing. God, Collin, I'm so sorry. You deserve so much better."

"Please don't do the *it's not you it's me* thing."

"I mean it." I twisted and untwisted my finger around a loose shirt thread. "You're amazing. If the timing had been different, if things had been different . . ."

"You love him, don't you?"

I sucked in a breath. "I'm sorry, Collin. I'm sincerely sorry."

Heavy silence weighed on my chest, and I was too tired to handle it after the nightmare this week had been. Thankfully, Collin didn't leave me drowning in it for long.

"I wish you would've said no to the date, but I did make it impossible. I like you a lot, Scarlett, but . . . I'm never going to be him, and he's what you want." He kicked at the ground. "It sucks, but I get it. What I don't get is why you're not with him."

"He doesn't want a relationship. Or, I don't know. He didn't before. I don't know exactly what he wants now." He said he could be more. The question was, what the hell did he think *more* meant? "When I told him I had feelings for him, he didn't return them."

"I wouldn't be so sure he still feels that way. A guy doesn't show up for a girl like that unless he cares. It's obvious to anyone who pays attention that he'd do anything for you."

I rubbed my arms. "I shouldn't have started anything with you. I'm so sorry."

"Maybe not, but I also came in pretty strong with a date you'd be too excited to refuse." He lifted a shoulder. "It is what it is." He pecked me on the cheek. "Take care of yourself."

"Thanks for being nice about it."

"I think you've been through enough." He waved as he backed toward the door. "I guess I'll see you in class."

The door shut after him and I buried my face in my hands. If I'd met him first, I would've fallen hard, and he would've been so good for me. But I didn't meet him first. I met my chaotic, grumpy biker, who burst into my life like a flash of lightning and left permanent marks I couldn't forget.

Marks I saw everywhere. Especially in my apartment. Everything was clean. Not even a splinter of wood remained. No evidence Todd had been here except the new security door that was likely invented to protect a vault. Ryker even replaced my bedroom door. No remnants of my nightmare, just my own space. Safer than before.

How does anyone get over someone like Ryker?

Sighing, I abandoned my apartment and trudged downstairs. I could use a drink and comfort food. Although I anticipated Ryker would be in his usual seat, my stomach flipped when I saw him. My mom sat beside the register, next to where I usually sat. Close to Ryker.

Sitting by her meant sitting by him. *How much can a girl take in one day?*

Mom pulled out the seat between her and Ryker and patted it. "Who came down a minute ago?"

Massaging my temples, I sank onto the stool beside her. "Collin."

"Oh, you should've told me!"

My shoulders slumped. "It doesn't matter anymore."

Mom's eyebrows shot up. "He ended it?"

Ryker's presence had never been more potent. I picked at my nails. "I did."

Don't look at him. My attention flicked to him briefly anyway. His expression? Unreadable. His eyes? Intense as ever. Intense, and a magnetic force I had to tear my gaze away from before I got sucked in.

Mom didn't miss a thing. Her eyes darted toward Ryker before returning to me. "I thought you said he was sweet."

"He was, but I'm not in a place to be in a relationship right now."

She quirked a doubtful brow and I cleared my throat as I racked my brain for any other topic. "Can we eat? I want all the carbs."

I didn't think she'd let it go so easily but she averted her eyes and twiddled her thumbs. Nervous. She was nervous?

I tilted my head. "What?"

Her sheepish expression raised alarms. "I wondered if you'd be willing to maybe let Mike eat with us tonight?"

Shoot me. "Oh."

"Please give him a chance." She gripped my arm, her eyes alight with hope. "I like him so much, Scar. He's good to me and he's been alone for days while I've been with you. One meal, and if you hate him, I won't bring it up again."

I inhaled and mentally scolded myself. I'd be so annoyed if she did this to me. I shouldn't do it to her. *Calm down the protectiveness, Scarlett.*

"Yeah, he can eat with us."

"Good." She squeezed my arm and stood. "Because he's outside."

I pouted. "How'd you know I'd agree?"

She shrugged. "You're a pain, but you have a big heart. You wouldn't say no to me."

Rude. "I say no to you all the time."

She didn't hear me over her excitement as she flitted toward the doors. I inhaled and reminded myself that if I could find a good guy like Collin, Mom could too. Our pasts didn't have to shape our futures.

Ryker nudged his foot against mine. "Say the word, and I'll make him disappear."

An unexpected laugh bubbled out of me, and the way it made his eyes shine caught my breath.

"I guess I should at least meet him before giving him over to you." His lips curved in a smirk I rolled my eyes at. "Be careful what you promise me, Ryker. I might hold you to it."

His eyes bore into mine. "Please do."

Afraid of what might happen if I continued sinking into those ocean eyes, I directed my attention to the man who entered the bar with my mother.

Not her usual type. Maybe that was a good sign, even if he wore khakis. Nice crisp shirt. Hair styled neatly. Big smile, and not a scowl in sight. Yeah, not her type at all. She and I had very similar types and well . . . obviously, Ryker was mine, and this guy was his polar opposite.

Mom pointed at a table. Meeting boyfriends was always awkward, but I didn't want my mom alone forever, so I returned the friendly wave he offered and slipped off my stool.

A worry line creased Ryker's forehead, and his gaze bounced between me and them. Butterflies making a mess in my stomach at his attention, I patted him on the shoulder. "I'm fine." I strode toward them.

Here goes nothing.

Chapter Thirty-Three

Fallen for Her

Ryker

The Todd incident scared Danny into taking care of himself. A double knee surgery wasn't fun for anyone, but never again did he want Scarlett in danger where he couldn't reach. She drove him to the hospital, but she had an exhibit for that art program she'd saved up for and it ended around the same time as the surgery. He insisted she go and assured her I'd give him a ride home. After lecturing me about updating her regularly and sending every last detail the doctor gave, she relented and left, and I hung around until the operation finished.

It went well. The surgeon was confident that with physical therapy, Dan would be up and walking around the bar again. I got him into his van and put the wheelchair in the back while he grumbled about the recovery time. His eyes drooped as I drove out of the parking lot. *Lingering anesthesia, probably.*

"You need anything before I take you home?"

Danny yawned. "Let's get a burger."

I took the next right turn to his favorite place. "You got it."

As usual, we picked up the food and fought over who would pay. He won by playing the *I had surgery, so what I say goes* card. Jackass.

I kept my burger in the bag, but Danny was starved from fasting before the operation. He munched on his burger while I drove to his house. The silence after he finished wasn't unusual. He and I both did well in comfortable silence.

Except this silence didn't seem comfortable, and I couldn't put my finger on why.

I cleared my throat. "You all right?"

"Why did Scarlett call you that night?"

Fuck. Not what I expected. Good thing the military taught me how to handle pressure. "I didn't ask. She called and told me what was happening, so I got there."

"But why you? Why not Collin?"

"I don't know, Danny, you'd have to ask her." I regretted the words instantly. Saying that transferred the heat to her. "I mean, like I told the cops, I saw her beforehand. Maybe she figured I was nearby. Doesn't Collin live a ways away?" I actually had no idea. I was grasping at straws.

"Yeah, he does."

Thank fuck. "I'm sure that's what it was, and she knows I'm always armed and ready for a fight. Collin doesn't seem like the fighting type."

"That's true." Danny frowned. "I guess I hadn't thought about it like that. I wish she would've called me."

"Shit, Danny, what could you have done?"

"I know." He scratched at his beard. "It irritates the hell out of me that I wouldn't have been able to help if she did call."

"Well, that changes now. That's why you got the surgery, right? For her?"

He nodded.

"Don't worry about it. It's in the past. You'll be the first on her call list now, as long as you do what you're supposed to with those knees. You'll be up and working the bar before you know it."

"It's shit to be useless, Ryker," he grumbled.

"You're not useless, Danny." I shook my head. "You're her rock. You know that. She's been staying with you, hasn't she?"

"Not the last couple nights." He huffed. "I wish she'd stop staying in that apartment. She hasn't slept since she tried being there again. She refuses to see reason. Told me she needs her own space to overcome it." He scowled. "She almost fell asleep making dinner last night. So goddamn stubborn."

Dammit. That sounded like her.

"She's gotta figure it out herself, Danny. At some point she will, or she'll be too tired to stay there. Something'll give. Be patient."

"Yeah, I guess." He pulled out his phone and tapped the screen. "She's been working with me on texting. Helps me stay in contact with her better."

I nodded and said nothing while he typed a message that'd likely go to Scarlett. I'd kept my distance the last several days. Despite the fact I didn't want to. *Despite the fact she dumped Collin.*

I wasn't sure what to do. I wanted to tell her the truth. What I said was too vague. She needed me to man the fuck up and flat out admit I wanted a relationship. I was so fucking worried about her and wanted to be there for her, but I wasn't sure it was the right time to tell her. She had so much happening and I didn't want to take advantage of her vulnerable state. I'd fucked things up with her too much to risk fucking up anything else.

I took Danny home and, per Scarlett's instructions, stayed with him until she arrived. She fussed over him, and they went back and forth bickering, but the truth was, he wasn't winning any fight with her. It made me feel a little better that even he had a hard time keeping up with Scarlett.

Although I wanted to check in with her about this not sleeping bullshit, watching her and Dan reminded me they needed family time. I let them be and drove home to take the dogs for a run and play.

After we got back, I jumped in the shower while Demon and Grayson passed out on their beds in the living room. I emerged from the bathroom to find a text on my phone.

Sugar: *I want to see you. Come over.*

She wants to see me. That was a good sign. I'd kept checking on her, but this was the first time she'd initiated. I was used to her demands. She rarely *asked* me to do anything. Bossy pain in my ass.

Me: *Be right there.*

I broke several speeding laws to get to her. On my way upstairs, I ignored the looks from my guys and Tammy. I entered the apartment, and the aroma of lavender assaulted my senses. Lavender incense. Lavender candles. Lavender oil. *Someone's trying to relax.* My heart ached. She was trying so damn hard.

"Before you lecture me." Scarlett's slurred words accompanied swaying as she rose from the couch, glass of whiskey dangling from her fingertips. "I unlocked the door when I heard your bike."

She knows what it sounds like. A smile battled with a frown as she stepped around the couch and stumbled. She caught herself on the armrest and whiskey splattered the ground, eliciting a giggle from her. "Oops."

I approached and cupped her elbow to steady her after she set down her whiskey. "How much have you had?"

"Like . . . barely any." She staggered, eyes glassy as she clasped the robe she wore shut. One step toward me, and she almost fell again.

I steadied her and clicked my tongue. "Clearly."

"Don't be all judgy," she whined. Her head dropped against my chest, where I wanted it to remain. "You drink all the time."

"I'm not judging you, Scar. I'm worried about you. Why'd you want to see me? Are you okay?"

"I wanted to see you because . . ." She circled her arms around my neck and pulled my lips down to hers. "This."

It'd been far too fucking long since I'd tasted her. So long, and yet, the memories rushed in like they'd happened yesterday. *Fuck.* I tasted alcohol on her mouth.

"Scar." I internally whimpered when I eased back and broke our kiss. "You're too drunk. Come on, you need to go to bed."

I tried to pick her up, but she dodged me and stumbled backwards toward the bedroom.

"I'll go to bed." She untied her robe, revealing bare skin underneath. "With you."

"Jesus, Scarlett." I averted my eyes and yanked her robe closed. "What are you trying to do to me?"

"I want you." She threw her arms around me and kissed me. I groaned, holding her close and backing her into the bedroom. If I got her into bed, she'd probably pass out. I almost had her there when she lifted my shirt. Soft, addictive hands glided up my chest and I nearly shuddered.

Instead, I snatched her wrists and narrowed my eyes. "Bed."

That vixen caught her delectable lip between her teeth. "You gonna spank me if I don't?"

If there was some deity, it hated me.

Sweeping my arms under her legs and back, I lifted her and carried her across the room. "Don't fucking start with me."

She pouted and my cock wept. *Too bad. Not until she's sober.*

"You don't want me anymore?"

"Of course I want you. I want you when you're fully conscious." I laid her on the mattress. "Not about to pass out."

"I wanted you before I got drunk, but I was too chicken to say anything." She fiddled with her robe strap. "Don't you want to fuck me?"

"I do, baby, but not like this."

Tears formed in her eyes, and she looked away. "You're making excuses."

"Sugar, it's not you." I crouched and turned her face toward me. "I'll stay the night and when you're sober, I'll show you how much I want you. Do you have any idea how hot this is? It's one of my fantasies to have you show up at my house wearing only a jacket. It's not easy to say no to you."

"Don't lie to me. I'm too much trouble and too damaged, I know." Her lip quivered and she stared at the ceiling. "I'm so fucking messed up. You can go. Please go."

Goddammit. My options were either make her cry or do something fucked up and I didn't like those. So I came up with a new one.

I lifted her, only to toss her to the middle of her too small bed. She squealed, and I climbed over her, sliding my hands up and down her sides and nuzzling into her neck. *Fuck,* I missed her.

She moaned and wrapped her arms around my neck, pulling me in for a kiss. She wouldn't last. As long as I kissed her and made her feel wanted until she passed out, I wouldn't make her cry. I kissed her slowly and gently, sliding my hands up and down her stomach, but never anywhere she might regret tomorrow.

As usual, she was stubborn. Didn't pass out as fast as I'd thought, but I knew her better than I knew my fucking self. She was my world.

I angled her head to the side and kissed her while I pushed my fingers through her hair. She hummed as I ran my fingers through the gentle curls. Within seconds, she mewed and slumped into the bed. Her kissing became sloppier. When her hands loosened, I broke the kiss.

"Ryker," she murmured, eyes shut.

I pressed a kiss to her forehead. "I'm right here, Scarlett."

Soft snores answered. I rolled off her, tied her robe, and covered her with a blanket. Her curls spread across her pillow, dark lashes long and tickling her flushed cheeks. *She's so goddamn beautiful.* I wanted to stay in bed with her, but I also didn't want to scare the shit out of her in the morning. So, I moved to her living room and stretched out on the couch, which was far too short for how tall I was. I'd had worse.

Scrubbing a hand over my face, I did my best to recover from the most attractive woman in the world throwing herself at me. She wanted us to have sex again, but what did that mean? That she wanted sex or more? Would it be too soon after everything that'd happened?

I wasn't sure but I was sure that I wanted her. The thought of living another second not having her as mine *tormented* me. I wanted her at my house loving on my dogs even though they liked her better than me. I pictured her lying in my lap while we watched TV. Waking up beside her. I wanted to fight with her, make up with her, hold her, kiss her, fall asleep with her.

Fuck. I should've realized sooner but I'd never been good at emotions or accepting anything good in my life. Scarlett petrified me. Only because I'd never wanted to be close to someone like this. Not until her.

But the truth was undeniable.

I'd fallen for her.

Hard.

CHAPTER THIRTY-FOUR

Like You Missed Me

SCARLETT

Throbbing headaches were my least favorite way to wake up, but I supposed I'd earned it.

I rolled over in my bed, away from the blinding light of my window. My eyes fluttered against the pounding in my head. I needed water.

Whimpering, I sat up and massaged my scalp, eyes squeezed shut. When I reached a point I could open them without them popping out from the pressure in my skull, I did.

A glass of water sat on my nightstand. A bottle of painkillers beside it. As much as I wanted to believe I'd done that for my future self, it didn't sound like me.

Then I remembered Ryker coming over. Me throwing myself at him.

I smacked my forehead. "Oh my *God.*"

Memories from the night before blurred too much for a clear image. Did he put me to bed? He must've put my robe back on me because the ties were tight around my waist.

Shit. *Way to embarrass yourself, Scarlett.* Retrieving the water and painkillers, I took both and gingerly rose to my feet, then gulped the remaining water. The aroma of eggs pulled me toward the kitchen, and I froze.

Ryker stood at my desk, rifling through drawings. Hopefully not the ones with him.

"What are you doing?"

He glanced back and shrugged, closing the sketchbook. "I missed seeing your new stuff."

"Oh." Not the answer I expected. "Um . . . what happened last night?"

A teasing smile played on his lips, and he approached me. "You tried to assault me."

I rolled my eyes. "Shut up."

"I'm serious. You kept coming on to me." He gestured to the stove, where eggs waited in a pan covered by a lid. "Made you eggs. How do you feel?"

"Thank you." I caught my lip between my teeth and moved to the sink to refill my glass. "Like shit."

"Not surprised. Were you drinking because you can't sleep here?"

I spun to face him, and my stomach flipped at the way he leaned one shoulder against the fridge, arms crossed. "Nosy much?"

"Danny's worried about you."

"Dan's always worried. What happened last night?"

"Nothing." He lifted the shoulder he wasn't leaning on. "We kissed a little. That's it."

"You put me to bed?"

"Yeah. You thought I was rejecting you because I didn't want you, which, by the way, will *never* be true." My heart skipped. "I kissed you until you passed out so I wouldn't make you cry." He rubbed the back of his neck. "I hope that was the right thing to do. I hate seeing you cry. I wasn't trying to get anywhere."

"I know you wouldn't." His expression softened, and his mouth opened, but my phone vibrated against the kitchen table. "Hold on." I held up a finger to Ryker and answered the phone. "Hey, Dan."

"Hey, honey, I made breakfast. You hungry?"

"You *what*? You're supposed to be taking it easy."

"I was careful. Do you want some or not?"

"I'll be right there." I sighed and hung up. "Sorry. It was sweet of you to make breakfast, but Dan did too, and yeah. You didn't do anything wrong. I mean—" My cheeks warmed. "I kissed you first. Sorry about that."

"I'm only sorry that you were drunk and hurting. Not that you kissed me."

Goose bumps spilled over my skin. "Did I cry?" He nodded, and I buried my face in my hands. "Shit. I'm sorry. I'm such a mess."

"Don't apologize, Scarlett." Ryker peeled my hands from my face. "It wasn't a problem. I told you I want to be here for you, and I mean it. Especially when you cry."

Mind racing, I lost myself in those blue eyes that caught my attention the very first time I saw him. I missed being close to him. I missed it like part of *myself* had been severed. He didn't let go of my hands, and his eyes never strayed from mine. He opened his mouth like he was going to say something. My phone rang again.

Breaking our eye contact, I picked it up, Dan's name once again illuminating my screen. "Hey, you okay?"

"Yeah, I'm out of orange juice. Get some from downstairs on your way over, would you?"

"Sure thing. I'll be right there." I ended the call and wrung my hands together. "I, um . . ."

"Gotta go?"

I nodded and he did as well. Neither of us moved. I couldn't think of another time we'd stared into each other's eyes so long without physical intimacy. Either I was delusional, or something in our stare had altered. It wasn't pure heat anymore, though of course that crackled in the background. There was something deeper too.

I gnawed on my lip. "What were you going to say?"

"Hmm?"

"Before Dan called this second time. You looked like you were about to say something."

"Oh." He sucked in a breath and averted his eyes. Whatever he wanted to say, he clearly lost his nerve. After opening and closing his mouth several times, he muttered under his breath.

Stepping closer, Ryker pressed a kiss to my forehead. "You're not a mess, Scarlett. Your tears aren't too much for me. None of you is too much for me." He stepped back but one of his hands lingered, his thumb brushing my cheek. "I'll, uh . . ." He cleared his throat, and his hand fell away from me. "I'll talk to you later."

The door thudded shut after him. What the hell was going on in that mind of his? He'd never been timid. Not to mention the need to know what he was about to say sparked curiosity that wouldn't be satisfied by anything but a direct answer.

On a normal day, I would've spent too long trying to decipher the great Ryker mystery. Unfortunately, my head throbbed, and my stomach turned in a way that told me I needed food and water.

I eyed the eggs on my way to eat breakfast with Dan. *Dammit.* Of course, he and Dan chose to make me breakfast on the same day. Did he think I didn't appreciate it?

It occupied my thoughts while I sat with Dan, unable to hide my hungover state. I anticipated a lecture, but his energy was directed elsewhere. He wanted me to move in with him and out of that apartment. He worried about me not sleeping. I worried too, but I wouldn't let fear control me. I wanted to conquer it, even if it took time.

After breakfast, I returned to my apartment, locked the door, and showered. The more the day wore on, the more the night before came into focus. Parts were fuzzy but I remembered. His lips against mine. His hands on me.

I asked my therapist how I could want Ryker so soon after Todd's death and she said that might be exactly why. Because he was *there*. He not only protected me but eliminated the threat. He made me feel empowered because he helped me enjoy sex again. Helped me get to therapy so I could recover. Reminded me I could be close to someone without being scared.

Maybe we could go back to how it was. For a little while.

The tender pieces of my heart argued about what a terrible idea that was, but he made me feel safe and *good*. I was desperate for that after drowning in sadness. Plus, I wanted to know what he was going to say earlier.

Before I overthought it, I got ready and drove to his house in the late afternoon. Didn't even bother to verify he was home. His schedule wasn't exactly normal. Being a bounty hunter, he made his own hours.

I'm trying anyway. I pulled in front of his place and the garage door opened as I climbed out of my truck. I grinned when the dogs rushed toward me, tails wagging and tongues lolling.

"Hi, sweeties," I cooed, hugging both and planting kisses on their heads. "I missed you."

They licked at me and nearly knocked me over trying to get close. I giggled and scratched behind their ears.

"We've been over the *sweeties* thing." Ryker stepped outside and my mouth dried. Sweat dripped down his shirtless torso, catching between the ridges of his abs and around his taut chest. He slowly uncurled wraps from his fists. "Demon's a retired military dog for fuck's sake. They're not sweeties."

I tried not to drool at the tattoos decorating his sexy body. "First of all, they are sweeties. I don't care what you say. Second of all, I wanted to say thanks. I remember parts of last night, and I appreciate you handling it like you did and staying with me. Sorry I didn't get to eat breakfast with you."

"Don't apologize. Danny's eggs were probably better anyway. And yeah, Scar. You can call me anytime. I'll be there." My breath trembled. He kept talking like he intended to always be near me. "You okay? You didn't have to come here. You could've said that over the phone."

"I wanted to talk." I clutched my long jacket around my naked body. "Can we talk?"

He inclined his head for me to follow him into the garage. I gulped at the muscles on his back, all swollen and bulging from his workout. "What do you wanna talk about?"

"I want to know what you were going to say earlier when Dan called."

Ryker hesitated in front of the door that led up to the house. He glanced at me over his shoulder. "It's nothing. I don't know why I was going to say it."

"Well, say it anyway. I want to hear it."

Ryker twisted the knob and pushed the door open, blowing out a long breath. "I'm back in therapy. Just . . . you know, you're not alone. We're both trying to fix our shit."

My mouth fell open. "Really? Why?"

He faced me now, mouth in a thin line. "I should never be so angry I lash out and say shit like what I said to you." I stopped breathing. "I know an apology can only do so much, and I'm not asking you to praise me for doing something I should've done a while ago, but I wanted you to know my apology wasn't just words. I'm doing the work too."

"Why?"

Vulnerability flashed in his eyes—quick as a lightning bolt. "I want to be a better man."

If any part of me doubted my next move, those simple words melted all hesitation. He ascended the stairs, and I blocked the dogs from following. I couldn't take my clothes off around them. It weirded me out.

We entered his house and when I closed the dogs out, he glanced back.

"You don't have to leave them down there. They miss you."

"I don't like them being in the room when we have sex."

His posture went rigid. Slow and predatory, he turned toward me. One sweep of his gaze over my body ignited the sparks that'd turn into an explosion and obliterate us both. His voice lowered to a rasp as he took a step toward me. "Are we having sex?"

I opened my jacket to reveal my nakedness underneath. "That was the idea."

I remembered what he'd said last night. His fantasy about me showing up in nothing but a jacket. He sucked in a breath, pupils overtaking his irises as he drank in my bare skin.

"You said you'd show me how much you wanted me." I shrugged off the jacket and it pooled on the floor around me. "Here's your chance. Unless you were bullshitting me."

"I wasn't bullshitting you," he growled.

Grabbing the nape of my neck, he dragged our lips together. Electricity crackled, the charge coursing through us more potent than ever. He backed me into the wall and ran his hands down to my hips, then up to my breasts.

"Scarlett," he murmured against my lips. "Let's talk about this."

"Since when do you want to talk?" I tugged at his shorts. "You've told me many times that I talk too much. Now look who's talking instead of fucking?"

His movements slowed and he pressed his forehead against mine. "I thought you wanted a relationship."

I very much did. But only with him. He was all I needed and right now, I'd take him however I could have him. I didn't want him to pull away because he thought I expected too much. I hadn't figured out what Ryker meant by *more*. More could mean anything, but I didn't care. I needed to be close to him.

"I only want you to fuck me." I reached into his shorts and stroked his cock. He groaned and dropped his head to my shoulder. "Fuck me like you missed me, Ryker."

He stared at me for so long without moving, insecurity bubbled up. It died off when he slammed his lips over mine and cupped my pussy. Two thick fingers pushed into me, and I whimpered as he thrust them in and out. My nails dug into his shoulders, my head thudded back against the wall, and I moaned for more.

Ryker obliged. He kicked off his shorts, lifted me, and buried his cock in my pussy. I almost cried when he plowed into me, pinning me to the wall with his cock inside me. Like coming home after being away too long. I clutched his shoulders, locked my legs around him, and begged him to fuck me until I was tender. I wanted to never forget how he felt.

He did as I asked. Fucked me against the wall, every thrust at the perfect angle. My nails pierced his skin as he moved harder, faster. Each thrust deliberate and calculated, like he wanted to show me he hadn't forgotten the spots that threw me into ecstasy.

I'd been so desperate for him, it didn't take long for me to reach my peak and scream his name. Ryker growled and sank into me faster while he finished. I loved his dirty talk, but we moved too quickly for it this time. Too desperate to feel each other again.

After a few minutes of catching our breaths, he carried me into the bedroom and dropped me onto the bed. I didn't recognize the expression he wore. One so buried in conflict. I set my hands on his face and frowned. "What's wrong?"

"Nothing." He stroked my jaw. "I really fucking missed you, Scarlett."

A flash of hurt I intended to ask about flickered in his eyes, but he sucked my nipple into his mouth before I could confront it, forcing a strangled moan from me instead of words.

CHAPTER THIRTY-FIVE

Mine

RYKER

No one else in the world made me both euphoric and ticked off. Every part of me rejoiced at having Scarlett again. The chemistry between us only gained power since the last time I'd touched her. We couldn't keep our hands off each other. Our recklessness almost got us caught by Danny. Twice.

I was flying high having my woman in my arms again. Except that I didn't. I'd been working on a speech to tell her I wanted a relationship and now she only wanted to fuck. I didn't see that coming.

I didn't know how to tell her, but worse, I was afraid. What if she didn't feel the same? I couldn't handle if she ended things now. I'd take being her friend over nothing.

Which was why I was ticked off. At me. Because I had the opportunity to make her mine, and instead, I sent her to a different fucking guy and almost lost her altogether.

This is karma. This is the punishment for fucking up so much.

It had to change eventually. *Didn't it?* If she had feelings before, she'd catch them again. I simply needed to be someone worth catching feelings for, and I was trying. Trying so much she teased me about it. *Why so talkative all of a sudden? Why are you always asking about my feelings?*

Because I fucking love you, dammit.

I'd never considered a future where I got frustrated because a woman chose to suck my cock instead of talking, but here we were. For now, it'd be a lie to say I didn't enjoy fucking her again. I couldn't get enough and neither could she.

As much as we didn't want to, we needed to be careful. Danny was cleared to work a couple hours a day, so he was in the bar more. Once he left, we either went upstairs or back to my place. It depended on the time. Tammy banned us from having sex during business hours because it was too loud.

Scarlett turned red when Tammy scolded us. While she was embarrassed, I wasn't. My woman liked to scream, and I liked to make her scream. I never wanted anyone to hear her scream before, but now it felt like a claim.

Tonight, I intended to make her scream a lot because her inner brat was out in full force.

She told me before I left to take the dogs for a run that she wouldn't wear the skirt I hated her wearing at the bar. Mostly because I hated how much attention it drew to her. She teased me about being jealous but promised she'd only wear the skirt for me.

A lie. A flat-out fucking lie. I returned to the bar and found her in that very skirt. Worse, her low-cut shirt barely managed to contain her marvelous tits, and she refused to change.

I tried to let it go. I really did, but then the flirting began. Flirting with customers right in front of me, along with a mischievous little smile that said, *I know I'm driving you insane.* If the bar hadn't been busy, I would've hauled her upstairs and forgone the "no fucking during business hours" rule. One guy in particular couldn't keep his damn eyes off her and I swore she gave him special attention to make it worse.

Although telling her what not to do usually blew up in my face, she was killing me by batting her eyelashes at that motherfucker. Against my better judgment, I grabbed her arm when she passed by. "At least stop with that one."

She blinked innocently. *Pain in my ass.* "What one?"

"You know which fucking one," I snapped. "Cut it out. Why are you flirting with him so much?"

She stuck her tongue out and twisted out of my hold. "Maybe I'm keeping my options open."

"Fucking asking for it, Scar," I growled.

She returned to work without sparing me a second glance. It took all my willpower to stay in my seat and not scare the guy off. Watching her flirt with other guys put me on edge. Sometimes, I wondered if she did it on purpose to punish me for not making her mine when I could have.

I startled when someone plopped onto the seat beside mine. Then I internally groaned. Hannah. Scarlett's friend. The extrovert from introverts' nightmares. Without asking, Hannah swiped my drink and took a sip. Girl was fucking weird.

"Hey, Ryker. Scarlett said you're about to rip someone's head off." She grinned. "Want to talk about it?"

"There's nothing to talk about." I snagged my drink from her. "She's trying to piss me off."

"Why do you think that is?"

Maybe because making up is so much fun. Or to punish me. Either way, it'd end the same.

Hannah had this mission to become my confidant. Always asking about my feelings. "This isn't a therapy session, Hannah."

"Ugh. You're so closed off."

Scarlett paused in front of us, hands on her hips. "Is he bothering you too?"

I scowled at the infuriating beauty. "Yeah, *I'm* the problem here."

Hannah giggled. "You guys are silly."

"I didn't know you were coming by." Scarlett held up a glass. "You want a Cape Cod?"

"No. I'm not staying. I only came to drop this off." She handed Scarlett one of her favorite jackets. "You left it with Collin last night. We never saw him again, so he gave it to me today to give to you."

Collin?

Scarlett's sass dissipated as she avoided my gaze. "Thanks." She stuffed the jacket behind the bar. "Sure you don't want a drink?"

"I'm good. I'll see you two later." Hannah blew a kiss and skipped for the exit.

Scarlett pointedly avoided my eyes. Turning to the cash register, she flipped through receipts. Redness crept up her neck and face.

I gave her three minutes to speak, and since she didn't, I did. "Something you wanna tell me?"

"No." She massaged her temples. "Nothing happened. I didn't know he was going to be there."

She ripped a fresh receipt off the register, and I reached over the bar to grasp her wrist before she walked away. "His presence doesn't mean you have to interact with him. Or leave your jacket with him."

"Nothing happened. Chill out."

Chill out. Oh, that was it. All night, I'd been trying not to snap, but that was the last straw.

The crowd thinned as the hour grew later. The asshole she'd spent the night flirting with left her a big tip and tried to get her number. She turned him down, thank God. It wouldn't change her fate, though. The mention of Collin had ended my drinking for the night. I substituted scotch for water. I wanted to be sober when I finally got her alone.

After I declined another offer for a drink, Scarlett braced her hands on the bar. "Still don't want a drink? Is this how you pout?"

A muscle in my jaw pulsed. "Don't push me, Scarlett. Not right now."

"You're ridiculous." She clicked her tongue. "He happened to hit the same club we were at and stopped to say hi. To be polite. That was it. I swear. You think I'd lie to you?" She shook her head and sashayed away. "Calm down, Grumpy."

Tammy's rule of not hooking up could get fucked tonight. I waited until Scarlett went into the back and snuck in after her while Tammy was occupied with a customer. I crept past the cooks and found Scarlett in the storage room, reaching for a bottle. She didn't notice me until I closed the door with a soft click.

She spun to face me and arched a brow. "Tammy has rules."

"I don't care about Tammy's rules." I stole the bottle in her hands and returned it to the shelf. "I have my own fucking rules to go over with you." Grabbing her hips, I pushed her against the wall.

She gasped, hooked her arm around my neck, and stretched on her toes to kiss me.

I planted my palm on her chest and pushed her back. "Ground rules first."

"Ground rules?" She wrinkled her nose. "Really?"

"I agree we shouldn't need them, but apparently we do."

"You're such a baby. Collin is a good person, and he was kind to me. If I want to have a three-minute conversation with him because we happened to be at the same place, that's my choice. I can talk to whomever I want."

"Not him."

"Ryker, that's bullshit and you know it." She crossed her arms. "You're doing that thing again. Trying to control me. Telling me what to wear and who I can talk to. It's not okay. If you want to hook up with me, you have to respect my decisions about what I do."

I frowned, clenching and unclenching my fists. I hated when she was right. I promised her I'd be better, that I wouldn't be an asshole. It wasn't that I wanted to control her. It was that I was selfish when it came to her and didn't want to share.

I refused to fuck up again, so I took a long breath. "You're right. I'm sorry." I swept my thumb over her lower lip. "But no more flirting with the fucking customers."

She flicked her tongue across the pad of my thumb, that mischievous glint in her eye back. "Why?"

"Because you're *mine*." I kissed her. Hard. I wanted her lips to be swollen when she walked out. I wanted it clear she wasn't available.

She moaned and circled her arms around my neck, but I caught her wrists and pinned them above her head. She let out a delightful sound that made my rapidly hardening cock stiffen.

"Listen and listen good." I bit her lower lip until she hissed, then released it. "You aren't going to flirt with customers anymore."

"You don't have a say." She licked her lips. "I'm not yours."

I slid my hand under her skirt and cupped her pussy. "You're not mine?"

She gasped and rocked her hips into my hand.

I nipped at her neck and rubbed her through her underwear. "Yes, you fucking are, Scarlett." I touched her until her thighs quivered around my hand.

Hooded eyes gazed up at me with all the power to fucking undo me. "You think I'm yours?"

I released her wrists and closed my fingers around her throat. "I know you are."

She flattened her palm against my cock and stroked me through my jeans. Her other hand covered mine and she squeezed, tightening my hold on her throat. *Fuck*, I loved when she did that. "Prove it."

I did not need to be told twice.

"You're mine, Scarlett. These are mine." I groped her breasts. She moaned, and I moved to her ass, gripping both cheeks and pulling her roughly against me. "This is mine." I drew away from the wall to smack her ass. She whimpered, and I returned to her pussy, pushed her underwear aside, and plunged a finger into her. "This is *definitely* mine."

"*Ryker.*" She threw her head back, expression twisted with pleasure I was about to take away.

Snatching her jaw, I planted my mouth on hers. She melted for me, grinding against my hand, my fingers pumping in and out of her.

"This mouth is mine," I murmured, grazing my fingers over her lower lip. "My lips to kiss." I set my hands on her shoulders and pushed her down. "My mouth to fuck."

Lips parted and cheeks flushed, Scarlett sank to her knees eagerly. My cock twitched in anticipation.

I undid my belt, and she fumbled with my jeans. "You should've told me you saw him."

"I didn't want you to be mad."

Whose fault is it she's worried about that? I forced myself to consider the part I'd played before responding. "I promised you I'd be better, Scarlett. How can I be better if you don't give me a chance? Would you like it if I saw Nat and didn't say anything to you?"

"No." She tugged my jeans and boxers down, freeing my cock. "I'm sorry." Big, brown eyes staring up at me, she swirled her tongue around my tip. "I'll make it up to you."

Sexiest woman in the whole fucking world. I wrapped my fist around her hair. "Damn right, you will."

She opened her mouth and sucked me in. Panting, I tightened my grip on her hair to keep her in place while I sank my cock down her throat. She gagged. I pushed deeper until she was stuffed full of me.

"You won't do that again, will you?" I eased back until only my tip remained in her mouth before I shoved back in.

She peered up at me with watery eyes and shook her head.

"Good girl."

I rocked in and out of her mouth, savoring the sound of her taking every inch of me. Her tongue gave special attention to the underside of my cock and sent me over the edge. Several quick thrusts later, I came down her throat, and she swallowed every drop like the good girl she was.

Pulling out of her mouth, I lifted her to her feet and set her hand over my cock before it softened. My other hand curled around her neck, and she blinked at me, mouth parted and mascara running. "This is mine." I petted gentle circles against her neck. "And this is yours." I curled her hand around my cock. "And this is yours." I guided her hand along my length, then under my shirt to my chest. "This is yours." I curled her arms around my head and kissed her.

She let out a soft mewl and knotted her fingers in my hair, deepening our kiss. I tugged on her ponytail so our lips parted and our eyes met.

"Don't fucking tell me you're not mine, Scarlett. I'm yours, and you're mine, sugar. All mine. So, go finish your shift quickly because I'm taking you home to pay for your shit tonight, and the longer you make me wait, the more creative I'll get with what I'm going to do with you."

Chapter Thirty-Six

Still in Love

Scarlett

Having fun pissing off Ryker used to come with a certain amount of guilt until I realized he did the same thing to me. I wanted to be mad at him for it, but I couldn't blame him when I did it too. Making up made fighting worth it.

He had a certain look I tried to coax out. One I'd grown familiar with. A look that said if I pushed him any further, he'd snap. I liked making him snap. Sex was amazing when he snapped.

This time I pushed harder and the glint in his eye proved it. His constant stare took on a new level of intensity that forced me to change my underwear. It should be illegal for the man to make me cream my underwear by staring, but I couldn't help but wonder what gears were turning in his head. What exactly he planned to do with me once we were alone.

He didn't say a word when I finished my shift. Only dragged me out of the bar and onto the back of his bike. He didn't say anything when we got to his house either. Nothing while we greeted the dogs. Nothing when he closed them out of the bedroom. The tension made me need *another* change of underwear.

Ryker peeled off his shirt, revealing miles of muscle on his way to the bathroom. "When I get out, I expect you to be on that bed with nothing on." He paused and narrowed his eyes at me over his shoulder. "Absolutely *nothing*, Scarlett."

I clenched and nodded. The moment he disappeared, I stripped. Cool sheets greeted me when I lay back in his bed. He returned in boxers. My mouth dried, a condition made worse as he crawled over me.

Striking eyes soaked me in with languid glances up and down my naked body. I pressed my thighs together, heart thudding.

Then he kissed me.

Ryker had a way of kissing that ignited my entire body, as if his mouth were all over me instead of in one place. After all his talk of punishing me, the kiss was soft. Deep, intimate, and unexpected.

"You want me to show you how creative I got, baby?" He spoke against my lips, hand drifting lazily along my waist and the side of my breast, back and forth at a teasing pace that pebbled goose bumps on my skin.

"Yes."

He snatched my wrists and pinned them over my head. His mouth returned to mine, one hand keeping my wrists in place while the other journeyed down. A quick grip of my throat, then it descended, tracing my collarbone, lowering between my breasts. He circled one without touching, and my body hummed in need.

"Ryker," I murmured.

"Scarlett." He nipped my lip. "Keep your hands where they are."

He sat up and I obeyed, curling my fingers around the bars of the headboard. With a belt, he secured my wrists to the headboard. He shifted back, straddling my waist, staring. Self-consciousness crawled up my skin. His gaze raked over me, lingering on my breasts. My mouth. My breasts again. All in utter silence.

I squirmed. "What?"

"What, what?" He cocked his head. "I'm allowed to look at what's mine."

I shouldn't have liked when he said that, especially since we weren't together. The growing pool between my legs didn't care. I lifted my chin because my bratty mood lingered, and I liked playing with him. "I'm not yours."

"You're still saying that?" He adjusted, hovering over me. One hand braced above my shoulder. The other took its time drifting down my body, circling my navel, teasing above my mound.

"It's true." I tried and failed to keep my breathing even. "I'm not yours."

"If you're not mine," hooded eyes focused on mine, and he sank a finger inside me, "why are you so wet for me?"

My eyes fluttered, a moan threatening to escape. I bit it back and shook my head. "Finding you sexy doesn't make me yours."

He plunged a second finger into me and thrust them in and out. After all the tension from the night, I was already sensitive. His thumb pressed to my clit while he fingered me, and I gasped and arched my back. His digits curled against my G-spot, stroking. I almost tasted sweet relief.

He stopped.

"Ryker," I whined, crossing my legs.

"If you're not mine, why should I let you come?" He kissed down my body, teasing me by almost putting his mouth over my nipple but barely missing instead. His attention moved lower and lower. Strong hands gripped my ankles and yanked my legs apart.

He flicked his tongue over my clit, and I jolted. "Say you're mine, Scarlett."

"No." I squeezed the bars of the headboard, barely able to suppress the sounds of pleasure on the tip of my tongue. "I'm not yours."

The man must've had the blueprints to my body. He licked, kissed, and sucked in all the right places at the right pace. If not for his unwavering pressure on my thighs, I would've ground against his face. His tongue flicked over my clit again and again, that intense pleasure building—

He pulled back.

"Ryker," I pleaded. "Don't stop."

"Say you're mine." He crawled up my body and bit my neck hard. "Now."

How much more of this can I take? My pussy throbbed, but I didn't want to end the game. "No."

Two fingers shoved into me and this time, I couldn't help it. I tipped my head back and moaned. He edged me to the brink of insanity. By the fifth time, I was dying, curling my toes and trying to press my thighs together for relief that wouldn't come.

"Ryker, *please*."

"You want my cock, baby?"

Are my soaked pussy and hard nipples not making it obvious? "Yes."

My mouth fell open when he obliged. He removed his boxers and positioned himself between my legs. My body tensed in anticipation. His tip pressed in, then the rest of him. My eyes rolled back. "*Ryker.*"

Slow, deliberate thrusts shoved me toward paradise. All the teasing had heightened my sensitivity, and it only took a few firm thrusts before my pussy clamped around him, my release teetering on an edge I *needed* to fall off.

He pulled out of me right before I exploded. I practically wept.

"Say you're mine."

I almost gave in. Almost. "No."

Ryker straddled my torso, cock wet with my excitement.

I hardly heard anything over the sound of my thundering heart. "What are you doing?"

"I'm going to fuck these tits because they belong to me." He positioned his heavy cock between my breasts, pushed them around himself, and thrust. "God, you have great tits."

Oh fuck, that's hot. He tugged on my nipples and my back bowed. He panted, thrusting faster and faster. Listening to him moan while he fucked my tits amplified the already intense need coursing through me. I couldn't help but mew.

"Say you're mine, Scarlett."

I shook my head. He pinched my nipples harder, the muscles in his abs contracting as he moved. Groaning, he sat back and stroked himself as he came on my breasts. Hot, white liquid spilled down my skin and he collected some with his finger.

"You have an awful lot of my come on your tits to not be mine." He brought his come-coated finger to my lips, and I sucked it clean. "You sure like tasting me and having me fuck your mouth a lot to not be mine."

Scooting down, he closed his hand around my jaw and kissed me. Heat coursed through my body, worsened by his tongue slipping into my mouth and caressing mine. His hand drifted between my legs, and I nearly cried.

"Tell me what I want to hear." He circled my clit, and my hips bucked. "Say it and I'll make you feel good."

I squeezed my eyes shut and sank into the bed. I tried to hold out. I did. However, two more teases were the last straw.

Body vibrating with need, I gave in. "If I'm yours, are you mine?"

"I'm yours, baby. I said that already. Your turn."

I caught my lip between my teeth and stared up at him. He stared back, eyes narrowed. My skin burned as he adjusted to kneel between my legs, cock pressed against my aching pussy.

He rubbed it against me without pushing in. "Say you're mine."

"I'm yours."

He smirked and shoved into me. All the teasing almost made one thrust send me over the edge. I cried out and lifted my hips to take him deeper.

He paused inside me. "Say it again."

"I'm yours."

"Good girl." He circled my clit and slammed into me. The bed creaked with his deep invasion, and I sobbed, my hands fisting.

"Again."

Oh, fuck it. "I'm yours, Ryker."

"Damn right you are."

Finally, he didn't stop. His thrusts remained consistent and so delectable, I cried out his name and came. Pleasure ripped through me, wave after obliterating wave that gained power because while I was sensitive enough to finish, Ryker wasn't. This was his round two, and he always lasted longer on round two.

That meant he didn't spare me. He fucked me through the orgasm, increasing its intensity so the tingles of pleasure spread all over my body, down to my curled toes. I couldn't tell if the orgasm ever ended but another built. I thrashed on the bed, the ecstasy dancing the line of too intense. It built higher and higher—the edge inevitable.

"That's right, baby." He grunted, shoving into me harder, his grip on my hips bruising. "That's fucking right. You come all over me again. Let me feel how much you're fucking mine."

I screamed out my release. My muscles quaked, no piece of me unaffected by the assault of pleasure that burst into my every muscle and nerve. Ryker pulled out before he finished and came on my stomach, covering me in more of him.

Climbing off the bed, he set his hand on my thigh, then dragged his palm up as he made his way toward the headboard. His lips lowered to mine in a deep kiss

I needed after the roughness.

He had this amazing way of knowing when I needed to be untied. He pulled back and caressed my cheek. "I know." He released my wrists and kissed both.

I locked my arms around his neck and guided his lips to mine. He threaded his fingers through my hair, deepening the kiss. It ended when he pulled back and slid an arm under my back, the other under my legs so he could lift me.

My brows furrowed. "What are you doing?"

He kissed my forehead and carried me toward the bathroom. "Cleaning you up."

My heart fluttered. I didn't know why. I didn't need much care after rough sex, though I'd heard that was unusual. For some reason, I didn't mind going to sleep right away without reassurance, but the fact he wanted to take care of me after how intense we'd been sparked butterflies in my stomach.

In the bathroom, he set me down in the shower and did something I never expected from him. He washed me.

Kneeling in front of me, he scrubbed a sudsy washcloth not only over his come but over my entire body. Gentle, consistent circles that calmed my overexcited nerves. My eyes shut, and my legs turned to jelly when he stood and washed my hair. Strong fingers massaged my scalp, and he pulled me back against him. A contented sigh escaped me as I let his body hold mine up.

"That's nice," I murmured.

His response came in the form of a kiss on my shoulder. Once he was done, he spun me around and dropped to his knees. Despite thinking I couldn't take more, he pulled my leg over his shoulder and changed my mind. I whimpered and fisted his hair. He was gentle, his movements slow and deliberate. Tantalizing and euphoric.

Once I reached yet another orgasm, he turned off the water and led me out of the shower. Another shock came when he dried me from head to toe.

Both of us naked, he carried me back to his bed and proved me wrong that I couldn't take more. He slid his fingers into me, put his mouth on me, all gentle and so contrary to his usual tactics. He didn't shove me into pleasure, he eased me into it. Hands drifted all over my body like a worship. Not one part of me went untouched or unappreciated. It sent my heart into overdrive and left me, more than ever, wishing this could be more.

Whether my hair was damp from the shower or from sweat, I couldn't tell. Either way, I was trembling by the time Ryker lay over me and glided his cock into me.

"Scarlett," he grunted, sinking his head into the crook of my neck while he slowly and gently rocked in and out of me.

This was unlike anything we'd ever done. It wasn't a fancy position that would make me scream. Not fast. Not rough. He moved in and out at a savoring pace, allowing me to enjoy every inch of him stretching me. A divine experience that rippled through my nerves until they all stood to attention for him.

I moved my hips with his, and he planted soft kisses all over my neck. He increased the pace—gentle but deep enough to rip moans from me. His fingers weaved their way between mine, and he held my hand over my shoulder as his thrusts grew more desperate.

"You're so fucking beautiful," he murmured.

A lump formed in my throat, and I tangled my fingers in his hair. His kiss was like his hips, slow and tender, tongue caressing my mouth, similar to how he caressed inside of me. Gentle sex usually didn't do it for me, but with Ryker, it was different. *Everything* was different with him.

He squeezed my hand and trailed his lips along my jaw and onto my neck, where a sensitive spot always made me squirm. He gently sucked and my legs locked around his waist. My climax built, my pussy clamped around him, and he let out a guttural sound that pushed me closer to the edge.

His rasped words against my ear knocked me off that edge. "That's it, baby. Come with me."

The sound of his voice always got me there. I gasped as the orgasm coasted through my body, every muscle humming with ecstasy. He sank into me and went rigid, groaning against my neck while his come emptied inside me.

Our chests heaved, and I melted against the bed, spent. My body refused movement. I couldn't even keep my eyes open. At least, not until Ryker's hand landed on my face. I opened my eyes and found him staring, his thumb rubbing my bottom lip.

"Scarlett," he murmured, then kissed me. Sweet. Cherishing.

My eyes stung when he massaged circles into my neck with his thumb. My chest swelled at his kiss that felt so . . .

So . . .

Loving.

Breaking the kiss, he pressed his forehead against mine. Powerful eyes took mine hostage, and my breath caught as I fought against the tears.

I loved him even more than I had before.

CHAPTER THIRTY-SEVEN

All of You

RYKER

I'd never been a great picture taker, but I got lucky one night. Scarlett didn't notice me snap it. Didn't know it'd been my background for weeks. Her on the couch, Grayson lying on her legs while Demon licked her. Her eyes were closed—the only downside—but she had a huge smile, her face scrunched up as Demon covered her in slobber. It was the cutest damn thing I'd ever seen. I couldn't help but capture the moment so I'd never forget it.

God, I'm so in love with her.

Love. I never thought I'd say that, but if I was honest with myself, I'd been in love with her for a while. Every interaction from the first moment I saw her pushed me in deeper, and I couldn't recall what dumbass version of me ever turned down a relationship with a woman so goddamn incredible. I should've been the one asking—no, *begging*—for a relationship.

Maybe it was time I did.

I couldn't take it anymore. The sneaking around. Not seeing her every day. Not waking up to her brown eyes every morning.

I was done.

My hands shook, but I was going to ask her to be with me. I couldn't wait for her to make the move. I needed to be with her. I needed to be the person she leaned on. The person she trusted. The person she spent the rest of her life with.

The person she lives with. Although too stubborn to admit it, she was a mess in that apartment. Any chance she got, she insisted we go to my place instead. On the rare occasions we stayed at hers, she couldn't relax. Jumped at every noise. Jolted if a door slammed. It fucking broke me to watch her try to force herself to be comfortable in a place she couldn't be anymore.

Which was why I planned to take two big risks today. Ask her to be with me, and ask her to move in. For her sake and mine. I was sick of not spending every spare moment with her.

Because she was tense, I texted her to let her know I was on my way. Then, once I parked, I texted again to let her know I'd turn off the alarm.

Inside, she opened the door before I made it to the top of the stairs. "Horny already?" She smirked. "It's barely ten."

"I'm constantly hard for you, sugar." I curled my hand around the nape of her neck and pulled her in for a brief kiss. "I don't know why this is a surprise."

"You should've called. I would've come to you." She pecked me on the lips. "I need to eat first, though. I'm making breakfast. Want some?"

I dragged out a kitchen chair and sat. "I'll take some if you have it."

"I'm not capable of cooking for one person. Or two." She smiled sheepishly. "I grew up cooking for several people. I learned from Dan and he always had friends over. I have no idea how much to make for a single serving of anything. Like, how much spaghetti do you even cook for one person?"

I couldn't stop my lips from curving up. She was fucking adorable.

"Better than not enough."

"Are you actually being positive?" She arched a brow. "Mr. I-don't-know-how-to-smile is finding a silver lining?" She flitted over to me and pressed the back of her hand to my forehead. "Are you sick?"

I *tsked* and tugged her down to straddle my lap. "Hilarious."

"I know. My humor is why you can't stay away from me."

"It is."

She rolled her eyes and peppered kisses down my neck, her hands twisting in my shirt.

Fuck, I love when she touches me. I palmed her ass and pulled her more snugly against me. "I'm serious, Scarlett."

She nibbled my neck. "Uh-huh."

If I didn't talk soon, her mouth would have me doing a different kind of talking. I eased her back. "I mean it. I love your sense of humor."

She tilted her head. "You're being weird. Normally you'd have my clothes off by now. What's wrong?"

"Nothing's wrong." I nuzzled her nose, and her brows furrowed. "Maybe I want to be with you like this. Eating breakfast and talking."

"You don't socialize."

"I don't usually. I never want to." My pulse raced and turned the rest of me into a fidgeting, anxious mess. "I want to with you."

It'd be fair if she rejected me after all I'd put her through, but *fuck, please don't reject me.* The rest of my life would lose all its color if she weren't in it.

"Are you trying to let me down gently?" Her arms fell to her sides. "Do you not want me anymore?"

Impossible. "No, Scarlett. I want you. All of you. All the way."

Her lips parted. "What?"

"I want to be with you. We're electric, Scarlett." I cradled her face, and a lump formed in my throat when her eyes glistened. "And I want to take that charge with me everywhere I go. I want to wake up with you and fight and make up with you. I want your sarcastic comments. I want that sense of humor and sass every second of every day. I want to make dinner for you and spend the night with you and date you and go to every goddamn art show you ever have so I can watch you become a world-famous artist. I want you to be mine." I pushed my forehead to hers. "All of you. Will you be my woman, Scarlett?"

Her wide eyes stared for so many seconds, I feared she might say no. My stomach tied into knots that wouldn't release unless she said yes.

"Yes." She kissed me and murmured against my lips, "Yes, I want that so much."

Everything in me unraveled, and I was glad for it. I'd reform with her. Mold into the kind of man she deserved.

"Fuck, baby, I'm so into you." I spoke between kisses because I wanted to be close to her. Now and every day of my life. "You're so important to me. I miss you when I'm not with you."

She whimpered and tangled her hands in my hair, pulling our kiss deeper. I slid my hand up her shirt onto her back. A huge sense of relief washed over me. She said *yes*. She was *mine*.

"Ryker." She tipped her head back, and I kissed down her neck. "I miss you too. I want to be with you all the time."

I told myself I wouldn't tell her I loved her right away. I'd do things right. Wait for a special moment. But I couldn't fucking wait anymore. I'd wasted too much time already and I didn't want another *should have* moment. *Fuck it.*

"Scarlett." I cupped her face, adrenaline buzzing through my blood. No one had ever given me a rush like she did. "I'm in love with you."

Her mouth fell open. "You are?"

"So fucking much," I whispered. "I love you so much."

She sniffled. "I love you so much."

Self-loathing had embedded itself so deeply inside me, I never believed I could love someone. More, I never believed someone could love *me*.

Then she spoke the words, and that lump in my throat grew. I crashed a kiss on the lips I'd never get tired of and always craved. Her arms locked around my neck and my chest swelled with a warmth and comforting sense of *home* only she could give me.

I wanted her to move in with me. I considered maybe all this was too soon, but we weren't normal. We did things our own way. We had from the start, and I didn't see a reason to stop now.

"Scarlett." I eased back before I got too distracted by her lips. "One more thing."

"What?"

"Move—"

It would've been perfect. It would've been the right time. Except the door opened because *I* hadn't locked it, and in walked Danny.

"Hey, honey, I was cleared to come upstairs final—" He froze.

We froze. I wasn't facing him, but Scarlett was. Her eyes widened. Silence stretched and I hazarded a glance back, but all Dan did was gape. We couldn't bullshit him on this. She was in my lap; my hands were under her shirt. We'd gotten away with a few things before, but there was no way out of this one.

"Oh, God." Scarlett slipped off my lap.

I stood and set a hand on her back as I faced Danny. She wouldn't take the heat alone.

"Danny, I—"

"No. I want to talk to her. You go."

I lifted my hands in surrender. "Danny—"

"Ryker." He gestured for the door. "Out. I want to talk to Scarlett."

"Go." Scarlett nudged me with her shoulder. "It's okay."

I hesitated but she nudged me forward again. Reluctant legs carried me out the door.

Then I waited. For three hours. *Three* hours. I had no message. Got no response when I texted. I almost walked back in but decided against it. Instead, I went home. Took the dogs for a run. Worked out. Anything to keep me busy, but after another two hours passed, I couldn't take it.

I didn't know what to expect or how mad he'd be, but I refused to lose Scarlett. Danny knew I wasn't good enough for her. I knew that. Hell, *anyone* would know that. But I'd become good for her, and I'd be damned if I let anything come between us.

When I got to the bar, Tammy informed me Scarlett was at Danny's, so I headed that way. I thought about knocking but I hadn't knocked on Danny's door in about three years. No point starting now.

Inside, voices drew me toward the kitchen where they sat at the table. Scarlett straightened and frowned when I walked in. "What are you doing here?"

"I need to say something."

I'd never done anything like this, but Scarlett was worth braving the unknown for. I faced Danny. "I'm sorry for going behind your back. I'm sorry for lying when you asked why Scarlett called me. I'm sorry for not being honest with you. I'm *not* sorry for being with her."

I set my hand on Scarlett's shoulder and squeezed. A smile twitched on her lips and provided the boost I needed to keep going.

"She's the best damn thing that's ever happened to me." I met Danny's gaze so he'd know how serious I was. "I want to be with her, and she wants to be with me, so you're going to have to be okay with that. She's a grown woman who doesn't need your permission. I don't need your approval. But I respect you, and more importantly, Scarlett respects you. We don't need your permission, but I want your blessing. I don't want anything to change between you and me, and I especially don't want anything to change between you and Scarlett. I'm crazy about her, but I won't drive a wedge between the two of you. I also can't stand to be away from her, so we have to work something out because I'm not going anywhere."

I'd known Danny for years and his stoic expressions had never bothered me. Right then, I could see why Scarlett hated that about both of us. It made a person want to squirm, but I held my ground.

Sweat collected on the back of my neck, and I spoke once more. "I'd also like to say I'll never take her out on a Tuesday." Tuesdays were their night.

The silence could've killed me, but he took mercy on me. Shook his head and chuckled. "What'd you think was gonna happen here, Ryker?"

Kinda thought you'd bring out the shotgun, honestly. "Uh . . ."

"Did you think I was going to tell her to stay away from you? Or you to stay away from her?"

"Well . . ." I scratched the back of my head. "Yeah."

"Even if I wanted to, it'd do no good. I know from experience with this one," he sent Scarlett a reprimanding glare she answered with an angel-sweet smile, "and I wouldn't anyway. I'm not upset you two are together. I could've done without the sneaking around, but I'm happy you're together."

My mouth fell open. "You are?"

"Of course. I was never wary of her boyfriends because I wanted her to be alone her whole life. I was wary because she always brought home shitheads. I wanted her to be with someone who was good to her, and she says you are."

My gaze snapped to Scarlett, whose cheeks turned pink, and something in me healed. I wanted her to feel that way forever.

"I'm not good enough for her either," I pointed out.

"No," Danny agreed. "But nobody will be, and you're as close as we'll get. Just don't hurt her, or we *will* have a problem."

"Wouldn't dream of it." I pivoted toward Scarlett. "Will you come out with me tonight?"

Her lips parted. "Out, like on a date?"

"Yeah, a date. Will you?"

"Yeah." She caught her lip between her teeth and stood. "When?"

I offered my hand. "Right now."

I'd never seen her smile bigger and took it as a personal goal to make it grow more every day.

She pecked Danny on the cheek before taking my hand. We strolled out together, and the second we were outside, she stopped and faced me. Standing on her toes, she stretched, her lips meeting mine.

"That was so sweet." She spoke between kisses. "You coming here like that. It was so sweet."

"Unnecessary, apparently." I slid my hands into her back pockets. "You couldn't have texted?"

"I'm sorry. We had a lot of talking to do. Lots of explaining and apologies." Easing back, that pink on her cheeks turned red. "Where are we going?"

"I—" I wanted to be with her, but I didn't know the first thing about taking a girl out. "I'm going to be straight with you, I'm new to this. I didn't make a plan. Partially because I didn't know what to expect when I showed up here. But I swear, I'll get better at this." I nudged her nose with mine. "I promise, okay? I'll read a boyfriend book, or whatever. I want to be with you, Scarlett. I don't give a fuck what we're doing."

She grinned then whispered into my ear, "Dinner's always good. Food can win anyone over."

My lips twitched up. "All right, dinner it is. Where do you wanna go? What's your favorite place to eat?" I was certain it was the bar, but I couldn't take her on a date there.

"My favorite?" She glanced at Danny's bar and lifted a shoulder. "I mean . . . What's your favorite place to eat?"

My gaze also drifted to the bar. The food and drinks were the best in town. "That's—I mean, that's a bad idea, isn't it? You always eat there. It's not romantic."

"It's not romantic to have our first date at the place we met?"

Well, when she put it that way. *God, I fucking love this woman.* "All right." I gripped her hand. "Let's go."

"But I don't want to sit at the bar. I want a table in the corner, where less people will stare at us."

"Deal."

Her fingers weaved through mine, and we entered the bar from the alley. Since it was a weekday, it wasn't too busy. I led her to a corner table away from everyone else, but it didn't help. My guys gawked at us. I pulled a chair out for her.

"Take a fucking picture," I snapped. They whipped their heads away.

Scarlett dropped her face into her hands. "*Ryker.*"

"What?" I pushed her seat in as she sat. Before I sat, I inched the chair beside her closer. "Do you want them gawking while we eat?"

"Of course I don't, but there's this thing called *manners*. You might've heard about them at some point in your life."

"Can't say I have." I twisted toward her and took both her hands.

Her attempt to hide her amusement failed miserably when our fingers laced together. A perfect fit. I'd never been so content to hold someone's hand. The damn woman made me soft.

"Are you guys . . ." Tammy approached the table, eyeing our joint hands curiously. "On a date?"

Scarlett sank back in her seat and covered her cheeks with her hands. "Yes."

"Fuck yes, we are." I yanked Scarlett's seat closer until our chairs bumped against each other. "We'll be going on a lot more of them."

Tammy's shoulders lowered, and she turned away with a heavy sigh. "*Finally.*"

"Hey, we wan—"

"I know both of your drink orders." Tammy waved her hand and didn't bother looking back. "Give me a break."

Scarlett and I grinned at each other, and I dropped my arm over her shoulders. Now that we were together, there was no reason to not have her close to me at all times.

"What do you want to eat, sugar?"

"I don't know. I was thinking about one of those ridiculously unhealthy burgers." She tapped her chin. "You?"

"I'll get the same." I leaned forward and brushed a kiss against her soft lips. "Because you know you make it look damn good."

Epilogue

SCARLETT

One month later

I tried to focus on the salad I was making, but two holes burned into the side of my head. "Stop looking at me like that."

He didn't stop. He never stopped. He was relentless.

"I'm serious." I glared down at Grayson, who sat beside me, waiting for scraps. "I'm not supposed to feed you outside your normal meal regimen. You know this."

Grayson licked his chops, and his whip-like tail wagged swiftly against the tiles.

How am I supposed to say no? "Oh, fuck it." I plucked a piece of chicken, and Grayson's eyes bugged, drool dripping from his mouth. "Don't tell Ryker."

The moment I tossed Grayson the chicken, and he chomped it, Demon leapt from his bed in the living room and skittered into the kitchen, tail wagging and puppy eyes in full force. I pursed my lips. He sat and flicked his tail.

"Fine, but I'm serious! Don't tell Ryker." I flung a piece of chicken to Demon, who jumped to catch it. "Now shoo. You'll get me in trouble."

At least this time, they listened. Ryker repeatedly lectured me that they'd listen better if I showed consistency by not giving them scraps, but *damn*. How could anyone say no to those faces?

The rumble of an approaching engine curved a smile on my lips. I peered out the windows overlooking the front yard and access road. Ryker pulled in on his motorcycle, and a few seconds later, the familiar groan of the garage sounded below.

After our first date, Ryker asked me to move in with him. I couldn't deny I wanted out of that apartment. Plus, I couldn't deny I wanted to spend more time with him. Maybe it was crazy that I'd said yes, but maybe we'd always been a little unconventional.

Telling Dan went better than I'd hoped. He understood the apartment was tainted now and wanted me out of there as much as Ryker did. With the help of Ryker's friends, I was out within two days.

Living with Ryker opened a new door for us. Sure, we had our small bickers, like any couple moving in together, but we resolved them as quickly as they started. The occasional disagreements were nothing compared to all the positives. Our intimacy ascended to a heightened level as we uncovered new layers of vulnerability, especially as we both worked through therapy.

While he'd been seeing a counselor, today was his first day in group therapy. Hence the special dinner.

As soon as the door to the garage opened, the dogs bolted. My heart swelled as they preened under Ryker's attention. I'd never get tired of seeing that adorable, soft side of him.

"Hey, sugar." He circled the kitchen island and approached me from behind, arms encircling my waist. "What are you making?"

"Chicken carbonara." I angled my head to meet his lips with mine. "You said you wanted to try it."

"Smells fucking amazing." He spun me around and pushed his forehead to mine. "What's the occasion?"

"You taking the group therapy plunge." I draped my arms over his shoulders and twisted my finger in his hair. "I'm proud of you."

"Well, shit, if you're going to cook a nice dinner every time I go, maybe I'll go more times a week."

My breath hitched when his lips planted on my jaw. My neck. His hands roamed over my spine and slipped into my back pockets.

My eyes fluttered as he placed a hot kiss against my pulse. "How'd it go?"

"Good." His lips lifted to my cheek. "Real good. Thanks for encouraging me."

"Always." I hugged him and settled my head against his chest, where the even beat of his heart warmed mine. "I'm glad it went well."

"Did you feed the dogs again?"

"What?" My head snapped up and I pulled away to check food I didn't need to check. "Of course not. You asked me not to."

He grasped my chin and turned my face toward him. "Are you lying to me, Scarlett?"

I shrank under a pout. "They were giving me puppy eyes."

He clicked his tongue and let me go. "Oh, for fuck's sake."

"What's wrong with them getting a treat? They're good dogs!"

"What am I going to do with you?"

I winked and flitted to the salad I needed to finish. "Whatever you want as soon as we're done with dinner."

"Fucking tease." He swatted my ass, and I squealed. "Danny called and asked if I could install the new grill tomorrow." He pecked my cheek, then sat on a stool across from me. "I'm assuming you wanna come sit with him while I do that?"

"Yeah, I talked to him already. Oh, and I have to go out of town in two weeks." I dumped my chopped cucumber, carrot, tomato, and onion into the bowl of lettuce. "Art show with René. I'm not in it. I'm helping out."

Ryker leaned forward on his forearms, and I caught my lip between my teeth. He made the simplest actions sexy. "For how long?"

"Four days. It's an extended weekend thing. I'll be back before you know it."

"Can I come with you?"

Butterflies tickled my stomach. "You want to?"

"I do."

"I thought art wasn't your thing unless it's mine."

"I want to go to be with you." *Melt.* "Besides, I'm appreciating it more thanks to you."

Cheeks warming, I tossed the salad. I'd never been with someone so supportive of my passions. When I moved in, Ryker took the week off to renovate an art studio with fantastic natural lighting so I had my own quiet space to work. It was my favorite place in the house. *Next to our bedroom, that is.*

"I'd love for you to come."

His lips twitched into a half-smile that never failed to weaken me. "Yeah?"

My blush intensified. The hold he had on me continued to grow, blossoming into something unexpected. My muse. When I showed René my drawings of him—approved by Ryker first, of course—she gasped and told me this was it. This was the masterwork she knew I had in me. Where I poured raw emotions, vulnerability, pain, and healing into every stroke. She was hosting a show for me in a few months. The subject: my own personal muse.

That muse only tried to distract me a couple times before dinner, but he couldn't resist my cooking. To be fair, I couldn't resist his either. He was a fabulous cook. We took turns and technically tonight was his turn, but I wanted to show support for his first day in group therapy.

The nice thing about living with Ryker was he couldn't stand things to not be neat, but he didn't hound me about it. He did it himself. The second we finished eating, he jumped up to do dishes. He always did, but I'd never been one to sit around. We fell into an unspoken agreement of him washing dishes and me drying and putting them away.

Once we were done, I dragged him to the bedroom to make him help me pick a dress for an art show the next day. He sat on the bed and pouted like a child with his arms crossed.

"You said I could do whatever I wanted with you after dinner," he grumbled.

"Stop being such a baby. The more you cooperate, the less time it'll take." I held a black dress on a hanger against my body. "What about this one?"

"Scarlett, they all look good. It doesn't matter what you wear, you'll look fucking gorgeous. Pick any damn dress." He patted his lap. "Then get your ass over here."

I posted a hand on my hip. "You're not helping."

"Why are you asking me? Ask Hannah."

"Okay, fine." I lifted a shoulder. "I'll call Hannah and ask her to come over right now, and she'll probably have a drink." I hung the dress in the closet and retrieved my phone from my pocket. "Meaning she'll probably stay late. Maybe even spend the night. We won't be alone *all* night."

He leapt off the bed and stole my phone. "I like the black one."

"Which black one?"

"The—" He rubbed the back of his neck. "The second one."

I narrowed my eyes. "The second dress was green."

"The second black dress."

I snorted and pulled out the dress with a plunging neckline. "This one?"

"I like that one when I'm with you, but I won't be there until later." He took it from me and hung it up, then plucked a different hanger. A red dress. *His* red dress, I should probably call it. "What about this one?"

"Uh, no, not that one." I lunged for it, but he held it out of my reach.

"Why not? I like this one a *lot*."

"Yeah, you like that one a little too much." I stretched on my toes, but Ryker grabbed my waist and raised the dress higher.

"What's wrong, Scarlett? Afraid I'll end up fucking you at another art show?"

My face burned. "I'm never wearing that dress in public again."

"Oh, come on. I love this dress on you."

"You love it, huh?" I never got tired of him telling me he loved me, and now the word stood out anytime he used it.

"Yeah." He hung the dress on the closet door, then hauled my body to his. "I love it." His stare infiltrated every pore, like it had the first time I saw him.

"Fine. I'll wear that one if you love it so much."

"Wear what you want, baby." He snatched my jaw. "I love anything you put on. Put on pajamas for all I care."

"Want me that badly, huh?"

"I'll always want you." He lowered his lips to mine, and my heart stopped as it waited. I could always tell when he was going to say it. I could see it in his eyes. "I love you, Scarlett."

My smile stretched so wide, my cheeks ached. "I love you too." I fisted his shirt and stood on my toes to brush my lips against his. "So much."

He lifted me and I wrapped my legs around his waist while he carried me to the bed. He pressed his lips to mine and spoke against them before he kissed me. "You're in my veins, Scarlett. I'll spend every day loving you more."

The kiss radiated through more than my body. That kiss was *everything*. Everything in the way I felt it everywhere, and this time I didn't only feel it physically.

This time, it radiated through my heart. My soul. In parts of me I hadn't known were there but blossomed to show me this love I had with him wasn't going anywhere, despite all we'd been through. Despite the fighting and the tears. Despite the hard moments.

Love wasn't always sunshine. Love was never letting go, even if lightning in a storm was the only guide out of the darkness.

Ryker and I? We were forever.

Thank you for reading!

Enjoyed this book? Please consider taking a moment to leave a review! They are highly important for indie authors to get recognition and visibility. Interested in staying up to date on future publications? Join Jaide's newsletter on her website.

About the Author

Jaide is an indie author who writes works her readers have dubbed 'therapy romance' due to the frequent focus on mental health rep. She writes across many subgenres of romance including contemporary, paranormal, urban fantasy, fantasy, and more. Writing since she was a young child, Jaide's inspiration stems from her love of music, books, nature, and escapism. If you would like to get to know Jaide more, she has a blog on her website.

patreon.com/jaideharley

instagram.com/jaide.harley

pinterest.com/jaideharley

facebook.com/jaideharley

tiktok.com/@jaideharley

Acknowledgements

To my honey, who kept up with my silly human needs like water and food while I was too focused on my book to think about it, thank you for going on yet another adventure with me. Through late nights and long hours when I overworked myself, you were always there to pick me up and restore me. Your patience when I disappear on my metaphorical boat to vividly hallucinate the next characters/scenes/plot I'm going to write is something I will always deeply appreciate. Thank you for encouraging me to submerse in my passions, and for making me the most perfect cups of tea along the way.

To my twin flame, without whom I would've collapsed and never gotten back up, the gratitude I feel for your friendship and love isn't something that can be reduced to words. You've not only been my greatest champion and supporter, but you've also been a friend unlike any I've ever had. Thank you for always punching imposter syndrome in the dick, and never tiring of me. It's a rare thing to feel seen in this world, but thank you for seeing me, and allowing me to see you too.

To my Discord cultists, my ultimate cheerleaders and hype team, I would be nowhere without you. Whether it was providing feedback for my books, making me laugh to the point of breathlessness, being a shoulder on the days imposter syndrome hit hard, or just simply being good friends, I'm so thankful for your existence and presence in my life.

To my patrons, without whom I wouldn't be a published author, my thanks are as endless as my longest updates. While I've dreamed since I was a child of being an author with a reading community, I never believed it would happen until you all proved me wrong. There are some of you who recently joined my Patreon and some who have been with me for almost five years now, and I'm unbelievably grateful for every one of you. I wouldn't have the means or time to publish and continue writing if not for your support. Thank you for proving me wrong, and giving me the greatest community of readers. Your value is immeasurable.

To my editor, Liss, and my proofreader, Makenna, this book could not have come together for publishing without you. Thank you for being patient and helping me take this from an early draft, to something I'm excited to publish. Your input is invaluable, and I'm so grateful for both of you.

Also by

JAIDE HARLEY

I Accidentally Summoned a Demon
Pre-published works on Patreon

9 7 9 8 9 8 6 9 3 6 0 4 8